The first fair wind

Aberdeen at the beginning of the nineteenth century is the setting for Agnes Short's sixth historical romance.

Orphaned Rachel grows up in the fishing community of Footdee, taken in by the warm-hearted Christie family – kindly 'Fiddly' (so called for his skill on the violin of an evening), his serene and competent wife, Bonnie Annie, and their brood of sons. Like the other fisherwomen, little Rachel gathers bait, coils the lines, wades into the icy sea at dawn to launch the boat, and carries full creels to market.

But James, the handsome eldest Christie son, hankers for a different way of life, more prosperous and more secure than fishing, with its dependence on tiny boats in the treacherous sea, can ever be. He dreams of building a fine stout ship and taking part in Scotland's growing trade abroad – sailing to London, even Europe. Fishing provides the Christies with just life's bare essentials: where can they ever find the money for such a venture?

Set in the bustling harbour and market, with its sharp breezes and pervading tang of the sea, this story of fisherfolk and merchants, of courage, love and endurance, is backed by Agnes Short's thorough research into, and knowledge of, the period of which she writes.

Also by Agnes Short

under the name of 'Agnes Russell'

Agnes Short

The first fair wind

Constable London

First published in Great Britain 1984
by Constable and Company Limited
10 Orange Street London WC2H 7EG
Copyright © by Agnes Short 1984
ISBN 0 09 465640 1
Set in Linotron Plantin 11 pt
by Rowland Phototypesetting Ltd
Bury St Edmunds, Suffolk
Printed in Great Britain by
St Edmundsbury Press
Bury St Edmunds, Suffolk

For Katy

'Mind now,' warned the woman, tugging the girl's hair back from her face with a broken comb, 'remember what I told ye. Do as yer Aunt Annie says. Nae lying late i' yer bed. Turn *roond*, will ye?' She took the thin shoulders and pushed.

Rachel transferred her patient gaze from smoke-blackened wall to smoke-blackened pot-shelf, and clenched her teeth against the pain as comb fought matted hair. Her eyes swam with sudden moisture, but she made no sound.

'I'd best cut yon tangle oot,' said the woman with a curse. 'Hand me the knife, will ye?'

Dry-lipped the child did as she was bid: whetted steel slashed out a chunk of hair, leaving her white-faced and trembling.

'My, what a sight ye are,' said the woman, regarding her ill-shorn victim with satisfaction. 'Ye werena blessed wi' looks and that's a fact.' She tossed the hank of hair on to the open peat fire and watched it flare up and sizzle into writhing ash. 'There,' she said, pleased – cut hair must be burnt to avoid ill-luck, and the Lord knew she'd had enough of that since the lassie came. 'At least ye'll carry nae vermin tae the fine city.'

Rachel stared blankly ahead of her, her eyes avoiding the murky glass of the window lest she see her mutilated reflection. What would they think of her in the Square? But her tormentor had not finished with her.

'See ye set the hooks neat i' the basket, coiled like I showed ye, and dinna go snarlin' a body's line or ye'll nae forget it.' One tangled line and the whole boat came home, the day's catch lost: no fish for the women to string in pairs in the smoke-shed or carry in creels on their backs to Aberdeen, no money or bartered goods in return. Rachel's small heart chilled with dread at the threat, bruises on shoulder blades and thighs stinging in anticipation. Suppose Aunt Annie was as heavy-handed as Frenchie Noble's wife?

'Did ye hear what I said, lass?' Rachel's head blurred

momentarily as the blow struck her ear. 'Pay attention when I'm speakin' tae ye.'

'Yes, Ma.' Jeannie Noble was not her mother, yet she was the only one the child had known.

'Yer uncle'll no' thank me for sendin' him a useless body, and him wi' enough bellies tae feed o' his ain. Do ye ken what I'm speakin' aboot?'

'Yes, Ma.' But I am not useless, Rachel thought, with a spark of spirit, small as the first sputtering light from Frenchie's tinder-box when he lit up his pipe of an evening. I'm not, I'm *not*.

'And tak' yon sullen look off yer face. They're nae wantin' a body wi' a de'il's aspect. Stand tall. Ye're a poor soul at the best o' times, but there's nae call tae show it. Hae ye yer shoes?'

'Yes, Ma.' The little girl indicated the cloth bundle on the earthen floor at her feet. 'And my Sunday petticoat.' It was a hand-down from one of the Noble girls, stained and threadbare, but better than her everyday garments.

'Then what are ye waitin' for? Awa' wi' ye. It's a fair step tae Aberdeen, and the sky black as sin. Ye've kept Andrew waiting long enough.'

'There's plenty time, Ma.' A thin-chested, spindly lad of fifteen with pale hair and mild, abstracted eyes emerged from the shadows beyond the box bed. 'It'll no' take us long.'

'It's a fair step,' contradicted his mother, 'and you wi' yer oatmeal an a'.' But the hard lines of her face relaxed momentarily as she looked at her favourite child. Andrew had won a bursary at Marischal College and was 'apprenticed to the University' as she would tell the other women when they worked in the smoke-sheds, or sat at their house doors shelling interminable mussels, or baited the sma' line from pails of the globular flesh. Unlike his brothers and the other village lads, Bookie Noble did not work in the family boat, even in the vacation: Bookie had long fingers, more suited to a clerk than to a fisherman. 'Bookie' was the village name for Andrew on account of his skill with reading – not the chap-books the older men guffawed over with their whisky and tobacco, and the apprentices sniggered at, hot-faced and daring, but real books written in Latin and Greek. His mother, however, always called

8

him Andrew, with a deference proper to someone who would one day be a doctor 'wi' a fine house i' the Guestrow'.

'Mind and work hard now, son,' she said, remembering her boasting and the shame should it come to nothing – though how could it, with Andrew so clever and willing?

'I will.' He adjusted the oatmeal sack and picked up a smaller cloth-tied bundle which contained his change of linen and his books. 'Good-bye, Ma.'

She clasped him swiftly against her breast, her eyes unusually moist. But under her embracing arms, he was too thin. 'Wait.' She reached up for a jar at the back of the pot-shelf and took out a coin.

'Here's money for the ferry, Andrew. It'll save yer strength and ye'll need all ye have for yer book-learnin'. You,' she said sharply to Rachel whose eyes had widened at the sight of such unexpected bounty, 'will go round by the Hardgate and the Green. There's nae call for ye tae idle in a boatie when ye've a pair o' feet tae yer name. But Andrew's a scholar.' Before emotion might overwhelm her, she thrust him out of the door. 'Awa' wi' ye both.' As an afterthought she aimed a cold kiss at the child's forehead. 'And mind ye behave proper, Rachel. Because if ye dinna earn yer keep, they'll put ye oot, and ye ken fine I'll nae have ye back.'

In her stomach Rachel felt the familiar grey weight that had been with her as long as she could remember, sometimes leaden as a November sky, sometimes paler, sometimes even bright at the edges, like a rock against the shimmering sea. That happened only in Andrew's company, but Andrew was at college now and the greyness was as much a part of her as her work-torn hands and mottled, chilblained feet. She accepted it, unquestioning, as a necessary part of her anatomy, and expected the same, or worse, at her Aunt Annie's house.

Now she slipped a hand into Andrew's softer one for reassurance, and looked for the last, deliberate time at the place which had been home for eight years of her life, ever since Jeannie Noble's husband had taken her in, the motherless child of his cousin drowned at sea.

'But we've daughters enough,' his wife had wailed, looking at the small, sallow face, pinched even then with hunger. 'And the house sae full there isna room to swing a herring as it is.'

9

'We'll manage fine,' her man had said, with a finality she recognized. 'Her father was a good friend, and wi' her Ma dead o' the fever, it's only right we should give his wee orphaned lassie a home.'

Home. Rachel looked at it now with no regret. One over-crowded room containing table, stools, pot-shelf, box bed and truckle. Salt fish and onions hung from the beams among oars and fishing-line, while the inevitable pot of skate-bree for Frenchie's rheumatism added its pungent aroma to that of mussel shells, smoking fish, and the indefinable smell of the shore.

Little enough to call home: but Andrew had been there and Andrew was the only one in the Noble household from whom she received any affection. To be sure, Frenchie was kind enough when he remembered to notice her, which was rarely – and usually in a mood of drunken benevolence, the same mood in which he had first brought her home, a fact which his wife never let him or Rachel forget. She had daughters enough of her own to bait Frenchie's hooks and those of her two fisher sons, without giving house-room to another. So when her sister Annie in Aberdeen sent word that her mother-in-law had died and she needed another pair of female hands, Rachel was the obvious choice.

Rachel was glad, and a little afraid. But surely nothing could be worse than Cove, and the woman she called Ma told her Aunt Annie had a fine new house in a square, built by the Council for the fisherfolk of Fittie – or, more correctly, Footdee. She was afraid already of Aunt Annie and of what would be required of her – but home with Bookie away was no home at all, and the college where he was a bursary scholar was in Aberdeen.

'Is it far from Footdee to the college?' she asked now as they left the little fishing cove behind them and struck northwards.

Andrew squeezed her hand in reassurance. 'Not far at all. Just a step away from the Castlegate and the Plainstanes where the Fittie women take their fish to market every day. Don't frown so, Rachel. I'll not be far from you. Like as not we'll meet often. You'll be carryin' fish to market for Aunt Annie afore ye know it, and I'll not be studying every hour of the day.'

Rachel glanced behind her to the huddle of thatched cottages, the green curve of Cove, the blue-grey mussel shells heaped in glinting mounds along the tight green turf. She had gathered and shelled thousands of those mussels, wading waist-deep in the rock pools, feeling along the crevices of submerged boulders, and later sitting with her Ma and the other girls, knife in hand on the turf outside the cottage door, splitting the shells open to extract the flesh. Her fingers had been slashed and scarred a dozen times while the others gossiped and she sat silent, concentrating on the 'sheeling' so that she might not be walloped for lagging behind. But she had never been to market. When the others shouldered their loaded creels and set off, laughing, she had had to scour the house pots, redd the floor, and mend the tippens for Frenchie's line.

Frenchie had forgotten to say good-bye to her, leaving, as always, before dawn, to get the lines shot before daylight 'and home again afore yon storm clouds gather'. But the sea, she noted automatically, was no more turbulent now than it had been at daybreak. Spray smacked up from the rocks at the cove mouth, showering pale green lace high against a frowning sky. Gulls drifted, mournful and predatory, waiting for the fishing-boats' return. Rachel knew she must never harm a plingie, for were they not the souls of drowned fishermen, to be treated always with charity? Secretly Rachel believed her parents to be among those wheeling gulls and would talk to them in whispers if she came across a pair resting, talons spread, on granite rock or driftwood. She fed them morsels from her pail of mussel shells, and even, on occasions, bread. Would they follow her to Aberdeen? Or would they think she had left them?

'Cheer up,' said Andrew kindly. 'There's nought to be afraid of. You'll not be asked to do anything you can't manage fine. Not like me: I have so much to learn, Rachel, I doubt sometimes I'll ever manage it.'

'You will, Andrew. I know you will. You will be a fine doctor one day.'

'Wi' a fine house i' the Guestrow,' finished Andrew, quoting his mother's perennial boast. 'I hope so, Rachel, for Ma's sake, but sometimes I wish . . .'

'What?' prompted the child, scurrying to keep up with his longer strides.

'Oh . . . nothing.' How could he explain the burden of his mother's expectations, or his own unadorned wish simply to learn and eventually to heal? He adjusted the heavy oatmeal sack across his shoulder and set his face to the north.

'Will you really have a house i' the Guestrow?' asked Rachel, eyes bright now with excitement. 'And will there be many mansions?' *In my father's house are many mansions* was a line which never failed to thrill her lonely heart with the splendour of the unknown.

'Many, many mansions,' Andrew assured her, slipping easily into the game they played together when the rest were sleeping and Andrew was working on, permitted the meagre lifespan of an extra tallow candle for his studies. Rachel would creep close to scan the letters and learn to hold the pen, and he would read to her till the flame guttered to smoke and darkness. 'And one of them will always be ready for you, Rachel, should you ever need it.'

'Thank you, Andrew,' she said, with quaint solemnity. 'I will not forget.'

'And if you visit me and I am not at home, you will leave a pasteboard card on a silver tray.'

'Why?'

'Because it is the custom among the great folk, and you must do as the fine ladies do when you visit me,' he finished, teasing. 'Besides, you will have a fine house of your own by then.'

It need not be *very* fine, thought Rachel, as long as it is mine, with a family of my own to people it and no cold corners or shivering loneliness, no empty stomachs or smarting eyes. There will be no one then to beat me, or to grudge me my existence . . . But first, I must go to Aunt Annie, in the Square. As the road lengthened behind them, Rachel's courage dwindled.

'I will miss you, Andrew.'

He recognized the plea behind the simple statement and shifting his burden from right shoulder to left, put his arm around her. 'I know. I will miss you too, Rachy. But we'll meet again, you'll see.'

'Tell me again the way I am to go when I reach the Hardgate. I fear Aberdeen is a big place and I wouldna want to lose myself.'

'You'll not lose yourself, silly. I'll be with you.'

'But your mother said . . .'

'I know what she said. But do you think I'd take the ferry and leave you to walk into a strange place alone? Not for ten sacks of oatmeal. No, I have a much better idea. We'll walk to the Square together and on our way we'll spend that money on a gingerbread mannie or a wee loafie in the Green. Would ye like that? Or would you rather buy an apple, or one o' they blood oranges from the Holy land?'

At the thought of spending so much sudden wealth, Rachel's apprehension receded and the next mile passed happily in a discussion of the relative merits of one titbit over another as Andrew described from his vigorous imagination the delights awaiting them in the Green.

But even that dream was not strong enough to blot out the reality of the coast road on a cold October morning. When the clouds spilled sudden stinging rain, and a lacerating wind whipped in from the north-east to drive icy needles into unprotected faces, both dipped their heads and thought of nothing but to fight their way to the nearest shelter, be it hedgerow or house eave, and sit out the worst of the storm – not only for their own sakes, but for the protection of Andrew's precious mealsack.

'Is there broth enough for the Cove lassie when she comes?'

Annie Christie looked up from the pot she was stirring with a heavy iron ladle and nodded. 'Aye.' She added salt, stirred once, slowly, from left to right and tasted the result. 'That'll heat her wee belly after the day's journey,' she said with satisfaction as she replaced the lid and swung the pot back over the fire.

'She's awfu' late, isn't she?' Fiddly laid aside the horse-hair tippens he had been repairing, setting each hook carefully into more horsehair for safety. 'There, that's the last o' the wee de'ils sorted. Perhaps I should walk a way along the road to meet the lass?'

'And have her terrified out o' her wits to be accosted in the twilight by a stranger? You leave her be. Like as not Jeannie's sent one o' her lads wi' the child to see her safe, and with the rain there's been today they'll have sheltered till the worst was past.'

'Aye. I reckon you're right.' He put the 'skull' of repaired hooks with the others in the corner beyond the box bed, then reached up to the shelf for his fiddle, polished glassy smooth by loving hands and much wear. Idly he plucked the strings, tuning each one to his satisfaction, then drew the bow slowly across the gut.

Annie wiped her hands on her apron, took up the heavy undergarment she was knitting for Davy, eleven years old and inclined to take cold in the chest, and settled into her chair near the hearth, where the firelight served to light her stitches and she could keep a watchful eye on the pot. She had lit the crusie lamp ten minutes before, so that James and the others could see for whatever job they were about, but when Fiddly's idle strumming took off suddenly into a cascade of tripping notes, feet tapped and heads nodded in time to the beat till someone broke naturally into melodious whistling.

It was James of course, at sixteen the eldest of the Christie boys. Tall as all the Christies were, bar Fiddly who had fathered them, James was dark-haired, firm-necked and straight, his face flawless as his mother's except for the eyes, one brown, one crystal blue. They gave a disconcerting sparkle to his expression, an air of mystery or teasing, so that even his mother was never sure what he might do or say next. Privately it worried her, as if the two colours were two different personalities doomed to discord and discontent.

'Awa' wi' your fancyings, woman,' Fiddly had reassured her when she mentioned her foreboding. 'He's a fine lad and a fine fisherman. He'll make a fine father, too, before ye know it, and he's happy enough and healthy. What more do ye want?'

Yes, thought his mother, as James whistled joyously and without self-consciousness, he's happy enough now, but I've seen him when the brooding is over his spirit. Then, though he says nothing, it is turmoil and tempest. Not like Maitland.

Maitland was her second son, tall as James, but with hair bleached pale by the summer sun and a seaman's clear, chameleon eyes, now grey, now green, now morning blue. But in Maitland's case they were the eyes of a dreamer, turned inward, more often than not, to the grand plans of ships which filled his head and which one day he hoped to build in more than the plywood scraps which occupied him now and filled every spare moment of his day. Already the shelf beside the hearth held half

14

a dozen models of square-rigged luggers, yawls, brigantines and, latest, a schooner modelled in delicate, painstaking detail.

'Ye can design yer father a fishing boat, Maitland,' Fiddly told him. 'One that'll keep out the sea and the cold, ride out any storm, and come home safe with a hold full o' haddock.'

'I will too, Da, one day.'

'And put me in a fine bed, while you're at it, lad, and a roof over my head, wi' a chimney for a fire where I'll have a pot o' your mother's broth simmering night and day.'

'What you want is an ark, Da,' said Davy, grinning.

'Then William and George can be the first o' the animals, two by two.' James ducked to escape the good-natured lunges of the twins, inseparable and almost indistinguishable except that William had lost two front teeth in the wood of the gunwale when a rough sea had caught him unawares, and George had a broken nose, memento of a similar mishap with a spar.

A house full of men . . . Annie looked at them with pride, then, remembering the Cove lassie, with a stir of apprehension. She hoped the lass would cause no disruption. But she was young enough as yet, the same age as Annie's daughter would have been had she survived the measles. She would take the place of that daughter, keep an eye on wee Alex, and help with the lines.

Annie's fingers flashed effortlessly in and out, weaving wool and needles in the pattern she had knitted countless times over the years of her marriage: six sons and a fisherman husband needed a never-ending supply of vests and drawers, thick thigh-length stockings, and tight-fitting jerseys. The evening hour was precious to her, with her family safe about her, five-year-old Alex already sleeping in the truckle bed he shared with Davy, the peat fire burning with steady warmth, the shadows friendly, and Fiddly playing her favourite air. She knew that later, when Bosun Brand and the others arrived, drawn as they always were by Fiddly's playing, there would be dancing in the crowded room, spilling inevitably into the Square. Then Davy would take up his mouth-organ, James would whistle, and Fiddly would leave his playing to pull her to her feet, one arm about her waist, and draw her into the dance. Annie smiled to herself in calm anticipation.

Fiddly Christie, seeing her private smile from across the

room, marvelled yet again at his good fortune. Not for nothing was his wife known as 'Bonnie Annie' to distinguish her from all the other Annies in the community of Footdee. Seventeen years of marriage had not marred the purity of her voice, the classic beauty of her face, nor the neat proportions of her figure. Half a head taller than Fiddly himself, and fifteen years younger, she had a quiet dignity which never failed to move him as it had done when he first saw her on the shingle at Cove, where his boat had fled for shelter from a sudden storm. It remained a mystery to Fiddly why she had agreed to marry him instead of some handsome youngster, had agreed to leave her family at Cove and follow him to his home in Footdee – for, in spite of his effervescent spirits and optimistic outlook, he was a humble man at heart and knew she could have had the pick of a dozen younger, better-favoured men.

James Christie senior, known as 'Fiddly' for his prowess on that instrument, was a wizened frog of a little man, all laughter and tapping feet, his skin pickled by salt and barnacled with the scars of old wounds, embedded fish-hooks, frost-splits, knife-cuts. With his greying hair and grizzled beard he looked nearer sixty than his forty-nine, until he took down his fiddle from the wall, which he did at the first empty moment. Then youthful exuberance spilled over with every dancing note, and the happy nature which had so attracted Bonnie Annie filled the house from earthen floor to rafters.

Something of his affectionate and carefree spirit lay in Davy, the fifth boy, though he was all thumbs with the fiddle. It was a 'mouthie' for him and he and his father together played a rare jig, till Bonnie Annie's face relaxed, her foot tapped under the hem of her sailcloth skirts, and she slipped naturally into song.

Tonight as the music swelled into the Square, doors opened and soon the Christie house was thronged with noise and neighbours. Cushnie Baxter and his sons, Red Willie, Wee George and Baxter's Davy (to distinguish him from all the other Davys in Footdee); Bosun Brand in whose boat William and George Christie sailed, for he had no sons old enough yet to help him; and, of course, Bosun's Jess.

'Jessica,' she had cried fiercely and tugged her sister's hair half out of her head when the child called her Jess, but it made no difference. For all her black hair and fiery eyes, Bosun's Jess she remained to all but Fiddly Christie's eldest son, James, who called her 'Jessica' with a solemn mockery which left her furious and unaccountably chagrined.

James could have had his pick of the girls of the Square – and a wife too, had he chosen to take one. At sixteen he was entitled by law to marry, and a strong wife was a useful asset to a fisherman. But James had no wish for such responsibilities. He was content to leave fathering to his father and to follow him, first to sea in the family boat, then to the tavern with the other men when work was done: he also, on occasions, to his shame and his father's ignorance, found his way to a certain house on the quayside where, with a precious portion of his share of the family earnings, he bought the brief favours of a lady known to all the lads as Bouncing Bella. But as for a wife, he had no need. Bonnie Annie prepared his hooks as she did her husband's and he wanted no other. Till her death the previous summer, their gran had helped them as best she could with the rest, but now the new lass from Cove would take over that job. As long as the household ran smoothly, domestic matters were no concern of his, and, beyond a fleeting curiosity as to whether the child would manage better than his gran had done, James felt no interest in her: until a sudden draught blew from the open doorway on a cry from Bosun's Jess, and James looked, with the others, towards the small, bedraggled figure with haunted eyes.

The journey had been longer than Rachel expected, and far more awesome. When the rain at last had eased, she and Andrew had set out once more along the rain-soaked highway northwards, past sodden meadowland and stubble, till they topped a rise and looked down on the shimmering sweep of the River Dee and the huddle of buildings at its mouth. Beyond, sea and sky merged in a uniform grey, flecked here and there with dirty white.

'There's the Castle Hill,' indicated Andrew, setting his sack down beside the road, 'and there, where the river meets the sea, is the headland where you'll find your village. See the line of the thatched roofs glinting?'

Rachel had looked, with an awe which increased the nearer

they approached the town. She had heard, of course, of the Plainstanes where women from the country round about cried their wares; eggs, butter, cheeses and the like. She had heard of the flesh market and fish market, the stalls which sold oranges, dates, and other wonders imported by sea from the ports of Europe and the Mediterranean. She had heard of the splendid new town that was to be built in the air above the old, with a street that ran on bridges, and grand houses for the gentry on either side. But hearing and seeing were two different things. As they entered the town by the Windmill Brae and threaded their way down the cobbled hill-slope between narrow huddling houses and the debris of departed day, Rachel felt fear gather in her throat so that even Andrew's offer of sweeties from the lamp-lit stall at the foot of the hill could not shift it.

Overhead, the engineering wonder of the Union Bridge carried what was to be the great new main street of the city high above them so that the child drew closer to Andrew for protection in the threatening shadows. A carriage bowled eerily overhead, a ghostly apparition in the twilight, and Rachel shivered.

'It's all right,' said her companion with a laugh. 'It's only one of the fine folk travelling home in style. Maybe the Provost himself – or one o' the baillies gone to see how his grand new house is progressing. Such mansions as there will be in the Union Street you cannot imagine, Rachy. Perhaps you will have a house there yourself, one day. Who knows?'

'Oh no! I wouldna like a road that's half-way in the sky. It might fall down, Andrew!'

'The best engineers i' the land have worked on that road, Rachy, and it cost thousands of pounds. It'll not fall down, and one day all the fine folk will live there.'

'Then we can have the houses they used to live in, i' the Shiprow and the Guestrow. That would suit me fine.'

Andrew laughed and took her hand as they traversed the deserted Green where straw drifted, whispering, over rain-soaked cobbles in the light of a single lantern. A scavenging cat crouched, evil-eyed and wary, till they had passed, and Rachel shivered again with apprehension.

'It's all right, Rachy. You'll get on fine in the Square, I know you will.'

But Rachel had not his certainty. Why should they like her? '*A poor soul at the best of times,*' Jeannie Noble had said.

Then suddenly they were at the harbour edge, the water black except where lamplight from a tavern or riding light cast a gleam across the surface. Masts and rigging threw skeletal patterns across a sombre sky, and from somewhere along the quayside, where a larger patch of light indicated an open doorway, the sound of a hammer echoed rhythmic and mournful across the water. The air smelt of salt and seaweed, laced with the familiar tang of fish. Rachel stubbed her foot against a bollard in the darkness and winced.

'Look where you are going,' warned Andrew. 'You'll not want to end up i' the water. You're wet enough as it is.'

But they had reached the foot of the Shiprow, where crowded alley-ways backed high, many-windowed houses in a sweeping curve from quay to Castlegate. Lights studded the darkness with amber, and from somewhere beyond came the sound of carriage wheels and jingling harness.

'See that fine house, Andrew!' cried Rachel, pointing up the Shiprow to where a lantern hung above an arched entrance. 'I will live in that one. Which will you have?'

But somewhere in the town a bell was ringing and Andrew had other matters on his mind. 'Look, Rachy, will you be all right if I leave you now? It is late and my landlady bars the door at nightfall. I dare not be locked out. It's not far for you, truly. Keep straight along the quay to the Fittiegait and you'll see the new fisher houses at the end. Anyone will tell you which is Aunt Annie's place.'

Rachel bit her lip hard to still the terror: not of the dark, which held no fear for her, but of that unknown, waiting woman with the household of men.

'Rachy, don't look like that – and never mind what I said. I'll come with you. If we run I might just have time, and if not, no matter.'

But Rachel had recovered. 'I'll be all right, Andrew. And you must not be locked out.' Cheap lodgings were hard to come by and Andrew must not risk losing his. 'I'll find my way alone. But you will see me again, won't you?'

'I'll see you, Rachy, I promise.' He bent swiftly to kiss her cheek. 'Take care, and dinna fret. They'll like ye fine i' the

Square.' He shifted the sagging meal-sack to the other shoulder and set off briskly up the curve of the Shiprow. The small, forlorn child in the ragged skirts watched his dark shape merge with the shadows of tenement and archway, to spring suddenly to life again in the lamplight of her chosen house. He turned and waved a hand before moving on into the smothering darkness beyond.

Left alone on the quayside, with only the lap of water against hull, distant male laughter from an unseen tavern, and that rhythmic hammer, Rachel pulled the tattered plaid tight across her bony chest, and set her chin high and her face towards the eastern tip of the harbour.

There were ships moored by the quayside, one with candle-light pale in a cabin window, another with a rear lamp in whose light two men sat cross-legged, throwing dice. There were bales on the deck behind them and more in the open hold. As she passed under the shadow of the prow she saw the splendid figurehead of a turbanned blackamoor with hoops in his ears and a wooden scimitar in his wooden cummerbund.

'All the spices of the Orient,' breathed Rachel in wonder, remembering Andrew's whispered stories. 'Tea from China, and precious silks . . .'

She asked the hammerman the way, standing in his lighted doorway till her silence attracted his attention. He was fixing a wooden plank on to the side of a huge ship's bottom, whose ribs curved upward like the cleaned jawbones of a whale.

Mouth bristling with wooden pins, he pointed eastward and mumbled, 'At the north pier. Ye'll hear the fiddle.' From the moment she caught the faint mew of distant strings, Rachel's steps lightened, till she stood in the open doorway of the Christies' low-roofed cottage and looked in returning apprehension at the scene of merriment – and at more menfolk than she had seen in one small room in her entire life.

'You must be the Cove lassie, and swum a' the way by the looks o' ye,' said a voice at her shoulder, and she turned to see a handsome girl some two years older than herself and already well on the way to womanhood, with black, unruly hair and brilliant eyes. 'My, but you're a wee yin.' The girl gave a shout of laughter, pushed her hard between the shoulder blades so that she almost fell over the threshold, and yelled above the noise of the fiddle music and chatter, 'Here's a water-kelpie, Jamie Christie, swum a' the way frae Cove to curse yer hoose!'

There was instant silence as every head turned towards the doorway where Rachel stood outlined against the night, her ill-shorn hair plastered to her head with rain, her eyes huge in their fleshless sockets, one hand clutching her cloth bundle, the other holding together the edges of her ragged plaid at the throat and both mottled blue with cold. Water dripped slowly from the hem of her skirt on to the earthen floor, where her bare feet glistened like new-boiled crab. Fear gathered in her eyes.

'The De'il tak' yer tongue, Jessie,' roared Bosun Brand, called 'Bosun' for his boasting, when drunk, of superior seamanship. He aimed a blow, but his daughter skipped nimbly back and laughed in his face, her eyes darting mischief.

'That's no kelpie, ye daft lass.' The crowd parted to show a small, wiry man with a grizzled beard and merry eyes, a fiddle tucked between shoulder and chin. 'And no way to welcome a wee lassie come a' the way frae Cove to live wi' us. Make way, lads, and let her through to the fire.'

As the men moved back, Rachel saw at the fireside the figure of a woman with a look of Jeannie Noble about her, but this woman was more handsome, and when her calm eyes met Rachel's fearful ones the child could not look away.

Like a terrified rabbit, thought Bonnie Annie on a sigh of resignation. What help was this that Jeannie had sent her? But she laid aside her knitting and stood up to greet the child. 'Come away in and dry yourself.' She reached out to take the sodden plaid from the child's shoulders.

Involuntarily Rachel flinched, a hand raised to ward off the expected blow. Annie and her husband exchanged one glance of startled anger, then both together moved to flank the child with instant protection.

'We'll bid you all good-night,' called Fiddly with an authority all recognized. 'We've family matters to attend to, as you see.'

'You too, Bosun's Jess,' said Annie as the girl lingered, her eyes taking in every detail of the new arrival. 'Unless ye'd care to lend yer fine petticoats to the lassie?'

With a flounce of the threatened skirts and a defiant toss of the head, Jessie left, but not without throwing a look of open flirtation in James's direction.

James ignored her. He was already opening up the fire to give greater warmth. 'Shall I fetch more peats, Ma?'

'No,' said Annie, who saw more than her sons gave her credit for. 'Let Maitland do it. You get down the tub from the roof-beams for me. William and George, fetch more water from the pump, and Davy, just look i' the kist and see if ye can find my woollen plaid. It's all right, Alex,' she soothed as her youngest child surfaced, startle-eyed, from his blankets. ''Tis only Rachel.'

'Here, child,' said Fiddly with gentleness, 'sit on this wee sunkie by the hearth till you're warmed through. There's nae call to be feart. See, I'll ladle ye a pot o' Ma's fine broth, and wi' a droppie o' whisky in it, that'll warm ye.'

'Later, Fiddly. The lassie must strip off those wet clothes first. We dinna want her taken wi' the fever when she's newly come to us, do we? Hae ye found that plaidy, Davy? Fine. Warm it at the fire for me and see ye dinna let a spark catch it. Now Rachel, lass, let's have those clothes off yer back so I can dry them for ye. There's nae cause to be scared. We're all friends here.'

Stripped of her pitiful assortment of hand-me-downs, Rachel was bundled quickly into the sweet-smelling plaid, but not before everyone in the room had seen the bruises and weals across the bare shoulders and buttocks. No one commented, but there was an extra tenderness in Fiddly's voice as he gave her the bowl of broth and urged her to 'drink up, ma wee lammie'. James and Maitland filled the wooden tub with water from the kettle, Davy heated a thick oat bannock at the fire, and the twins kept up a flow of chatter designed to divert the child's attention from her physical discomfort and to set her at ease – though the result was more baffling than anything, as Rachel had yet to learn the art of listening to two voices telling the same tale, now speaking in unison, now changing in mid-sentence from one voice to another.

'There's a man found a mermaid at Thurso,' 'so the mannie wi' the black coat was tellin' Bosun Brand . . .' 'saw a figure like an unclothed human female,' 'sitting on a rock extendin' into the sea,' 'combin' its light brown hair . . .'

'And for a' the world,' put in Fiddly with a twinkle, 'like a wee lassie frae Cove.'

Rachel, the broth finished and for the first time in her life up to her armpits in hot water with not only her body soaped but her head too, felt the beginnings of a happiness she had felt only momentarily before, and then only in Andrew's company.

'I'd like fine to net a mermaid one day,' said a twin.

'I wouldna,' put in Wee Alex from the safety of his bed. 'I'd be feart.'

'You're feart o' anything,' teased William.

'Even your ain reflection i' the water pail,' added George.

'Whereas you two,' said James solemnly, 'would happily sit all night i' the kirkyard if ye had a relative to guard.'

There was general laughter at some private family joke, but the twins said quickly, 'Other folk are feart o' the snatchers,' 'and what yon Medical Society students do to the bodies.'

'I'm nae,' said Davy cheerfully. 'What's a body anyway? Only a shell, wi' the soul fled.'

'Wheesht,' warned Annie, 'ye'll scare the child.'

But Rachel was reminded only of Andrew and his whispered stories. Andrew was a doctor-student and meant no one any harm – and he had promised to see her soon. She felt fear melt out of her with the cold, and, when Annie bade her step out of the tub to be rubbed vigorously with a dry cloth so that her flesh tingled and her hair crackled into new life, Rachel felt like a new-born chick emerging from the dark constriction of its shell.

'There now,' said Annie with satisfaction, 'you look a new lassie.'

'Aye,' said Fiddly, 'our little mermaid has cast off her scales i' the splash of a water tub, hasn't she lads?'

It was James who answered for them.

'She has that, Da – and emerged a beautiful princess, just like in the stories.'

From that moment, Rachel loved him.

'Ye'll nae be called to bait Fiddly's line, nor Jamie's,' explained Annie the following morning when the menfolk had left in time to shoot their lines before sunrise. 'I do those myself. Davy doesna have a line yet, so he helps wi' Maitland's when he can.

23

That leaves William's and George's for you. I'll give ye a hand till we see how quick ye are. Can ye gather mussels?' Rachel nodded. 'Then ye'd best start there. The tide's low and there's a mussel scarp i' the rocks behind the house. Take yon pail and see what ye can fetch me, while I attend to Wee Alex.'

That was the beginning of a new life for Rachel. She slipped easily into the routine of the Christie home and was as easily accepted, for when she realized she would not be chastised for every shortcoming, real or imagined, she threw heart and soul into pleasing her new family, from Fiddly, to whom she showed the devotion of a stray to the one who has adopted it, all the way down to little Alex, whom she tended with the solicitude of a loving mother. But above all she sought Bonnie Annie's approval, for she remembered Jeannie Noble's warning, '*If ye dinna earn yer keep, they'll put ye oot,*' and the fear that she might somehow fall short of Bonnie Annie's expectation filled her child's heart with dread. More than anything on earth, she wanted to stay in the Christie household.

The house, as Jeannie Noble had promised, was a fine new one in the new village of Footdee, laid out the previous year by the Town Council for the accommodation of the pilots and whitefishers and their families, so that the land of old Footdee could be used for harbour development. On the headland behind the north pier, the new village was close enough to the shore to please the fishermen who liked to go the shortest possible distance to launch their boats, while its spacious and airy situation endeared it to the womenfolk. There was room enough for the men to dry their lines, for the women to spread their washing, and for the bairns to play: and all within walking distance of the town with its market and its wealthy customers for the fish on which the little community depended.

The houses were laid out in two squares, their backs to the outside world and blank of windows, their faces turned inwards. Each cottage consisted of one room, one story high, its unceilinged rafters neatly thatched with straw, weighed, measured, and paid for at the Weighhouse on the quay at 7p the stone. There was a pump in each square for water, and ample space for the inevitable middens and the heaps of discarded mussel shells.

The Christies' house was at the north-eastern corner of the

north square so that Rachel had only to step outside the door and round the side of the house to find herself on the grassy headland, with the bent grass rattling in the wind and at her feet the surf lifting, green-flecked and foaming, to boil over on to the sand and recoil once more in a rush of rattling pebbles and indrawn breath. It was the sighing rhythm which had measured every moment of her short life.

Inside, the house contained much the same as Jeannie Noble's: a box bed, a kist or two for clothes, a table and benches, fishing creels, coiled ropes, and sailcloth, as well as cooking pots and the wooden bowls from which the family ate. But there was a contentment in the Christie house which there had never been in Jeannie Noble's. Pondering, Rachel decided it must come from the fiddle which Annie dusted so reverently every day, taking it down from its central position on the dresser and replacing it only when she was satisfied that it could shine no brighter. Certainly the fiddle was the source of the happiest moments in the Christie household, rivalled only in Rachel's estimation by the times when the family took turns to tell stories at the fireside, of fairies, or witches, or the sea.

Then Fiddly would take out his tinder-box, strike flint against flourish, and light up his pipe, while Annie knitted, Maitland whittled away at his ship-models, and little Alex's eyes grew huge with pleasurable terror at the threat of bogles or Old Nick. The twins, thirteen and fearless, were the best raconteurs, delighting in the gruesome and the frightening, till Annie warned them they would give the wee ones nightmares. Then they would laugh and offer to take bets as to who would dream the most terrifying dream, which of them would wake first, sleep last, or any other wager which sprang to mind. For not a day passed without William or George laying bets on something, be it only who would come next through the door. It was a harmless enough game and the wagers, whether made in fish, fowl, or currency, were paid only in pebbles from the earthenware jars they kept for the purpose. At first their game had mystified Rachel, for the Noble household had held no such flights of exuberant imagination; then she realized that each one of the Christies had an individuality beyond the shared involvement in the fishing which was their livelihood.

Fiddly had his music, and Davy too; Maitland his model ships; William and George their wagers; even little Alex showed a particular talent and delighted in drawing charcoal sketches of birds and fishes which were astonishingly true to life. As for James . . . Rachel could not define what it was that set James apart, except that he was sixteen and taller than his father, that he lived a life separate from and far more exalted than hers, and that on the rare occasions when he spoke to her she tingled with pleasure for hours afterwards.

But it was Bonnie Annie, beautiful and calm, who ran the household with a silent strength which encompassed all of them: she who held the purse-strings and whose word was law. Bonnie Annie rarely spoke but her silences were always companionable, with a quality which eased the tiredness and soothed the small worries of the day. Not like Jeannie Noble's silences which had carried the brooding threat of a thunder-cloud and invariably presaged storms. When Annie did speak it was quietly and to the point, so that by the end of a week Rachel knew exactly what was expected of her.

She slept by the fireside, curled up small under the plaid in which Annie had wrapped her on that first evening, seeing pictures in the embers, or looking up at the dim shapes of oars and netting in the rafters, the shadowed strings of onions, rush-pith for lamp-wicks and Annie's bunches of dried herbs, till her eyelids grew heavy and finally closed. Even then she would listen contentedly to the rhythm of the sea at their backs, to the fire's purr, or the breathing round her: sometimes a muttered half-sentence from little Alex, caught up in the excitement of a dream, a soothing grunt from Davy beside him in the truckle bed, the soft murmuring and movement from the box bed where Fiddly and Annie slept, the doors closed on their privacy, and sometimes a distant snore from beyond the sail-cloth partition where the four older boys slept in bunks like ship's bunks, ranged along the wall among the wooden chests that held the menfolk's best clothes and the dresser which was Annie's pride. The Christies were lucky to have their house to themselves: many of the houses in the Square held two families, a few of them more. But then Fiddly had his own boat, sons to sail it and to fish with him, and in a good week they could earn £1. More in summer.

26

Before first light the household was awake, all except Wee Alex who was allowed to stay abed till the rest were gone. Rachel's job, when she had rinsed the sleep from her eyes with water scooped from the pail, was to coax the fire awake and see to the porridge pot, while Annie drew the ale for the lads' breakfast, packed oatbread and cheese for their 'piece', helped Fiddly and her sons into their working clothes of tight woollen jerseys, canvas whole-fall trousers tied at the knees, woollen stockings drawn over them, and leather sea-boots, made to measure and reaching well up the thighs. Then it was time to launch the boat in the dark hours before dawn.

All round the Square, doors opened as the fisherfolk set about the day's work. Rachel and Annie, like the other women, helped to manhandle their boat from shore to water and, skirts looped, calf-deep in water, held it steady for their menfolk to embark. They watched as Maitland pulled on the oars, James heaved the sail aloft, and Fiddly steered, while young Davy stowed the coiled lines neatly in the bow.

They watched as the twins embarked in the Brand boat, and watched again till the tiny craft were safe over the harbour bar and dipping in the troughs and hillocks of the open sea, the sky light now at the edges. When the sea lifted them high enough, the little fleet, tiny as Maitland's models, was outlined black against a paler sky.

Only then did Annie turn back towards the Square and home, to start the long round of never-ending tasks.

Rachel's next responsibility was to visit the Christie 'scarp' of mussels in the rock pools north of the harbour mouth and collect enough for the day's bait. When the store ran low, she and the other girls scoured the coastline north to the Don mouth, or south along the banks of the Dee in search of more, or of sand eels which did almost as well. Her pail filled, she would carry it back to Annie and together they would sit, the pail between them, knife in hand, shelling each one, dropping the flesh into a second bowl and reaching for the next shell with a dexterity that quickened as the task progressed. They sat outside if the weather was fine enough, exchanging gossip with their neighbours, all engaged in a similar task. The Brand family lived several doors away on the northern arm of the Square, but Jessie often joined them, invited or not, or called her pleasantries from her own doorway for all the Square to hear.

The Brands were a rough lot: Bosun was drunk as often as not, his wife a huge woman, red-faced and black-haired, with arms like hams.

'I hope Jessie doesna grow like her mother,' Annie said one evening over the supper table after the girl had been particularly pert.

Fiddly laughed. 'She'd make a fine armful if she did.'

'And smother a man into the bargain,' said William, his mouth full. 'I'll wager my best marble old Bosun's been overlaid a dozen times,' added George, giggling, 'and three more that he was only saved from suffocation by the whisky in him.'

'Boys! I'll not have you talk so. And you in Bosun's boat, too.'

'Sorry, Ma.' ''Tis common gossip.'

'All the more reason not to repeat it. But young Jessie's a fine looking girl – I hope she doesna go to the bad.'

'She'll go whichever way she chooses, that young madam,' said Fiddly indulgently, 'and enjoy herself every inch o' the way.'

'Just so long as her companion does the same,' said Annie.

'And what do you mean by that, Ma?' asked James, off-hand.

'Only that there's some lassies a lad is better off without, however fine-looking they may be.'

James shrugged and took another hunk of bread, but Rachel saw the wink he gave Maitland and for the first time since her arrival felt the grey weight in her chest. Rachel was in awe of Jess: in her presence she felt small, plain, and inexperienced. Even at the 'sheeling' Jess excelled her, knife flashing over shell, hands darting from pail to basin, and always with a flow of derisive chatter, gleeful gossip or, failing all else, a snatch of song, the bawdier the better. Rachel was both humbled and fascinated by the older girl.

The mussels shelled, they were set aside till the boats' return, to bait the hooks for the next day's fishing. At first, Annie did it herself with Rachel's close attention. Then Rachel was given a stretch to bait and, as she proved adept at securing the mussel flesh and coiling the line carefully in the wooden 'skull' so that no hook tangled with another, she was given a greater stretch of line. But first there was the market.

When the cry went up that the returning boats had been sighted, the womenfolk went down to the shore to meet them, anxiously watching as the little vessels negotiated the harbour bar where river flood met tide-waters, causing sudden hazards of sucking trough and rolling breakers. In an onshore wind the spray slapped house-high from the pier, and the ships were lost from sight in the furrows before riding the crests in precarious triumph. Annie watched in silence, rigid with fear, suspending breath and motion, till the danger was past and her menfolk safely home. Then it was time to unload the slippery stream of haddock, each with the definitive thumb-mark of St Peter. There would be other fish among them – skate, ling, whiting, mullet – but it was the haddock Annie packed into the creel for market. The creels loaded, they were heaved up on to the women's backs and together they set off for the town.

At first Annie went alone, leaving Rachel to tend the house and the fire and look after Wee Alex, while Fiddly and the boys stretched out the lines to dry, looping them over poles in front of the house, cleaning the hooks of any debris and checking for weaknesses, so that they were ready for baiting on Annie's return.

'You should take the lass with you,' said Fiddly. 'Teach her the ropes straight off. She's bright enough. She'll learn.'

'But she's such a peely-wally wee thing. I fear she'd not be able to shoulder the basket.'

'She may be little, but she's wiry – and tough, too, I'll warrant, behind yon timid eyes.' When Annie hesitated he went on, 'Look at me. I'm small enough and look what I can manage. Six strapping sons for a start – and six more if I'd had my way.'

'Enough o' that, Fiddly,' warned Annie, though her voice was tender. 'Another month or so, and I might give the lass a try. If she continues to thrive.'

Rachel did. The food was much the same as it had been in Cove, but there she had been left to forage for herself as best she could when the rest were finished, whereas here both Annie and Fiddly went out of their way to see she ate.

'Ye must grow strong and straight if ye're to be a fisher's wife and carry his creel to the market,' teased Fiddly.

Rachel looked up through lowered lashes to where James sat at the far end of the trestle table, both elbows resting on the scrubbed wood, the broth bowl cupped in his big hands. He caught her eye and winked, and she felt a glow of pleasure spread through her thin little body.

'Maybe she'll nae choose to be a fisher's wife,' he said, teasing, 'but wife to a merchant wi' a grand house on the quay.'

'And why not?' said Fiddly as Rachel blushed, tongue-tied. 'She's a fine wee lassie, and a merchant needs as good a wife as a fisherman.'

'Aye,' said Annie, ladling more broth into Rachel's bowl. 'Drink it up, lass, to give ye strength.' She swung the cauldron back over the smouldering peat and replaced the lid. 'There's money in trade and it needs a good woman to take charge of it.'

'You're right, Ma,' said James, breaking off a hunk of the flat, brown loaf in the middle of the table and speaking through the crumbs. 'There's plenty o' money in the sea – and not just from the wee darlin's we pull out of it. Take a boat with a big, empty belly, fill her with goodies in a foreign port, and, gin ye dodge the Frenchies and the Customs men, there's a fine fortune for the making.'

'There's been brandy run at Torry again,' said a twin, 'and the Customs men couldna catch them.'

'It doesna have to be illegal,' said Maitland earnestly. 'There's silks, tobacco, tea, and spices all fetching a fair price, as well as brandy wine. A ship is all ye need, and men to sail her.'

'We're fisherfolk,' said Fiddly, 'nae floatin' shopkeepers. Leave trading to the likes o' Atholl Farquharson.'

'I'd nae trust my goods in any ship o' his, Da,' said James. 'Did ye see yon brig he sends to London? Old, patched-up, leaking, and overloaded till the gunwale's awash with sea-water. 'Tis a wonder she hasna sunk.'

''Tis greed keeps her afloat,' said Maitland, 'but 'tis wicked to risk men's lives so. A seaman deserves a good ship under his feet, and I'd like fine to build one, one day.'

'They say Atholl Farquharson's nae a man to cross in the way o' business,' said James, his strange eyes suddenly bright, 'leaking ship or no. He's rich, he's sharp, he's ruthless – and he canna abide competition.'

'Then it's lucky he'll find none from us,' said Fiddly firmly. 'We're fisherfolk and happy to be so.'

Davy began to play softly on his mouth-organ, *Three times round went the gallant, gallant ship, Three times round went she, Three times round went the gallant, gallant ship, Till she sank to the bottom of the sea . . .'*

'Listen to Davy, Da,' cried James, triumphant. 'Fisherman or merchant, if his ship founders the sea'll drown him just the same, with no questions asked first as to whether his hold's full o' fish or fancy draperies for the ladies.'

'Don't talk so,' gasped Annie, touching iron for protection. 'I'll have nae word o' drowning, do ye hear?'

'Sorry, Ma.' James looked momentarily contrite, then his disconcerting eyes lit up again with enthusiasm. 'We may be fisherfolk, but that doesna mean we canna dream of other things now and then. Tell them, Maitland.'

'Da . . .' began his brother, and looked to James for support, but James only nodded encouragement. 'We've been thinking . . .'

'Nae again?' crowed George. 'It's nae good for ye, lad,' added William, 'it strains the brain.'

'Leave him be!' said Annie sharply. Maitland had always needed protection from the twins' teasing, being too abstracted to realize till too late what they were about. Maitland was the quietest of her sons and because of that she still felt a particular tenderness towards him, though he was almost a grown man at fifteen and should not need a mother's coddling. But she knew he was also the cleverest of them all, which was protection of a kind, as well as provocation. 'Let the lad tell us,' she said, 'and you two can fetch more peats, since you're so full o' energy.' She took Fiddly's pipe and tobacco from the pot-shelf and handed them to him, before resuming her seat at the table.

Encouraged, Maitland continued, 'There's plans for the harbour development, Da, with Commissioners appointed. A new wet dock's to be constructed, and new dry and graving docks. The piers are to be extended, to deepen the channel so that the merchant ships can come and go freely, and . . .' He took a deep breath before continuing, in a rush, 'there's that land at the flood-mark for lease, where Hall's have yon wee dockyard and shed.'

31

'Aye, so there is,' Fiddly packed tobacco into his pipe and waited, eyes twinkling, for the lad to continue.

'Well, if we could maybe lease that, we could build a boat – a brig of ninety tons or so, for the coastal trade.'

'Aye,' said Fiddly solemnly, striking flint against flourish, 'we could that, or a 500-ton three-master, or a man o' war, guns and all, for the King's fleet. *If* we had the wherewithal.'

'But they're to sell off the building materials, too, Da. Their whole stock in trade – timber, plank, iron, tar, pitch, even the shed that holds them.'

'And what do ye think we'd use for money?'

'We could borrow, maybe, from the Whitefishers?' The Whitefishers Society was a benevolent body to which they all contributed so that funds might be readily available to help the widowed and the sick.

'We could, Da,' agreed James. 'Maitland's made a first-class model, good as any boat Hall's have built. He's got a book, too, with instructions. We could draw the plans and . . .'

Rachel listened, enthralled, her embarrassment forgotten. She had seen that book: *The Shipbuilder's Repository, a Treatise on Marine Architecture*. Had watched Maitland study the tables of measurements and proportions, had admired the tiny model ship he had constructed out of carved wood and twine. The possibility that he might actually make the same boat in proportions large enough to put to sea had not occurred to her, but if James was to have a part in it, then all things were possible.

'If we had the money, James and I could . . .'

'No,' interrupted Fiddly with unaccustomed sternness. 'I've never borrowed in my life, lads, and I dinna look to you to start.'

'But Da, we'd pay it back soon enough. There'll be good money from the herrin' come summer.'

'And trade's good,' put in James. 'Maybe not to foreign parts as yet, wi' the Frenchies everywhere and the privateers, but all up and down the coast it's flourishing. Freight charges from Banff are up to three shillings the barrel bulk, and that's just for transport. If we bought our own goods, Da, and traded . . . I tell you, there's profits to be made.'

'And risks to be taken. Did ye not hear the *Jean* went to pieces in St Andrew's bay only last week, and her cargo of iron sunk to the bottom? A hundred tons of it. What profit is there in that?'

'But they hope to save the iron, Da. Bosun Brand was sayin' . . .'

'Bosun says a deal too much and like as not in his cups, so dinna any o' ye listen to him.' Fiddly puffed once, twice, at his pipe till the tobacco flared into satisfying fumes, then continued, more gently, 'Let me tell ye a tale, lads – you too, lassie – and listen carefully.'

The door opened on a rush of night air to set the tallow candle swaying.

'Come away in, Willy and George,' called Annie. 'Put they peats down i' the hearth and listen to yer Da.'

Obediently the twins set down their burden and crowded on to the bench at the table, expecting entertainment, as Fiddly gathered his thoughts. Quietly Rachel collected the wooden drinking bowls and plates and began to wash them in the basin kept for the purpose, while Bonnie Annie took up her knitting. Her fingers were soon flashing silently over wool and needles, while her eyes were fixed, like all eyes in the shadowed room, on Fiddly's wizened face. The candle on the table guttered and died. Someone poked the fire into added flame and the cauldron sang softly into the silence.

Then Fiddly spoke. 'There's nothing certain i' this world but what ye have in yer hand, and that's like as not to fly awa'. Before your Ma and I were married . . .'

'Not that, Fiddly,' interrupted Annie. ''Tis long past and done with, and no cause to open old wounds. Tell a different tale.'

'Nae, Annie, I've not mentioned it in a' these years, but I mean to do so now. And you listen, lads, and listen well. Before your Ma and I were married, we had hopes o' a fine new house. Nae this one, but a better, planned by our own Whitefishers Society. Plans were drawn, tenders called for, the builder chosen. Your Ma and I were promised, and I'd paid in good money, regular, to the Society. Then, before yon houses could be built, the treasurer found there was nae money after all. It had been lent out to the Gibbon brothers for their fancy shipbuildin' schemes and they'd lost it all, with the rest o' their fine assets and promises.'

'How, Da? Did the ships go down?'

'Never you mind the ins and outs o' it, lad. The Gibbons were bankrupt, the Whitefishers the losers, and your Ma never got her fine new house.'

'It didna matter, Fiddly.'

'*It did to me*.' Fiddly's face was stern with rare, remembered bitterness. 'I'd promised ye a fine new house and I'd failed ye.'

'But we have a fine enough house now, Fiddly.' Annie's eyes were troubled as she saw his face. 'And a fine family to fill it. There's nae cause for regrets.'

'Maybe not for you. But this house is the Council's; it should hae been the Whitefishers', and would hae been, but for borrowing.'

'What happened to the Gibbons, Da?' asked James.

'It's no matter. But what is, is this. Ye'll nae borrow money, do you hear me? For 'tis not only the borrower who suffers if things go awry, but those he borrows from.'

'But Da,' persisted Maitland, 'that's nae the way o' business. We borrow to build, and what we build earns more than we borrowed – and I've planned a fine boat, a brigantine with two masts, square-rigged sails, and a hull built for storage *and* speed.'

'Besides,' added James, 'it's nae every day there's land to lease on the quay and practically at our own door.'

'*No*. We're fisherfolk, not gentry. We'll have no debts. *Or may my boat be a bonnet to me*.'

There was silence at the utterance of this solemn oath. In the shadows Annie touched iron again with an indrawn breath, while Rachel bit her lip against the memory Fiddly's words called up: her own father had found his boat a bonnet to him as it capsized and pinned him underneath. After that, there could be no more talk of Maitland's plans.

'But I mind clear as day, Jamie,' Fiddly told his son later that evening, after several mugs of ale in Cushnie's tavern, 'how disappointed your Ma was. I'd like fine to buy her her own house one day. There's fine old properties for roup every week now, wi' the grand folk wanting to build i' the new town. For instance, Fordyce of Culsh's house is up for sale. Ye ken that fine place i' Castle Street? What grand views o' the harbour she'd have from yon house. There's nae chance o' me bidding for it, nor much o' you doing it for me, Jamie, but I dinna want

34

to think o' her in the poorhouse or dependent on charity if I go afore she does. Promise me, Jamie, ye'll care for her and the wee ones?'

'Of course, Da.' Jamie would no more think of doing otherwise than swim to China, but the glimpse of such a responsibility, remote though it was, filled him with a dread which he hastened to dispel.

'Drink up and sing, Da, like ye usually do. Ye're in a rare miserable mood the night, and no mistake.'

Fiddly grinned, slapped his son on the back and laughed aloud. 'Aye, ye're right there, son. And I'd best snap out of it afore I addle every egg i' Fittie. Cushnie! More ale for me and my fine son. *"I came to the Cross and I met wi' a lass; says I, my wee lass are ye willing to go? To tak' share o' a gill? She said, sir I will . . ."* Come on, lads, all o' ye together, *"For I'm the wee lassie who never says no!"'*

Later, when Fiddly had ambled home, still singing, James headed for Bouncing Bella's lodging. Her energetic favours would surely scatter the cloud which his father's words had spread at the back of James's mind, and he knew she would wait for payment till another day.

'Sure my lad,' she had told him on that first occasion, 'a young and lusty fellow, handsome as you are, is welcome any time.' But as he made his way along the quayside in the lamplight of moored ship and riding light, with the water lapping against quay and bow, Fiddly's words lingered. *'If I go afore she does'* . . . *'the poorhouse'* . . . He had never heard his father speak of such things before, and though every fisher lad knew the sea was hazardous and his calling more so, it was a danger never spoken of: James could no more imagine home without Fiddly than the sea without water.

As for himself taking his father's place, that was impossible to imagine. He loved his Ma and his brothers, even that wee scrap of a Cove lass had his affection, but he wanted to remain one of them as an equal, carefree and without responsibility, not weighed down by his father's mantle. He had other hopes . . .

As the old year drew towards the new, there was no more talk of leasing the yard at the flood-mark. Maitland continued to carve

35

his models and to study the great book which he had contrived to borrow, no one knew how, from someone at Hall's. He and James talked in the evening while they sorted hooks or spun horsehair for new tippens, of ships in the harbour, of cargoes and trading posts, of timber from St John's, flannels and muslins from Hull, brandy from across the Channel. Rachel, crouching over the stocking or shirt she was mending, listened as she had listened to Andrew Noble's fairy stories in Cove. She knew, as they all did, that they were fisherfolk not merchants, but those tales of foreign ports and cargoes of strange spices and oriental silks were more than tales to her. They were promises of a future which would encompass all those barrels and bales she saw daily on the quayside, with their scents of nutmeg and cinnamon, oranges and cloves – and somehow, James Christie, Captain . . .

At Old Yule she joined happily with the rest of them in the traditional celebration, though as always Jessie Brand was in the forefront of everything, preening herself in her Sunday finery as she served the customary dish of fermented oats – or sowens – to the menfolk, joining with gusto in the 'boat to burn' ceremony when the bonfire on the shore was followed by a grand meal of roast beef.

Wide-eyed and eager, Rachel watched it all, quick to help when she was needed for cooking or serving or clearing away dirty pots, quick to join in when Fiddly's music rang through the Square with Davy's mouth-organ and, later, Annie's singing.

'Here's a wee gift for ye,' said James, coming upon Rachel where she sat on her creepie-stool at the fireside, tending the sowens. He held out his closed fist, palm downwards, and grinned, his eyes sparkling, one blue, one brown in the firelight. 'Well, aren't ye going to take it?'

Rachel bit her lip in blushing pleasure and held out her hands. She felt something cool and smooth against her palm and saw a perfect, pearly conch shell, its curling lip as delicate as a baby's ear, the surface gleaming pink and blue and turquoise like summer dawn on a quiet sea.

'I got it from a sailor on the quay,' said James, offhand. 'A lassie must have some kind o' gift at Old Yule.'

'Thank you,' breathed Rachel, overwhelmed. 'It's beautiful.'

'And fit and proper for a wee mermaid, eh?' teased Fiddly. 'Put it to your ear and hear the singing. Well, aren't ye going to give Jamie a kiss for it? Or is it every day ye get a present from a fine young gentleman?'

Shyly, Rachel stood on tiptoe and kissed James's cheek. His young beard was soft as silk and his flesh warm. Rachel felt the touch of it long after on her lips, and treasured her shell as if it had been a pearl.

Jessie, seeing the exchange from the doorway, called, 'And what about me, James Christie? Can you no' see I've a fine new gownie that needs a kiss for good luck?'

James looked at her with level eyes. 'Aye. Alex, give the lass a kiss as she's needing one. I reckon Wee Alex is nearer your age,' he added, as he made to push past her into the Square.

'I'm not a nursemaid,' she retorted, eyes flashing, 'nor a mother neither, to need a bairn's kisses. Not yet,' she added, with an upward thrust of her well-developed breasts.

James felt the warmth of them through his jersey, and in spite of himself felt the stirrings of an excitement hitherto reserved for Bouncing Bella. 'Away wi' ye,' he said angrily, pushing her aside. 'I've no time for lassies that think they're grown women. Away to your skipping and your ball.'

Jessie, scarlet with humiliation, turned her anger on the nearest object. 'What are ye gawping at, ye daft quine? Shut your mouth, or I'll do it for ye!' Then with a final furious look at Rachel she turned on her heel and flounced out of the house.

Fiddly laughed. 'She's a silly wee lassie, yon Bosun's Jessie, but she's good at heart.'

'You're over generous, Fiddly,' said his wife, 'as ye always are. But she'd best be careful – I'll not have her in my house if she canna behave decent.'

'Come now, Annie, 'tis Old Yule and no time for animosity. How about a dance wi' me, if Davy'll carry the tune for a while?'

In the dancing merriment which followed, the incident was forgotten, but when, a few days later setting out for the mussel beds, Rachel found a hare's foot in the bottom of her pail, she had no doubt who had put it there. Trembling, she threw it on to the furthest midden. Her short life had seen plenty of childish cruelty and spitefulness, and though she wondered,

37

briefly, what she had done to make Jessie Brand ill-wish her, the hare's foot thrown away, she thought no more about it.

In May, the small-line fishing gave way to the great or deep-sea fishing, and the menfolk were away for up to three days at a time. The Christies beached their winter fishing boat and went to sea in a large thirty-footer, owned jointly with the Brands. This time Fiddly, James, Maitland, William and George went together, young Davy being left unwillingly at home, and Bosun the sole representative of the Brand family in the boat.

'When those wee sons of his grow a bitty older, there'll be no room for more than three Christies, and we'd best start looking for another boat,' said Fiddly, but without anxiety. There'd be time enough to start worrying in three or four years' time. Meanwhile, it was Annie who worried: for with so many of her family at sea in the same boat anxiety was natural.

They took food for three days at a time with them; bread and dried fish, ale and cheese, all to be eaten cold, since on the undecked boat there was nowhere to cook or prepare a hot meal. For the deep-sea fishing the men baited the lines themselves, at sea, and the womenfolk took the opportunity this gave them to cut peat for the winter's supply, wash blankets, or catch up with other jobs that the winter schedule left no time for, while they awaited their menfolk's return with the next batch of fish for sale.

Rachel enjoyed the summer. She liked the flat expanse of sand warm under her feet when the tide was out, the perfection of the herring gulls drifting white against an azure sky, the smaller black and white terns like little fishing boats riding the swell, the bird prints in the sand, and the thousand bubbles of sand eels as she trod the tide-washed shallows with the sun at her back, the grasslands a rich velvet on her left hand, the glinting sea on her right, and ahead of her the curve of coastland stretching northwards into a sunlit haze of sandy headland and gleaming sea. She gathered driftwood for the fire, finding out those pieces which had been polished smooth by the sea, collected sea-shells and fragments of polished glass, emerald, amethyst, and once a brilliant sapphire blue. She found sand-eels and mussels for bait, heaping them into her pail to carry home to the mussel scarp at the back of the house, and gathered seaweed, or dulse, to twist round a poker and roast over the fire.

Sometimes if the day was fine, she helped Annie to carry the benches and table out of doors and scrub them down with fine sand, or to wash the heavy shirts and blankets which were spread on the grass to dry in the sun and wind, with the bent grass rattling on the headland and the spray flying high. Sometimes when the men were home again, the work done and the Square full of families enjoying the mild evening sunlight, Maitland would help her to read or she would practise writing in a careful, rounded hand, while Alex lay on his stomach on the grass and sketched his pictures of the animals and birds he saw around him, Annie knitted, Fiddly sucked his pipe and talked lazily to James or Davy, the twins whispered together or disappeared on to the shore to play elaborate games in the rock pools, and Davy played softly on his mouth-organ till the sun sank beyond St Nicholas' kirk and the light left the sky.

These were the moments Rachel loved best and she would look up from her copybook and glance quickly from face to face of 'her' family, ticking them off in her mind, and lingering always longest on James's face, his dark hair silky in the evening light, his young beard soft as the breast feathers of a thrush, till he looked up, caught her eye and winked or pulled a face, and she would look quickly away, blushing. James teased her as his father did, but he was kind as they all were in their ways; and gradually, wonderingly, the child realized that she was happy. Though she had no particular friend, the Square accepted her, until she was teased no more and no less than any other child.

Fiddly watched her with satisfaction. 'She's a quiet wee thing, yon Cove lassie, but she's a good lass for a' that.'

'Aye, and hard working,' agreed Annie. 'I couldna ask for a better. The Lord knows what Jeannie was about, treating her as she did.'

'Jeannie had aye a quick temper and a heavy hand. Not like my Bonnie Annie, eh?' He slipped an arm round her waist and kissed her on the cheek.

'Away with ye and your flattery, and in front o' the bairns, too.'

'They're nae watching – and if they were, what's wrong wi' them knowing their father fancies their ma?'

39

Nothing at all, thought Rachel, overlooked in the shadows beyond the 'skulls' where the next day's lines lay neatly coiled. She had been checking yet again that nothing was snarled or twisted, for Jeannie Noble's threat still lingered. But with Annie's praise in her ears she felt reassured, and doubly so to think that Annie and Fiddly were in harmony. Not like Jeannie Noble and her man. Rachel shuddered, remembering how the Nobles' marital violence had inevitably spilled over to spend itself on her. Perhaps it is the same with love, she thought, wondering. Perhaps the happiness is not from the fiddle after all, but from the way he and she are like one person. It was a concept new to her, and one which insidiously took over the substance of her dreams. She still dreamt of a home with her very own family to fill it, but for the first time the dream included a husband who would love her as Fiddly Christie loved his Annie.

Rachel went regularly now to market with Annie, and it was here on a grey day in autumn that she met Andrew. She had seen him only once since her arrival in the Square a year before, and that briefly, when he had called on his way home at the end of the University session. She had found him changed, more solemn and preoccupied than before; or perhaps it was she who had changed? And when Fiddly drew him in to join them round the family board and teased her about the friend who had come to call on her, she was tongue-tied with embarrassment. Only when she walked with him along the springing turf of the Fittiegait back towards the town did she recapture something of their old intimacy. She loved him still, but he was no longer the only tenant of her heart – and as for Andrew, study occupied all his waking hours.

'For as well as Latin and Greek, I must attend outside lectures in anatomy, physiology, chemistry, and I have joined the Medical Society, too. Their weekly meetings are awesome, Rachy. The human body is an endless marvel . . . I have so much to learn and so little time to do it in.'

Rachel knew what he meant, for every waking moment of her own life was filled with one task or another as Annie trusted her with more and more of the household duties, till she judged her strong enough and ready to go to the market.

As soon as they had hauled the boat far enough up the slipway to be able to unload the catch in safety, Annie and Rachel would load the creel to the brim with the day's catch and pile the extra into a narrow-necked basket called a murlin.

Then Fiddly and James would heave the heavy creel on to Annie's back, Rachel would take up the murlin, and together they would set out along the Fittiegait towards the town, then up Shiprow or Marischal Street to the Plainstanes and the rows of countrywomen crying their wares.

Annie's stance was a good one on the corner with the Shiprow, and her customers were for the most part regulars who knew she sold fresh fish at a fair price.

'Remember, Rachel,' she told the child on the first day, 'never sell a marred or stinking fish. There's some who keep back what they canna sell and try again the morrow, over and over, but word gets around and I'll not have folk saying the Christie fish isna fresh. That way we can charge a steady price. Now watch me well, be polite, never swick wi' the change, and keep a sharp eye on the siller. There's light-fingered bodies everywhere.'

'Yes, Auntie.' Rachel looked apprehensively round the crowded square: baskets of vegetables and eggs; joints of beef raw-red on iron hooks; chickens, cheeses, pats of butter shaped between wooden moulds into fancy patterns, onions, heaped creels of glinting fish, some spilling in silver-slipping streams on to the cassies; fishwives in their blue skirts, sailcloth aprons and black shawls, hair tied back under kerchief or heavier plaid; and the customers: townsfolk, innkeepers, menservants or maids sent to buy for their employers' table, sharp-eyed housewives hunting a bargain. Everywhere the scents of fresh produce mingled with the herbs from the herb-woman's bundles, the smell of fresh fish, and the smokier tang of Findon haddock and 'smokies' (strung in pairs in the smoke-sheds of the neighbouring fishing villages till hard-fleshed and yellow). There were hake, stone-flattened and wind-dried, and skate, prized for its aphrodisiac as well as its medicinal properties, salmon from the Dee, and partans, grey-shelled, pincer clawed, moving endlessly in a layered heap of claw and shell. The crab-seller had decorated her stance with seaweed and painted shells. But the fishwives from the coastal villages favoured the Green and, with relief, Rachel saw no one she recognized from Cove.

Dogs rooted in the garbage, dodging hurled stones and abuse, small boys did the same, larger lads pushed importantly through the crowd on errands for people rich enough to pay them for their trouble, while further down the street, on the edge of the throng, carriages stood empty, waiting to transport people of importance home. How would she ever be able to keep a sharp eye on anything with so much going on? Rachel felt beleaguered and at bay, the murlin of haddock at her feet a pitiful barricade against a hostile world.

'One more thing,' said Annie, unwittingly dealing the *coup de grâce*. 'If a townie jeers at ye, take no notice. They like fine to torment the folk from Fittie, because they ken we're nae like them and nae wish to be neither. But dinna heed. Look straight ahead of ye and ignore them.'

It was while following this advice as the group of lads came up the Shiprow chanting, 'One, two, three, what a lot o' fisher-nannies I see,' that she saw Andrew and, fear forgotten, cried out his name. Heedless of dray horse or porter, he was ambling across the Castlegate, an open book in his hand, but he looked up instantly and saw her.

'Rachy! I never thought to see you here. I was on my way to Marischal Street to see Dr Dyce. He gives a class in the principles and practice of midwifery, and I have a question to ask him. But, where was I? Oh, yes. On my way I chanced to look into Brownes the booksellers and I am afraid I was diverted. Most fortunately so,' he added, remembering manners. 'Good morning, Aunt Annie. You remember me from the spring?'

'Aye, you're Jeannie's boy who's to be a doctor, and talking like one already. You did right well, Andrew, to win yon bursary. Your Ma must be fair proud o' ye.'

'She is, and she sends her fond wishes,' he improvised, mentally rejecting his mother's 'And dinna go near yon sister o' mine wi' her fancy ways, gin she sends the lassie back. We're well rid o' her.'

But Rachel is well rid of us, he thought, noting the girl's rounder face and figure, her well-kept hair and clear eyes, no longer clouded, as he remembered them, with secret pain. It had been his mother's doing, he had always known it – though, he argued loyally, she had many troubles and a burdened life; it

42

was not her fault. But he was glad his aunt and Rachel got on well together.

'I'm right pleased to see you again, Rachel,' he said now. 'You look well.'

'I am, Andrew.'

'And what about the letters? Are you keeping up with them? Rachel's a rare skill with reading, Aunt Annie, and with writing, too.'

'She didna tell us herself – she's a shy wee mousie – but my Maitland found her out. He gives her a lesson now and then. It's a good thing to be able to read and write a fair hand. But will ye no come back wi' us? We'll not be long afore we've sold all, and you'll be right welcome.'

'I'd like fine to do that, Auntie, but I have to be back at the college in an hour for Dr French's chemistry instruction. He is to deal with the principal processes and their application to pharmacy, and I must not miss it.'

'Then when you've a free hour or so ye must visit us again in the Square. I know Rachel would like that.' On an impulse she added, 'And the lass may walk some o' the way with ye if she chooses. But mind and dinna lose yourself, Rachel. I'll wait for ye here.'

'Thank you, Aunt Annie.' Rachel slipped a hand unselfconsciously into Andrew's and set off with him towards Marischal Street, her tongue miraculously loosened.

Jessie Brand, watching from her stance further along the Plainstanes, bit her lip in jealousy. Why should that peely-wally Cove lass with her flat chest and her chopped hair get to walk out with a fine student laddie like him? Whoever he was, he was too good for her. And so was James Christie, though she'd seen the way Rachel looked at him.

Jessie Brand, at thirteen, was as tall as her mother, and as well endowed, though Jessie's breasts were firm and high, her waist still trim. She had her mother's lusty appetites and her mother's ready tongue, but she also had what her mother was too lazy ever to entertain – ambition.

'I'll not spend my life in a shack like this,' she would say, casting scornful eyes over the rough-walled, earth-floored in-

43

terior of their crowded home. Mrs Brand was no housewife, and the room that under Bonnie Annie's hand was cheerful and welcoming in spite of the overcrowding, the plain furnishings, and the inevitable paraphernalia of Fiddly's trade, was, in the Brand household, merely a dirty, cluttered and sour-smelling enclosure where uncleaned fish hooks vied with unwashed children and rotting mussel bait to perfume what air was left when the fire had finished smoking into every crack and cranny. No one, least of all Jessie, thought to attempt to change matters. The only way to change was to move out into a better.

'I'll marry a merchant or a shipbuilder,' Jessie boasted. 'I'll have a great house on the quay. I'll buy my gowns from the best haberdasher and ride in a fine carriage.'

'You'll marry naebody if ye spend all day bletherin', 'stead o' earning yer keep,' Ma Brand would retort, with a smack round the ears for good measure. 'For naebody'll have ye. And if I catch ye round the back o' the boatsheds wi' yon Baxter laddie just once more, I'll skelp your backside black and blue.'

'Save yer strength,' retorted Jessie, unabashed. 'He's nae worth it, yon lad, and I've bigger fish to fry.'

Now, watching Rachel and the unknown student, Jessie set her jaw in determination. The student was tall and fair-featured, as far as she could see. He walked straight, with a fine set to his shoulders and though his clothes were shabby enough, he wore them with an air of authority.

'As if he knows where he's going,' she realized, 'and has nae doubt he'll get there. I wonder if he's yon Cove lad that visited i' the spring? Grown taller? But whoever he is, if Rachel can walk wi' him hand-in-hand, then so can I.'

Jessie had good reason for confidence: so far, every lad she had picked out for her attentions had succumbed willingly to her as yet inexpert but fast-blossoming wiles. Every lad, that is, but James Christie and it would not be long before she persuaded him, too, to go round the back of Hall's boatyard with her – and she might let him go further than the rest. Her young eyes aged with calculation. Already she had discovered the power of offering and withholding at the most vulnerable moment; she would use that power to get her what she wanted. At the moment, she wanted the Cove lassie's student.

'If ye like, Bonnie Annie,' she said, sweet-faced as only she knew how to be when self-interest required it, 'I'll tak' yon Cove lassie with me and show her how to sell at the door. I can see ye've a fair bittie yet to sell, and I've nae so much that I canna dispose of it to the professors in the Guestrow or the Broadgait. The Baxter wifie usually cries her wares in yon streets, but she's sick the day and telt me I could tak' her place,' lied Jess with accomplished innocence. 'The lass can maybe bring yon wee murlin o' fish wi' her, and I'll guarantee to see she gets a good price.'

Bonnie Annie regarded the Brand girl with cool eyes. She saw through her wiles, of course: the doe-eyes widening, the unruly hair transformed by some inner will-power into beguiling curls, the round cheeks rosy with innocent goodwill. The girl was after something. But whatever it was, James and Maitland both were safe at home and Rachel was a sensible child. She would not easily be diverted from her own straightforward path, and it might be useful for her to learn the knack of door-to-door trading, young though she was. Rachel had an air of innocent honesty about her which should stand her in good stead with the servants of even the most suspicious households – but it might also expose her to exploitation and, if nothing else, Jess would see the child got a fair price.

'All right,' she decided, 'but not for long, mind. And see ye tak' good care o' the lass or ye'll have me to reckon with.'

Jessie Brand, like most of the Square, stood a little in awe of Bonnie Annie, and even had the woman not been James's mother and therefore to be propitiated, she would have warranted the girl's respect.

'I'll see she comes to nae harm, Mrs Christie, ye can be sure o' that,' said Jess in her best Sunday-innocence manner, a manner in which she greeted Rachel on her return and retained, to the child's astonishment, until the pair of them had passed out of view of the Plainstanes and merged into the bustle at the far side of the square.

'Well,' said Jess, stopping and turning to block the child's path, 'what have ye done wi' him?'

'Who?' asked Rachel, baffled.

'Why, yon student o' course. The lad you were hanging on to like a hooked haddie on a line.'

'Oh, *Andrew*.' Rachel blushed with remembered pleasure. 'He is going to the college, to a lecture.'

'A lecture, is it?' jeered Jessie. 'I thought yon students were too high and mighty to speak to the likes o' you and me. Except in the way o' pleasure.' She laughed. 'Not that they've money enough to buy it, from all I hear.'

'But it was Andrew,' explained Rachel, not understanding the implication of Jess's remark. 'I lived in his mother's house in Cove.' Her small face clouded momentarily at the reminder. 'Did you not see him when he came to the Square? He's to be a doctor one day,' she added, with pride.

'Then when he is,' said Jess humbly, changing her tactics, 'I'd like fine to meet him. I've a great respect for yon doctor-mannies wi' their coloured medicines and their pills. Is it true,' she went on, steering Rachel towards the Guestrow, 'that they buy dead people to cut them up and see what's inside?'

Rachel shivered at the reminder of an aspect of Andrew's life which she preferred to forget, but, 'That is Andrew's affair,' she said loyally, 'and I have not asked.'

'Then I'll ask him myself,' said Jess, satisfied that a sufficient link had been established. 'He'll be coming to see you in the Square again, like enough, wi' you and he being *related*.' She relished the word with private satisfaction. After all, if they'd been brought up in the same house, that made them good as brother and sister. 'And if he doesna have the time for visiting, we'll search him out for ourselves one day, you and I. I ken where the professor folk live and there's nae reason why they shouldna buy their fish from you and me.'

'But . . .' Rachel was aghast at the idea of venturing un-invited on to such august territory, 'we *couldn't*. I mean, suppose . . .'

'And why not?' interrupted Jess with a toss of her curly head. 'I'm nae feared o' any professor mannie. They're folk same as us, and folk need to eat. And if any fishwife's been callin' her wares afore us, we'll show them we've cheaper and better to offer. You watch me, Rachy. Sell it cheap, see, till you've got 'em hooked, then you can ask a bittie more. "This isna fish today, ma'am," ye say, real ingratiating, "'tis men's lives we're selling." That'll get them, especially if ye add a bit about an uncle drowned or a boatie smashed to pieces on the rocks.' She

46

assumed an expression of mournful endurance, hitched a corner of her plaid to cover her hair, and intoned, "'Tis only a month back I lost my brother and my father to the waves . . .'"

'Don't say that!' Rachel looked quickly about her for cold iron to touch and avert the ill-luck which Jessie's words would surely bring down upon them. 'It is wicked to tell such lies.'

But Jessie only laughed. 'They're nae lies, they're persuasions. All in the way o' trade. Besides, folk do drown, boats do get smashed. I've seen it often enough and so must you have done, even in Cove. Well,' she finished, challenging, as Rachel refused to meet her eyes, 'haven't ye?'

'My father drowned,' said Rachel quietly, 'and my mother almost.' She remembered hearing from Frenchie Noble in one of his benigner moments how her mother had run screaming into the waves in an attempt to snatch her husband from his capsized boat, had failed, and had died a week later of grief and the fever brought on by immersion in an icy sea.

'There you are,' said Jessie, triumphant. 'They willna be lies when you tell them. Come *on*, will ye, or they'll have done their marketing afore we arrive. There's merchants and lawyers live in they streets, and professors too, and ye canna keep them waiting all day. You see yon fine housie wi' the turrets and the wee bit garden all railed in neat and private? We'll try yon first.'

Rachel looked ahead of her along the narrow cobbled street with its high houses, its archways into darkened close or airier garden, and, to the left and gable end to the street, the building which Jessie had indicated. It was an imposing structure with many windows, a carved crest over the square entrance way, and overhead a pair of turrets. Through a first-floor window Rachel caught the flash of firelight on crystal chandelier and the warmer gleam of polished wood.

'Are you sure we should, Jessie? It looks awful grand.'

'Why not? I'm nae scared. And call me *Jessica*: we're dealing wi' gentry in these parts. Now ring on that bell and leave the talkin' to me.'

Mrs Abercrombie's parlour, or withdrawing room as she preferred to call it, was her particular pride, with its polished panelled walls and polished floorboards most satisfactorily covered in the centre of the room by an India carpet of the finest workmanship – and so it should be, remembering what it had cost, if not in actual silver, then in ingenuity and courage. It was not easy for a shipmaster to avoid both privateer and government exciseman on the high seas, especially with the French hostilities making the German ocean more hazardous than ever. The Chippendale chairs and sofa-table had been more easily come by (a country client uncomfortably deep in debt) and the sofa, upholstered in pink brocade, she had ordered herself all the way from London, with the firescreens and the chandelier.

Christian Abercrombie had not quite forgotten that she had been born plain Kirsty Main of Torry, but she worked hard to erase the memory and to establish herself, by all the means she knew, firmly in the forefront of Aberdeen society. To that end she had invited guests and, in their honour, dressed her stringy person in a deep pink teagown of an unsuitably youthful cut and topped her hairpiece with a cap – 'for all the world like a frill on a saddle of lamb', as Euphemia Farquharson unkindly reported afterwards.

For her daughter Clementina's benefit there were Clemmy's friends Madelina Farquharson and Louise Forbes, and for her own, their mothers. All six ladies were engaged in the serious business of discussing what they should wear for the forthcoming dance at the Queen's Rooms. This involved not only a study of the newest fashion reports from the London papers together with the newest patterns, but the latest information in the columns of the *Aberdeen Journal* as to what materials were readily available in the town. They were also drinking tea.

'I shall tell Mr Abercrombie,' said his wife, setting china teacup back into china saucer with the unconscious care of one not born to such refinements, 'that the newest cargo of Hyson tea is so much better than the last. Would you not agree, Mrs Forbes?'

'Certainly, my dear. So much fresher. But then it is a wonder to me that anything can arrive fresh when it has been rolling about for months in the hold of a ship.'

'Tea-chests do not *roll*, Mamma,' corrected Louise. 'And if any cargo shifted as you imagine it to do, the poor ship would sink!'

'Dear Louise is so clever,' fluttered Mrs Forbes, deflated. A plumply pretty woman, innocent of all book-learning, she was

48

in turn baffled and intimidated by her angular, intelligent offspring.

'Such a pity the East India Company has the monopoly,' said Mrs Farquharson, helping herself automatically to a fourth ratafia biscuit. 'My husband would enter the tea trade himself otherwise, and import tea direct.'

Euphemia Farquharson's father had been a county gentleman, if only a younger brother, and she considered herself to have conferred a favour on the merchant classes by her marriage. She had been a good-looking woman in her time, and was still handsome in an imperious fashion, the authority of which was increased by her stature (built like a figurehead on a Spanish galleon, Abercrombie had said after their first meeting) and by the undoubted excellence of her dress.

Her husband, Atholl Farquharson, owned a lucrative share in a whaling company as well as several ships that traded between Aberdeen and places as far-ranging as London, Jamaica, and the Baltic Sea. He was known to drive a hard bargain, to sail close to the wind, and to be evil-tempered when crossed. He was, however, rich, and Euphemia appreciated money. The fact that her husband's riches accrued from dubious, if not downright dishonest, trading methods in no way disturbed her.

'Of course,' agreed her hostess politely. 'Who would not wish to engage in something so profitable *and* appealing?' Though what Farquharson needed with more trade when he had more than enough already, she could not imagine, except that some folk were never satisfied. She made a mental note, however, to encourage Clementina to take more notice of the Farquharson boy, in spite of his buck teeth and unfortunate complexion. 'But no one has the monopoly of the silks and taffetas, I am happy to say,' she went on in her best hostess manner. 'William Mackie has just received a most extensive assortment from the principal manufacturers in Britain, though I have not seen them myself.'

'So has James Roy,' retorted Mrs Farquharson. 'He imported them on one of our ships. I urge you to look at both before you come to any decision. And you, Mrs Forbes.'

'Quite right,' agreed Mrs Forbes, 'a wise precaution.'

'It gives one such an advantage when it comes to bargaining,' went on Mrs Farquharson and proceeded to relate some transaction with a tobacco-buyer in which her husband had triumphed.

As if that woman needed to bargain, thought Mrs Abercrombie enviously. She could have the pick of the bales and not feel the loss, whereas she herself still had a long way to go before she could relax, what with Clementina needing clothes for the new season, Fenton to be educated, and her husband no help at all. They'd both have to marry money, it was the only way. Mrs Farquharson had a daughter as well as a son: it was a pity Madelina was older than her own Fenton, but they could not afford to be too particular, and Fenton would grow.

At that moment there was a hasty knock at the door which opened to admit a maidservant, out of breath and flustered. She bobbed a quick curtsey before gabbling, with no pause for verbal punctuation, 'Cook says to tell ye there's two fisher lassies at the door ma'am wi' a basket o' haddies and they're fine and clean not like the last wifie and there's nae stink nor nothing like that and knowing the master's liking for a good bit haddie shall she try and get some cheap like for the dinner?'

'Mairi!' said Mrs Abercrombie sternly. 'How many times have I told you not to barge into the room when I am engaged with visitors? You will knock, pause, and when I call you, enter. And you will speak only what is necessary. Do you understand? I do not need a detailed report of everything that passes for kitchen conversation! If Cook wishes to ask whether I require her to purchase fish for the master's dinner, than say so. Now try again. Tell me, *briefly*, what you came to say.'

'Yes, ma'am.' The girl lowered her eyes, twisted her work-reddened hands in front of her none-too-clean apron and said in a rush, 'Cook says there's two clean fisher lassies at the door and would the master fancy them if Cook can get them cheap?'

Mrs Forbes smothered unfortunate laughter, the girls clapped hands to mouths and turned away to hide their giggles, while Mrs Farquharson merely sat a little straighter, raised one quizzical eyebrow and allowed herself the ghost of a smile.

Mrs Abercrombie's usually sallow face flushed with fury, but, remembering her company, she said, through tight lips, 'Thank you, Mairi. Tell Cook she may do as she thinks best.

Now go. *Really!*' she exploded when the door had closed again, 'that girl is impossible. She will have to leave at Martinmas.'

'Oh no,' drawled Mrs Farquharson, 'do keep her, if only as a conversation-piece. I found her *too* amusing.'

'And she was quite right, Mrs Abercrombie,' said Louise from the window through which she had been peering with undisguised interest, 'they do look clean enough. The fisherfolk are not all flea-ridden, in spite of general belief.'

'Louise!' protested her mother. 'Not in the drawing-room.'

'One of them is really quite pretty,' said Madelina Farquharson wistfully. She had inherited her mother's size, with her father's undistinguished features and colourless hair.

'In a vulgar sort of way,' agreed Clementina, staring down at the two figures who stood in the angle of the building where kitchen and hallway met to form a little courtyard of sun-warmed flagstones, sheltered from the wind. Across the yard was a patch of garden with a herb bed and apple tree before an arched entrance led into the street.

'Come away from that window,' ordered her mother sharply. 'I will not have you staring down into the close like a common busybody.'

'They're going now, anyway,' said Madelina, turning back to the company and the tea-table. 'Shall we discuss that pattern for a gown you mentioned, Mrs Abercrombie? It sounded particularly attractive.'

'Yes, please show it to us,' urged Mrs Forbes. 'Dear Louise needs something up-to-date for the new season, and perhaps it will inspire her.'

'I know what I want, Mamma, and I've told you so a dozen times. A plain grey merino with no fal-de-rals and suchlike nonsense.'

'But Louise dear, you must at least *try* to be feminine. I declare if she had her way she would wear a redingote and pantaloons like some dreadful French revolutionary. She is so intelligent,' she sighed as Louise turned away in disgust. 'Such a pity she was not a boy.'

Privately Mrs Abercrombie agreed. Louise Forbes unsettled her, with her forthright speech and unashamedly masculine tastes. It was a pity Clementina had to consort with her, but her mother was harmless and Maxwell Forbes was an eminent lawyer in the town, a friend of Mr Farquharson and fellow-member of the Aberdeen Club to which she hoped Abercrombie might be elected, one day . . .

'I will look out the pattern at once, Mrs Forbes,' she said. 'I think there is just time to study it before Mr Abercrombie comes home.'

Outside in the yard, Jessie Brand was well satisfied.

'What did I tell ye?' she said, hitching the creel higher and making for the archway which led back into the street. 'Did ye see the brass cooking-pots shining? And the chicken roasting over the fire? I could smell brandy, too, I swear it, and expensive tobacco. I told ye we'd find the rich folk, didn't I?'

'You said we were going to the professors' houses,' reminded Rachel, with a mixture of disappointment and relief. She had been nervous that somehow, by offering a professor her fish, she would spoil Andrew's chances at the college; but now that that danger was past, she regretted the lost opportunity of contact with Andrew's separate world. She would have liked to see how he lived.

'Professor or merchant, what's the difference as long as there's money?' said Jessie. She stopped in the archway and pointed to her right along the street to the Netherkirkgate some fifty yards away. 'Do ye see yon shoppie wi' the painted signboard and the barrels? Yon's Abercrombie's the wine merchant, and that fine house behind us is where Abercrombie lives. Did ye not hear yon daft quinie say, "Mister Abercrombie likes his haddie"? Used to be a fisherman, my Da says, over Torry way, wi' his own boat an' all, till he took to smuggling and made himself a fortune running brandy and claret wine under the noses o' the Customs men. And his missis no better. You'd never think to look at them that they were once like us.' Jessie's voice held a mixture of admiration and envy which dissolved suddenly into laughter, loud and taunting.

'And here's young Abercrombie coming out o' the shop now, with all the airs o' the king o' the herrings and him still wet behind the ears. Going home to yer mammy are ye, townie?' she jeered, and deliberately blocked his path as he made to pass her under the archway.

The boy blushed and hesitated. He was pink-faced and beardless, about Andrew's age though not so well-grown, in a neat grey coat and breeches, a bundle of books under one arm. Rachel thought he looked mild-tempered and kind, but Jess was bent on torment.

'Please let me pass,' the boy said, and made to walk to one side. Jessie side-stepped neatly to block his path again.

'Give us a kiss and I'll let ye by,' she said, her fresh face alive with mischief. George Abercrombie, coming to the door of his shop to see what the noise was, saw a dark-haired, round-cheeked, and lively lassie with wickedly laughing eyes apparently accosting his son with, from the look on Fenton's face, an improper suggestion – but before he could intervene an imperious voice called from the building beyond.

'Fenton! Come inside the house this instant!'

Jessie gave a shriek of delighted laughter. 'Bedtime for the bairnie! But remember, laddie,' she called after him as he slipped past her and ran, 'when she lets ye out to play, I'll be waiting.' Then she gave Rachel a playful push and pranced out of the archway into the street.

'A spirited lass,' noted Abercrombie with secret admiration, 'with something about her. Not like those peelywally friends o' Clementina's.' Sighing, he turned back to his shop, his barrels of rum, brandy, and claret, and his waiting customer – a gentleman from Deeside in search of a suitable accompaniment to the season's venison. Abercrombie was sure he could come to most satisfactory terms.

But when the gentleman had left, the bargain sealed, Abercrombie felt a moment's regret for the bygone days in Torry, with a dark night and an ebb-tide, when the only sound was the faint brush of oiled rowlocks and the slap of water against bow as he rowed across the harbour mouth to Pocra and the waiting pack-horses, their hooves muffled with sacking, their drovers silent. His wife had been spirited as that fisher-lass then, keeping watch for the exciseman and helping to man-handle wooden kegs in the light of one shrouded lantern. Now her energies were expended in social climbing and grandiose ambitions for the children.

Abercrombie, too, had ambition, but of a simpler kind. He wanted to build up his business into an empire to cover all

Scotland – and England too if he lived long enough. He had leased the Netherkirkgate shop ten years ago – the damp-walled ground-floor room and cellar of a decaying tenement building, with two rooms above it for his family. He had expanded since then to fill one of those two rooms with snuff and tobacco of a superior quality, and the other with chests of choice teas, on his wife's suggestion, and the ledgers of his growing enterprise. Fenton kept these up to date, or had until his enrolment as a Bajan student at the college a month back. Abercrombie had a steady contract with the Shore Porters to convey his barrels from the quayside, and another with the carrier to take deliveries inland. With a lad for the rough work and his own strong arms, he could manage the rest till Fenton should finish at college and join him. Five years ago he had leased part of the house in the Broadgait, and the furbishing of it to Kirsty's taste was a constant drain on profits. Now she wanted him to buy a stance in the new Union Street and build a shop there, but he had dug in his heels. The Netherkirkgate shop suited him. When Fenton came of age he'd have a fine sign put up over the door – '*Abercrombie and Son*' and one day, '*Vintner to His Majesty King George III*'.

But in spite of his expanding business, George Abercrombie remained a simple man with simple tastes, and he found his wife's assumed refinements both indigestible and depressing. He was too heavy a man to sit with ease on her new-fangled chairs, had she allowed him to do so, and his bulk required more to fuel it than her chicken consommés and ratafia biscuits if he was to carry a keg of brandy on his shoulder from carrier's cart to cellar. In consequence he spent as much time as possible on his own territory in the Netherkirkgate shop, or with his fellow merchants, booksellers, or publishers in the nearby Lemon Tree Tavern. He thought with longing of the old rooms over the shop, the porridge and salt herring and shared ale. Kirsty had been different then. It was a pity that wealth had made her envious and carping, always wanting more. Like the fisherman's wife in the vinegar jar, he thought, remembering childhood fairy tales. Look at her ideas for the children, for instance: an honest trade was no longer good enough for his daughter's husband, or for his son. Fenton was happy enough in the vintner's, but no, his mother wanted him to be a lawyer and would not leave the idea alone. Abercrombie sighed at the prospect of strife to come.

But he had promised to be home early for his dinner today, and must not forget, though there was still time to have a word with Farquharson in his office off the Shiprow. That last consignment of claret had been six weeks overdue. He whistled the lad to guard the shop and, thumbs in ample waistband, set out towards the Castlegate and the splendid vista of the new street.

'It'll be a fine avenue one day, wi' grand houses on either side,' said Jessie as she and Rachel made their way back through the town towards the harbour and home. 'We'll tak' our fish there then, and not bother wi' that lot.' She jerked her head derisively behind her to the mesh of tenements and closes which they had threaded in their efforts to get rid of the day's fish. They had traded the last for bread and eggs from a farm lassie on the Green, and Jessie was well pleased.

'Ye did well, Rachy,' she said, with rare generosity. 'I reckon you've a good face for sellin'. I'll tak' ye with me again.'

That was the beginning of a strange friendship: the older girl brash, fearless, her tongue ever ready with a sharp rejoinder, her pert eyes ever seeking out male admiration and as like as not rejecting it with mocking laughter or a jeer of derision. She was merry and cheerful, good company while things went her way, but if she was thwarted or her jealousy aroused, she showed the claws and spitting temper of an alley cat.

Rachel, in contrast, was shy, modest, always politely spoken and never hurtful. She was honest where Jessie was not. Her word given, it was never broken. Jessie could not see the virtue of such honesty, except where it worked to their advantage, but she recognized its value in the market-place and used Rachel accordingly. Jess knew which houses would respond best to Rachel's quiet offering, which to her own forthright approach, and together they built up a thriving trade.

Rachel admired Jessie's flamboyant beauty, her dark hair and flashing eyes, her full red lips and the shapeliness which reached voluptuous proportions as she blossomed into womanhood. In spite of the fishwife's apron and the creel on her back, heads turned in the street as Jessie passed, while Rachel went unnoticed. Though this reminder of Ma Noble's words – '*a poor soul at the best of times*' – still had power to wound, she accepted it as she accepted Jessie's authority in most matters concerning the world outside the Square. Yet if Jessie overstepped the mark in some matter of trading, Rachel would dig in her heels with inflexible obduracy and refuse to give in.

'It is not right,' she would say, pale-faced but determined, 'you must not sell a basket of fish with good ones only on the top layer,' and eventually Jessie would capitulate. It was not that she could not have persuaded her if she'd a mind to, but it wasn't worth the risk. Though Rachel would never carry tales, it wouldn't do to let word of shady dealing reach Bonnie Annie's ears. She would surely forbid Rachel to cry fish with her again, and Rachel was her best way into the Christie household.

Rachel was also the perfect foil for Jessie's looks and Jessie knew it. On the rare occasions when any man spared a glance for Rachel, Jessie's eyes gleamed bright with annoyance and her full lips narrowed. She was fond of the Cove lass, with the rough and ready affection of daily contact and work shared, but she was jealous of her too, though she would have scorned to admit as much. For deep in her heart she envied Rachel her air of quiet dignity, the way the gentlefolk spoke to her, her ladylike manners, and most of all, her position in the Christie house.

'Don't think to marry one o' they Christie boys,' Jessie warned her. 'I've seen you make cow's eyes at Jamie if he so much as looks at ye. But I marked him down for myself years ago and I'll have him. And that student lad o' yours too, if I've a mind to.'

'Andrew?' said Rachel, startled. She had not seen Andrew since that day in the Castlegate when she had first gone into the town with Jessie.

'Aye, Andrew Noble, if that's his name. I'll have them both, see if I don't.'

'But that is not right,' protested Rachel. 'Two husbands are not allowed.'

'Who mentioned husbands?' Then at Rachel's shocked expression, Jess gave a shout of gleeful laughter. 'If I have a husband, I'll choose *him* for pride – I'll have the other for pleasure!'

Rachel was appalled. Jessie was her friend, but sometimes she behaved like a . . . Rachel was ashamed even to think the word. The idea of her marrying James or Andrew was dreadful – she did not know which was the worst. As for the 'having', Rachel blushed at the very thought of it. 'Jess shall not have James,' she vowed over and over, 'nor Andrew. Not if I can help it.' But how could she help it when they were all three of them older than she was, and free to marry whom they chose? She walked the rest of the way home in troubled silence.

'Did ye hear, Da?' announced James at supper. 'Yon whalers brought in the best catch ever. A clear profit of £10,000 between four ships.'

'Even wi' a crew of fifty apiece, that's a fair bounty,' added Maitland enthusiastically.

'And a fair stink from yon whale-oil factory,' commented Annie. 'When the wind's in this direction it turns my stomach.'

'Maitland and I were thinking, Da,' began James, but Fiddly interrupted.

'I know what you're thinking, and no. I'll have no son o' mine going to the Greenland seas and changing his line for a harpoon.'

'Whales are fish too,' began Maitland, 'and we'd only need to go the once. Then with the profits we could find an empty slipway and . . .'

'No. I've told ye afore: we're fishermen, nae traders. If you're so keen at earning money,' he added, 'ye can buy us a yawl for the summer fishing. Yon Brand boys are growing fast and we'll need to look around for another boatie wi' room to take us afore we know it.'

'But Da, that's what I mean,' persisted Maitland. 'With money we could *build* a yawl, to learn our way about, and then move on to bigger ships.'

'Maitland's designing a bow, Da, which is going to be better than anything in the harbour.'

'Designing is one thing, doing another. Yon boat-building's skilled work and neither of ye are shipwrights, nor mast-makers neither, nor smiths, nor sailmakers, nor ropemakers, nor . . .'

'All right, Da,' interrupted James, 'we're a pair o' ignorant

57

fisher lads fit for nought but to haul haddock from the sea. But we can dream, can't we?'

'And we can learn, Da, from those who do know,' added Maitland. 'I've spent time at the yards. I've seen how it's done, and with the whaling money we could . . .'

'Whales are treacherous beasties,' interrupted his father, 'and the seas they dwell in the same. I've heard tell o' ships trapped in the ice and crushed to splinters by the swelling of it. Of whales thrashing so fierce in the flurry that they pull men and boats after them, under the sea; and they say the dying song of the creatures is pitiful to hear. Nae, lads, you stick to what you know. You're good whitefishers both, and there's no call for ye to dabble in dangers ye ken nothing of.' But, seeing their crestfallen faces, he added, more kindly, 'We'll maybe spend longer after the herrin' this summer, gin Bosun agrees. There's profit there, and we've the skill to take it.'

'Besides,' said Annie, closing the subject, 'yon Greenland boats are gone for months at a time. How would your Da manage without ye? He canna sail the boat alone.'

But though the whaling industry was closed to the Christie boys, it brought prosperity to others. There were soon five whaling companies in Aberdeen alone, and profits continued to rise.

Profit was also to be found in coastal trading, which grew rapidly as goods were shipped from abroad via London, Hull, Newcastle, Leith and Glasgow. There was a brisk trade in all manner of goods from wheat, barley, and flax to dye-stuffs, drugs, silks, china, and fruit. And, of course, wines. Harbour commissioners were appointed, and additional quays constructed to accommodate the growing number of ships. The north pier was extended nine hundred feet seawards and a south breakwater built, while the hammering from Hall's shipbuilding yard intensified, and other smaller yards sprang up on the Inches and the quay. A lifeboat shed was built south of Footdee and men were recruited to man and maintain it for a guinea a year.

'There's to be a slipway at the first stair, for speedier launching,' said Fiddly one evening on his return from inspecting the progress of the new pier. 'That'll be right handy. I offered myself for the lifeboat,' he added with a note of disappointment, 'but Captain Freeman was only needing six men and them already chosen. If any drop out or prove unfit, he'll consider me, but I reckon I'm too old for him.'

Annie was silent, her face carefully controlled in the expression Rachel had come to recognize as fear when the men were at sea and the wind howled in the rafters, when the surf thundered at their backs and the spray leapt thirty feet into the air from breakwater and pier, or on a clear day with a calm sea when the boats were late back from the fishing. Seeing Annie's pale, taut face, Rachel felt the same fear in her own breast for those she loved. But James was speaking.

'I put my name forward too, Da, with a dozen others,' he said cheerfully. 'I wasna chosen neither, and I'm young enough. But no matter: at least we'll be spared the training, and yon lifeboat hasna the monopoly. We'll still help as we've always done, Da, with hand or boat, if need arise.'

'Aye lad, and we'll maybe move faster, too. Yon lifeboat's a flatbottomed tub o' a thing by the looks o' her.'

'And she'll be no help when the ships are washed agin the pier. Remember yon Danish boat, when her masts tipped over so far we grabbed hold o' them from the quayside and pulled the men ashore that way?'

'Aye, and the hull smashed to pieces on the rocks,' put in William and George. 'There was fine driftwoood in the bay for days after.'

Rachel listened, a prickle of fear at the nape of her neck. It wasn't only staved planking that the tide washed on to the shore after a wreck, but seaboots, caps, tobacco pouches, jerseys, the pitiful, salt-soaked remnants of a life now lost. A week after that talk of shipwreck, though she did not see it for herself, there was the body of a seaman.

'His name was sewn into his shirt,' Jessie reported with relish, bursting into the Christie house one afternoon when the menfolk were on the shore redding the lines after the day's fishing, and Annie with them. Rachel had stayed behind to finish a piece of work that had been promised for the morrow. 'So it doesna matter', Jessie went on, 'that the sea and the fishes between them have ta'en his face. Mind and stitch the name large and clear in yon shirt you're sewing,' she added, devilment in her eyes. 'Whose is it, anyway?'

When Rachel made no answer, she caught up the garment and held it up to her own ample front. 'Too big for Davy, too small for George or William . . .' The twins were grown tall now, square-built and strong. 'It wouldna be for . . . James, would it?' Rachel dropped her eyes and Jessie crowed with delighted triumph. 'It *is*. Here's a "J" clear as can be. But ye'd best stitch "Jessica" if you can spell that much, for I telt ye way back that Jamie's mine.'

'Give that back to me.' Rachel leapt to her feet and snatched at the garment, but Jessie whipped it out of reach.

'Not till ye promise to do as I say. Stitch "Jessica", or I'll . . .' but before she could finish, the doorway darkened behind her.

'And what may you be doing, Jessie Brand?' demanded Annie. 'Tormenting Rachel again, is it? Well ye can just give yon sewing back to her and get out the house. A great girl like you – have ye no work to do o' your own without preventing other folks doing theirs?'

'Not if I can help it,' retorted Jessie, tossing the shirt to Rachel. 'Remember what I telt ye,' she warned and flounced out of the door.

'And what did she mean by that?' asked Annie as Rachel resumed her seat and bent her face over her work to hide her burning cheeks. 'Never mind,' she went on, as Rachel sought unsuccessfully for a truthful answer that would give nothing away, 'that girl's aye up to some mischief or other. Dinna you heed her.' She bent over Rachel's shoulder to inspect her work and nodded, satisfied. 'That's fine and neat, lass. You've done well. Now put it aside and give me a hand, will ye, Rachy? They'll be home soon enough, and the meal not ready. Just give yon pan a stir for me and check the seasoning while I warm the griddle. I've a pile o' herrings that'll cook a treat in oatmeal.'

'What's ado wi' Jessie Brand?' asked Fiddly, behind them. 'I passed her i' the Square just now and she swung her behind at me for a' the world like a quayside trollop. Had she come from here?'

'Aye,' said Annie, 'I sent her packing.'

'It's time yon lass was married,' said Fiddly, reaching for his pipe and tinder-box. 'She's old enough and ripe for it, by the looks o' her. I'm surprised she hasna hooked a lad by now.'

'She's saving herself,' said William from the doorway. 'For the man o' her choice,' added George. 'Poor sod.'

'That's enough o' that kind o' talk,' warned Annie.

'She's got her eye on our Jamie,' piped up Wee Alex, emerging from the box bed where he had retreated with a slate and chalk to draw in peace. 'She telt our Rachy to sew "Jessica" on Jamie's shirt.'

Annie looked sharply at Rachel who was stirring the broth with particular attention. The girl's head was averted, her eyes downcast, but Annie, remembering the scene she had interrupted earlier, looked suddenly thoughtful.

'Wash the chalk off your hands, Alex, and dinna hide in yon bed again, do ye hear? I've telt ye often enough. As for our Jamie, he's more sense than to fall for a daft quine like Jessie Brand.'

Nevertheless from that day Annie watched both girls with particular attention until, towards the end of Rachel's third year in the Square, she said suddenly, 'Rachel lass, it's time you had a new gown. You've grown awfu' tall this last year, wi' a shapely figure too, in the right clothes.'

It was true. Rachel was taller than Fiddly now, and though her bundled clothing concealed it, her breasts were full and rounded, her waist trim. Her hair, too, had changed; no longer nondescript and spiky, it was long and thick with a sheen like polished sandalwood. Her eyes were a calm blue-grey.

'I've a gownie yonder i' the kist,' went on Annie, 'put away these fifteen years and more. I was slim as you once, Rachy, till the bairns came to thicken me. But I reckon yon gown would fit ye fine, wi' a bit o' stitching here and there.' She opened the lid of one of the chests beyond the looped sailcloth partition and lifted out a blanket or two, a fold of white linen ('for my winding sheet'), then a thicker fold of pale-blue woollen material.

'There,' she said, pleased, as she shook out the creases and held it against her. 'It's good cloth and laid up in camphor, so there's nae moth in it. If you're prepared to work late a few nights, you and I together can make a fair job of it, I'm sure, and wi' new ribbons it'll do ye fine.'

'Well, lass!' said Fiddly in astonishment when she stepped from behind the partition in the completed garment at Old Yule. 'I never thought when I took in a wee drowned scrap o' a

61

quinie frae Cove that she'd grow to be a beauty. Let me kiss ye, Rachy, for good luck.' He hugged her tight against his chest and kissed her cheek. His beard was wiry, his skin leather-rough, but she felt the loving protection in his arms and knew he meant every word.

'Thank you, Fiddly,' she said, her eyes moist, and kissed him in return.

'Well, lads, aren't ye going to give Rachel a kiss too, for her fine new gown? Or are ye all struck dumb by the sight o' her?'

It was not far from the truth, for Rachel in her new dress which exactly matched her eyes was not the Rachel they had grown used to – a mousy, quiet thing in nondescript browns and greys, pinned up in a shapeless bundle of aprons and layered petticoats, her hair tied back by a kerchief. This Rachel was elegant and slender, in a dress which emphasized the soft blue of her eyes and the soft curve of her figure, her hair looped into a chignon at the nape of her graceful neck. Under the silent battery of eyes, Rachel blushed and unwittingly added the final touch.

'She's beautiful,' thought Maitland in astonishment, 'and I never noticed.' He kissed her as the twins did, swiftly on the cheek, but the memory of her figure against the sailcloth background was to stay with him long after.

Davy was more demonstrative. 'You look like a princess,' he said, grinning, and hugged her with unabashed affection. 'I'm right proud o' ye. But where's James? He must kiss Rachy too.'

'Away at the bonfire,' said Wee Alex, but James was in the doorway, as he had been for the past five minutes, startled into silence by the new Rachel. He remembered, as his father did, how she had been when she came to them – large-eyed, ragged, with great weals and bruises on her skinny figure. She was now no longer the foundling to be teased and protected as one would any smaller sibling; she was suddenly an individual, with her own privacy and rights. James was vaguely disturbed, and at a loss how to treat her.

'Well come away in, lad,' called Fiddly with mock impatience. 'Can't ye see we've a lady in a fine new dress waiting for her good-luck kiss. Or have ye forgotten how to kiss the ladies?'

James grinned and stopped forward. 'Let me look at ye,

62

Rachy.' He took her shoulders in his hands, then kissed her lightly on the forehead. 'There's for luck,' he said and released her, but it was his murmured 'You look lovely, Rachel,' that lingered with her throughout the celebrations, to keep her eyes bright and her cheeks aglow.

Annie, watching from the fireside where she was busy with the sowens, was well pleased. But she was less so later on that evening, when the bonfire had died on the shore, the embers had been carried triumphantly round the Square, and the meal of beef and sowens was over. Fiddly had taken up his fiddle to play for the dancing; doors opened all round the Square, lanterns were hung on door-frames or poles, and soon the darkness throbbed with stamping, swirling shapes as more and more fisherfolk joined in. Maitland asked Rachel to dance; then she was claimed by William, George, and Davy in turn, then by Maitland again, till she was flushed and panting, her hair delightfully dishevelled and her face alive with happiness.

It was a cold, black night with a frost-clear sky and stars, the sea quiet under a sliver of rising moon, but no one was cold for long as the fiddle music sang joyously to the stars, Fiddly's foot beating rhythm, one or other of the men punctuating the whirling intricacies of the dance with a cry of atavistic pleasure. Annie, behind Fiddly in the doorway, looked on with simple pleasure, until she saw that brazen Jessie Brand in a scarlet bodice with the buttons popping and her skirts flying higher than they ought, seize James's arm for the reel and refuse to let him go. There was ale and whisky, cheese and bread, and as the music raced faster, so did the laughter and the dancing, till Fiddly drew his bow in a final chord and fell back onto the bench, face streaming sweat, to call for 'a gallon o' best ale to put back the life in me'.

But Jessie too had 'fallen', exhausted, big breasts heaving, and James could do no other than catch her. The crowd moved to block them from sight before Annie could see further, and when Fiddly, refreshed, took up his fiddle for the next reel, James and Jessie Brand were no longer of the company.

Rachel, slipping round the house to fetch more peats for the fire, saw them in the shadows of the back wall. She snatched up a single peat from the stack and sped back without a sound, but Annie saw all in the girl's face. Anger swept her outside and round the house, where she wrenched the locked pair apart and boxed both smartly about the ears.

'The whole Square knows you're heading for a whore, Jessie Brand, and if your own ma won't beat the sense into ye, I'll do it for her,' she cried, with another smack. 'And as for you, James Christie, I'm ashamed o' ye. Get back in the Square where I can see ye, and dinna leave my sight again the night!'

Jessie laughed in Annie's face. 'He's a grown man. He'll do as he chooses,' but when James pushed past her towards the Square without a word, she hurried after him, crying, 'Jamie, wait for me.'

With satisfaction, Annie wiped her bruised hands on her apron front as she watched them turn the corner of the house. James, she was glad to see, looked suitably ashamed, and she'd stopped them before anything irreversible happened. With a girl like Jessie Brand, any man was vulnerable, given the whisky in him and a clear night; and though James was old enough to know better, he was also young enough to take what was offered. But it was Rachel she worried for. She had seen the look of betrayal on the girl's face, and it was a look she would not soon forget.

'Dinna grieve,' she said gently, late that night when, the music over, everyone had gone to their beds, including James. 'It's some men's ways to be frisky when a lassie leads them on. It means nothing. It'll be all right, Rachy, you'll see. It'll be a good year.'

But Rachel knew, with a grey premonition, that the happiness of early evening, with Fiddly's music and James's words sweet in her ear, would not come again.

At first it seemed that Annie was right. The weather was milder than anyone remembered for many years, with none of the violent storms and bitter winds to be expected in the early months before the spring. In the harbour, whaling ships prepared to set out for the Greenland waters, taking on provisions and crew till the final farewell ritual of garlanded merriment. There were five of them on that first day of April, when Rachel rose, as usual, before dawn, and the rest of the household with her. The wind was westerly and gentle, the sea calm.

'We'll find good fishing the day,' said Fiddly, pleased. 'And we'll be back early wi' a fine catch for ye, lass.' He kissed her, as he always did before setting out, and called James and Maitland to hurry themselves. 'There's William and George gone already. Do ye want Bosun's boat to catch the best fish afore ye're out yer beds?'

'Coming, Da,' called James from somewhere inside his jersey as he struggled to pull it down over his head. Mild though the weather was, it could be cold at sea. 'And dinna worry. Bosun hasna your knack o' finding out the shoals. They'll wait for ye, the silver darlings.'

Rachel, packing the bread and cheese for their 'piece', watched James through lowered lashes as he pulled on his boots, first right, then left, leather tops reaching half-way up his thighs. His young beard gleamed chestnut in the light of the crusie, dark hair and eyebrows glistened with water-drops from the morning dousing above eyes alert with humour. Maitland seemed pale and weak beside him, though she knew him to be strong as James was, and as tough. But James loved the sea whereas Maitland loved his dreams . . .

'Come on lads, or am I to go without ye?' Fiddly winked at Rachel and added, 'Or shall I take Rachy with me in your place? She'd be a fine mermaid to lure the fish to my line wi' her singing.'

'She's nae boots,' said Wee Alex, bleary-eyed from sleep. 'And nor have I, or we'd both come with ye.'

'Time enough for you, lad, when these great lazy brothers o' yours are past it.' With a good-natured slap on the shoulder, he pushed James and Maitland before him, under the low doorway and out into the morning darkness of the Square.

'Bye, lass.' Fiddly kissed Rachel on the cheek and followed. Rachel watched the three of them stride towards the quay, two tall lads and a smaller, older man silhouetted black against an indigo sky. But the sea to the east was gleaming with the gold-streaked promise of dawn and the wind at her back was soft. Annie and Davy were gone ahead already to launch the boat.

Rachel took up her mussel pail and moved round the gable end to the shore.

She loved the silent time before the dawn, the sand clean and

65

cool under her feet, the surf curling and drawing in endless rhythm, while beyond the rim of foam the sea stretched limitless till sky and ocean merged into infinity. To her left the long line of the shore stretched in a clear-cut line of turf and cliff past the Don mouth and Black Dog northwards to Newburgh, the sand a pale band between darkened shore and glinting sea. To her right was the curve of the bay where it met the north pier, stretching like a protective sword from Pocra pier, the warning flags at its tip, guarding the entrance to the harbour. Across the neck of water made by the pier and the southern breakwater were the grassy cliffs above Torry, the rocks of Girdleness and Greyhope Bay. She could see the small shapes of cows grazing on the slope above the breakwater and, as she watched, from the harbour mouth came the bobbing, valiant shape of Fiddly's boat. She would know it anywhere, the squat hull, the dark sail, the figures at tiller and lines. The other boats were already on their way to the horizon, but the Christies were making good time. Soon she saw the boat far out to sea, a tiny wooden model, lilting gracefully over the billows, dark sail full, bow spraying foam.

Then came the first of the whaling ships, slipping slowly past the harbour bar to anchor in the bay until all five of them rode gently on the heaving water, while the wind freshened and the light strengthened in a troubled sky.

'We'll be back early,' Fiddly had said and they were, though not with the catch they had expected. 'But with the wind veering towards the south-east and a storm threatening, we thought it best to make for home. I see yon whalers are still riding at anchor: they'd best watch out if the wind veers any more.' Annie's creel was barely filled, and none to spare for a murlin. But Rachel had a creel of her own now, and with William and George's share of Bosun's catch there was enough for them both.

'We'll not be long,' said Annie. 'Mind and see Wee Alex gets into no mischief, and keep the fire in. I've a thick broth cooking for your dinner. And if the snow comes, as it threatens to do, mind and keep warm, Fiddly. I dinna want you taking a chill in your chest, nor Davy neither.'

'Awa' wi' ye, woman,' he said affectionately. 'You're aye fussing. The lads and I have work to do. Jamie's line lost a deal o' hooks – a dogfish like as not – and the boat's nae ridin' like she ought. Maity's going to upend her and see what's ado.'

'Well mind what I say, Fiddly, and dinna get wet. Watch him for me, Jamie. He's an obstinate wee devil.'

'I will, Ma,' said James with a grin.

She pulled the shawl over her head, adjusted the creel on her back and set off towards the town, Rachel at her side. At the Weighhouse, Rachel turned her head and saw James raise a hand in farewell. Fiddly and Maitland were already busy at the boat, retrieving the soaked lines to be cleaned and made ready for the next day's fishing.

If there's to be any, thought Rachel later, as the wind shifted further to the north and storm clouds blotted out the light. Then suddenly the grey mass burst, to spill a veil of snow over market-stall and open basket. The cassies at their feet were patterned with huge flakes, piled one on another in layers of thickening white.

'We'd best pack up here and try the Broadgait,' said Annie. 'This snow'll keep the customers inside, and by the colour o' yon sky there's a fair storm gathering. Thank God our boat is safe at home.'

It was as they stood at the corner of Netherkirkgate crying their wares into the narrow quiet of the snow-blanketed street that they heard the first shout.

'There's a whaler adrift off Girdleness!'

'The *Oscar*'s adrift!'

The Christies heard the shout with the rest of the Square and, snatching up caps and jackets, ran outside to see what was ado.

'Not you,' ordered Fiddly as Alex made to follow. 'Nor you, Davy. Ye mind well what your Ma said.'

'But Da,' protested Davy, 'I'm *fifteen*!'

'Stay wi' Alex. I dinna trust him. But I trust you, Davy.' Davy, dejected, turned back to the fire and James's broken line which they had been mending, while the rest of the Christies ran with the others to the north pier. The wind, miraculously, had dropped but a little snow fell, soft and silent, over the huddle of watchers on the headland. The sky overhead was leaden, the sea the same, the few pale snowflakes hanging here and there like suspended foam over the heaving surface. Inside the harbour, in the cradle of pier and quay, the water was calm, but even here there was a stirring as of impending disaster.

Beyond the harbour mouth, dipping and rolling on the swelling sea, rode the whaling ships; four of them a good distance out, the fifth, the *Oscar*, drifting dangerously near to the rocky waters of Greyhope Bay on the southward side of the harbour.

'What's she doing so close in? She put to sea this morning,' said Fiddly, 'wi' the rest o' them.'

'Aye,' said someone in the crowd. 'But the *Oscar* hadna all her crew and came back to meet them.'

'They're on board now, God help them, but with nae wind and the incoming tide, they'll wish they'd stayed ashore.'

'What'll we do, Da?' asked James quietly. 'They'll be washed on to Girdleness. They'll never pull clear. And we canna stand here idle and watch them go to their deaths.'

'A dozen Leith oysters there's a storm coming,' said William. 'The king o' the herrings they'll no' get the lifeboat out,' added George. 'Just look at yon sky.'

'She's dragging anchor.' 'They canna get her round, wi' no wind and the incoming tide flowing strong.' 'She'll not clear the Girdleness.'

'Come on, lads,' decided Fiddly. 'We'll launch our boat. Thank God we havena upended her yet.'

'But Da,' protested James, 'if the lifeboat canna put to sea . . .'

'We'll not put to sea, Jamie, just cross the harbour. We've ropes enough: we'll maybe be able to help them ashore.'

Others had had the same idea, and already the loaded ferry-boat was pulling across the harbour basin from north to south. Beyond the point, in the comparative safety of the open sea, the *St Andrew* rode the swell with the *Middleton* and *Latona*, their anchors still holding – though the fourth ship, the *Hercules*, was dragging uncomfortably close as the sea heaved and rolled under the swelling tide, and the first hint of the approaching tempest rattled the bent grass in a flurry of stinging sand.

'Pull hard and fast for the south shore, lads,' cried Fiddly as the surface of the water was lashed suddenly into a thousand catspaws. The little boat dipped and rose alarmingly under the unaccustomed weight, for as well as the five Christies there were others, anxious as they were to reach the southern cliffs.

'She's struck!' The cry came from the headland as the boat touched shore, and before they had disembarked and beached the boat out of reach of tidal waters, the threatened tempest broke in a crash of surf and whining winds.

Blizzard mingled with leaping spray to lash the wooden whaler as she creaked and writhed, trapped in the rocks of Greyhope Bay, a mere two hundred yards from the shore. The noise was deafening: howling wind, raging, roaring surf, screams of terrified onlookers, pitiful cries from the helpless ship. Then, with a crash like a thunderclap, the ship's hull cracked.

'She's breaking up!'

'Oh God, oh God!' There were forty-four men and boys on board.

'Someone help them! Please!' A woman clutched Fiddly's sleeve, her eyes streaming tears of terror. 'My son is on that ship, and my husband too.'

'We'll try, woman,' said Fiddly, 'but their lives are in God's hands now. Have ye the rope coiled, James?'

'But Da, look at the breakers. No boat nor man could survive in a sea like yon.'

'But if they attempt it, we can at least help them.'

'They're cutting the mast!'

Through blinding snow and leaping, lashing spray the crowd watched in sudden silence as seamen hacked at the mainmast, already tipping at a dangerous angle that threatened to roll the ship over.

'It'll fall shorewards, as a bridge. Then we'll be able to reach them.'

Hope sprang again in the watchers' hearts. There was a swelling crowd on the headland now, heedless of the snatching wind and freezing snow. Many of those watching had sons, fathers, or husbands aboard, men they had waved on their way only that morning, on a calm sea. The waters of Greyhope Bay were boiling now with black and grey-foamed venom, snatching at rope and sailcloth, snarling at porthole, smashing bulwark and forecastle with splintering fury. A fusillade of barrels

69

catapulted shorewards, jettisoned suddenly as the *Oscar* rolled and a hawser snapped.

'Jump!' screamed a woman's voice. 'Swim ashore!' and among the bobbing shapes of water-casks and bottles, a head appeared.

'Now!' cried Fiddly, and waded into the surf, coiled rope in his right hand. His arm came up in a swinging arc and the rope rattled seaward to smack, useless, into the water in a mesh of tangled debris.

'Look out! The mast!'

With a deafening crack, the mast fell, dragging sail and rigging with it, showering men like water-drops on to the rocks or into the boiling sea. Fore- and mizzen-masts followed. But all fell sideways on to the ship, not shoreward. As the masts fell, the ship rolled over, gurgling water jets from porthole and hold, and the sea was peppered suddenly with the heads of those who had sought refuge in the rigging and found only the sea.

'Swim!' screamed the onlookers, as one by one the heads disappeared, swamped by the waves, or the cascade of debris from the *Oscar*'s deck: harpoons, coiled lines, spars and oars, and, with a thundering roar, one of the ship's guns, a six-pounder, fitted for defence against privateers. Some managed to grab hold of a barrel or spar, only to have it snatched from them by the surf, or to be lifted, helpless on the swell, and dashed against the cliffs, while in the thrashing shallows shoremen shouted encouragement and held out boathooks or spars in a vain attempt at rescue. James and Maitland between them dragged a man ashore, only to find him dead, his head cracked open like a hen's egg by a hidden rock. George and William pulled in another, while from the forecastle of the *Oscar*, still jutting sideways through the surf in a welter of tangled spars and rigging, came the frantic cries of Captain Innes and a handful of men, still clinging to the splintered remnants of their ship.

'But one of them's no' but a laddie!' Fiddly Christie re-coiled his rope, waded deeper into the turmoil, and threw . . .

'My but it was bleak i' the town today.' Annie Christie pulled back her shawl and shook her hair free of melted snow. 'Where's Fiddly and the others?'

'Gone to the wreck on the Girdleness.' Davy was still bitter at being left behind, but there had been compensations. 'You should have seen the storm, Ma. Yon whaler, the *St Andrew*, cut both her cables when the sea threatened to drag her after the *Oscar* on to the rocks.'

'But she got under way with stay-sails and mizzen, Ma,' put in Alex excitedly, 'quick as you please, set fore- and main-topsail, and beat to windward along the coast. You should have seen her ride the breakers!'

'Aye, Ma. It was tremendous seamanship and she made harbour, too, wi' the *Middleton* and *Latona*.'

'But the *Hercules* is on the beach, Ma. Did ye no' see her? Dragged anchor all the way to the pierhead and knocked off her rudder. Davy and I watched her.'

'Are the crew all safe?' asked Annie, her voice quiet. They had heard already in the town of the Girdleness disaster. Only two hands saved, and the rest feared lost. There'd be too many widows and fatherless children by nightfall; the first bodies were already lying on the steps of the Sugarhouse, waiting to be claimed.

She and Rachel had seen the melancholy procession from the Shiprow as the ferry-boat brought the townsfolk, living and dead, home from Greyhope Bay; had seen the lifeless, battered bodies oozing seawater and blood laid out on the snow-covered steps in Sugarhouse Lane; had passed stricken women, white-faced and weeping, their children crying at their heels. It was a sight that wrung Annie's heart with an anguish which only the warmth of her own hearth could comfort. Pray God there were no more . . .

'Aye, Ma, they're safe enough. We helped them ashore,' he finished proudly, 'Davy and me.'

'Good lads.' She took the lid off the pot and inspected the day's broth. 'And I see you've kept the fire in right well. I hope your Da will not be long. There's a fair gale blowing and the snow building up fast in the town. It's nae a day to be abroad. Run and see if they're coming, Rachel lass, afore ye take off your shawl.'

But when Rachel stepped out into the Square she saw a picture that was to stay with her a lifetime. A tight group of men, whitefaced and silent, was moving slowly across the

71

Square carrying something on a sailcloth sling between them: four men, one at each corner. Then she saw the faces and her heart leapt with dread. Annie heard her gasp.

'What is it, Rachy?' But she already knew. Waxen faced and trembling, she took in the stricken faces of her four sons as the water dripped slowly from the sailcloth bier on to the snow of the yard. Snowflakes had already settled on the lifeless face, frosting eyebrow and beard with premature white.

'I'm sorry, Ma,' said James, his face streaming tears, 'I didna' watch him.'

'A dreadful affair,' said George Abercrombie, looking up briefly from the close print of the *Journal*. 'I see subscription papers have been left at the usual places. We must do what we can. I will call in at the News Room this afternoon and leave £10.'

'Remember how many others will be giving,' said his wife. 'With charity lectures and a play, surely £5 would do?'

'Very well.' Privately George Abercrombie intended to give what he chose, but it was not worth domestic discord to say so.

'It must be terrible for the families,' said Fenton Abercrombie, his young face grave. 'I wish there was something more we could do.'

'I don't see why,' argued Clementina with a toss of her beribboned head. 'They're not like us. They're fisherfolk: they expect to drown.'

'Clementina! How can you be so callous when there are whole families bereaved?'

'I'm not callous, Papa,' pouted Clementina uneasily, 'merely practical.' She turned on Fenton who had started the trouble. 'They *do* expect it, Fen, just as they expect us to get up a subscription for them afterwards. You know they do.'

'Because they follow a calling whose risks they accept,' argued Fenton, pink-cheeked, 'that does not mean they forfeit all sympathy.'

'Well said, son.'

'Apologies for speaking,' said Clementina sulkily. 'I did not know you felt such an affinity with *fisherfolk*.' She uttered the word as if it were unclean.

'I'll have you remember, lass,' said her father, 'that your own grandparents were fisherfolk and don't you forget it.'

'No, Papa.' She lowered her eyes: fortunately so, or her father might have recognized rebellion. For Clementina, like her mother, intended to forget everything that lay behind them in their rise to prosperity and to concentrate only on what lay ahead. With that in mind, she said, after a suitable pause, 'May we go to the play, Papa? The proceeds all go to the widows and orphans.' When he did not immediately answer, she continued, 'The Fraser girls are to take the female parts and it will be such fun – and the Farquharsons are sure to go.'

'Perhaps,' temporized Abercrombie, who disapproved of such frivolities as a waste of time, especially for Clementina who, he thought, was quite frivolous enough already. As for Farquharson, he wouldn't trust the man as far as he could throw him – and there were plenty who would like to throw him into the harbour at midnight. But the Farquharson boy was harmless, and a good enough match for Clementina – if only to get Abercrombie reduced freight-charges on his regular shipments from London and Leith.

'It is to be *Love-a-la-Mode*, Papa, and the play of *Douglas*. Do say yes?'

'As long as I am not expected to accompany you.'

'Of course not,' said Mrs Abercrombie, satisfied. 'Fenton shall come with us in your place.'

'Then if you are to claim my son on Monday, I reserve the right to his company now, my dear. Come, lad, there's a proposition I want you to go over in the office. With your book learning, you'll be able to help me.'

Fenton had just completed his third year at the college, and his father was looking forward to his help during the vacation, particularly as he had expansion in mind.

'I have been thinking, Fenton,' he began when they had left the house behind them and were walking down the narrow, cobbled slope of the Netherkirkgate towards the low shop door. 'With people moving into Union Street, there'll be properties on the market.'

'Morning, sir.' Archie, the odd-job lad, touched his bonnet in deference to the master, then resumed sweeping the shop floor with redoubled vigour: Mr Abercrombie did not tolerate slacking.

Down three steps from street level, the shop door stood open so that barrels and counter were clearly visible to any passer-by as well as, through the small-paned window, the assortment of bottles and glasses on counter-top and shelves. Abercrombie was generous in the samples he gave prospective customers in the interests of trade, though shrewd enough to scent out and discourage the younger, more brazen element intent merely on tippling free. The shop was stone-floored, low-ceilinged, dark even on the sunniest day, so that a lamp was kept burning in the interior, touching barrel and cobwebbed bottle with glinting shadows. Abercrombie liked to think the light gave the atmosphere of a private wine-cellar on a rich estate. His wife merely thought it gloomy.

At the back of the shop, steps led upwards to the store-room and 'office'. It was in the latter that Abercrombie liked to sit, among the tea chests stamped 'Green Hyson' or 'Bohea', and turn over ideas at the deal table under the window. From here he could look down on the street with its bustle of black-hatted businessmen, red-gowned students, professors, dray horses, porters, errand boys; and he could pick out a magistrate or councillor from the Town House round the corner or an officer from the barracks on Castle Hill – all potential customers – as well as the country gentlemen on horseback, or strolling nonchalantly from the direction of the Athenaeum. If he spotted the latter, Abercrombie would be downstairs and at his own shop door before they reached it, to bow, greet them deferentially, and persuade them, if they needed persuasion, inside.

'I've been thinking, Fenton,' he said again as he and his son emerged into the store-room, Fenton to perch on a tea-chest, his father to occupy the only chair. 'With more space we'd have scope to extend our range. We've done well enough from wines and I like the trade, but since we took to tea as well, for your mother's sake, we've done even better. I am thinking of expanding to cover a range of high-class groceries: coffee, demerara sugar, spices, flour, all of the best quality, with dried fruits, perhaps, and suchlike.'

'What about customs duty, Papa? And shipping costs?'

'That's what I want to discuss with you. I see Farquharson's quoting 2s 6d the barrel bulk from Leith, but he doesna have the monopoly; there's aye competition if ye shop around, and we need a regular contract. Best of all would be our own ship, like in the old days, only larger, of course. I've thought more than once o' buying shares in a brig, but there'd be running costs, crew's wages and natural hazards to take into account, as well as the risk of privateers . . .'

Fenton Abercrombie listened dutifully, only half his attention on his father's words. Three years at college had changed Fenton from a mild-faced boy to a mild-faced young man, fair-haired, clear-complexioned, his beard no more than golden down along his jawbone. Rachel had been right when she had thought him gentle-tempered and kindly. Fenton had an affectionate, undemanding heart, without ambition. He had also an honest and unwavering appreciation of right and wrong, independent of any teaching, and a strong streak of compassion. It was this last which prevented him from putting the *Oscar* tragedy out of mind.

He could not forget the families of those drowned whaling men, or the men themselves, fighting in the icy surf for breath while the sea battered them, filling ears, brain, throat, lungs with bubbling seawater, dragging them down to oblivion in a string of helpless bubbles. Fenton's horror of drowning had been with him since earliest childhood and still had the power to wake him, sweating, on a stifled scream.

'. . . there's a brig for sale at the Lemon Tree on Saturday, 120 tons and in part-shares. There's no harm in having a look at her for future reference, and we can ask about those theatre tickets on the way. After all, the entertainment *is* in a good cause.'

Somewhere in the street outside a girl's voice, high and strident, was crying 'fish'. Fenton was reminded of that occasion more than three years ago, when two fisher lassies had so affronted his Mamma by blocking his way. One of them had been dark-eyed and remarkably pretty. He hoped she had lost no relatives in the disaster.

After the wreck of the *Oscar*, James Christie changed. The loss of his father cast a shadow over the whole Square, for Fiddly had been well-loved, but whereas with time the Square regained much of its normal vigour, in the Christie household the healing process was more painful and disfiguring. For with Fiddly's passing, joy had fled the house: his fiddle lay unplayed on the dresser shelf and there was no longer music at the end of the day. Instead, the family drew together in a kind of silent mourning from which only Annie stood apart. Anxiously they watched her while she went about her daily tasks with stoic endurance, her face pale and drawn, her eyes dull with pain. She rarely spoke. When she did, her voice was unwavering, but they all knew her anguish, even nine-year-old Alex, as they lay awake in the darkness and heard muffled weeping from the closed box bed.

It was Davy who rescued them. That evening they worked, as usual, in muted silence, each one busy about some task. Rachel stood at the pot-shelf under the window, rinsing the supper dishes in a wooden basin and catching the last of the light from a fading sky. At the table, James had lit a candle the better to see the horsehair intricacies of the tippens he was repairing with Davy, and in the same pale light Maitland was carving the delicate mastwork of yet another model. George and William, whispering together, were inspecting a herring net they had hauled down from the rafters in preparation for the summer season, and Wee Alex, as always, was sketching something on a slate. The squeak of his chalk, the rustle of herring net, the scraping of Maitland's knife, and the swishing of water from Rachel's basin were the only sounds against the fire's murmur and, beyond the house wall, the muted rhythm of the sea. Suddenly Davy crashed back the bench, stood up, crossed to the fireside where Annie sat in her usual chair, the usual knitting immobile in her hands, and put his arm around her shoulders.

'Come on, Ma,' he said, at the same time coaxing and gentle. 'Dinna grieve.' He drew her head to rest against his young chest and hugged her. 'Ye have us, Ma, and ye ken fine Da wouldna like to see ye sad. He couldna abide a doleful house, remember? Sing, he used to tell us; be happy. We canna have folk saying the Christies are not grateful for what they have – and we have each other, Ma. We love you,' he added quietly. 'We'll care for you, all of us. So smile, Ma? Please?'

Annie closed her eyes and let her head rest for a brief, exhausted moment against Davy's chest, Davy who was the one most like his father, then, with a long shudder, drew away from him to sit erect and calm.

'You're right, Davy,' she said. 'Your Da was aye cheerful.'

77

She took up her knitting and drew the wool firmly for the first stitch. In silence the others watched till her hands were flashing with almost their old speed, the click of needles adding its customary rhythm to the evening's sounds. There was an audible releasing of breath, as tension relaxed and noises hitherto muted expanded to normal volume. The twins no longer whispered, Maitland grumbled aloud at the intricacies of the model's rigging, and Rachel clattered the wooden bowls with deliberate noise. Then Davy put his mouth-organ to his lips, blew a tentative note, and launched into 'The Bonny lass of Fyvie'. After a moment, the twins joined in, humming in unison, and Wee Alex added the fluting high notes of a penny-whistle. It was a brave effort, bravely answered. For, softly at first, then strengthening, came Annie's clear voice from the fireside. *'There's many a bonnie lass, In the Howe o' Auchterless, There's many a bonnie lass in the Garioch, oh . . .'*

Only James remained silent, and Rachel, watching him from across the room, felt her heart twist with pity at the pain in his eyes.

'Rachel,' said Annie the next morning, 'it's nae fitting for you to sleep by the hearth now you're a grown lass. Ye must come in wi' me.'

And though Rachel knew by the quality of the silence beside her that Annie Christie lay awake for long stretches of the night, she heard no more tears. But in the drawn control of Annie's face she read a grief no amount of singing could dispel.

Once, returning early to the house after the morning's search for bait, she came upon Annie standing motionless, staring into space, the violin held lovingly in her arms and such a look on her face as brought the tears springing to Rachel's eyes. But when Annie saw her, she said only 'I must keep it polished,' and laid the instrument gently back on the shelf. In her grief, she carried herself with dignity, but the sorrow aged her, and Rachel watched the strong lines of her figure take on a new frailty.

Change was in James, too. He was no longer carefree with the exuberance of youth, no longer teased her or joked with his brothers. Nor did he frequent the alehouse or the more dubious quarters on the quay. Instead, grave-faced, he spent every leisure moment with the family in the Square. As his father had done, he took out the fishing boat each morning, with Maitland

and Davy and Wee Alex now to make up the numbers. On the morning when they set out for the first time after Fiddly's death, Rachel feared for Annie's newly found composure, but the older woman somehow remained dry-eyed and straight as together they pushed out the boat, bare legs immersed to the knees in icy water.

'Mind and take care of Alex, now,' called Rachel, and together they watched as Davy pulled on the oars, James took the helm, and Maitland and Alex busied themselves at the ropes till the small brown square of sail rattled aloft, caught the morning wind, and filled with a snap of canvas to carry them breasting through the billows at the harbour bar and on into the open sea. Behind them came William and George in the Brand boat, and a handful of other small craft. The twilight air was crisp, the sea already blurred bronze from the rising sun which, even as they watched, touched masthead and sail with a golden gleam. Seagulls mewed in a swirling cloud behind the boats till they were out in the roads of the bay, then veered back to shore to drop, spray-footed, into the shallows, or perch on the tarred pillars of the north pier to wait for flotsam from the coastal trading ships, and for the fishing boats' return.

Like Annie, Rachel knew that she too would find no peace now till the boats were safely home. Fiddly's death had been a frightening warning of the treachery of that sea which lured by its loveliness, awed by its majesty, and soothed by its sighing rhythm. Its breakers had claimed first her father and then the man whom she had loved as a second father. She lived in daily dread that a third sacrifice would be demanded, and when, hours later, the boat beached and James stepped safe ashore, her young heart overflowed with relief.

And love. For secretly, scarcely acknowledged even in her weakest moments, Rachel loved him. Since the day she had arrived in the Square and he had called her a princess she had loved him – as she loved Andrew Noble and as she would have loved anyone who was kind to her. But over the years that love had changed from an innocent, open affection to an inner ache and a yearning which she strove to hide from all the world, and most of all from James.

He was a grown man, seven years her senior. He was handsome and, till Fiddly's death, had been exuberant and

79

carefree. Rachel knew there was not a girl in North Square who had not set her cap at him, nor in South Square neither, and as for Jessie Brand – Rachel's heart lurched at the thought. But Jess would not have James. She, Rachel, plain though she was, would somehow prevent it . . . and somehow, someday, win him for herself. But in spite of her bravado, Rachel remembered Old Yule and the locked shapes behind the peat stack with a dread which would not leave her. Jessie had succeeded once. Why not again? For with William and George working in the Brand boat, daily contact was inevitable; Rachel and Jess collected the day's catch together, and though it was usually William and George who heaved Jessie's creel on to her back, it was not always so, and she had seen Jess's pert eyes and pouting lips and heard James's laughter as he lent a hand to 'load' her. Since Fiddly's death, however, there had been no such levity. James's attention was focused only on his family.

In May, the small fishing boat was laid up for the summer and James, Maitland and the twins went in the Brand boat to the deep-sea fishing. Davy had hoped to go too, in his father's place, and Wee Alex, but the first of the Brand lads was ready for the sea and there was no room.

'Never mind, Davy,' said James. 'You've a line of your own and skills. We'll find a place for ye somehow,' and with the memory of the *Oscar* disaster still fresh in everyone's mind, Davy found a place in one of the South Square boats and earned his share of the summer's catch. Annie and Rachel both had fish enough to sell.

Then it was time for the herring fishing. Nets were dragged down from rafters and mended long into the night – and mended again when they came back ripped by an encounter with rock or dogfish. It was a good season's fishing: at the end of it they had even saved a little.

'But it is not enough, Rachel,' James told her one afternoon when, inshore fishing resumed, the others were mending the lines in the open air, for the autumn day was clear. Rachel, newly back from market, was preparing the evening meal. James himself had come inside to put away his coiled line and, seeing Rachel at the fireside, had lingered. He found it soothing to watch her preparing vegetables or kneading dough, restful to watch her graceful movements and calm face; and with the turbulence of doubt and the new ideas inside him, he needed calm.

'With a family as large as ours and father dead,' he said, thinking aloud, 'there is too much at risk. Suppose our fishing boat were to capsize?' At Rachel's gasp he said, 'Nay, lass, ye ken fine it happens, and why not to us? 'Tis not the fisherfolk's oath for nothing . . . *a bonnet to me*.' He paused, remembering those lost and the frailty of their own boat on a rough sea. 'I promised Da to care for you all, and I will, but there's nae *security*, Rachy, and that's what I want for Ma. If Maitland or I were to follow my father . . .'

Her heart lurched at the thought, but she said firmly, 'There are the twins, good fishermen both, and Davy and Alex.'

'The twins think only of each other. They're good-hearted, but feckless; and Davy's young. As for Wee Alex . . . No, Rachy, 'tis my burden, and I canna bear to think of Ma – or you – joining the crowd at the town soup-kitchen, or taking charity from the Whitefishers.'

'It'll not come to that, I promise you. I can work for both of us,' said Rachel proudly. 'But should the worst happen, it is our own Society. There would be no shame.'

'Happen not, but there is shame to me when I look at Ma and see the sorrow in her, and all of my doing.'

'Not of your doing, James, and she knows it is not!' cried Rachel. 'We all do. You've no cause to despair, James, and no right. It was the sea's doing and the storm's doing – and his own valour's doing,' she finished sternly. 'Dinna forget that.'

James took down his father's pipe from the shelf and busied himself with tobacco and tinder-box. 'No,' he said quietly, 'I won't forget. Nor will I forget the promise I made him. My father promised Ma a house once.' He spoke as if to himself. 'He told me he'd like fine to buy her one wi' a view of the harbour. "There's nae chance o' that," he said, "and nae much o' you doing it for me, Jamie," but I *will* do it. I owe it to him. This house is fine enough, Rachy, but it belongs to the Council. I've thought a lot about it over the summer months, and I want our *own* house – not one room with only an earthen floor, but a stone-built house on the quay, with room enough for my brothers and my brothers' children together. And I want a livelihood that canna be snatched from my mouth by a careless wave. Oh Rachy, if you could have seen his face . . .' and James bowed his head, unashamedly, in grief.

'And will you not marry?' she asked after a moment, and waited, breath held, for the answer. A fisherman needed a wife.

'What would I want wi' marrying? I've family enough to care for.' On his face she saw new lines of responsibility overlying the guilt and grief. She already knew he blamed himself for Fiddly's death, for she had heard him moan, 'I should have watched him,' over and over on those first nights after the tragedy – and she now realized he saw atonement only in the achievement of Fiddly's dream.

'But I canna see how I can keep my promise, Rachel,' he went on. 'We've nae money to spare and never will have, unless . . .' But he left his sentence unfinished.

By the end of the year, however, James's hesitation had hardened to decision. 'It seems to me . . .' he said, looking round the family gathering at the end of the supper, 'No, Rachel, leave the dishes and listen . . . It seems to me that it is time to look ahead. I have thought a lot over the months since my father's death. I promised him to care for you all and I will – but we've worked all year at the fish and what have we to show for it. A *couple o' pounds* put by! Nae enough to bury me with! I want something more solid to rely on than a shoal o' fishes that can swim away afore we net them, or a cockleshell o' a boat that can be swallowed by a single wave, nae bother.'

No one spoke, not even Annie, quiet-faced in the shadows beyond the lamp, though it was her husband's livelihood that was being scorned.

'She's a fine wee boatie, to be sure,' said James, seeing her expression, 'and has served us well, but she's old and big enough for no more than three. I know William and George have lines and as long as there's room in the Brand boat, can shoot them and bring home a catch. But the Brand lads are growing. Come summer, there'll be room for no more than three of us in the great-line boat. Come autumn, there'll be no place for the twins in the sma' boat, neither.'

'But we've our own lines and hooks.' 'We'll manage fine.'

'Aye, I know. We're nae propertyless men, thank God, but we're nae jobbing fisherfolk neither. I want more for the Christies than that.' He looked up and caught his mother's steady gaze. She knew what he was going to say and remembered, as he did, his father's solemn oath. But his father was dead, and his mother did not know of that other oath when he had sworn to care for her and the little ones. She had not heard his father's wistful voice when he talked of a house in Castle Street with a view of the harbour.

James straightened his shoulders, avoided his mother's eyes and said clearly, 'We will build a ship.' At their gasp of awe, he went on quickly, 'I am convinced our future lies in trading. We canna hope to buy a vessel ready made for us – and I scorn to buy a paltry share in someone else's enterprise. So we must build one for ourselves, plank by plank, and . . .'

'But we're fisherfolk,' interrupted his mother, 'nae shipwrights.'

'Fisherfolk need vessels too, Ma,' said Maitland kindly. 'And we can learn. I've spent many an afternoon in the shipyard at Alexander Hall's. I know what's involved, and I'm handy enough wi' the saw.'

'He's right, Ma,' said William and George together. 'Ten oysters to a mussel Maity's models are better than anything in the builder's yard. He should ha' been a shipwright.'

'And will be, one day,' vowed Maitland. 'I promise.'

'And so will I,' put in Wee Alex. 'I'd like fine to draw ships.'

'What sort o' ship will we build, Jamie?' demanded Davy. 'A fishing yawl? Or one o' they trading brigs like they're building in Hall's yard?'

'We'll need to find a yard o' our own,' put in the twins, 'And good timber.'

'And ye'll need to find a deal o' money,' said Annie, unable to keep silence. Excitement evaporated as they saw her stern face: Annie Christie held the purse-strings. 'Remember what your father said about debt.'

'I'll not forget, Ma,' said James quietly, his strange eyes gleaming. 'We'll need a yard, o' course, for the building, but there'll be land for lease at Pocra come Lammas. Maitland and I had a look around today. As for the money, we'll earn what we need somehow.'

Annie dropped her eyes to the shirt in her hands. She was unpicking her husband's name before making it over for Davy, and lingering over every stitch. James was a fine lad and she loved him, but his ways were not her husband's. As she made no comment, he went on, 'We canna just go on in the old ways, Ma. Maitland's nineteen: he'll be wanting to marry soon, and the twins too. We'll need more than one fishing boat to feed us when the wee ones come along, and we canna depend on the odd piece o' pilot work, not with a family our size.'

'I'm nae planning to marry,' protested Maitland, blushing: he had yet to walk out with a girl.

'Nor me,' said the twins, embarrassed, pushing each other playfully so that the plates rattled on the trestle table and a wooden basin shot to the floor. ''Tis James who'll marry,' they added, emerging tousle-haired from the tussle, 'if a lassie not four doors away from here has her way.'

'Shut your mou' the pair o' ye.' James, hot-cheeked, aimed a blow at the nearest twin.

'Ten haddies to a herrin' Jamie'll be the first to take a wife,' taunted William, dodging the blow, and George added, 'Another ten it'll be to a lassie whose name begins wi' a "J".'

This time James's hand found its target. With a clatter William pushed back the bench and retaliated, George joining in, and mugs and platters scattered in the general mêlée.

'Boys! Boys!' cried Annie with something of her old authority. 'I'll have no fighting here. Make up and be friends – or grown men that you are, I'll tan the hides off the lot o' ye.'

But, order restored, Annie's shoulders slumped once more in the lines of habitual sorrow which stirred James still with guilt. Averting his eyes, he repeated, 'We will build a ship. A small one to start with, of ninety tons or so. There's a schooner in the harbour for sale in part shares, and Maitland and I went over her. Seventy-six tons, oak built, carries a large burthen on an easy draught, ideal for our purpose. We haven't the money to buy her, but we had a close look at her construction and we reckon it's feasible to build a similar. We're nae carpenters, we'll need to learn new skills, but we know what we look for in a good vessel.'

'A brig, Ma,' put in Maitland, 'for the coastal trade. I'm working on the plans already; soon I'll have a model made.'

'But we're *fisherfolk*,' protested Annie for the last time. 'It's fishing that we know.'

'Aye, Ma,' agreed James, 'but we also know the sea. We've

been content too long to let it give when it chooses and take when it chooses. It's time we learnt to use it to better advantage. The sea *owes* us, Ma. And I'll see we claim our debt, or may my boat be a bonnet to me.'

A shudder ran through the company before James said quietly, 'I'm sorry, Ma, but my mind's made up.'

'It's all right, Ma,' said Davy reassuringly. 'Jamie'll not put us to risk.'

'I've thought it all out.' James's eyes were hard with resolution. 'We still have our wee boat. Maitland can take her to the sma' line, wi' Davy and Alex, and George and William have their places i' the Brand boat a while longer. We'll have money enough to live on, though little enough to save.'

'And you?' said his mother quietly, though she already knew his answer.

'I'm to Greenland, Ma, for the whaling. Just this once,' he added as he saw her face. He remembered, as she did, Fiddly's voice saying, *'No son o' mine goes to the Greenland seas'*.

'Once?' she repeated sadly. 'When the danger gets you, the adventure and the thrill o' the chase, you'll be trapped for life. Besides,' she went on, changing tack, 'who will take ye on, wi' nae experience and nae money neither?' Places in the whalers were highly prized for the chance they gave of adventure and riches.

'Cushnie Baxter's cousin is first mate o' the *Middleton*, and he's spoken for me. I'm sorry, Ma, but I signed on today.'

There was a moment's silence before Annie said quietly, 'And suppose there are no whales? What then?'

'That's a chance I must take. Dinna be angry wi' me, Ma. It's the *only way*.'

The *Middleton* sailed on the first of April, a year to the day since Fiddly's death. There were crowds at the quayside to see her put to sea, among them Rachel and the Christies. Rachel had put on her blue dress for the occasion and knew she looked her best – though nothing could compensate her for the ache of James's leaving.

The farewell party was in full swing when they arrived at the quayside, two tall women flanked by five sturdy, bearded men and Wee Alex who, since his inclusion in the family boat, inspected his soft cheeks daily and without success for the longed-for hair.

At the quayside the *Middleton* swarmed with activity. The painted figurehead was beribboned and garlanded. A ribboned hoop, in the centre of which was the model of a ship, had been hung between the masts. Somewhere a fiddle played, and everywhere there was merriment.

For weeks now, ever since the crew had been signed on, they had been working to prepare the ship for the Greenland seas. In the graving dock her hull had been caulked with oakum and melted pitch, and given two coats of tar to the waterline. Provisions had been tendered for and bought: cheese and sugar, hempseed oil, ships' biscuit, apples, salt beef, barley, whisky, rum and dried peas. Water barrels had been filled, gunpowder and shot loaded for the eight guns which were her defence against privateers, harpoons had been checked, ropes coiled, sails patched and mended, a medicine chest compiled. Everything had been prepared for the voyage, which could stretch from two months to four, or even six, if the whales avoided them. But now all was ready to sail on the first fair wind.

'First stop Lerwick in the Shetland Islands,' James told them, 'to lay in eggs and butter for the voyage, and hire men to row. To buy woollen stockings, too, for those as needs them.'

'You've stockings enough, James,' said his mother, biting

back emotion, 'and you'll not find better if you go to Timbuctoo. Rachy knitted them herself.' Rachel lowered her eyes lest James see the love in them, but he said only, 'Good, I'll need them. There's fields of ice in the Greenland seas, so thick ye have to pull the boat wi' ropes sometimes, walking on ice floes like giant paving-stones.'

'*Must* ye go, James?' said Annie, dreading the moment of parting. It had been a whaler that had caused Fiddly's death.

'It's the only way, Ma. We'll make no money otherwise, and it's just this once.'

'Will ye promise me that, James? On your word of honour?'

James hesitated: suppose the whales were scarce? But he could not refuse the plea in her eyes. 'I promise, Ma. Now smile for me. I'll not be gone long, and when I return, it'll be with enough to buy all the timber we need for a whole fleet o' ships. You'll see.'

'And if the whales dinna choose to be caught?'

But James refused to be deflated. If any whaler came home 'clean', it would not be the *Middleton*. 'Then I'll pursue them till they do. Now take a tot o' the captain's whisky and drink to our success.'

Then the cry went up that the pilot was ready, and the tug-lines in place; and all visitors spilled ashore in a cascade of squealing children, envious lads and tearful, brave-faced women.

'Good luck,' said Annie, reaching up to kiss him good-bye. 'God go with you.' Her cheeks were wet against his young beard.

'Take good care of her.' James stooped to kiss Rachel's cheek in farewell. 'You too, Maitland.' He clasped his brother's hand, 'And mind and work on those plans.'

'I will.'

'And I'll help,' said Alex eagerly. 'Maity's teaching me . . .'

'Good lad.' James ruffled his hair affectionately. Then, 'See and care for Ma,' he repeated as he took his leave of George and William.

'We will.'

But Davy's arm was already round his mother's waist, his other encircling Rachel. 'Dinna ye worry, James,' he said, 'we'll be fine. Just see ye hurry back wi' a fortune.'

Through the crowd behind them pushed a dark-haired, buxom lass in a scarlet bodice and petticoats, her cheeks flushed pink by the sea wind.

'Have ye no farewell kiss for me, Jamie?' Without waiting for his answer, she reached up and kissed him full on the lips. 'And there'll be another, and a better, when ye come home,' she promised as she released him. But he brushed her aside with a brusque, 'Good-bye, Jessica,' humped his canvas roll of belongings on to his shoulder, and made for the gangplank.

Once on the deck of the *Middleton*, James felt his eyes moisten as he saw the family group encircling his mother and Rachel with protective care. His mother stood erect, sad-faced, her dark hair touched with grey, and dignity in every line of her grey-clad body. Beside her, Rachel looked fresh-faced and young, slender as a harebell in that blue dress which suited her so well. Yet, seeing them together, James recognized for the first time the same strength in the Cove lassie's bearing as in his mother's, the same calm dignity, the same beauty and, for a moment, surely the same love in her face? Troubled, he looked away as orders were shouted, ropes loosed and coiled, and the helmsman stood, feet planted firm and eyes on the harbour mouth while seamen swarmed the rigging. Then, as the tugropes tightened, the ship slipped out into the channel and moved majestically eastwards in a flurry of screaming gulls, towards the pierhead and the open sea.

When James looked back, the tight-knit group stood where he had left them, waving: then, as the tugs cast off and the pilot boat turned back, the ship met the swell at the harbour bar and the deck tipped and rolled, spray smacking high from the figurehead. When he looked again it was the scarlet flash of Jessie's gown which caught his eye, her raised hand and laughing, mocking face. His ear burned suddenly with the memory of her breath, his nostrils with the animal scent of her. Then, as the ship left the shelter of the harbour behind and breasted the billows of the bay, he leapt for the rigging and forgot all else in the exhilaration of raising sail on mizzen and main. Ropes cracked in the wind, the pennant flew straight from the masthead and the sea parted at their bidding, while the shantyman's voice came clear from the afterdeck, *'I'm bound now for Greenland and ready to sail, I hope to find riches in hunting the whale . . .'*

The house without James was bleak indeed. Everywhere Rachel saw evidence of his presence: his pipe, his line coiled in its 'skull', his bed; and though the normal activity of the household left her no time to brood, sadness weighted her heart with something of the old, remembered grey. The days slipped past with no news, and anxiety replaced grief. Suppose the *Middleton* had foundered? When wind rattled casement or sent sand showering on to table and cooking-pot, Rachel and Annie exchanged a swift glance of alarm, then each retreated into her private prayer of 'Keep him safe'.

But both found compensation in the new urge to save. 'For if James is sailing a' the way to Greenland to find money,' said Annie, 'the least we can do is save what we can at home to put to his.' *Lest*, the unspoken corollary, *he forget his promise and return again to the whaling.*

So while, as usual, the boys put to sea each morning before dawn, Rachel and Annie redoubled their efforts, scouring the shore for flotsam, making a handful of meal fill the space of two, scrimping and patching to the limits of ingenuity and, in the market, haggling with a new obduracy for a still better price. Slowly, one by one, the pennies accumulated.

'What are ye savin' *for*?' demanded Jessie Brand some two weeks after James's departure. 'Is it for your wedding kist?'

Rachel continued up the Shiprow in silence, the creel heavy on her back.

'It *is* for your kist, and nae a bad idea. I'd best be saving for mine too,' Jess went on, delighting in the girl's discomfiture, 'now that the mourning's past for Jamie's Da.' Since that public kiss on the quayside, Jess had a new confidence when she spoke of James, whose absence could neither confirm nor deny her claims. 'There's James away to the Greenland seas,' she went on conversationally, with a sideways look at Rachel's pinkening face, 'seeking money to set himself up wi' a wife, and I wouldna like not to be ready when he comes home.' Still Rachel said nothing and Jess continued, deliberately teasing now, 'Is it Maitland ye're to have? There's nae much o' the man about him, but I've seen the sheep's eyes he makes at ye – ye can snare him, nae bother, and he's better than yon daft twins. James'll be glad to see ye well settled, and so will I. For James and I'll have family o' our own to concern us soon enough, wi'out troubling our heads over brothers and sisters. Wi' the money James brings back, I reckon we'll find a house on the quay or maybe in the Castlegate, or there's plots o' land to feu off Union Street. Golden Square's a grand name, wi' a fine ring to it, and there's gardens, too . . .'

Jess continued to boast and tease as they made their way up the hill, but Rachel bore the wounds in proud silence. James had kissed Jess certainly and it *might* be true . . . but she remembered the ship they were to build and, '*It's not, it's not,*' she repeated over and over in her head. She longed to tell Jessie so to her face, but that would reveal the secret she was sworn to keep, and she had no course but to endure.

The Plainstanes were more crowded than usual, with unaccustomed activity at the doors of the Reading Room.

'What's ado?' demanded Jessie of a hovering errand-boy, seizing him unceremoniously by the sleeve.

'I dinna ken, except that there's to be a holiday wi' illuminations and fireworks, and a bonfire big as St Nicholas' kirk.' Then, spying a gap in the crowd, the lad squirmed out of her grip to disappear eagerly into the throng like a weasel into a drystone dyke.

Jess tried again, this time accosting in her demurest manner a young gentleman in beaver hat, tail-coat and nankeen breeches.

'The tyrant Bonaparte is overthrown,' she reported gleefully to Rachel, 'and there's to be a grand celebration. The placard's on the wall of the Reading Room and yon crowd's pushing to see it. Monday it's to be. I wish my Jamie was here to see it wi' me. Such junketing as there'll be.'

Napoleon overthrown! Rachel's heart swelled with relief and hope – for hadn't James said the Frenchies were a plague to the trade routes, the French privateers as much danger as the sea itself? Now the trade routes would be open and ready for James's ship when it was built.

'What are ye gawping at, Rachy?' said Jess with a playful push. 'Get on wi' ye or we'll sell no fish the day. Or are ye planning to be trampled underfoot on the Plainstanes?'

The Christies, like the rest of Aberdeen, many wearing the lily and the white cockade, attended the celebrations in the Castlegate, stood in the heat of the bonfire as 'Napoleon' burned on the forty cartloads of timber supplied by the Council, marvelled at the fireworks, the Bengal lights, the extravagant transparencies of goddesses and patriotic emblems, the variegated lamps and the more humorous representations, such as that of a Dutchwoman pulling on a worsted stocking under the slogan 'Thank God – Aberdeen Hose Again.'

While Davy took his mother's arm, the twins and Wee Alex disappeared into the crowd with a group of young folk from the Square, and Rachel found herself with Maitland at her side.

'Come, Rachel,' he said, taking her hand, 'we'll see the lights better from the far side of the square.' But when they reached the indicated spot their view was the same, only the company was different. Annie, Davy, and the rest had disappeared, and when Maitland slipped an arm casually around her waist, Rachel was reminded suddenly of Jessie's taunts: *'There's nae much o' the man about him, but I've seen the sheep's eyes he makes at ye.'* Stealing a sideways glance, she studied him as he in turn watched the gyrations of the corporation fireworks coruscating above the Plainstanes: he was tall as his brothers, pale-haired, with clear grey eyes and a boyish look to his face in spite of his beard. He turned, caught her eye, and smiled, and she saw the gentle intelligence of his face in the crackling flare of naphtha and magnesium. Fireworks sputtered overhead like hail on taut canvas, and they laughed. His arm was still round her waist. Remembering Jessie, she might have moved away, but in the crowd of merrymaking strangers, loneliness swelled suddenly to blot her heart with the old, familiar grey and she had need of human warmth.

Maitland drew her protectively close as the crowds pressed tight about them, the bonfire roared in orange and vermilion splendour, and unexpectedly the first drops of rain fell. Then, as the shower grew heavier, sizzling and spitting in the flames, they spotted Annie and the others sheltering in a distant doorway and ran, laughing, to join them, faces rain-sparkled, hair clinging in tendrils at brow and temple.

'Home,' ordered Annie. 'I'll not have Davy taking cold i' the chest again, and Alex isna strong.'

'I am so,' protested Alex. 'Just because I chose to draw, 'stead of idling wi' the other lads . . .' but his mother would not be dissuaded. 'Rachel, you come with me while Maitland finds yon daft pair o' twins.'

Gathering her family about her, Annie Christie moved inflexibly away from the crowd towards the Shiprow and the harbour.

'Mind and bring them straight home, now,' she called after Maitland as he moved obediently away. 'It's good to celebrate once in a while,' she pronounced when they were all safe home again, 'but I like fine to be back at my own hearth, wi' the kettle singing and the fire bright. You're to take a glass o' toddy, Davy, for your chest, then we'll away to bed.' Even those who would gladly have stayed longer in the Castlegate did not gainsay her.

Rachel lay awake in the box bed beside Annie long after the others slept, remembering Maitland's arm around her waist, Jessie's taunts, and James's dear, absent face. For not all the jollity of celebration, with its promise of peace, increased trade, and profit, had been able to suppress anxiety.

The *Middleton* was to sail to Lerwick, take on its complement of oarsmen, and sail again for the Greenland seas. How soon could they hope to hear? Had she felt it justified, Rachel would have used one of their precious pennies at the Reading Room, but she knew Maitland or the twins would hear what news there was, at quayside or tavern.

As for Maitland, she loved him as she loved Davy and the others: he was a dear, kind friend whose company she valued and whose time had been willingly given over the years, to teach her reading and simple arithmetic, and to perfect her writing till she had as good a hand, she knew, as any lady. But he was no more than friend. Following Jessie's words and the bonfire celebrations, Rachel observed him as she had not done before, and what she saw disquieted her. Often when she looked up from some task, it was to find his eyes upon her, and it seemed to her that he went out of his way to sit beside her, to walk with her, to engineer occasions when they would be alone.

On one such occasion, finding her alone in the house making oatcakes for the supper, he came up behind her, encircled her waist, and murmured something which she did not catch. She twisted away and calmly busied herself at the griddle, asking about fishing matters, for it was almost the deep-sea season, and with a light laugh he took down the herring net from the rafters and carried it out of doors to be spread out for inspection when the twins returned. Perhaps it was nothing; perhaps she imagined deeper meaning than there was; but Rachel took care not to be alone with him again. She had no wish to hurt him.

In truth, there was little privacy for anyone in the busy life of the fishing community. The small line fishing ended, the boats were beached and the larger yawls prepared for the deep-sea season, but in all the work that this involved, a part of Rachel's mind stood back and thought only of James.

In May, it was reported from Lerwick that some forty Greenlandmen were in harbour there, en route for the whale fisheries. Maitland and the rest beached the small boat and found what places they could for the deep-sea fishing. They were away three days at a time, days in which Rachel and Annie, left together in the Square, felt anxiety stretched to insupportable tension in which they started at the least rattle of casement, shuddered at the least breath of wind, and offered endless, silent prayers of supplication. But the fisher lads returned safe, unloaded their catch, and put to sea again; and still there was no news of that other, longer venture – till a day in mid-July.

'The *Hope* has arrived in Peterhead,' reported Maitland, returning late after a long session with a torn herring net. 'Bosun Brand had it from the mannie-i'-the-black-coat himself.'

'The first ship o' the season on its way home with a full load,' added George, taking his place at table and reaching for the bread.

'The *Hercules* has ten and the *Letitia* fourteen,' said William, raising the broth bowl to his lips and drinking noisily. 'A dozen hoppin' chickens Jamie'll have the same.'

'A brace o' grouse he'll have a load o' sealskins, too.'

'And the *Middleton*?' asked Annie, addressing Maitland.

'One.' Maitland took up a knife to cut bread and avoided his mother's eyes. Rachel's hand trembled as she ladled more broth for William, filled a bowl for Davy, another for Alex. One whale. There would be no profit for anyone in that.

'There's time enough, Ma,' said Davy, the optimist. 'The *Middleton*'s a good ship wi' a good crew. Like as not they've

93

been unlucky so far wi' other ships getting ahead o' them. Another week, and they'll be hauling them in thick and fast.'

'Aye, like as not,' agreed his mother, but without hope. It was a judgement. She should not have let James go: they were fishermen, not whalers, as Fiddly had told them. Greed had been suitably rewarded.

'How much oil do ye get from one fish?' asked Wee Alex, his eyes anxious over the rim of the broth bowl.

'That depends how big it is,' said his brothers. 'And how old.' 'Ten tons, maybe.' 'Perhaps less, perhaps more.' 'But as well as the blubber, there's the baleen and the two jawbones.' 'Only the creng's discarded . . .'

But Rachel was no longer listening. One whale. She did not know how the profits were shared out, but knew enough to know a seaman in a crew of forty would get little enough from one fish: for the Greenland whale, or bowhead, was smaller than its Pacific counterpart, the cachelot, though just as dangerous. James would come home poorer than ever, his hopes shattered, his ship-building a vanished dream.

One fish. Even Davy could not long sustain enthusiasm, and they finished the meal in silence. But a week later came better news.

'Eleven!' cried Alex, rushing in from the Square ahead of his brothers. 'Jamie's ship has eleven fish!'

Their relief was premature. Before two weeks were out, the *Aberdeen Journal* reported the wreck of a whaler, the *Royalist*, crushed to pieces by prodigious masses of ice, its barrels of oil burst, its crew drowned. Even in the triumph of a full catch, success could be snatched away.

The August days slipped by and still no news. One by one the whalers turned for home, bringing reports of those left behind. Full catches were reported. A good season. No mention of the *Middleton*. Soon it would be the end of the deep-sea fishing. By September, everyone knew, the ice grew dangerously thick in the Greenland fisheries. Ships could be trapped by ice floes, locked all winter in their merciless grasp, beset by frost, hunger, disease, madness . . .

Then, on a Tuesday towards the end of August, the cry went up from the headland, 'Whaler ahoy!' The *Middleton* was safe home at last, with fifteen fish: 160 tons of blubber to be boiled down in the factory in the harbour, as well as whalebone for corsets and other products. Now, surely, James's share would be enough?

Rachel could not go to the quayside with the rest for fear of witnessing the meeting of Jess and James; could not join the scramble of joyful women and squealing kids for the overwhelming fear inside her. But it was Alex who swarmed the mast first and secured the precious garland with its ribbons salt-blown and tattered, and its tiny, crusted model ship. He bore it proudly home, for luck, James cheerful at his side.

Rachel heard the whistling from far away and her heart swelled suddenly full with a joy which obliterated Jess, the parting, everything; and when he seized her waist in triumph and swung her high she laughed as he did with the joy of a safe return and a full purse. Then he set her down again, held her shoulders in his two hands, looked for a timeless moment into her eyes which were swimming with welcome, and kissed her for the first time, on the lips.

'Oh Rachy, but it's good to be home.'

'Tell us about the whales, Jamie.' 'Is it true they fight worse than demons in the flurry?' 'Was the ice really high as a house?' Behind him in the doorway Davy, Alex, and the twins clamoured for tales of the whaling voyage, and only Maitland was silent. He and Annie had come in behind the others. Had they witnessed James's greeting? If so, it had made Annie well content, for her face was lit with happiness. Maitland's was paler, but smiling too, and if anything troubled him it was soon forgotten in the talk of James's adventures in the Greenland waters, his earnings, and their future plans.

'Did ye get the yard?' demanded James, the meal over.

'Aye. That piece o' ground at Pocra, behind Dixon's tattie patch. It's nae ideal, but fine for a start. £5 feu the year and a five-year lease.'

'Is there access to the water?'

'Aye, there's a wee lane at the side big enough to take a hundred-tonner. If we build much larger, we'll have to cross Dixon's patch to the water, but he's a good neighbour, there'll be nae bother.'

James was satisfied: good neighbours presented no problem. 'And is there space for timber?'

'Aye, and an adjoining building that'll serve fine for a planning loft.'

'And the plans themselves?' Now that the money was safe in his hands, James could not wait to start the venture.

'Complete,' said Maitland, 'though no one's seen them yet but me. Not even Rachel.'

'Then show us,' cried James, with a thump of fist on table, his face alive with triumph. *Now!*

Maitland swept aside the debris of supper and unrolled a stiff and crackling paper whose curling corners he weighted with mug and knife.

'This is a brig,' he began modestly. 'I know with all the talk o' the East India Company's losing their monopoly to India we should maybe be building larger, for the spice trade,' he went on, half teasing, half serious, 'but we'll come to that in a year or two. Meanwhile, this is what I have in mind.'

Rachel lit another candle and in the light of this, the fire and the crusie, they studied the drawing.

There were three plans: the sheer, the section cut through keel, stem and stern part; the floor plan, the horizontal on which the whole frame was erected; and the body plan, a section cut amidships, perpendicular to the sheer and floor plans.

'She's awfu' wide-bottomed,' said William, studying the plans and George added, 'There's a deal o' planking there.'

'A merchantman needs both capacity and strength,' explained Maitland, 'if she is to carry the cargo safely from one port to another without damage to cargo or ship.

'It's the science of water-displacement,' he went on, in his element now. 'We don't yet know what cargo our ship will carry, but whatever it is, it is best to build with a long floor, the lower futtocks very full, the upper near and straight. We need a good depth in the hold, with wing transoms carried pretty high, and the upper work must be kept as low and snug as possible if she is to take the ground well, carry a good sail and quickly answer the helm . . .'

Annie listened intently, the lines of doubting softened, until she too was caught up in the new excitement.

'And what about speed?' she asked. 'Will she no' be bottom heavy?'

'Not with the right mast height and spread of sail,' said James.

'We'll have the main mast here,' said Maitland, indicating his carefully drawn plans, 'and the foremast here. The bowsprit to make an angle of 36° with the horizontal . . .'

Enthralled, Rachel listened with the rest of them as Maitland explained measurements and timber requirements, how to get the proportions right, illustrating each point first on the plans, then on the delicately carved model which later he set lovingly in the centre of the dresser shelf, beside his father's unplayed fiddle. She knew that tiny model held their future, a future she would fight for with every talent she possessed.

'We will call her the *Steadfast*,' said James when candle and lamp had both burnt out, 'to remind us of our aim.'

That night, when Davy took up his 'mouthie' and played, one by one the Christie family joined in with whistle, voice or gentle humming till Annie's habitual mask of sorrow was broken by a smile and she, too, sang.

That was the beginning of a new life for the Christies. In September the family fishing boat was taken out as before to the sma' line fishing, but now it was William and George, with Davy and Wee Alex who put out to sea each morning, as Fiddly and their brothers had done before them. James sold their half-share in the summer herring boat and put the money towards the *Steadfast*, and the Christies' connection with the Brands was at an end. Annie and Rachel baited the boys' lines, helped to launch the boat, took the catch to market as before, and helped when they could at the Pocra yard. Even ten-year-old Alex did his bit, hanging around the larger quayside building-yards on rough days when Annie refused to let him go to sea, picking up what jobs he could and noting every part of the process of ship-building in readiness for the day when he, too, would be at work on the hull of a schooner or brigantine. Meanwhile he helped Rachel scour the water-line for flotsam and jetsam, gathered seaweed to augment the meal-pot; hawked bundles of split driftwood at the area doors of houses in the better part of town; scraping together and saving every penny to buy timber for their ship.

'We must buy only good wood,' insisted Maitland, 'and suited to our purpose. Nothing shaken, druxy, or with rotten knots.'

'There's a timber sale on the Links tomorrow,' said James. 'We've money enough, and if it runs out, I'll ask the Whitefishers for a loan.' This time Annie made no objection, not even when James and Maitland returned with the news that they had bought the entire stock, at 4s the cubic foot.

'And all good wood, well-seasoned, not a druxy piece among it,' James reported, jubilant. 'We'll shift it to the yard tomorrow.'

Their piece of land behind Dixon's patch was rapidly taking on the guise of a shipyard as James and Maitland assembled the materials for their enterprise – axe, adze, saw, auger, with wooden pins, cotton padding, oakum, and pitch. When their brothers returned from the fishing, they lent a hand to stack the timber, grading it into thicknesses and lengths, while from first light till last, Maitland and James worked on the developing *Steadfast*.

First the plans were laid out and enlarged, the model cut again in plywood, till the brothers felt confident enough to transfer theory to practice and lay down the first timber framework of their ship. Then there was the calculation of exact measurements for every plank and beam, and the cutting of each piece to size. It was a tedious process, for they had to learn each skill by trial and error, but gradually the little ship took shape as the keel was laid in place and the first ribs raised.

When she had finished the 'sheeling' and the day's mussel pails were full, Rachel carried food to the brothers in the building yard, and again when she returned from the town, her creel empty. Sometimes, uninvited, Jess came with her.

'That's a fine boatie you've got there,' she would tease, arms akimbo and head tipped mockingly on one side. 'I can see the daylight clear as clear through her ribcage. Yon'll let the water in and out again easy as a sieve . . .' Or 'Which way up is she? I canna tell,' or 'Yon's a braw witch's tub ye're making.'

James ignored her, and when even her most insulting taunts brought no reaction, Jessie would retire, baffled and petulant, as she had been forced to do when the *Middleton* had sailed triumphantly into harbour and James had been claimed under her nose by his mother and idiot brothers.

'Yon Christie lads are a' gone fou,' she would complain, 'and James is worst of all. I reckon yon icebergs addled his brain. Ye'd think he'd tak' a wife now he's head o' the house wi' money in his hand, 'stead o' playing with a toy boatie like a bairn. For yon'll never sail.'

Secretly Rachel was delighted at Jessie's defeat, for since that incident on the quayside and Jessie's boasting, she had daily dreaded its fulfilment. Since his return from the Greenland fisheries, James had retreated into the world of his family and his shipyard, and for all her brash effrontery, Jess could not break through the barrier.

One evening in late October, however, she deliberately waited till Maitland had left on some errand, then slipped from her hiding-place behind the shed and into the lamplight where James worked on the skeletal hull of the *Steadfast*. The ribs were all in place now, bolted firmly to the keel and curving up like the rib-cage of a whale against the darkening sky. Tonight the first of the cross-timbers had been fitted, low on the keel, and James was securing it in place with wooden pins and great care.

'It's awfu' late for ye, Jamie,' she said, wheedling, her eyes large and ingenuous. 'Ye must be lonely out here i' the dark and the cold with only yon skeleton boatie for company.'

James continued to whistle softly to himself and made no answer.

'I've brought ye a pie, see, and a draught o' best ale,' she said as he continued to hammer at the hull. 'Will ye no take a wee rest, Jamie, and talk to me? Like ye used to?'

She ran a sensuous hand up his bare arm and made to encircle his neck, but he wrenched angrily away, with a violence that sent her staggering.

'Take your whoring to the quayside, woman, where ye'll find better custom.'

'At least I'll find *men* there! Folks i' the Square, James Christie, say it's time you wed and fathered sons o' your own now Fiddly's dead, but ye couldna father a jelly-fish, not if they lifted ye on!'

James gripped her forearms till the thumbs bruised her flesh, but she laughed into his face, her breasts swelling full against his chest, her breath hot on his cheek.

'Go on,' she taunted, 'shake me. It's all ye ken how to do.'

In the darkness of Pocra pier, tension quivered on the edge of violence, while water lapped against pierhead and from beyond the harbour came the relentless beat of sea on shore. It was a moonless night, the sky layered with racing cloud, a sharp edge to the wind. Behind them the lantern guttered in its casing, and Jess's cheeks were wet with spray. Their breath came loud and laboured, then, with a tremendous effort of self-control, James thrust her from him with an oath. 'Get home!' he snarled, with such suppressed fury that Jessie snatched up her offering of ale and left, reserving a derisive flick of the hips till she turned the corner of the yard.

From that evening she feigned unconcern, but she wanted James as a cat wants the cream it can smell but cannot reach, and she was sure she could get him if only he would let himself be 'got'. She had felt the banked passion behind his violence, sensed that, once released, it would be all she hoped for, knew her only rival to be that half-built ship. But how did you fight a *ship*?

'I'll get him one day,' she vowed, 'I swear it!' But for the moment she did not know how to proceed. Tried methods had failed, and she had not imagination enough to explore the untried. Bafflement made her short-tempered.

'Where's yon student laddie o' yours?' she demanded of Rachel on a frosty day in late autumn. 'He's over passionate, isn't he? Leaving ye all these months with not a kiss to warm your pantin' wee heart? Or does he not love ye like he used to do?'

'He is studying,' said Rachel. She had not heard from Andrew since the spring and then only briefly, to say that he was working as an assistant in the public dispensary. '*You* would not know what that involves,' she said, with a rare edge to her voice. 'But 'tis a long, hard course if ye mean to be a doctor as Andrew does. There's not just Latin and Greek to learn, but chemistry and anatomy and natural philosophy, and then he must be apprenticed, like as not, to a practising physician. He'll come when he can.'

'Then I hope he comes soon,' grumbled Jessie. 'I'm hungry

for a man wi' something more to him than yon wet herrings i' the Square.'

Rachel did not answer. Remembering her friend's boasting, she feared for Andrew as she feared for James. When Andrew did come, as he must one day, she resolved to guard him somehow from Jess's wiles. For it was common knowledge Jess had 'tried' every unmarried lad from sixteen to thirty in North and South Squares – and had not always stopped at the unmarried. But few had the spirits to match her own and those that had, she tired of.

'Ye'll be an old maid yet,' grumbled her mother, 'and your looks willna last much longer. If ye're nae careful ye'll find yoursel' passed over, for all yer vaunting. Then where'll ye be?'

'In a fine house in Union Street,' retorted Jessie, 'built by yon architect fellow everyone's talking of.'

'In a whorehouse on the quay, more like,' snapped her mother. 'Now get on wi' ye to the town and sell yon fish afore it's stinking.'

In the Broadgait the conversation was also of houses.

'It is time we moved to larger premises,' said Abercrombie. 'There is just the place for sale in the Guestrow.'

'The *Guestrow?*' cried Clementina, dismayed. 'But Papa, all the best people are moving into the new street. Surely you could buy a stance there – or take one of the shops in the new Union Buildings?'

'All the best people, as you say, may be moving into newfangled mansions with porticoes and Grecian columns, but the best businessmen are staying where the trade is, in the old town,' grunted her father. He liked the old houses, as he liked a good solid table of old-fashioned oak and a good solid spread. Though the elegant mahogany dining-table, he noticed, was loaded today with more than its usual meagre fare. He tucked the napkin securely under his chin and took an appreciative mouthful of thick mutton broth.

Mrs Abercrombie directed a warning glance at her daughter. 'Mr Farquharson says Union Street will one day hold all the trade of the city,' she said, sipping delicately at her broth.

Clementina was to marry the Farquharson boy in the spring. 'And that it is wisest to get in at the beginning.'

'Aye, if ye've the prior knowledge and the resources as he has, the swindling devil – all the town knows he sold yon land of his at twice the value when the new road was built. Nae wonder he's money to burn on daft mansions big enough to house an elephant. But I've a good clientele in this part of town, as the other merchants have, and it'll be a while yet afore we all move out. Besides, the house I have in mind is in a good position in the Guestrow, at the Union Street end, south of Barnett's close, and is at present possessed by an *advocate*,' he added slyly. 'Cellars with catacombs for the stock, shop space on the ground floor and twice the rooms we have here. A first-floor dining-room, my dear, and a splendid second-floor drawing-room, *and* a water closet, flushed by a pipe from the guttering.'

Mrs Abercrombie's expression changed to one of wary interest. A water closet . . . She knew for a fact that Mrs Forbes had none. As for the Farquharsons, who were building a house in the West End, with a separate wing for Robert, designed by the local up-and-coming architect, Archibald Simpson, she could not hope to compete with them – but at least Clementina would live in the right part of town. Remembering the purpose of the meal, she said cautiously, 'Perhaps you are right, my dear. Shall we look over the house tomorrow?'

'As you like.' Abercrombie had waited a long time for the right house and had already inspected the Guestrow premises from attic to cellar. Living over the shop, he would be able to supervise every detail of the expansion he planned, and, with the tyrant Napoleon safely out of the way in Elba, the East India Company's monopoly to India ended, and more improvements talked of for the harbour, it was a good time for development in all sorts of trade. The Farquharson connection would be useful, too, if it led, as it ought to do, to better rates. If it did not – and Atholl Farquharson was a grasping bastard – then he would make those other arrangements he and Fenton had discussed. The decision made, he allowed himself to relax.

'I think, if you can spare it my dear, I will take another ladle of that delicious broth.'

Mrs Abercrombie smiled with relief. The lunch was going well, and the arrival of stovies and an excellent piece of boiled beef ensured success. A more cynical man would have suspected an ulterior motive in his wife's pandering to hearty masculine appetites, but Abercrombie's mind was otherwise occupied.

'Where is Fenton?'

'He is lunching with the Forbeses,' said Mrs Abercrombie complacently. 'Mr Forbes has kindly suggested that when Fenton's studies are complete, there might be a place for him in his legal office.'

'There's a place for him here,' snapped Abercrombie. 'He's already had an extra year at the college because o' your nagging, woman, and he'll get no more. So ye can forget your high falutin' ideas,' he finished, 'and leave the boy alone.'

'But there is no *harm* in the law,' persisted his wife, 'and Louise is a pleasant girl, in spite of her unfeminine interest in learning. She and Fenton are quite intimate.'

'Louise and Fenton are friends, Mamma,' put in Clementina impatiently. 'Nothing more. They talk about tedious things like the rights of the poor, when goodness knows the poor are well enough off. Why, there is even talk of closing the public soup-kitchen this autumn because the harvest is so plentiful.'

'The honey, I know, is excellent,' agreed Mrs Abercrombie, deciding to shelve the question of Fenton's future in the interests of domestic peace.

'Honey? What has *honey* to do with it?' demanded her husband. 'Or are the poor of the parish to live off beehives?'

'I mentioned honey only because I know your partiality for Athole-brose, my dear,' said his wife smoothly. 'But for today Cook has made you your favourite apple pudding, with orange-flower water and a touch of brandy.' She caught Clementina's eye and gave the briefest of nods.

'Papa,' began Clementina, 'Miss Cruickshank in Broadgait has dresses new from London, very elegant and fashionable and ordered purposefully for the Assemblies next week. Madelina Farquharson, I know, has purchased two in the newest winter colours, and Mamma and I thought . . .'

The Square was busy on that afternoon of crisp sun and racing clouds. Shawled women sat on creepie-stools at their doors

103

baiting lines, others knitted, pared vegetables, or shelled un-ending mussels. One toothless old woman sucked noisily at a clay pipe while nursing a fretful grandchild, and two small girls skipped nimbly through the intricacies of hopscotch. From close at hand came the rhythmic hammering of some boat-repair, and the air was sharp with fish, seaweed, and the peat-reek of many fires.

Like the other women, Rachel and Annie had taken their stools into the thin sunlight of afternoon and were engaged in making ready the last of the lines for the next day's fishing, when a sudden hush transformed the busy Square into a place of statues, staring. All eyes turned to the southernmost corner where, in the gap where south side met west, had appeared a trio of townsfolk in walking outfits. After only a moment's hesitation, the first of the three stepped forward into the silence.

'It's Andrew!' cried Rachel, starting to her feet, only to subside again in consternation at the near ruin of Davy's line. Quickly she re-coiled the newly baited section into the 'skull', setting each hook in its allotted place, and laid aside the portion still to do, while watching silence hung over the Square and Rachel's were the only hands that moved.

'It's Jeannie's boy, right enough,' said Annie at her side. 'But who's he brought wi' him? Two townies by their finery, and ill enough at ease.'

Who would not be ill at ease, thought Rachel, with a square full of strangers, staring. She remembered her own arrival at Fiddly's door, Jessie's mockery and the way all eyes had turned on her till she thought she would melt into nothing from sheer terror.

'This is Miss Forbes, Aunt Annie,' said Andrew, indicating the tall, thin girl with the intelligent face, 'and this is Fenton Abercrombie, a fellow student and a friend. I came across them quite by chance as I was making my way here, and as Miss Forbes expressed an interest in your village, I took the liberty of inviting them to accompany me. My aunt, and my cousin,' he finished, with a smile at Rachel.

'You are welcome,' said Annie with dignity, setting aside her work. 'Please come inside where you'll be spared the scrutiny o' folk wi' nought better to do than mind other folk's business. I canna offer ye tea,' she said to Louise when they were inside the one-roomed cottage, Louise in the only chair and the others on benches and stools, 'for 'tis a habit we havena adopted as yet.' And wouldn't, as long as tea cost 7s the pound. 'But I can offer ye hot toddy or a draught of good ale, and there's fresh baked bread.'

'Aunt Annie's oat-bread is excellent,' said Andrew. 'You must be sure to try some, Miss Forbes; and after our brisk walk in the fresh sea air, toddy would not come amiss, I know.'

While Annie swung the simmering kettle further over the fire and busied herself with the whisky jar, Rachel set out bread and cheese on wooden platters, and the pat of fresh butter she had brought back that morning from the market in exchange for the last of their haddock. From under lowered lashes she saw Miss Forbes's eyes roving over walls and rafters, pot-shelf and dresser, taking in every detail, and in spite of herself she felt her cheeks redden. Why should they come here to inspect and criticize? To sit disdainfully in their city finery and find fault? She fancied the girl's lip curled in distaste as Annie set the steaming toddy glass at her side, imagined the young man set his fine breeches unwillingly on the bare wood. As for Andrew, in his thread-bare clothes and frayed linen, could he not see they were showing him up? Using him as an amusing toy to relieve their boredom? Silence smothered the company till Rachel wished Andrew had not come.

Then the young lady spoke, in a voice at once respectful and forthright. 'I confess I thrust my company uninvited upon Andrew and on you, Mrs Christie, out of pure curiosity. I had heard so many tales in the town about how the fisherfolk live, many of them too scurrilous to be true, that I could not lose the chance to find out for myself. You see, Mrs Christie, I believe there is too much injustice in this world, too much oppression and exploitation, especially of us womenfolk.'

Oppression? Rachel's eyes widened in astonishment. Surely not of Miss Forbes in her grey merino walking-dress and hand-made leather boots?

'I noticed, as who could fail to do, in the Square just now, that all the work here is done by the women. Why, I even saw a woman carrying a load of peat on her back! While the men no doubt smoke their pipes and drink their ale in idleness. I do not mean to be impertinent, Mrs Christie, but how can you tolerate such exploitation?'

Annie looked at the girl's animated, indignant face for a long, cool moment, then said, with a hint of amusement, 'You think we should lie late in our beds and rise to sit in idleness ourselves?'

'No, no,' said the girl impatiently. 'It is not your working that I find an exploitation, but the disproportion between your work and that of your menfolk. You even *carry* them to their boats on occasions, I believe.'

'And so would you,' said Annie grimly, 'if wet feet meant pneumonia and death.' Rachel knew she was thinking of Davy, whose cough still troubled him.

'They must go to sea before dawn,' explained Andrew, who had grown up in a fisher family, 'and spend several hours in an undecked boat, in the cold. If a man is soaked at the beginning of such a journey, what might he be like at the end of it? Fever is rife enough without encouraging it.'

For a moment the girl looked disconcerted, then returned undaunted to the attack. 'Yet the women carry more than a man's weight on their backs. It seems to me they carry a man's work, too.'

'My menfolk leave before dawn,' said Annie, her eyes cold now with the glint of battle. 'They put in a day's work before you townsfolk are out o' your beds. They have work enough to do on shore after that, if their boats and tackle are to be seaworthy for the next day's fishing. Just because ye canna see them, that doesna mean they're nae at work. Why I've two lads building a ship wi' their bare hands this minute, and they'd be at it twenty-four hours a day if I didna stop them.'

'A ship?' said Fenton with interest. 'How enterprising.'

'Yes,' agreed Rachel proudly, 'and when she is finished, she will ply the coastal trade, for profit.'

'Nevertheless, it seems to me you women are exploited,' persisted Louise, ignoring the interruption.

'Exploited? Rubbish! How many townswomen have our freedom? How many townsmen give all their livelihood to their wives to manage, as our men do? How many townswomen have the family fortune, such as it is, entirely in their own hands to save or spend as they think fit?'

'Is that really so, Mrs Christie?' Louise's face took on a look of absorbed fascination. 'You must tell me exactly how you manage . . .'

'Louise is never happier,' said the young man, smiling at Rachel, 'than when pursuing some imagined injustice or social deprivation, and Mrs Christie does not seem to mind.'

It was true. Looking at the two women, locked now in heated argument, Rachel realized she had not seen Annie so animated since the old days, before Fiddly's death. 'I am glad you came,' she said. 'You have done her good.'

'I came to say good-bye,' said Andrew, taking her hand and squeezing it. 'I am to go to Edinburgh for a while, to study anatomy.'

'But I thought . . .' Rachel was dismayed. Edinburgh was so far away, and though she rarely saw Andrew, the knowledge that he was here in her town had been comfort enough. 'Is there not anatomy in Aberdeen?'

'Of a kind, of course, but in Edinburgh the training of doctors has progressed far ahead of what we have here. Why, we have still no common faculty for medical studies but must find what lectures we can, where we can, whereas there the classes have been collected into one faculty for almost a century.'

'But we have had professors of medicine for generations,' protested Fenton Abercrombie, 'both at King's College and at Marischal.'

'Aye, but merely nominal, with no tradition of lectures.'

'Then must you go to Edinburgh?' ventured Rachel. She had not realized till now what a prop it had been to her to know, should there be illness in the family, that Andrew was at hand to treat it.

'Aye, Rachy,' he said quietly. 'I must go, if I am to learn anatomy as I want to learn it.'

'Anatomy? That's cutting up bodies, isn't it?' said a cheerful voice from the doorway as Davy, with Alex at his heels, arrived home from the yard. 'James says he'll be late, Ma,' he added, unabashed by the company. 'He's buildin' a ship,' he explained to the room in general, 'and it's takin' awfu' long. You're Rachy's Andrew, aren't ye? From Cove?'

'Davy,' said his mother sharply, 'where's your manners? With Miss Forbes here and Mr Abercrombie. You too, Alex.'

'How do you do,' said the brothers, in chorus; then, while Alex foraged in the bread crock before retreating with his chalk and slate to the box bed, Davy joined Rachel and Andrew. 'How many bodies have ye cut up, Bookie? 'Tis well kent yon Medical Society robs all the graves o' Aberdeenshire in the cause o' study. Why, only a week back they say two o' your number drove all the way from the country wi' a corpse propped up atween them in the carriage! Did ye have a hand in that affair, Bookie?'

'I am sorry, Davy,' said Andrew, smiling, 'but I am bound by an oath of secrecy not to tell.'

'On pain of expulsion,' added Fenton, who understood how dangerous an enterprise it was to secure a fresh body, since it was common knowledge in the student community that each member of the Medico-Chirurgical Society was bound to take his turn.

'Oh well,' said Davy cheerfully, 'I wouldna want ye to break your word. But I'm nae superstitious, and bodies dinna worry me. Ye can have mine when I'm dead, and welcome.'

'Davy!' cried his mother, appalled. 'Dinna talk so!'

'Sorry, Ma,' said Davy, momentarily contrite. He crossed to the hearth and put a swift arm around her shoulder in reassurance. But when he rejoined Andrew's party he went on, more quietly lest his mother hear, 'Still, I meant it. A body's no use to a man when he's dead, and if Bookie's Society wants to borrow mine for a whilie, it's welcome. I'd like fine to be there, though,' he added, grinning. 'Then I'd peer down from heaven and see just what it is that gives me that twinge i' the chest on a frosty morning.'

Before Andrew could answer, the door opened again and a girl's voice said sweetly, 'Oh dear, I am sorry, Rachel. I didna know ye had company.'

Jessie Brand had been inside, feeding one of her numerous siblings, when the arrival of Andrew's party threw sudden silence over the Square. Crossing to the doorway to see what was amiss, she spied a trio of townsfolk in walking outfits. It was too good a target to miss. She opened her mouth to jeer, and then thought better of it – for wasn't that Bookie Noble,

Rachel's student laddie? The fellow with him had a familiar look to him, too.

Hastily she had smoothed her hair, splashed water on her face till the skin glowed, draped her best shawl at the right angle across her shoulders, and stepped out into the Square.

'I'm sorry, Mrs Christie,' she said now, with her demurest expression. 'I wouldna have troubled ye, but Ma's suffering with the cough again and I wondered if ye'd a drop o' honey syrup, as ours is spent.'

Annie Christie looked at her with level eyes. Mrs Brand had been robust enough half an hour earlier, and Jessie never spoke in that sweetly innocent voice unless she was after something.

'Come in, Jessie,' she said with scant courtesy. 'I'll have a look.'

'It's Andrew Noble, isn't it?' said Jessie, unabashed and seating herself on the bench beside him. 'Who's to be a physician-mannie? You'll know best, then, what to do for a cough, wi' all your studyin' and practice.'

'Little enough practice as yet, I'm afraid,' said Andrew, 'though I have worked at the Dispensary for some months now. You should tell your mother to call there herself if her cough grows troublesome; she need not worry about the cost, for treatment is free to those who have not the means.'

'Oh we dinna worry about the fee,' retorted Jessie with a toss of her head. She had no wish to be labelled a pauper in front of townsfolk. ''Tis of no concern to us.'

'Really?' Louise Forbes, left without her informant while Annie searched through her medicine shelf for the cordial, transferred her interest to the new arrival. 'What is the average income of your family, Miss . . . er . . . Jessie? How many are there of you, and how many working men?'

Jessie looked at her in astonishment. She was little older than Jess herself and a deal plainer, and though she had a fine merino gown and hand-made boots that did not give her the right to act like a magistrate, or the mannie-wi'-the-black-coat, as the fisher community referred to their minister. Nosey bitch, she thought, bridling; two can play at yon game.

'I expect ye ken the exact amount of *your* father's money, miss,' she said sweetly, 'and what *your* mother does wi' it? You tell me first, and we'll compare.'

'She's right,' said Andrew Noble's friend, smiling. 'You are a trifle impertinent, you know, Louise.'

'Never mind her, Miss Forbes,' said Annie, returning from the far recesses of the room and her medicine chest. 'I'll be happy to tell ye, if only to set right your notions of how we folk live, for ye have the oddest ideas. As for you, Jessie Brand, here's yon cordial ye were asking for, in case your ma gets taken wi' the coughing; and if ye're as rich as ye say, ye can buy me another to replace it. If not, I'll have it back tomorrow. Now away home wi' ye,' she finished firmly, and resumed her conversation with Louise.

Jessie, however, did not go. She was studying Bookie Noble's friend and wondering why he looked familiar. He was about Bookie's age, she reckoned, though better dressed. There was money there. Jess hovered on the threshold, reluctant to leave.

'I am sure the cordial is excellent,' said Andrew, reverting to the question of her mother's cough, 'but do remember to tell your mother about the Dispensary, won't you? There is a vaccine clinic too,' he explained to Rachel, 'for the prevention of smallpox, and one day I hope we will have discovered similar methods of preventing all such fatal diseases.'

'You don't work in yon vaccine place yoursel'?' asked Jess, drawing away from him in apprehension. 'I dinna want to catch anything.'

'You are quite safe, Miss . . . er . . . Jessie,' said his friend. 'Andrew has been vaccinated, and there is no danger.'

'Fenton is right. We take the greatest care to prevent any spread of infection and . . .'

But Jessie was no longer listening. Fenton. Fenton *Abercrombie*! Of course. She bit back a smile of gleeful memory, and in the flip of a herring's tail transferred her attention from Andrew to the new young man.

Andrew was to be a doctor and one day rich: but Fenton was rich now. Andrew was Rachel's friend and from a background close to her own: Fenton's family were well off and no doubt snobs. But Fenton was weak and susceptible. She could see it in his face as he eyed her full breasts and trim waist, and, remembering that encounter in the archway of his own yard, she reckoned she could manage him, and any opposition from his family into the bargain, if she chose. Idly she weighed the pros and cons as she lingered in the doorway, hand on hip and breast arched to best advantage. Then Andrew spoke and settled the matter.

'I will be away in Edinburgh at least a year, Rachel, then I mean to go to London to take an exam. When I return, I hope to work in the fever hospital here.'

The *fever* hospital! Jess was having nothing to do with fever. If he didn't catch it himself and die, he'd infect his family, like as not. Rachel could have him, and welcome. With a shudder of revulsion, Jess abandoned Andrew for cleaner, richer fields.

'Haven't we met somewhere before?' she asked softly, sidling closer to Fenton Abercrombie where he sat awkwardly perched on the wooden bench, the half-drunk toddy in his hand. 'Remember? I mocked you, blocking your path in your own gateway. You never did give me that kiss,' she added, her eyes teasing, 'but I'll maybe get a chance to block your way again.'

Fenton swallowed, blushed, then said, 'I do remember. I knew your face the moment you stepped through the door. Do you live far from here, Miss . . . ?'

'Call me Jessica,' she murmured, a watchful eye on Annie Christie, but Mrs Christie was safely absorbed in discussion with that Forbes girl, and the others were listening only to Andrew. Jess moved closer to the Abercrombie boy till she felt his thigh against her own and, even through the thicknesses of flannel petticoat, felt the trembling that shook him. 'Are ye still at the college?' she asked, her eyes wide and innocent. 'It must be awful hard studying all day.'

'You see, Rachel,' explained Andrew earnestly, 'there are things in Edinburgh that I cannot find here and that I must learn. How else am I to fit myself, as I hope to do, to combat illness as it must be fought?'

'I know, Andrew. But I will miss you.' Rachel's eyes brimmed with sudden tears at the thought of their parting. 'Edinburgh is so far away.'

'Remember the many mansions?' said Andrew gently. 'Where you are to come and visit me? How am I to buy even one small room if I do not work?'

'And if his work is in Edinburgh, Rachy,' said Davy kindly, seeing her trouble, 'then he must go there.'

'Of course.' She shook away grief and smiled, remembering

her own work and how much there was still to do before the Christie boat was finished. Time would pass soon enough. 'I wish you well, Andrew.'

'Thank you, Rachel, and do not worry. I'll be back before you know it.'

'And so will my sons,' announced Annie, rising to her feet, 'and the lines not baited nor the meal ready. You must excuse us, Miss Forbes.'

'Of course. But I hope you will allow me to call on you again one day, Mrs Christie? I found our conversation most enlightening.'

'If you please to come, ye'll be made welcome,' said Annie, 'though you'll not mind if I ask ye to go, as I do now. We're exploited, remember? Wi' a deal o' work to get through.'

'I know,' grinned Louise, 'and thank you for sparing me so much of your time. Come along Fenton,' she added with a touch of asperity, for he and that fisher girl seemed not to have heard the sounds of general departure. 'Good-bye, Mrs Christie. Till our next meeting.'

'You will come again then?' murmured Jess and laid her hand surreptitiously on Fenton's arm. 'Please? I'll be watching for ye.'

Fenton quivered at her touch. 'And I for you.' His face was flushed as he stepped out into the darkened Square.

Fenton and the Forbes girl visited the Square again, some two weeks later, and again at the turn of the year. On both occasions Jessie Brand intercepted them and exchanged a few smiling words with the Abercrombie boy, though on neither did she cross the Christie threshold: Annie Christie saw to that. But Jessie was well pleased. She had seen the look in Fenton's eyes when she greeted him, and if he did not come again to the Square before too long, she knew where he lived and would find an excuse to seek him out. If Annie Christie thought to keep Jess away from Fenton Abercrombie – or anyone else – by the shutting of her door, the stuck-up harridan would find herself mistaken. As for her precious James, he could rot in hell.

Old Yule came and passed without incident. For though there was once more singing and celebration in the Christie household, there was little time for relaxation with so much to be done on the *Steadfast*.

But on a morning towards the end of January the Christies knew to a man that there would be no fishing that day and little enough work in the shipyard either. The frost the previous night had been intense, the ice on the water pail was half an inch deep, the window crusted so thick it was impossible to see outside, even when Alex breathed hard on the surface and rubbed. Then with morning came a freshening: water surfaced the frozen pathways, frosted grasses were suddenly dew-laden, and the still air stirred with uneasy warmth.

'I don't like it,' pronounced James, turning his face to the wind that Friday morning and studying sea and sky in the half-darkness before dawn. Since his father's death, James had made it his business to decide whether the fishing boat would put to sea before William or George donned sea-boots and waterproof clothing. Today there was blood in the sky and the sea's surface heaved uneasily with reddening foam. 'There'll be a gale before sun-up. Just look at yon sea.'

William and George, clad only in long-sleeved woollen vests and fisherman's trousers, joined James beside the blackened wedge of peat stack. Spray licked over the cliff edge and bubbled across the drying green, laying gleaming spittle over night-hardened turf. In the distance, to the north, the dark line of coast met surf in a grey wall of spray, and the noise of the sea was a monotonous, threatening drone.

'East-south-east,' said George. 'And strengthening,' agreed William. 'We'd best make fast the boat, or a lobster to a Finnan haddie we'll find it blown into the Castlegate afore we know it.'

Already thatch from cottage roofs was shredding and tossing high overhead in a whirl of sea-birds, as the wind strengthened to a screeching, snatching gale. Seas heaved in mountainous crags of water which smashed against pier and cliff in one continuous roar.

'Aye,' said James. 'We'd best all stay indoors.'

But an hour later every male in the Square was scrambling for sea-boots and waterproofs as the cry went up, 'Ship in distress!' The door burst open on a rush of sand and spray through which Bosun Brand's wind-battered face appeared only long enough to shout 'Two ships! Making for harbour and both in difficulties!' before he was gone again, leaving turmoil behind him.

'*No!*' cried Annie, starting to her feet and shaking so violently that she clutched the chair arm for support. 'Not again . . . not all over again . . .' She finished on a cry of despair which sent Rachel speeding to her side.

'We *must* go, Ma,' said James quietly, pulling on the second sea-boot over the stockings Rachel had knitted him.

'There's a brig and a schooner in difficulties,' called William from the open doorway.

'The lifeboat's being launched,' added George, 'but with seas so huge, they'll need all hands on shore to help.'

'It'll be all right, Ma,' said Davy. He pulled a thick sweater over his head and tucked it hastily into his belt. 'My other boot, Rachel. Quick!'

But Annie, quivering uncontrollably now, was moaning over and over to herself, 'The sea will take them, I know it, the sea will take my boys.'

'Hush, Ma,' Davy put his arm round her in hasty comfort and farewell. 'If we were helpless in a storm at sea, would you have other folk stand by and do nothing? See to her, Rachel.'

But when they had gone, running to join the rest on the pierhead, only Alex forced rebelliously to stay behind, Annie was taken with a shaking so violent that neither shawl nor the whisky toddy that Alex made under Rachel's directions could quell it. Rachel knew the storm and the shouting had brought back the pain of Fiddly's death with intolerable memory. There could be no comfort for Fiddly's loss, only hope for those left to her, and this Rachel did her best to provide.

'They'll come to no harm, Auntie,' she said firmly. 'James'll see to that.' *But James had promised to watch over his father . . .*

114

'The sea will take them, I know it,' Annie moaned, over and over, shivering with undiminished violence. 'Nothing can save them.'

Nothing could save the crew of the brig, sunk off the Girdleness, while the lifeboat floundered, powerless to assist, and the schooner battled clear of the Girdleness only to be wrecked in the bay of Nigg. Two hours later, from the south-east, under square sail, try-sail and jib, came a smack racing for shelter. That, too, was swept on to the rocks of Greyhope, the crew drowned.

It was a sombre group that fought its way home in the snatching wind, spray-drenched, defeated, as the short day ended without further wreckage but with no diminution of the wind's force.

'Off wi' your clothes this instant,' cried Annie, galvanized out of shock and into frenzy by the sight of her sons, teeth chattering and water dripping from every crease and corner of clothing. 'Rachy, heat the blankets. Alex, top up the kettle and stock the fire. Oh Davy, Davy, how could ye get so wet.'

'He'll be fine, Ma, wi' a good glass o' toddy inside him,' said James, 'and so will we all.'

But when, dry-clothed and warm again, inside and out, the family had at last gone to bed, Rachel heard coughing in the night, felt Annie stiffen in the box bed beside her, listening, and shared Annie's fear.

The morning brought renewed gales, tremendous seas, and two more ships, fighting their way to the harbour and elusive safety. The first, a little smack, navigated superbly to ride the hazards of the Girdleness and harbour bar to reach their haven. The second followed, only to be struck on the beam fifty yards from home and smashed to pieces on the stones of the pierhead. And still the gale raged unabated, throughout that day and into the night.

But by morning the wind had died, leaving the seas clogged with debris, a battered landscape, and the near-death of James's hopes. For at the little shipyard they found their carefully graded timber scattered, snapped like matchwood and crunching underfoot, the skeletal hull blown off its blocks, its ribs buckled, the planning shed gutted and roofless, door banging loose, and where there had been neat plans and diagrams, a sodden, unidentifiable hotch-potch of oozing pulp.

For a long moment the Christie men stood in appalled silence. Then Maitland dropped to his haunches beside the shreds of paper and broken model on the floor of the shed, and began to pick them over with anxious fingers, searching.

'All my plans ruined,' he mourned, 'torn to shreds. But there must be something I can piece together and dry out . . .'

'Aye,' said Davy with determined cheerfulness, 'we'll soon set things right again, you'll see. And at least the wee model of the *Steadfast* is safe at home.'

'But the scale model's gone and the plans,' moaned Maitland. 'Weeks of work lost. Months . . .'

'Come on, Maitland,' rallied William. 'I'll bet ye ten wet kippers it's nae as bad as it looks.' 'And a dried skate wi' your name on it,' added George.

But James's mouth had set now in obstinate determination. 'We can at least try to retrieve something. No one does any other work till we've set things right.'

Every Christie from Wee Alex to Bonnie Annie helped. Scattered wood was painstakingly reassembled, sorted into the still-serviceable and the useless, and stacked once more. The bruised *Steadfast* was righted, replaced upon her blocks, her splintered ribs removed. One was found to be shattered, one snapped in half, others bent or cracked. Each damaged rib was unbolted, discarded and the keel made good.

In the roofless shed, Rachel collected strewn papers, smoothing and sorting them, retrieving what remained of scale-plans and calculations, while Annie swept and set the room to rights. William and George together replaced the roof, hammering new planking over the gaps, while Maitland collected broken plywood sections of his working model and made what he could of them. They worked in silence for the most part, retrieving what little they could of six months' work and hopes.

'It is best,' said James quietly, 'to find out the weaknesses early. Yon ribs were feeble or they'd not have cracked. We must build a ship which will not founder in a storm, but be strong enough to ride out the tempest and come into harbour, safe.'

'Like yon little smack,' said Alex.

'Aye, she handled well. As ours will.' But later, at the end of the day, Rachel saw his dejection and lingered behind the others when he sent them home.

'Oh Rachel, Rachel.' He spread his hands in a gesture of despair which embraced shipyard and shed. 'Will it never be done with, the scraping and scratching, the makeshifts, the borrowings? We are back where we started and the money already spent.'

It was true. The whaling bounty, the savings, even Annie's burial money, had gone on leasing and stocking their yard – but the yard was still theirs, the plans still good, whatever the setbacks.

'It is no matter,' she said fiercely, though her heart ached for him. 'We'll find it somehow. You cannot give up now, with so much achieved. You *must* go on . . .'

'But we will need sailcloth and anchor chain, rope for the rigging, so many things. I think, sometimes, that I am wrong to bring such hardship on you all, for a dream. Perhaps Ma was right after all. We are fisherfolk . . .'

'You said yourself that even fisherfolk may dream!'

'Aye, so I did.' He looked at her ardent, determined face, her shining eyes and pink-flushed cheeks, and, putting out a finger, lifted her chin and studied her. 'You're a strange lass, Rachy.' She saw his eyes deepen in the darkness, saw the tenderness of his face. 'I've never known a lass like you . . .' Then with a sudden laugh, he broke the spell. 'We'll build that ship, Rachy, somehow. I swear it.'

With a lighter step he took her hand and, whistling cheerfully into the twilight, led her back to the Square and home.

When news of the shipwreck reached the town and subscription lists were opened for the bereaved, Louise Forbes decided to call upon the Christies again. 'For,' as she told Fenton Abercrombie, 'the storm blew for three whole days and no fishing boats could put to sea. I must find out how they manage on such occasions.'

Fenton willingly offered to escort her, and together they settled on a ham and a cheese as suitable gifts, in thanks for all the time and help Mrs Christie had given Louise in her researches. One day Louise intended to write an article about the

Square for the *Aberdeen Journal* under the pseudonym of 'A Lady'.

'It is very kind of you, Miss Forbes, but I really cannot accept,' said Annie, though without her old authority. Since the day of the storm when the trembling had taken hold of her, she had aged in a dozen little ways which Rachel noted with sorrow and compassion. Annie stooped where she had stood straight, was paler, more hollow-cheeked, the hair at her temples suddenly white. Even her hands had changed, the skin shrinking over knuckle and tendon, fingers slowing over tasks once done with ease. And when she sat at the fireside, as she did now, her head still quivered with the residue of that violence which had shaken her from top to toe when her sons went out into the storm.

Quietly, Rachel had taken over what tasks she could while the older woman sat immobile, her hands idle. Rachel said nothing to the boys, but there was no need. They all saw the change in Annie and were solicitous and gentle.

'Never you fret, Ma,' James had said when the twins and Davy put to sea for the first time after the storm. ''Twill not be for much longer. When the *Steadfast* is finished we'll have no need o' the fishing, and no need for you to work so hard, either. We'll have a house in the town then, where you shall sit by the fire in a fine new gown wi' a maid to serve you tea in a china cup.'

'I'm fine as I am, James, and I couldna ask for better care than Rachel gives me. There's only one thing I lack, and that no one can supply.'

James bit his lip, knowing she referred to his father, but she went on sadly, 'You'll build yon ship and I'll not stand in your way, but 'tis for your own ambition, Jamie lad, and none of mine.'

James was silenced, but not deterred. His mother had worked hard all her life and deserved a little rest and comfort now her children were old enough to provide it, which he meant to do. Meanwhile Rachel did her best to relieve Annie of what tasks she could.

Now, seeing the older woman's pride, she laid aside the shirt she was stitching and said, 'Take them, Aunt Annie: the gifts are offered in friendship, not in charity. It would be discourteous to refuse.' Besides, the ham would feed the family for many a day, saving precious pennies for James's ship.

'Rachel is right,' urged Louise Forbes. 'I came as a friend, to ask how you fared in the recent storms, that is all. I know there was no fishing for several days.'

'No,' sighed Annie. 'We have had lean days, but they will pass, as they always do.'

'Ma,' cried Wee Alex, bursting unceremoniously through the door. 'James left his best knife on the pot-shelf and I am to take it to him. We've cut the new rib-timbers to size,' he added proudly, 'and they're all ready for fitting.'

'How is the ship progressing, Mrs Christie?' asked Fenton, remembering the family's enterprise.

'Too slowly,' she said with a touch of her old asperity, 'and what is achieved is as soon undone.'

'The storm did a great deal of damage,' explained Rachel, 'and not only to the ships at sea. It was a setback for us, certainly, but nothing,' she finished with vehemence, 'that we cannot overcome.'

'You should ha' seen the mess,' said Alex cheerfully. 'Our wee ship all smashed up. But me and James soon sorted her. Come wi' me and I'll show ye, if ye like.'

'Thank you, I would like to. If, that is, the ladies can spare me?'

'Go along, Fenton,' said Louise impatiently. 'Mrs Christie and I have things to talk about.'

'Mind and dinna keep James waiting, Alex,' warned Rachel. 'And bring Mr Abercrombie back again before it's dark. Miss Forbes will not want to be late home.'

'I'll find my own way, Rachel,' smiled Fenton. 'Do not worry. After all, I am not entirely a stranger to the Square.' Deep in his mind was the hope that *she* might be watching for him, as she had promised to do. If she was, she would join him somehow, and they could find their way back, slowly, together.

Rachel, newly home from market some few weeks later, was setting bowls and plates on the trestle table in readiness for the evening meal when James strode into the house, threw his bag of tools across the room with an oath, and slumped into his mother's chair at the hearth. Annie was at a neighbour's, on some trivial errand, and Rachel, for once, was alone.

'What is it, James?' she asked quietly, and when he made no answer but laid his head back against the wooden bars and closed his eyes with a groan of despair, she crossed swiftly to his side and laid a hand on his arm. 'Tell me,' she said.

'Oh, Rachel.' He took her hand in both his and held it to his brow. 'Your hand is so cool and refreshing.' But after a moment he released her, crashed fist on chair-arm and said, with returning anger, 'Will it *never* be done with? First the storm damage. Now our best saw blade has snapped in my hand and we haven't even the money to replace it.'

'A *saw* blade? Is that all?' Rachel laughed with relief. 'I thought at least the woodworm had eaten your timbers!' But James was right about the money. Since the January storm the fishing had been barely sufficient to feed them, and there had been little enough pilot work either. It had been easy to persuade Annie to stay at home and leave the marketing to Rachel, for there was barely enough to fill one creel. In spite of Rachel's relentless bargaining and the unexpected bounty of the Forbes ham, there had been nothing to spare for the *Steadfast*. Without that ham, in fact, they would certainly have gone hungry, for the twins were big men, with hearty appetites, and James and Maitland too; and young Alex was at the age when nothing seemed to fill him for more than an hour. As for Davy – he was thinner than he ought to be. Though smaller than the others, he had been wiry and tough as his father until the storm. Now he needed better food than they could provide to regain strength and vigour, though his cheerfulness was undiminished. Remembering Davy, Rachel's brow creased with worry. They could borrow a saw, no doubt, until they had the means to buy another, but she knew it was the long-term poverty that weighed, with his responsibility, on James's mind, as it did increasingly on hers.

'Was I right, Rachel,' he asked now, his voice tired, 'to hazard everything on an unbuilt ship?'

She could not bear to see the doubt in his eyes, those disconcerting eyes which could be at the same time mischievous and tender, as blue and brown combined, and lest her own will snap she turned away to resume her preparations for their meal.

'You said yourself it was the only way,' she said coolly, adding salt to the broth pot, 'If ever we were to have any kind of security or comfort. And you *will* succeed one day, I know it.' She set the griddle to heat at the fire, rolled back her sleeves and began to mould the dough into shape.

'I used to know it, too,' he groaned, watching her. She stood at the table, her back to him, while firelight lit her bundled hair with amber and gold. She wore a brown dress, neat at the waist above rounded hips which, as she leaned forward to roll the dough were, suddenly, disturbingly provocative.

'You cannot give up now, James,' she said without turning her head. 'Not with the yard hired and the timber paid for.' She turned, crouched, and slid the first cake deftly on to the griddle, then sat back on her heels, her face heat-flushed, and, pushing a stray tendril of hair back from her forehead with a floury hand, said, 'You *must* carry it through.'

At the back of his mind, behind the despondency, he thought wonderingly, 'She is *beautiful*,' but the thought merely increased his trouble.

'Seeing Ma as she is, and Davy, and you, Rachel, doing the work of two – no, do not argue for I know it to be true – then I feel I have let Da and all of you down. I have failed you.'

'No, James!' she cried fiercely. '*Not* failed! You have worked harder than any of us. You have thrown your very soul into that ship, and we'll not let you lose heart now. The *Steadfast must* be launched.'

She knelt in the firelight, her face on a level with his, her eyes unwavering. She had said 'we', but all the drive, the loyalty, the dogged perseverance sprang, he realized, from her. The others caught and echoed it, but Rachel was the source . . .

'Yes,' he murmured wonderingly. He looked deep into her eyes, searching for what he thought he had glimpsed once on the quayside when the *Middleton* sailed. There was a patch of flour on her cheek. He reached out a tentative finger to brush it gently away, as the door burst open and Alex erupted into the room.

'There you are, Jamie! I've been looking for ye. Maity says he's borrowed a saw from the Hall's mannie, but only till tomorrow, so will ye hurry – and Jamie, guess what? There's such a ship building there as ye never saw! Nearly 600 tons of her, and specially for the East India trade. We'll build a ship like that one day, won't we?'

'Aye,' said James with a sigh, and rose to his feet. 'But away back wi' ye to Maitland now, and help. Tell him I'll be along directly.'

When the boy had gone again, in a gust of breathless excitement, James said, 'You see, Rachel? Where would we find money for a ship like Hall's?'

'We'll find it,' said Rachel. She too was on her feet again, the spell broken, but the trembling warmth still with her, deep inside. 'There's the herring fishing. The boys did well at that last year.'

'Aye, but our share of the boat is now sold – remember?'

'Well, there's the stockings.' During the last year she had knitted for the manufactory in Schoolhill, in what spare time she had. It brought in little enough, but it helped. James, however, would not listen.

'I've told you, Rachel, it's slave labour. You'll do no more of it, not now Ma's ailing. We'll find some other way, somehow. You work hard enough.'

And so do you, thought Rachel, watching him stride across the Square towards the quay. From twilight to twilight, without rest or, she suspected, happiness.

Please God, she prayed in sudden anxiety, bring him success to his endeavours, and grant him peace of mind.

'It is *too* much!' exploded Abercrombie, smashing a fist on to the table with such force that papers scattered piecemeal, and a ledger, precariously balanced on one corner, fell with a thud to the floor. 'Damn and blast the man,' he added, 'for a grasping miser. Well, pick it up, pick it up, lad. Don't stand there gawping like a dottled grandda. Give it here!' He snatched the ledger from Fenton's nervous hands, leafed through it impatiently, before slamming it open on the desk in front of him. 'See!' he said, jabbing at the page with an accusing finger. 'Freight charges: Leith to Aberdeen. Three shillings the barrel bulk a year ago, and *that* was sixpence up on the previous year. Now the man has the nerve to ask for four! And his son not married to Clementina above a month. So much for his special rates! No doubt he hopes to milk me for every penny he's spent on that ridiculous palace of a house he's building in the new street – but I'll not pay for his vaunting extravagances and he'll carry no more freight o' mine.'

'Please sir, the mistress says to come for your dinner afore the soup's cold. It's nae awfu' thick the day, and it willna hold the heat.'

'Get out, girl,' said Abercrombie, but without resentment. Since moving into the new house Mairi had been a useful messenger between shop, office, and his wife upstairs. The cellars were ideal, too, for stock; the layout of the premises was all it had promised to be. Fenton would graduate from the college at the end of the month and join him, and when the new sign arrived, '*Abercrombie and Son, Vintners, Tea Merchants and High-Class Grocers*' in scarlet and gold paint, he would be well pleased. And, he had thought until this morning, he would also be well on his way to the achievement of his dream.

'Where's the *Journal*? Ah, this is what we want.' He spread the newspaper on the desk, obliterating ledger and offending dockets, and jabbed a finger at an advertisement embellished with the motif of a ship in full sail. 'I told you we'd need a ship of our own one day. "Two tenth shares in the schooner *Margaret*, 90 tons, upset price £250 . . ." A bit small, perhaps, and overpriced. "Vessel on the stocks for sale, 147 tons, ready for launching, for roup at the Lemon Tree Tavern, Saturday noon." Better. Or what about this one . . .'

'Make him go up, Mr Fenton,' pleaded Mairi in an anxious whisper from the doorway. 'The missis is fuming fit to scald hersel' and she's clippit my lugs already the day.' But Fenton had matters other than his mother's anger on his mind.

'Remember, Papa, when I escorted Louise Forbes to Footdee? I had occasion to visit the Christie shipyard where they have an ideal vessel building now, here in the harbour. We might be able to buy a share in her at advantageous terms, for I know the Christies are in financial difficulties.'

'As are we all until the Council chooses to pay its debts,' muttered his father, but his voice held wary interest. 'Well, go on, boy. Tell me about it.'

'A brig, Papa, two masts, square-rigged. I've seen the model and she'll be fast, I promise you, *and* carry a good cargo on an even keel. She's no more than half built as yet, but with extra investment they could finish her within a year. They have not advertised, of course, but I know they need the money and . . .'

'Not advertised?' interrupted Abercrombie. 'Then suppose we bought our way in, private like, and Farquharson none the wiser? It'd be worth it to see the look on his face at the launching! I like the idea, Fenton, and I'll not pour money into Farquharson's pockets any longer than I can help it, the swindling . . .'

He was interrupted by a crash from the doorway as Mairi beat a tattoo with a pair of panlids. 'Mistress says "Upstairs or else",' she said, pausing for breath, and crashed the lids again.

'All right, all right. Is there to be no peace?' Abercrombie heaved himself to his feet, called through the office door, 'Mind the shop, Archie. I'll be down again directly,' and with a hand on Fenton's shoulder, steered him towards the stairs. 'Good lad,' he said, 'Good lad. We'll go and see this ship o' yours as soon as we've pacified your mother.'

'I hope she'll be a long time i' the building,' murmured Jessie Brand, slipping her arm with pretended shyness round Fenton's waist. 'And that you come and inspect her *often*.'

They stood in the shadow of the Christies' planning shed, between its wooden walls and the narrow lane which led to the Fittiegait, touched now by the softening colours of the setting sun. It was an evening of muted pinks and greens, the harbour waters calm with resting seabirds, the surf a curling lip of foam on the wide-stretched sands, and the only sound the steady hammering of someone working late in the Christies' yard. Fenton had fulfilled his duties an hour ago, inspecting hold and bulwark, measuring the capacity of the ship in which the Abercrombies now owned part-shares.

'I will,' said Fenton with fervour, '*often!* I would come every day if it were possible and if you were here to meet me.' His arm tightened as he drew her closer.

She laid her head on his shoulder and whispered, with a tiny sigh, 'I would like that too . . . but it wouldna be right, Fenton.'

'No, Jessica. I know that, but . . .'

'But what, Fenton?' She lifted her face to his, her dark eyes huge and innocent in the moonlight, the sweet oval of her face outlined with delicate shadow. Her curls clustered thick and silken under his fingers as he framed her face, wonderingly, in his hands and gently kissed her.

'You are beautiful,' he murmured, 'beautiful . . .'

She nestled against him, her hands slipping soft and caressing over his chest, and wondered if James could see them? Perhaps if he were working on a ladder, high up . . . 'Am I?' This time her raised face and full, parted lips were more than he could bear.

'No, no, we mustna,' she gasped, pushing against his chest and twisting her head away, but only after allowing him a kiss sufficiently deep to leave him tortured with desire. 'It would be wrong.'

'Oh God, Jessica. Do not torment me so, I beg of you.'

But it was a game at which Jessie Brand was adept, and Fenton, she judged, had been brought to just the right pitch.

'I must go,' she said quickly. 'Ma will be in a right rage if I'm still out when she gets home.'

'Please, Jessica, say you will meet me again.'

'I am not sure that I ought to, Fenton.' She turned away from him and bowed her head. 'I dinna like to make you angry, as I always seem to do when . . .' She stopped, waiting. For a moment he did nothing, then reached out a hand, as she had known he would, and taking hers, drew her gently towards him.

'I am sorry, Jessica, if I upset you. And I am not angry. It is just that . . .'

'What, Fenton?' She looked up at him, wide-eyed.

'I love you,' he said, simply, and Jessie Brand offered up a silent cry of triumph before saying sadly, 'You think you do, but . . .' She plucked at the buttons of his jacket in pretended modesty.

'But what?'

'I am only a fisher girl, not a lady like your sister's friends. I have no fine clothes, no pretty jewellery.'

'What does that matter? Why, my own grandmother was "only a fisher girl" and as for my sister's friends, they are nothing compared to you.'

'You just say that,' she said, pouting prettily, 'because I am here and they are not.' She plucked again at his buttons, but this time making sure he felt the soft pressure of her hands against his chest. 'When I am away, you will forget me.'

'Never!' he vowed vehemently. Jessica was the first girl he had ever loved, and he loved her with a consuming mixture of romantic idealism and physical desire which left him helpless. He was naive and innocent, trusting and honest – and powerless in her shrewd, experienced hands. This time when he kissed her she led him on to the very edge of self-control before emerging, breathless, to gasp, 'No, Fenton! No! I must go home.'

But she allowed him to lead her across the open space behind the Christies' shipyard, his arm around her waist, her head on his shoulder, and to kiss her once more, in the open moonlight. She was enjoying her triumph, and if James Christie saw them, so much the better: it would serve him right.

Will I ever win James? thought Rachel, standing unseen in the shadow of the wooden shed which housed their store of tar, pitch, and working tools, and where Maitland worked on his plans and calculations. It was a sturdy wooden structure, repaired and strengthened since the January storms, though not big enough to house Maitland's aspirations, for with Abercrombie's encouragement he was already planning a ship twice the size of the little *Steadfast*. Though James had refused to sell more than four-tenth shares in the ship, the ready money had relieved him of immediate worry. It had not, however, led to relaxation: in fact the contrary, for with the legal document drawn up James took his new position as chief shareholder seriously. 'The ship will be launched with the least possible delay,' he vowed, 'so the shareholders can begin to find a return for their money.'

On her journeys to and from the market, Rachel was already noting which goods were loaded on to the Farquharsons' *Flora* and *Dora*, and the ships of the Aberdeen and London line; what cargo was unloaded on the quay or stored in the Weighhouse to await collection, so that when the time came they could choose the best freight for their own ship. Maitland, she knew, thought only of the ship's design, James of the practical details of its completion and sailing, and the others were still busy at sea. Someone should be concerned with the ordinary business of cargo, and Rachel, with her knowledge of the commerce of the Plainstanes and what she learnt by observation on the quay, took up the task willingly and with a keen intelligence which would have surprised both James and Maitland had they known of it. Rachel, however, kept her observations to herself until such time as they might be needed.

Meanwhile, sails must be ordered, ropes for the rigging, and the capstan, the anchor chain, the anchor. The figurehead young Alex was making, carving out of a block of timber set aside for the purpose. It was, by common consent, to be a mermaid.

'Then you'd best use Rachy as your model,' said Davy.

'Aye,' agreed the twins. 'Remember the day she came, and Da called her a mermaid?'

Unexpectedly, Rachel blushed. But it was not at the memory of her public scrubbing in the family tub, nor of the twins' chatter and Fiddly's affectionate teasing: she remembered James likening her to a beautiful princess in the stories. She wondered if he too remembered? But he was checking dimensions of the figurehead with Maitland and said only, 'We'll need to buy paints.'

Now, in the shadows, Rachel watched the man who had assumed his father's responsibilities and his father's cares, as he had promised Fiddly he would do, though it left him no time for youth or pleasure himself. James sees me, she thought sadly, only as another responsibility, a sister perhaps, no more. Beside the shed and stretching in a triangle from the dunes at her back to the boundary with Dixon's land was the piece of ground they had leased: a rough-turfed stretch of sandy rubble, seeping seawater where the ground dipped, sprouting bent grass on the hummocks, but flat and open and – by means of the little lane which separated it from the timber yard to the west – within launching reach of the harbour. The harbour was peaceful tonight, bare masts like winter trees at rest, the sky a deep and darkening blue as the frost gathered and the first stars appeared.

Beyond their own little shipyard the larger slipways of

Alexander Hall and the Duthie brothers stood silent in a darkness lit only by the riding lights of ships at anchor and the Christies' hanging lantern, while on Girdleness the lighthouse winked its regular signal to any ships at sea. When, years ago, she had stood in the doorway of that shipyard, a half-drowned, shivering child, she had not dreamt she would be involved with a shipyard herself one day, and so involved that it swallowed up every ounce of her emotional strength, every moment of her day. For the Christie yard was *her* yard as it was James's, *her* ambition as it was his, and through the achievement of that shared ambition, somehow, she had thought James and she would find each other.

Now, for the first time, she felt that certainty waver. He did not need her. He hardly noticed her except as a fellow-Christie and a fellow-worker. His work absorbed him utterly.

The ground under her feet was crusted with ice, and ice crystals gleamed on grass and timber where the lamplight fell. James worked in the light of a lantern, sawing through a length of spar, and the steady rasp of the blade blended with the slap of sea on pierhead like some bizarre melody over a solemn bass, until the severed portion fell with a crack, and James stood upright, panting but triumphant.

Behind him, dark against the harbour water and the grey hump of the headland above Girdleness, stood the hull of the ship they were building, its outer shell complete now but for bowsprit and figurehead, its sides curving gracefully into the solid wedge of keel and supported by wooden props at intervals from bow to stern. Each piece of timber had been carefully fitted, ends neatly slotted into rabbets in stern post or bow. Had they been building for the tropical trade, they would have nailed metal plates over the wood to protect the timber from serpents, but for the coastal trade it was not necessary. Nor for the Continental trade which, said James, they would attempt one day.

Rachel remembered those words as she watched James set the new-cut wood aside and choose the next length. The hull looked finished but it still needed deck and rigging, masts and sails; and if they worked as carefully as they had so far done, it might be as long again before the ship was launched and before the Christie brothers had time for anything or anyone but the

Steadfast. With a small sigh, Rachel stepped forward out of the shadow.

James turned his head at her footfall. 'Rachel?'

'I've brought your supper, James. Where is Maitland?' She had expected him to be in the planning shed, but though the door stood open she saw only papers and scale-models on the trestle that served for drawing board and desk.

'Gone to the Bay Tree to see a man about the deck supports. He'll not be long.'

'It's only sowens tonight,' she said apologetically, 'but there's cheese, too, if you want it.'

'Put it down somewhere, anywhere.' He spoke with the impatience of excitement, not anger. 'It can wait – at least until I've shown you the deck. We have fitted almost six feet of it already.'

He climbed a ladder at the ship's side, swung a leg over the gunwale, then turned to help her after him. Rachel put down covered pot and basin, kilted her skirts in one hand, and climbed the ladder. From her new height she had a sudden view of starlit sea and lamplit harbour, of the town in silhouette against the night sky, before she slipped over the gunwale and down into James's steadying arms and the belly of the ship. The wood was smooth under her hand, the high curving sides like some giant cradle above whose edge nothing was visible but stars and moonlit sky. It was quiet and a little chill; beyond the wooden cradle was the rhythmic soothing of the sea and, close at hand, James's breathing.

'Come,' he said softly and, taking her hand, led her to the stem of the ship where, supported on timber beams, the first small stretch of deck had been laid. Under the timber roof it was dark and suddenly warmer with the clean, dry scent of new-cut wood. James leant an arm against the timbers behind her shoulder.

'This is the hold,' he said 'where the cargo will lie.'

She looked up at the shadowed timber so close above her head, at the curving sides, and beyond to the long, undecked portion still open to the night sky, and tried to imagine it roofed in and full to the gunwales with barrels and bales and those crates she had seen stacked on the quayside labelled '*Danzig*', '*Rotterdam*', '*London*' or '*Leith*'. There would be lanterns suspended from hooks in the roof, swaying with the ship's rhythm, and a companionway leading up through a hatch to the deck. She felt a sudden shiver of pride and excitement.

'But you're cold.' James put his arm round her shoulders and leant back against the hard wooden hull while Rachel scarcely dared to breathe, as warmth flowed through her from his sheltering arm. The hull cupped them together in a warm and gentle hand, and she knew now the source of that sudden pride and excitement. It was James's emotion, spilling over and flooding into her. She turned her head to look at him, but he was looking at the *Steadfast*, stretching away from them, deckless, under the starlight.

'One day,' he said, 'this little ship will make our fortunes. Who knows what these planks will bear? Dutch flax, cheeses, indigo, even brandy perhaps, or Brussels lace. We can carry our own goods abroad and bring back in exchange all sorts of luxuries. Fine silks for Ma, so she can sit at her fireside like a lady; and one day even tea. We'll build another ship after this one – a bigger and a faster. Then another, with cabins fitted out with oak panelling and elegantly carved furniture. We'll send them to the world's end with the Christie flag at the masthead, a Christie man at the helm, and a mermaid for a figurehead. And you, Rachy,' he said quietly, turning towards her, 'what would you like me to bring home for you?'

His face was disturbingly close, his eyes no longer blue and brown, but an opaque velvet darkness in which she read tenderness and teasing.

'Well?' he murmured, his breath warm on her cheek, his eyes holding hers so she could not look away, while her lips parted and her face lifted wonderingly to his.

'James? Are you there?'

Maitland's head and shoulders appeared silhouetted above the gunwale. With a thud he dropped down into the body of the ship. Rachel felt the planking vibrate at her back as James curled forward out of the darkness of their corner and stood upright again. 'I was showing Rachel the hold,' he said calmly. 'Come and see for yourself how the support beams stand firm and true. She's going to be as good as any brig i' the harbour when she's finished. Abercrombie agrees.'

'Move over.' Maitland joined Rachel in the small space

between deck and bilges, bending his head as James had done to accommodate the crossbeam. 'Aye,' he said after a moment's inspection, 'but Abercrombie's nae infallible. I think I'll just check the positioning of yon supports.'

'Remember the *Betsy May*,' said James, 'and how we measured every inch of her? We canna go wrong having modelled ours on her.'

Listening to the brothers, Rachel knew herself forgotten in the absorbing question of the *Steadfast*'s construction, a discussion which continued uninterrupted as they shinned over the gunwale, handing Rachel deftly between them and down the ladder to the ground, then across the open space to the planning shed, Maitland retrieving the lantern on the way.

Neither noticed her departure, but Rachel was content, nursing the small shred of happiness secret inside her; content once more to wait in patience for the slow and tedious completion of their ship. Then, with the *Steadfast* launched, there would be time, surely, for sweeter, closer relationships? Meanwhile, she would continue to work as they all did with unbending resolution to swell the family purse and the family pot.

By the end of March, the hold was completely decked, hatch-covers and companionways in place. Then work began on the superstructure. Sails were delivered from the sailmakers, rope for the rigging, and finally came the masts, to be laid carefully in the shipyard ready for fitting when the boat was safely afloat. James and Abercrombie fixed the launching date for early September, and Rachel drafted an advertisement to be inserted in the *Journal* when the time came: '*The Brig* Steadfast *now ready to take in goods for London. Intending shippers are requested to make Customs House entries as soon as possible. Speedy passage guaranteed . . .*'

Abercrombie had 130 firkins of butter and 24 hands of raw sugar already ordered for the return trip, as well as dried fruit, spices, and fresh oysters to be collected at Leith. The cargoes had been discussed at length both in family conclave and with Abercrombie, and it was at Rachel's suggestion that the oysters had been ordered, to sell fresh in the Abercrombie shop.

James was to captain the ship on the first voyage, with William and George, Davy and Wee Alex. Later, perhaps, they would hire seamen at the quay, but for the maiden trip it was to be all Christies. Only Maitland, already at work on designs for the next ship, was to stay at home.

By mid-August everything was ready bar the smaller fittings which would be added, with the masts, when the vessel was afloat. Rachel was stitching the company pennant to fly at the mast-head: an emerald-green and silver mermaid on a background of azure, a silver 'C' in the north-west corner. James applied for Council clearance to run the vessel on rollers from the yard by way of the little side lane to the water, and in the Christie house excitement ran unbearably high.

'We'll have whisky and cheese for the launching,' said James, his strange eyes gleaming, 'and all the Square must come. We'll set it out in the office at the yard, you'll play your 'mouthie',

Davy, and there'll be dancing and singing. Will ye not be proud, Ma, to see our own ship trading on the high seas?'

'Aye, and proud to see ye safe home again,' said Annie, unable to keep the apprehension from her voice. The ships wrecked in last year's storm had been coastal traders and though months of tranquil weather had eased her anxiety, the strain still showed in that quivering head and those twitching, slowing hands. The August days were long, the evenings mild and still. Bathing machines on the beach found ready custom, and children splashed in the shallows till warmth left the sun and seabirds gathered, squealing, on the glistening sands at low tide.

On one such evening in mid-August, Rachel sat outside in the last of the setting sunlight, busily sewing, Annie beside her, her hands idle over the knitting in her lap. The twins, William and George, had vanished somewhere with a group of cronies, but the others remained. Maitland and Alex had spread papers on the trestle table and through the open door Rachel saw them working steadily at plans for the next ship they would build, while James leant against the door jamb, watching them and making the occasional remark. Davy, sitting cross-legged, sailor-fashion, on the turf, played softly on his mouth organ a plaintive, yearning tune Rachel had not heard before. Davy was walking out with a girl from Stonehaven, fifteen miles down the coast, and saw her only rarely when she came to market or when, as on the occasion when he had first met her, the fishing boat was driven inshore to shelter from a squall. But it was the deep-sea season now and between trips their only meeting-place was on the Green.

'You'll like her, Ma,' he said now, laying aside his mouth-organ and coughing the dry cough which was always with him, in spite of Annie's dosing with honey syrup. 'She's a fine lass.'

'Aye, 'tis time one o' ye was wed,' said Annie, 'and if your brothers willna, it had best be you – though I'd like fine to see James married,' she finished, with a sideways glance at Rachel whose head was bent over her sewing with exaggerated uncon-cern. Behind them, in the doorway, James shifted weight from one foot to the other before saying lazily, 'I've other things to do, Ma – and there's time yet.'

'Time for some, maybe,' said Annie, 'but others willna wait.

Just watch ye dinna leave it too long and find yoursel' alone. It's nae good to be alone,' she finished, and Davy took up his mouth-organ again to play something lively before melancholy took hold.

From across the Square Jessie Brand watched them, envious as always of the tight-knit family group. What was it about Annie Christie that kept her menfolk at home? She'd been 'Bonnie' right enough once, but not any more, and Rachel was nothing special either. Jessie's brow creased with resentment. As for that James Christie, he thought himself too good for any lass . . . but she'd show him there were grander folk than he begging for her favours. Remembering Fenton Abercrombie, Jess smiled. That campaign was going well. She thought with satisfaction of the red merino shawl he had bought her, and the gold chain and pendant which she kept hidden under the straw mattress of her bed.

'You watch your step, girl,' her mother had warned, 'or you'll be put out the house. Your Da'll not have a whore under his roof for all the Square to mock at, nor a kept woman neither.'

But Jess was playing for higher stakes. Fenton was a simple soul, honourable and upright; she could handle him, no bother. It was that other who had her baffled. She stared at James Christie until the evening deepened to summer darkness, and one by one the indwellers took up their stools and chairs and went inside to bed.

The northern nights were short at midsummer, the darkness pale, and it was late before the Christies turned in. Rachel, as always, was the last to go to bed, banking the fire, setting the morning porridge pot in the embers, filling up the kettle. Her tasks done, she had unpinned her hair and was brushing it with long, steady strokes when the ground leapt suddenly under her feet, every bowl and basin on the pot-shelf danced in clattering confusion, a china dish smashed to the ground, while bench, chair and table moved of their own accord and the door struggled violently against its frame. From the darkness outside came a heavy rumbling noise and the distant jangle of discordant bells.

'God Almighty!' James shot upright in his bed beyond the partition. 'What the hell was that?' William and George were

134

already on their feet, pulling on trousers over flapping shirts. Alex's tousled head appeared above the blanket, his eyes jerked open by the tremor, and from the box bed came Annie's voice, sleep-blurred and frightened. 'What is it? Is someone hurt?'

'It's all right, Ma,' said Davy, reassuring. He had been lying fully clothed on his bunk bed, thinking of his Stonehaven lass, when the bed shook under him, precipitating him to the floor. Now he flung back the doors of her bed and said, 'Just wrap a shawl round you and come outside.'

'Outside? I must get dressed first.'

'Why are the bells ringing?' Alex mumbled, still half-asleep.

'Get up!' ordered James, 'and outside all of you. You too, Ma, and never heed your clothes. *Quick!*'

Bewildered, Annie wrapped a blanket tight around her shoulders to cover flannel shift and bare feet. 'But why, James?'

'I think it is an earthquake. Outside, before the house falls!' William, George, and Alex were already in the Square; Maitland, stopping only to snatch up his precious model ships and roll of plans, followed; then Davy leading Annie, unwilling and anxious. Rachel cast a swift glance round the room, checking the fire would be safe, no lamp was left lit. She stooped to pick up a piece of broken china lest someone step on it, and James caught her roughly by the arm. 'Leave it, Rachel, and come out. Do you want to get killed?'

The Square was rapidly filling with people in every stage of disarray, frightened women, squalling infants, bewildered children, querulous old men, against a background of discordant, intermittent bells, agitated livestock, and that distant, grumbling roar.

'The ground cracked open.' 'The clock fell.' 'The dresser moved by itself, I tell ye.' 'It's a death-omen.' 'There was a knocking, right enough.' 'And the dogs howling.' 'Aye, 'tis ill-luck for sure.'

The half-dressed, motley crowd moved uneasily under the pale night sky, anticipating disaster yet unwilling to stray far from what little property they had, while men cried, 'Keep away from the building,' and 'There'll be another shock for sure!' The moon was high and clear, and the air mild, the only unusual sight a pale vapour gathering in the west, beyond the town.

'I want my bed!' wailed one of the Brand children over and over, and received a clout for its pains; a dog barked on and on, unheeded; men gathered in worried bands of twos and threes, conferring.

Suddenly, pushing through the crowd, came a young man, distraught, crying 'Jessica! Jessica! Please God you're safe!'

Fenton Abercrombie had been walking the pierhead when the shock came, unable to find rest in his own house, unable to keep away from where *she* was, finding solace in moonlight and calm seas for the tortured ache of his remorse and longing. She had told him she could not see him again if he persisted in his amorous advances. 'It is not right,' she had said, 'not outside marriage.' But how could he help himself when he loved her so, and she was so delectably appealing? She is right, he thought, we must not meet again. Ever. Yet what would life without Jessica be but a dreary round of tea-chests and customs forms, brass measures shovelling careful portions of best this and special that? His heart would be dead, all purpose lost.

In the sombre rhythm of the night waves curling endlessly on shifting sands, he had heard the echo of his own despair. Until the ground vibrated under his feet, shaking him instantly alert. Earth cracked, stones bowled across the beach, rocks fell, the sea boiled with a thousand sudden swirls and eddies, and from beyond the town came a grumbling roar, as of a distant giant woken angrily from sleep.

In a moment his mind filled with pictures of devastation, of whole families buried under fallen masonry, of crushed bodies and weeping – and he was running before he knew it, back along the pierhead to Footdee and the Square.

'It's safe to come inside now, Ma,' said James, taking Annie's arm. 'The tremor's over, no one's hurt, and no more damage than toppled furniture and jangled bells. William's gone to the Customs house to check, but I reckon it's safe enough to go back to our beds.'

'Aye,' said Davy behind him, 'there's nought more we can do. Where's Maitland?'

'With William and George.' But the twins appeared in the half-darkness of the open Square and reported together, 'An earth tremor. No damage.'

'I saw Maitland last by Pocra,' volunteered Wee Alex.

'The *Steadfast*! Alex, stay with Ma,' ordered James. 'See the pair o' yet get to your beds. You too, Rachel.'

But all Rachel's hopes were bound up, as his were, in the *Steadfast* and not even James's anger would keep her away.

'I'll not be long, Aunt Annie!' Rachel snatched up her shawl and ran out into the Square after the others. If the *Steadfast* were damaged now, when she was almost finished and so close to launching . . . She remembered the jangling and crashing of pots in the cottage and the shattering plate, pictured similar havoc in the little shipyard, the *Steadfast* blown on her beam, her glossy planking staved.

They found the shipyard in disarray – logs rolled into unaccustomed places, ladders fallen – but the precious ship stood where they had left her, proudly propped on her supporting posts, her newly varnished hull unsplintered in the moonlight, her gleaming deck immaculate, the dark shape of her figurehead provocative with shadows. Rachel breathed a long sigh of relief as James said quietly, and for them all, 'Thank God'.

Maitland was standing in the shadow of the figurehead, one hand against the wood. He turned his head at their approach, but said only, 'I think the line of the prow could have been sharper, to cleave the wave with less resistance. I'll work on it for the next ship.'

No one heeded him. They were too busy studying the hull of the *Steadfast* for any hidden damage, circling her slowly in the moonlight, running exploring hands over varnished wood and caulking. The night air grew still around them and touched their skin with unaccustomed warmth, while beyond the quay the harbour waters now lay smooth as rippled silk. William mounted the ladder and dropped on to the deck. George followed.

'We'll just check that everything's in place.'

'I'll be with you in a minute,' said James. He laid a cheek briefly against the ship's side where it curved gracefully above

137

him. 'You should not have come, Rachy,' he said, but without anger. He added quietly, 'I don't think I could have borne it if she had been staved.'

There was the sound of hurrying footsteps approaching from the direction of the Shiprow. They came past the Weighhouse and on until a man in a greatcoat and beaver hat, out of breath and anxious, emerged from the lane beside the yard. George Abercrombie, jerked awake by the earth tremor, had scrambled into his clothes, ascertained that his shop and its contents were undamaged, and then come straight to Pocra pier to check on his second investment.

'Well, Christie?' he demanded, striding across the turf towards them. 'Tell me the damage, so I know the worst.'

'Nothing, sir, that I can see.'

'*Nothing*? Splendid!' Abercrombie laughed aloud with relief. He had had visions of his investment splintered, his savings gone. He slapped James on the shoulder, shook Maitland by the hand, embraced Rachel and Davy together, one arm round the shoulders of each, then demanded to see for himself that the *Steadfast* remained intact. James held the ladder for him as he went aboard, the twins handing him down on to the deck. Maitland followed. James had one foot on the ladder to follow after, when there was a movement from beyond the shed and, in the half-light of a moon and the northern night, two figures emerged from the lane, a man and a girl, hand in hand.

'I came as soon as I could,' said Fenton, with a mixture of anxiety and elation, 'to find out if all is well.'

'Aye,' said James slowly, his eyes on Jessie Brand. She wore a shawl over paler petticoats, her hair was dishevelled, her face strangely triumphant. 'And what did *you* come for?' he asked, without expression.

'Jessica and I are to . . .' began Fenton, just as his father's head appeared above the gunwale of the *Steadfast*, outlined against the sky, but the rest of his sentence was lost as another, slighter, tremor shook the turf under their feet. Rachel stumbled and James put out a hand to steady her; Jess squealed and Fenton clasped her close. As the shiver died away the four stood face to face in silence, while dust settled on distant hills and from above their heads came Abercombie's voice, incredulous.

'*What* did you say?' The hiccuping aftermath of the earth-quake ignored, everyone waited for Fenton's answer.

'This is Jessica, Papa,' said Fenton. 'She and I are to be married.'

Rachel felt James's hand stiffen in her own, and when she looked quickly at his face, she saw he was pale with shock, his eyes fixed on Jess's face. Jess stared back, defiant, a taunting half-smile on her lips, her eyes gleaming bright in the moon-light, while on Fenton's face was an expression of bemused and wondering joy which wrung Rachel's heart with pity. She liked Fenton. He was always kind and courteous to her, and she did not want him hurt. But his father was clambering down the ladder.

'*Married?*' he thundered, when he stood, breathless, on the still-settling turf. 'You'd best explain yourself, my lad. As for you, lass . . .' He stared, studying her with sudden interest. The lad had taste, after all: a spunky, strapping girl with a bit of spirit about her. 'As for you,' he said, more quietly, 'you'd best get on home. These lads'll see you safe.'

'I will see Jessica home myself,' said Fenton, white-faced but calm. 'I came only to make sure the *Steadfast* was undamaged. As you, sir, are here to take care of that, you will excuse me. Come, Jessica,' and taking her arm he led her back the way they had come.

'Well, smack me wi' a wet herring!' said George, when Abercrombie, too, had left, swearing and muttering, for home. 'I've lost a bet!'

'Aye,' said William, 'but I reckon I have too.' He slapped James reassuringly on the shoulder. 'Cheer up, Jamie lad. There's more fish i' the sea. But I could have sworn it was *you* she wanted,' he finished, puzzled.

It is, thought Rachel with misery, and James knows it. Poor Fenton. And poor James.

But James merely shrugged and turned his back. 'I'm for my bed,' he said, and walked away.

'Come on, Rachy,' said the twins, each taking an arm and swinging her between them. 'It's nae the end o' the world, in spite o' yon earthquake.'

But, remembering that look on James's face, she feared it was the end of her world, whether Jess married Fenton or not.

'Marry? A *fishwife's* lass? I'll see ye dead first!'

'I am of age, Mamma,' said Fenton, white-faced but firm. 'I intend to marry Jessica.'

'He *can't*, Mamma,' wailed Clementina. 'I'll not have *her* as a sister-in-law. What'll the Farquharsons say? Why, she sold us haddock at the door. The whole town knows her! And the house will stink for ever after . . .'

'She'll not live here. I'll have no reeking fish-lass lording it in *my* house!'

'But Mamma, she will be my wife.'

'Then you'll be no son of mine, nor your father's. And you'll get nothing more from us. Tell him so, George.'

But Abercrombie refused to be drawn. 'She's a good enough lass, Kirsty, healthy and strong. She'll be a help to the business. A hard worker, I'll warrant, as fisherwomen need to be – you should know that.'

But his wife side-stepped the reference to her own origins in renewed attack. 'Fenton is to marry the Forbes girl and be a lawyer, like her father is. If you will not tell him so, then I will. Do you hear me, Fenton?'

'I do, but it makes no difference, Mamma. I must marry Jessica.'

'Must? Ah . . . I see how it is. She's trapped you. She's carrying your bastard bairn. But there's no need to marry her, Fenton.' Mrs. Abercrombie's voice changed to one of wheedling reason. 'Your Papa will pay her off, and no more to be said. No doubt money's all she's after.'

'I'll pay her nothing,' snapped Abercrombie, losing patience. 'Nor you neither if you keep on wi' your bitching. Fenton's made his choice. As far as I'm concerned, it's a good one. I'm sick to death o' your wittering pretensions, woman. It's time we brought honest sense back into this house, and that girl's no worse than you were when I married you. Remember that.'

Kirsty Abercrombie was silenced, but only for a moment. Then, drawing herself up straight and calm, she said, with a withering look, 'Then I hope you will have the grace to wait at least a year before you marry.' A year might bring the lad to his senses.

'Not a year, Mamma. Six months.' Fenton would have

married her immediately, but Jess had stipulated six months in order, she said, to collect a trousseau for which Fenton had promised to pay.

'Very well, since there's no hope of your seeing reason. But I tell you now, Fenton, I will not receive that fish-girl in my house!'

'In that case,' glowered Abercrombie, 'You'd best keep to your room, for Fenton's bringing her to dinner. Tomorrow.'

'Six candlesticks on the table, Rachel,' boasted Jess, preening. 'I wore my new taffeta, the one Fen bought for me. And there was *four* courses, wi' silver serving-dishes.'

Mrs Abercrombie, deciding attack was preferable to ignominious retreat, had aimed to overwhelm her son's upstart little fisher lass with condescending opulence: but she had misjudged her adversary. Jess, in her new dress of crimson taffeta, with Fenton's engagement pearls at her throat, her dark hair newly washed and gleaming, and every inch of her exuding youthful impudence and vitality, had outshone everything in the room, including Mrs Abercrombie and Clementina, hastily summoned, without her husband, to provide moral support.

Unabashed by her frigid reception, Jess had eaten her way heartily through all four courses, and when the Abercrombie women rebuffed all attempts at conversation with frosty monosyllables, Jess had merely shrugged, laughed, and said to Mr Abercrombie, 'I see your womenfolk aren't used to talking, Mr Abercrombie, or maybe they're too much in awe o' *you*,' and she gave him a deliberately flirtatious look, 'but I canna abide to sit silent, can I, Fenton? Not when there's so much *interesting* to talk about. Yon ship o' the Christies, for instance, that you've a share in – how soon do you reckon she'll be trading? And will ye tell yon customs mannie of everything you put in the hold? Come on now, Mr Abercrombie,' she teased as he opened his mouth to protest, 'everyone i' the harbour knows how ye came by your fortune – and admires ye for it.' She gave him a coquettish look from her fine eyes. 'Your secret'll be safe wi' me and Fenton.' She took Fenton's hand and squeezed it, with an intimate murmur pitched just loud enough for Mrs Abercrombie to hear, 'Isn't that right, darlin'?' Before he could answer, she demanded pertly of her host, 'What *are* ye planning to smuggle i' the Christie boat?'

'I might manage a length of lace for the prettiest lass in Footdee,' said Abercrombie, rising gallantly to the occasion, while Mrs Abercrombie fumed with silent fury.

'You should ha' seen her, Rachy,' reported Jess, triumphant, as Rachel sat at the house door shelling mussels. 'Wi'out a word to her tongue all evening. She'll be nae bother. Nor yon whey-faced prig of a Clementina. When I'm married to Fenton, I'll have a husband as good as hers, a house i' Union Street, a gig, *and* a maidservant. I'll nae be seeing much o' ye then, Rachy. Except when we come to inspect our ship.'

'*Your* ship?' Rachel could stand the parading of house and carriage without undue annoyance – her own dreams had long ago distilled into a more personal and single-minded ambition – but this last taunt was too much. '*Our* ship,' she corrected, 'in which Mr Abercrombie *senior* has a minor share.'

'Hoity toity,' jeered Jess. 'When all the Square knows ye couldna hae built it at all wi'out the Abercrombie money.'

'As all the Square knows', flashed Rachel, 'that it's the Abercrombie money you're after when you marry Fenton.'

'And why not, wi' him beggin' me to have him? I'm doing him a favour and there's nought wrong in marrying money. Take my advice, Rachy,' she went on, with sisterly kindness, 'and do the same if ye get the chance. There's aye merchants on the quay, long i' the tooth maybe, but fat i' the purse. Stroll down there and roll an eye at them now and again. Or give your hips a swing. That'll set 'em off.'

'Hold your tongue, ye daft quine,' said Annie Christie, appearing in the doorway behind Rachel. 'And away to your work so honest folk can get on wi' theirs. For ye'd best not fall out wi' your Ma, Jessie Brand, till you're safely married to yon poor lad – if he doesna see sense in time. There's been no agreeance, mind, and there's many a slip . . .'

'Crabby old cow,' muttered Jess, but *sotto voce*. She was still a little in awe of Annie and mindful of her connection with James. She picked up her pail and swaggered nonchalantly back to the Brand's house, singing. She had no fear of losing Fenton Abercrombie, agreeance or no. She knew how to play him too well to let him slip the hook.

But when Fenton next called in Fisher Square it was at the Christies' house. He found Rachel and Annie alone; the twins and Davy were at sea and would not be home till the morrow. James and Maitland were at the slipway, putting the last touches to the *Steadfast* ready for launching the following week, and Alex, as usual, was helping them. With no more she herself could do until the ship was afloat, Rachel had taken advantage of their absence and of the fine weather to shake out the blankets on the green behind the house to air and, hair tied up in a kerchief, was busy with besom and duster when Fenton arrived.

'Do you never stop?' asked Fenton. 'Surely on a day like this you could be allowed a rest?'

It was certainly a mild day, the air calm, the sky a shimmering azure haze over a rippling sea. The bathing machines on the beach were plying a steady trade. In the distance a single ship, tiny as Maitland's models, serenely rode the high wire between sea and sky.

'Only when we have visitors,' said Rachel, smiling. In truth, she was so keyed up with excitement as the day of launching drew nearer that only activity could keep her sane; but she welcomed Fenton's visit both as a reason to relax and because she enjoyed his company. She pulled off her kerchief and shook free her hair. 'Come and sit in the sun, Aunt Annie, with Mr Abercrombie, and I will bring us all a draught of cool ale.' She carried Annie's chair outside and set it at the door, while Fenton brought a bench for himself and Rachel.

'Well,' demanded Annie, 'what have ye done wi' Miss Forbes today? Or has she no more questions to ask me?'

Fenton looked discomfited. Louise had had a few terse words to say to him on the announcement of his engagement. 'Don't be a fool, Fenton,' had been the gist of it, with, 'Not that I ever thought as Mamma did – you and I are friends, that is all. But I would be a poor friend if I did not speak honestly to you, as I do now. You are a fool. I'll grant you she's a beauty – I remember her years ago selling fish at your mother's door and she was a beauty even then – but she's an acquisitive, calculating beauty who will make your life hell. Don't say I did not warn you.'

'Miss Forbes is otherwise engaged,' he told Annie uneasily. 'She attends lectures now, in midwifery and child health, and spends a great deal of her time studying. Which reminds me of the purpose of my visit. Ah . . . thank you.' He took the offered mug of ale and drank with appreciative relief, before unfolding the newspaper he had brought with him. 'I thought, Mrs Christie, that you would be interested to hear this item from yesterday's *Journal*. *"On Friday 6th inst. Andrew Noble, late Medical Student in this city, appeared before the Court of Examiners of Surgeon's Hall to whom he gave great satisfaction and received a Diploma, as Member of the Royal College of Surgeons, London."'*

'But that is wonderful news,' cried Rachel. 'Andrew a surgeon! With a London diploma! It is what he always dreamed of.'

'Aye, Jeannie's lad has done well,' agreed Annie. 'She'll be rare proud of him,' but there was a reticence to her enthusiasm which made Rachel study her with new concern. It was not like Annie to be grudging in her praise, and hitherto Andrew had been a favourite. It was clear, however, that something in Fenton's news had disquieted her, for the trembling of her head had grown suddenly more pronounced, and Rachel saw her fingers were plucking at the folds of her skirt.

'Is anything wrong, Aunt Annie?' she asked. 'Is the sun, perhaps, too hot for you? If so, we had best go back inside.'

'No, lass, there's nothing wrong, and it was generous of you, Mr Abercrombie, to bring us the news. I suppose that means the lad will be coming back. Or will he stay in London? What is usual in these cases?'

'I really cannot say, Mrs Christie,' said Fenton. 'But I always understood Andrew wanted to work here in the Infirmary when he had qualified. At least, I understood so from his letters to Louise.'

Letters? Rachel was unexpectedly jealous. She had had no letter from Andrew in all the time he had been away, nor had she expected any: but to hear that he had written to Louise Forbes put his silence in a different light.

'Andrew was kind enough to offer to help Louise with her studies,' Fenton explained uneasily, sensing from the silence of both women that all was not the unadulterated joy he had expected. 'He corresponds with her on medical matters.'

'Studies are best left to the men,' said Annie, rising, trembling from her chair. 'The sun is a little hot after all, Rachel. I think I will go inside.'

'Of course, Auntie. Thank you for calling, Mr Abercrombie, and for bringing us the news, but if you will excuse me I must attend to my aunt,' and Rachel hurried in anxiously after her.

With these hasty thanks and adieus, Fenton found himself alone. Troubled, he set aside the empty tankard, refolded the newspaper and stood up to go. The visit undertaken in a spirit of happy anticipation had not turned out at all as he expected.

At the yard a little later, Rachel found Maitland, for once, alone. Apparently James and Mr Abercrombie were somewhere in the vicinity, arranging final details for the launching in two days' time.

'The masts are ready for fixing as soon as she's afloat,' reported Maitland. 'We checked them today and everything's in place for stringing the lines.'

'I'll just leave your dinners here, then,' said Rachel, putting down the flagon and basin on the table in the office and turning to go.

'No, don't hurry away.' Maitland blocked the doorway so she could not pass. 'You have been avoiding me for too long, Rachel. In fact, ever since Jamie went to the whaling. Don't think I have not noticed. And don't tell me it is all imagination, for I know it is not.'

The shed they called the office was a plain wooden structure, with one window facing west, through which the evening sun cast long shadows over trestle table and drawing-board. A shelf on one wall held Maitland's models, his carving tools, the wooden sections from which he calculated sizes of ship's timbers. Another held the boxes in which were kept the bills, dockets, and other papers of which they seemed to have an increasing number. On the table were spread out the draught plans for the *Steadfast*, much creased now and grubby with months of consultation, and among them, on whiter paper, the sheer section of an unfamiliar hull.

'What are you working on, Maitland?' asked Rachel, deliberately matter-of-fact. 'Is it to be our next ship?' But he would not be diverted.

145

'Rachel.' He stretched out a hand and took hers, unwilling, in his. 'Look at me.' Seeing the moment could no longer be avoided, she looked into his mild and honest eyes, blue now with the echo of his worn blue shirt, open at the throat to show firm-muscled neck, weather-tanned to a golden hue that was darker than his sun-bleached hair and beard. His face was tender and at the same time pleading.

'Say you love me a little, Rachel?'

'How could anyone not love you, Maitland, when you are so kind and gentle? I am very fond of you, as I am of all of you.'

'Fond? Is that all?'

Rachel lowered her eyes and tried to draw away, but he still held her hand. 'Rachel? Oh, I know we grew up together; perhaps you still think of me as a brother? But we are *not* brother and sister, Rachel. We are no blood relation, and are free as any strangers to love one another if we choose.' His voice was mild, full of reason, as if he spoke of people in a book, she thought, not of *us*.

'I know, Maitland, but . . .' She hesitated, unwilling to hurt him, unwilling equally to encourage his dream – and surely it was only a dream? He still held her hand, but she felt no passion in the slender fingers, no throbbing urgency of desire.

'Then say at least that you will try to think of me as more than a brother, one day?'

'Please, Maitland, let me pass,' she faltered. 'Your mother will be waiting.' She tried to pull her hand away, but instead of releasing her he cupped her chin in his other hand and made her look at him again.

'In a moment, Rachel. When you have promised.'

'But I *can't*,' she began, struggling to twist free, just as the doorway darkened behind them and James arrived.

'Sorry if I intrude,' he said gruffly, 'I'll come back later.'

'No,' cried Rachel in agitation, 'don't go! Maitland was only showing me the new plans.'

James pushed past her to the shelf and began to root through the contents of the nearest box. 'Abercrombie wants the figures by tomorrow. Where's that damn quotation for anchor chain?'

'I brought your dinner, James,' she said, pleading silently for understanding, but he took the bread and cheese without a word and turned back to his papers.

'I'll take some of that too,' said Maitland with deliberate cheerfulness. He drank from the ale flagon Rachel had brought and, setting it back on the table, said, 'And now, while James settles how much it cost us to launch our first little ship, let me explain what I plan for our second and bigger. See how I have lengthened and narrowed the bow? I reckon that with this narrower stem we'll have speed *and* stability. I'll have to compensate for the lost hold-space somewhere, but I'm working on that now. With so much competition on the trade routes, speed is an essential part of the design.'

Miserably Rachel listened, her eyes on the neatly drawn plans and every sense in her body directed to that other figure with his back turned, across the room. Maitland's explanation ended and still James had not spoken. It was time for her to go back.

'James, I . . .' But there was nothing she could say. 'Goodnight, Maitland.' Despairing, she walked out of the shed.

Maitland came home alone that night. James, he said, had gone for a walk along the quay. It was late before he returned. Rachel, lying sleepless in the box bed beside Annie, heard his careful tread as he picked his way through the sleepers to his own bunk beyond the partition, and at last closed her eyes in troubled, restless sleep.

The day of the launching brought a crisp east wind with scurrying puff-ball clouds in an azure sky. The harbour was choppy with a thousand cats' paws, and the tide smacked white and foaming against pierhead and quay.

All the Square turned out to see the ceremony, from the smallest whining child to the oldest, most toothless, pipe-mouthing granny. Jessie Brand wore her new taffeta gown and lorded it insufferably over all of them, one arm in Fenton's, in the other a lace parasol which she ostentatiously tipped to frame her thick, beribboned hair to best advantage. Her mother sailed behind her, monumental in black watered silk with purple trimmings, '. . . A present from dear Fenton.'

'For a' the world like a tar barrel,' commented William behind her back. 'Or a sea-lion,' grinned George, 'pregnant wi' twins.'

147

The entire Brand menagerie followed at her heels, preening and prancing 'like a set o' turkeycocks'. Only Bosun was missing. 'Wetting his whistle in the Bay Tree, like as not,' said Annie Christie, 'and who's to blame him wi' his womenfolk making such exhibitions o' themselves?' She wore her best dress, a plain grey wool, and Rachel the blue merino which suited her so well. Even the boys had dressed for the occasion, faces scrubbed, beards still glistening with water drops, collars white as the clouds above them, dark jackets brushed and neat. James wore a rakie-step hat, like the other shipmasters, Davy a bright silk handkerchief knotted at the neck. But they both leant a shoulder with the twins and Maitland when it was time to manhandle the *Steadfast* on to the 'ways' or wooden rollers. Then the brothers took up the heavy ropes attached to the ship and pulled her out of their yard, down the little side lane and across the Fittiegait to the quayside, a score of local lads running beside shouting advice and helping on the ropes, trundling the ship over the 'ways' which Alex and Davy took up the moment she had rolled over them and replaced at the front, in quick, unbroken succession, until the bow with its brilliant figurehead protruded over the waiting water.

Annie clutched Rachel's arm and she felt the older woman's anxiety tremble with her own – suppose the ship capsized? Or sank, ignominiously, in a string of bubbles? But when the brothers set their shoulders to the hull and heaved, the *Steadfast* slid effortlessly into the water with no more than a token splash, silver figurehead glinting in the sunlight, the timber of hull and deck watertight and gleaming.

'Ma, will you name her?' James handed Annie a bottle. Still trembling, but erect, she stepped forward, said, 'I name this ship the *Steadfast*,' and cracked it over the boat's hull. As the libation split in a spray of aromatic foam, there was an audible sigh of pent breath released, then cheers and celebrations.

'Well done, lad,' said Abercrombie, slapping James heartily on the back, 'and you too, Maitland. But we must all drink a toast to the success of our venture.'

Leaving Alex proudly in charge of the *Steadfast*, now securely tethered to the bollard on the quay, the main party adjourned to the Christies' yard where Rachel had earlier set out bread and cheese and ale on the table in the office. Abercrombie had provided whisky and a side of cold beef which Rachel was soon carving into slices, thin as she could make them so that there would be enough for all. But she set aside her knife and raised a glass with the rest of them. 'The *Steadfast!*'

'She's splendid, Rachel,' said Fenton, 'splendid. Papa's really pleased. I told him he couldn't buy shares in a better ship, and I was right.' Fenton had already drunk liberally to the ship's success and radiated good humoured tolerance. 'A pity Mamma and Clemmy wouldn't come to see her launched.'

'Out of the question,' his mother had announced with icy finality. 'Eat from the same table as that girl's family? They'd think it gave them free licence to come a-calling here!' 'Mamma is quite right,' Clementina had agreed. 'Besides, my husband would never consent.'

In that last remark she was not entirely correct: there was at least one member of the Farquharson clan who would have welcomed a private report on proceedings at the Christie slipway. No one at the launching, however, had eyes for anything but the ceremony and the celebrations which followed, and the watcher in the closed carriage further along the quay went unremarked by everyone but young Alex, keeping proud and conscientious guard over the newly launched *Steadfast*; and he assumed only that some passing gentleman's admiring eye had been caught and held by the magnificence of the Christie ship.

'She's a mag . . . magnificent . . . ship,' said Fenton now, putting an arm around Rachel's waist and hugging her. 'Mamma and Clemmy *should* have come, but they're stuck up,' he confided, in what he thought a private whisper, 'and would not, because of Jessica.'

'What's because of me?' demanded that young lady, mindful of her new superiority but jealous as always of Rachel's friendships.

'It's because of you, dear,' said Fenton happily, 'that I am enjoying myself so much. Let me fill up your glass and we'll . . . we'll go and find Papa. I want to drink to his business succ . . . successes.'

But Jess had spied someone else whose health she meant to drink. 'He's over yonder, by the window,' she said. 'Rachel will show you.' Then taking the refilled glass in her hand she sailed in glittering splendour to confront James Christie.

'Congratulations,' she murmured, standing too close. She raised her glass, keeping her eyes fixed on his. 'Your dream ship hasna sunk – yet.'

'Congratulations to you,' countered James, his disconcerting eyes veiled with mockery, 'for the same reason.'

'This is no dream,' she retorted, holding out a hand from which flashed an ostentatious diamond. 'Nor this,' and she touched the matching stones at her throat. 'Just cause there's no agreeance and ye havena been invited, doesna mean there'll be no wedding.' She tossed her fine head in disdain. 'We grand folk go about such things differently. It's to be a *select* affair, wi' only the best folk asked. Just you wait till ye read it in the *Journal*, that's all.'

'I will,' rejoined James, 'if I live long enough.'

'Which isna likely if ye plan to sail in yon bathtub,' snapped Jessie and flounced away, hips deliberately taunting, to position herself between Fenton and his father in what she considered the place of honour at the gathering. When her mother approached, she was seen to send her packing 'wi' a flea in her ear' to the far side of the room.

'Silly wee bitch,' commented Annie Christie. 'It's nae wise to fall out wi' your own folk. She reckons hersel' too good for the Square now, but yon other lot reckon themselves too good for her. She'll come a-begging one day, you'll see, and be glad to be taken back where she belongs.'

Rachel, watching Jess's triumph from across the room, took no comfort from that. She saw only that Jess had succeeded in snaring one young man and apparently intended to snare another, for she harried James Christie relentlessly, attacking, retreating, attacking again, until Fenton Abercrombie called her to take her leave and drive home with him to the Guestrow. James joined Maitland and old Abercrombie, who were already discussing the design of the next ship which was to be built on larger, faster lines than the *Steadfast*.

'Though mind and keep the cargo space plentiful,' warned Abercrombie. 'We need speed right enough, to beat our competitors, but we need the capacity too.'

'Rachel has plenty of ideas for that department,' said James, calling her over to join them. 'Tell Mr Abercrombie what you have in mind for that tobacco shipment, Rachel, and the preserved fruits you talked of.'

'We need density of value,' explained Rachel earnestly. 'And by that I mean a bulky article that sells cheap is not worth the transport if we can get a better. Spices are good, for instance, as long as they keep fresh.'

'She has it all worked out,' said Maitland admiringly, 'down to the last square foot of cargo space, and for the new ship, too.'

'Good lass,' said Abercrombie. 'See ye keep her – and dinna let some dashing merchant mannie snap her up for a wife.'

'We'll keep her, dinna worry,' said Maitland with a fond look, but James had other things on his mind.

'Time enough to plan the second ship when we're sure of the first.'

'Which we will be, as soon as she takes to the sea. You'll tell me, James, won't you,' said Maitland, 'exactly how the *Steadfast* handles? I'll want to know every detail.'

'We'll tell you; ye'll not find a better seaman than Davy for a working report. But first we must fit her for the sea. There'll be no delay, Mr Abercrombie, I promise you. The cargo is booked, and, thanks to you, guaranteed. We'll have a full hold and, God willing, a good profit. Come the end of the month she'll be ready to sail with the first fair wind.'

The *Steadfast* sailed, four weeks later, for London.

It was quiet with them gone: no more frenzied activity at the yard, none of the endless drudgery of the white fishing, and the household diminished to three. James had wanted to sell the little fishing boat now that the *Steadfast* was launched, but on that point Annie was adamant. 'We'll keep the wee boatie. You'll need it soon enough,' and James did not argue. That fishing boat, small though it was, was a kind of insurance, for while Abercrombie guaranteed the value of the cargo shipped in the event of loss at sea, that boat guaranteed the Christies a livelihood.

But now the Company was in operation there was business to be done; shipments to arrange for the outward voyage, with customs clearance and payments. And on the ship's return there would be goods to be disposed of: best merino cloth in the latest colours, French brandy, West Indian tobacco. The tobacco merchant in Nicholas Street had already placed an order for the next voyage. Maitland had no head for business, being pre-occupied as always with his designs for ships, so it fell to Rachel to take charge of the growing volume of business transactions, which she undertook with eagerness and genuine pleasure, not only for James's sake, but for her own. She found she had a natural ability for organization and after their initial surprise at finding themselves confronted by a woman in the Christie office, and a young and attractive one at that, her dealings with prospective customers proved both cordial and productive. Rachel's training in the market place had prepared her for quiet and courteous bargaining with a core of inflexible determination where the good of the Christies was involved. For long ago she had adopted them as 'her' family and fought for them all in her quiet, unassuming manner, as fiercely as any tigress for her cubs.

The bargain struck, Rachel would enter the items in the ledger bought for the purpose. She had already sorted through the accumulation of papers in the office and put them into order, making herself as useful as she could in the new family business while she awaited the *Steadfast*'s return.

The first trip, James had said, would be a long one. There would be matters to settle in London, agents to contact, customs procedures to learn. 'After that, we hope to do the trip in 5 days at the most, unload and load again, and be back here inside two weeks.'

There had been an infectious excitement in his voice to which only Annie seemed impervious, and now that James had gone, Rachel was disturbed to see a recurrence of the trembling which had so afflicted Annie at the time of the storms the previous year. Once she heard her muttering to herself and caught the words, 'All my eggs in one basket', and when the sea haar rolled in thick and dank the day after their sailing, Annie was brittle with anxiety. It was no good for Rachel to explain the *Steadfast* would be far down the coast by now: Annie already saw her smashed to splinters on some rocky headland, the boys' bodies waterlogged and lifeless.

Maitland did his best to cheer her, but it was not Maitland she wanted: it was those others, in peril, at sea.

Rachel looked with compassion at the woman who had taken her in and brought her up as one of her own. 'It'll be all right, Auntie,' she soothed; 'they'll be home safe enough and soon. You'll see.'

'But yon ship's no but a few planks, Rachel, knocked up of an evening by ignorant fisherfolk. Who's to say she willna split apart when the first wave strikes her?'

'I say,' said Maitland, indignant. 'I designed and built her. She's a good ship and strong, so dinna worry, Ma.'

But Annie continued to twitch and shake in spite of all the reassurance Maitland and Rachel could give.

'Yon Annie Christie's dottled,' said Jessie with matter-of-fact directness on a morning some two weeks after the *Steadfast* had sailed. 'I reckon she's slept wi' the moon in her face.'

In spite of her elevation to the fringes of city society, Jessie still lived, much to their mutual irritation, with her mother in the Square, and would do so, said Fenton firmly, until her marriage. He saw in the arrangement his only hope for bringing the marriage forward. Mrs Abercrombie entirely agreed, hoping against all reason that one or other of the pair would see sense and withdraw from the contract. Jess herself could not have said why the waiting was necessary, except that it gave her the chance to lord it over all those bitches in the Square who had called her an old maid or worse, and to show the menfolk that she had been right all along to set a higher price on herself than they could offer. The real reason lay unacknowledged, even by Jess. But it was the high point of her day to dress herself in the finery her doting Fenton provided and stroll up and down outside the Christies' door, as she had been doing today till Rachel appeared, shawled for the town, a basket of stockings on her arm. Since the departure of the *Steadfast* she had spent every spare moment knitting stockings for the manufactory in Schoolhill: it passed the time, kept anxiety at bay, and brought in pennies, albeit few, which she used to stock her office in the shipyard with pens, ink and ledgers.

Jess eyed the basket with condescension. 'I'm glad I dinna have to slave for my living now,' she said, adjusting the folds of her new silk shawl. 'But I'll walk wi' ye a bittie o' the way, to take the air.'

'As you like,' said Rachel, 'but I'll not wait for you. I don't like to leave her alone too long.'

'You should put her in the Bedlam Hospital,' said Jess, 'where she belongs.' Rachel ignored her. At the corner of the Square she turned as usual to wave to the tall, gaunt figure in the doorway of the Christies' house, but when Annie raised a frail hand in acknowledgement, her heart twisted again with compassion. 'She's not well, that is all.'

'She's dottled,' corrected Jess. 'Daft as a brush. Look at her, wi' her head shaking, aye talking to herself and picking wi' her fingers at nothing. She's nearer Daft Annie than Bonnie Annie now.'

'She's worried,' said Rachel, leaping to Annie's defence, 'and so would you be if those you loved were at sea with all the hazards of fog and tempest, and only a few wooden boards between safety and disaster.'

'Aye,' agreed Jessie, 'she's need to be worried, wi' a cockleshell of a boat like yon *Steadfast*.' She smoothed the folds of her new taffeta skirt with unashamed vanity. 'One smack of a wave and crack!' She crunched a mussel shell under her heel. 'She'll splinter like yon shell. But I hope she doesna, for we Abercrombies have a deal o' money tied up in yon ship and we wouldna want to lose it.'

'*We* Abercrombies?' cried Rachel. 'You're not an Abercrombie yet!'

'Rachel's right,' interrupted Maitland, meeting them unexpectedly as they emerged from the Square. 'You're still plain Jessie Brand, and if you take my advice,' he went on as she opened her mouth to fly at him, 'you'll guard yon foul tongue or ye might stay plain Jessie Brand a deal longer, in spite o' your borrowed plumes.'

'They're nae borrowed, Maitland Christie, they're my own, and better than anything you and your stuck-up brother could buy. Why, ye canna even clothe your own mother decent, and as for yon precious Cove lass, she's worn yon same rags since she was washed up at your door, an ugly, half-drowned kelpie naebody wanted – and no better now.'

Maitland put a protective arm around Rachel's shoulder, but

154

she shook it off and, eyes hard with anger, said clearly, 'You were always a stupid lass, Jessie Brand, and if you measure affection by the yard, be it of taffeta or homespun, you've grown stupider with age.'

'Not so stupid as I canna see what's under my nose, like some folk,' flared Jess, furious with the jealousy which always assailed her when any man preferred Rachel to her – even a man such as Maitland Christie with his book-learning and his boring, superior ways. 'It's nae you she loves, ye daft loon,' she snapped, turning her venom on Maitland, 'it's yer brother and good luck to her. She'll need it.' She turned on her heel, and flounced back into the Square to continue her parade before a more susceptible and envious audience.

After the tempest of her departure, Rachel and Maitland stood for a moment in rooted silence, then Maitland said quietly, 'Is it true?'

The grass was cool and crisp under her feet and she saw that autumn had already touched the older branches with yellow. Beyond the grass lay the pier and the harbour waters, choppy today in the brisk east wind. Automatically her eyes sought the sea beyond the Girdleness, straining for the well-known outline of the brig, with her mermaid figurehead and fluttering pennant with the silver 'C' of the Christies. She could not answer.

'Oh well,' shrugged Maitland with a little laugh which pierced her heart, 'I think I have known it all along. You have no call to feel guilty on my account. It *is* James, isn't it?'

Rachel, her back to him now, her eyes on that empty sea, said only, 'I am sorry.'

'So am I.' For a moment she misunderstood, till he added quietly, 'Perhaps one day he will see it too.'

'You'll not *tell* him!' she cried, appalled. 'Promise me you will not? *Please*.' It was bad enough to love James unrequited, but to have him know it would be humiliation too deep to bear.

'I promise,' sighed Maitland. 'And now,' he went on with deliberate cheerfulness, 'you'd best go about your business and I about mine, or we'll neither of us be done afore dinner and Ma'll start her fretting again.'

After that, things were easier between them and had it not been for the continuing anxiety of Annie over the *Steadfast*, Rachel would have been happy in the new friendship which developed between herself and Maitland. Awkwardness had been dispelled and, looking at his clear, untroubled face, Rachel wondered, briefly, if her rejection of his tentative advances had not been as much a relief to Maitland as it had been to herself. Certainly he seemed more at ease in her company than he had been for many months, as she was in his. With no more need to fabricate reasons for leaving the office whenever Maitland appeared, or for avoiding his company except in the company of others, she was able to concentrate freely on putting their paperwork in order and making everything, as she said proudly, 'shipshape'.

'You've done a fine job there, lass,' said Abercrombie, on a morning some three weeks after the *Steadfast* had sailed. He had asked for an account of the lastage for the return trip, and she had produced it immediately, with details of cost and bulk, including what was to be offloaded at Leith and what taken on in its place. 'I see you've bales o' cloth for James Roy,' he said with satisfaction. 'Ye did well to win that order, and it'll be one in the eye for Farquharson. Roy's shipped wi' him for years. Serve him right for overpricing, the cunning shark,' he finished with a grin. 'Now Maitland lad, let's see how those designs o' yours are coming along. I've a mind to put my money into more o' your ships, if only to keep Atholl Farquharson on his toes.'

Farquharson was one of many who had lent money to the city for development at advantageous rates; money which it seemed increasingly, in the light of the city's threatened bankruptcy, would not be repaid. Consequently his business methods were becoming even more grasping and dubious as money grew short. In contrast, the Abercrombies' obvious prosperity, with their own ship and expanding trade, was increasingly hard for Farquharson to bear, especially when the *Steadfast* sailed triumphantly into Aberdeen harbour on a morning in early October, with a full and undamaged cargo.

'She handled like the dream she is, Maitland,' reported James, 'whether fully loaded or in ballast. Have you orders enough for the next trip?'

'Aye. Rachel's done wonders winning new custom for us.

She's a rare touch wi' the merchants. I reckon they fall for her lovely eyes,' grinned Maitland, 'so I leave all that side of it to her now. She's done a rare job with the book-keeping, too, and drafted a new announcement to go in the *Journal* as soon as you give the word. Show him, Rachy.'

'The papers are all in the office,' she said, suddenly shy. 'Would you like to fetch them?'

'Nay lass, stay where you are,' ordered Annie, restored almost to her old self by the safe return of her sons. 'There'll be time enough for paperwork in the morning. I want to hear all about yon foreign parts ye've been to, Jamie.'

'You should see the ships i' London, Ma,' said Wee Alex, wide-eyed with the memory. 'Huge three-masters, wi' decks and gun'placements, poops big as houses, and mainmasts high as a church steeple.'

'There were East Indiamen, too, Rachy,' put in William and George, 'and men-o-war to guard 'em, as well as all manner o' merchant ships.' 'Some small as ours, some five times bigger.'

'Did ye see the bows o' the East Indiamen?' asked Maitland eagerly. 'Are they narrower than ours, or higher?'

'I'll draw one for ye,' offered Alex. 'I've done some sketches already,' and he produced a sheaf of papers from his pockets. 'Great wooden platforms, built o' solid English oak.'

'You're awful quiet, Davy,' said Annie as the others crowded round Alex and his sketches. 'Did ye not enjoy the trip?'

'Aye, Ma. But I'd like fine to have called in at Stonehaven.' He turned away to cough, before resuming, more cheerfully, 'We'll be ashore a few days, though, and I'll likely see her i' the Green. I bought her this,' and he produced a lace collar, white as foam, with butterflies worked in the points. 'Do you think she'll like it, Ma?'

Annie took the delicate scrap in her hand and studied it. 'Aye lad, she'll like it.' The sadness in her voice made Rachel look up in concern, but Davy had his arm round his mother's shoulders, consoling her.

'It's all right, Ma, dinna fret. You said yourself it was time one of us married, and I'll bring her to live here wi' us. It'll make no difference, Ma, I promise ye. I'll still be here.' But for Annie, at least, something of the happiness of homecoming had disappeared.

Rachel, too, felt an awkwardness, for after the first exuberance of welcome, James had avoided her and she was at a loss to know how she had offended. She had shown him the results of her work in the office and he had praised her. She had demonstrated how he could put his finger easily on any piece of information he required, and he had praised her. She had shown him the draft announcement: '*The* Steadfast. *The undersigned make offer of their grateful thanks to the Importers of Goods from London on the first, triumphant voyage of the brig* Steadfast *of Aberdeen and take this opportunity to acquaint them and all interested parties that they are resolved to sail for London every fourteen days. They can with propriety recommend the vessel to the Public as being substantial and good, and those who order Goods to be shipped by them may rely on every attention and care being paid. Signed: the Managers: James Christie, Master, George Abercrombie, Merchant. Apply Christie's shipyard, Footdee, or to the Captain on board.*'

'I would have put in the freight rates,' added Rachel, 'had I known them, but . . .'

'No, no,' interrupted James, 'it is fine as it is. We will negotiate the rates individually, according to bulk, and perhaps give a small reduction on a regular order. What do you think, Maitland?'

Maitland, of course, was with them. For since his return James had never been with Rachel without somehow including his brother in the company. Maitland's words still rang with warning at the back of her mind. '*I am sorry. Perhaps he will see it too.*' But if James saw anything, it was flawed by the false assumption of her preference for his brother, and Rachel was powerless to open his eyes. Maitland had given his word and would not tell. As for Rachel herself, she had too vivid a memory of Jess and James together and of Jess's openly vowed intention to 'get' him, to have any confidence that, if he did tell, the knowledge would make any difference. James wanted Jess, she was sure of it – and as for that young lady, she had long ago declared her intention of choosing one man for pride but another for pleasure. So Rachel nursed her longing in secret, and turned a brave face to the world. The bustle of unloading and restocking the *Steadfast* was occupation enough for all the family.

The hold had to be emptied, and crates and packages delivered or stowed in the Weighhouse to await collection. There were freight charges to be collected and goods to be sold, shore porters to be hired and paid. The galley must be restocked, gear checked, water-barrels filled. Goods must be taken on to fill the hold for the next trip. Maitland was in charge of the loading though in reality it was Rachel's organization and Rachel's drive.

'Be sure to keep a good watch,' warned James, 'that nothing contraband comes aboard. Insist on a true and just description. Any customable articles must be specified, permits and clearance obtained at the customs house. Remember now! We don't want any trouble.'

'I'll keep a good watch, dinna worry.' There was no need for either of them to voice the idea at the back of both their minds: Abercrombie, their shareholder, had made his fortune by smuggling.

But Abercrombie, apparently, was as anxious as they were to stay above the law. 'Keep on the right side of the customs men, lads,' he told them, when he visited the shipyard two days before the *Steadfast* was due to sail again. 'And watch that you're not made use of behind your backs. There's folk as would think nothing of planting something, so as to get you into hot water wi' the authorities.'

'We don't man the *Steadfast* wi' Christies for nothing,' said James. 'You'll find no traitors here.'

'It's nae the crew I worry over,' said Abercrombie. 'It's the sharks on shore.' Their eyes followed his as he looked through the window of the office, along the quayside in the direction of the town, past the Weighhouse with its upper balcony and supporting posts, past the larger shipyards, to where the offices of the Aberdeen and London Shipping Company shouldered those of Atholl Farquharson further up the Shiprow.

'You've done well to win the Roy consignment again, and that tobacco order for Berry's. But they'll not like it over there.' He jerked his head expressively towards the Shiprow. 'Remember he'll have men in Leith and London too, no doubt, so keep a wary eye on your competitors and a good watch on your ship.'

'Night and day,' James assured him. 'Turn and turn about.'

'Good lad.' Leaning back in his seat, George Abercrombie

hooked thumbs into waistcoat pockets over his expansive girth. He was well pleased. The returns on the first trip promised excellently: if the ship continued to prosper, his investment would pay regular dividends. 'Now where are those plans o' yours, Maitland, and the wee models. It's time we settled our next venture. What about the bows o' this one, with the after-deck o' that one?'

In his office off the Shiprow, Atholl Farquharson narrowed his eyes. A rat-faced fellow at the best of times, he now took on the sly look of a conspirator intent on some particularly devious crime.

'We may have to teach those upstarts a lesson,' he said in the slow, quiet voice which never failed to make his son's palms sweat with nervousness. Robert Farquharson had inherited his father's physical characteristics, being over-long of nose and over-short of chin, with the same sallow complexion and colour-less hair, but he had none of his father's arrogance or unscrupulous drive. Consequently the note of malice in his father's voice set him quivering with fear: not of what might be required of him, for he was as amoral as his father, but of his own inadequacy and his father's wrath.

'Undercutting my rates. Taking my customers. I hear he has even approached the linen mill.' Farquharson spoke calmly, as of the weather in a temperate clime. 'I do not think, Robert, that we should allow it to continue much longer. Do you?'

'No, Father,' spluttered Robert too hastily. 'Certainly not.'

'Then find out what cargo they have lined up here and what is to be taken on at Leith. See one of our ships is close by.'

'Keep a tight watch, mind,' warned James as he left the *Steadfast* in the hands of William and George. 'Alex and I will be back by dawn. No drinking! Keep a clear head and a clear eye.' James had taken seriously Abercombie's warning, and the *Steadfast* at her moorings below the Weighhouse had been attended constantly, day and night, by a relay of watchful Christies.

'Aye, aye sir,' chorused the twins, slapping each other on the shoulders. 'Ten Spanish doubloons to a bawbee we'll stay sober as judges both – even if it is our last night ashore.'

The *Steadfast* was to sail on the morning tide.

'I still say you should not go, Davy,' protested Annie, mixing a potion from the bottle of honey syrup and standing over him while he drank it. 'Your cough is no better, and will not be as long as ye feed it wi' sea air and haar.'

'There's sea air at home, Ma,' said Davy cheerfully, 'and a deal more haar than we'll find in the open sea. Besides, the life suits me – and we'll be back again afore ye know it.' Davy spoke with the ebullience of a lover fresh from his true love's company, for with gruff approval James had packed him off to the Green, 'to see yon lass o' yours while ye can,' and Davy had not returned till the evening meal was almost over. But behind the happiness Rachel saw a new pallor to his face. The bones were too prominent, the eyes too bright, and in spite of Annie's physic, he coughed too often.

I wish Andrew would return, she thought with gathering anxiety. Andrew would know what to do. But since that notice in the *Journal* of his exam success, they had heard no word. That Andrew would return one day, Rachel was sure: meanwhile all she could do was watch and wait – and hope that by some miracle Davy's cough would go away and Annie's shaking cease.

For when the first joy of the boys' return had passed and the *Steadfast* prepared to put to sea again, Rachel had been dismayed to see the agitation return. Annie talked to herself, her head quivering with frightening violence, her fingers plucking so hard at the folds of her skirts that the cloth was worn in several places. But if ever Rachel asked what was troubling her, Annie Christie would start, recollect, and draw herself up straight and tall with something of her old manner.

'Nothing, child. Away to your work and leave me to mine.'

But Annie Christie did little work now. Her knitting as often as not lay idle in her lap and there were no longer any lines to bait for the fishing. Instead she pottered over what little cooking there was to do, or stood for long minutes immobile, staring into space. Once Rachel came upon her, as she had done long ago in the days after Fiddly's death, standing by the dresser, the violin cradled like a child in her arms, crooning quietly to herself; and with dread she remembered Jess's words, 'She's dottled', her tee-name no longer 'Bonnie' but 'Daft'.

Yet Annie Christie retained enough of her old self to command continued respect: in public, from the Square in general, and in private, from her sons. On one point only did they go against her wishes: on the continued sailing of the *Steadfast*.

When, early the following year, news broke of the city's bankruptcy, other men than shipmasters thought with varying degrees of desperation of methods outwith the law. For though the trustees would allow the city's creditors a modest dividend of what was owed them, for some it was not enough. George Abercrombie had been shrewd enough never to allow his creditors too much rope. Though payment for the last supply of claret was still outstanding, he would survive that, especially with the new contracts the Christie lads had wangled under Atholl Farquharson's very nose: regular shipments of salmon to London, with a bonus for speedy delivery – a master touch, that, and the Cove lass's idea by all accounts – and James already working on a similar contract with a tobacco firm for the return trip. Good lads, all of 'em, worth supporting. As soon as he'd money enough put by, he'd order a third ship, for himself this time. With the city's difficulties, no doubt businessmen unluckier than he would fall by the wayside and there'd be fresh opportunities there, too. He might extend his premises, take in more stock – and show Atholl Farquharson that two could play at empire-building.

Abercrombie chuckled at the memory of Farquharson's face when he had told him he'd put no more business his way. '"I've made other, more satisfactory arrangements," I said,' he reported gleefully to his wife. '"With a more reliable company." He went positively green wi' fury.' Mrs Abercrombie was torn between pleasure at the Farquharsons' come-uppance and anxiety for Clementina.

'Do you think that was wise, in the circumstances? After all, he is Clemmy's father-in-law.'

'That didna stop him overcharging for my freight, did it? *And* adding on for this and that – "special handling" extra, "perishable goods" extra. He'll be making folk pay to look at him next! But not me, lass.' He rubbed his hands with satisfaction. 'I've made my own arrangements and they suit me fine. What's more, yon trustees can pay nought on their owings and we'll still survive. Not like some. Who knows, lass,' he added with something of the old gleam in his eye, 'wi' a bit o' wangling, I might even get ye yon shoppie ye fancy, in the new street.'

Atholl Farquharson took the news of the city's embarrassment less cheerfully. His many and devious enterprises had included a regular contract for lime and other building materials, which was still unpaid. The loss could be absorbed and he had already received payment in other, less tangible benefits: but the blow was a painful one, especially in view of the reported prosperity of certain business rivals. Anger made him, as always, venomous. On a morning in early April he summoned Robert to his private office off the Shiprow.

'How is your wife?'

Robert looked startled: he knew his father's opinion of Clementina – a silly creature without the looks to excuse it, and her miscarriages had not helped. 'Well enough, Papa,' he said cautiously. 'Why do you ask?'

'Concern, my dear boy, for family unity in these difficult times. I have thought her a little pale lately, a little too withdrawn. I want Clementina to feel absolutely at home with us, do you understand? And her mother, too. I know there has been friction there, but it must stop. I want ease and confidence between our womenfolk, my boy, and Clementina must tell you *everything*.' Seeing his son's look of disbelief, he snapped, 'See to it, Robert. Keep in with the Abercrombies, *all* of them. Even that fisher lass that Fenton plans to marry, unless someone stops him in time. *Especially* her,' he amended on a sudden thought. 'A talkative girl, I believe. A little too inclined to boast, your mother says, but sometimes that is no bad thing.' He narrowed his eyes as always when scheming someone else's downfall and repeated thoughtfully, 'Especially her . . .'

Jessie Brand was to marry Fenton Abercrombie at the end of April, at the Abercrombies' house in the Guestrow.

'There is no need for anything elaborate,' Kirsty Abercrombie had decreed when Fenton, at Jessie's prompting, had suggested St Nicholas' kirk and the new Aberdeen Hotel. 'A minister's all that's necessary, and family friends.'

'Why ye canna have a wedding frae yer ain hoose I dinna ken,' said Ma Brand, a tankard of porter in one hand and her clay pipe in the other. 'When yon laddie bought his wife's ma a fine black gownie, special-like.'

'It's nae the way o' the gentry,' snapped Jess, increasingly impatient with her mother and her home. 'And I'm to be gentry too, now – you remember that. Mrs Abercrombie and I drove to the dressmakers in a carriage today,' she added, omitting the information that that lady had spoken not a word the entire trip, except to order the cabbie to wait at the door. 'We chose a tea gown wi' real lace.' Her mother continued to sip porter with unabashed enjoyment, imprinting a foam moustache above her own, darker one. 'And dinna slurp, Ma! It's nae polite.'

'Shut yer mou' or I'll belt ye one,' retorted that lady. 'You're nae married yet. And there's still time for the poor wee laddie to escape!' Ma Brand laughed delightedly at her own wit. But Jess, for once, did not respond to the challenge. Since 'hooking' Fenton Abercrombie she had had all she had aimed for – clothes, jewellery, even leisure, for he had forbidden her to touch the fish again, willingly handing over to her what she claimed she would have earned – yet her discontent and irritation increased, the closer the date of her wedding approached.

'Ye should ha' let me fix it,' said her ma now. 'An agreeance, wi' the whole Square asked. I'd ha' baked ye some rare scones wi' oatcakes and salt herring and whisky. Aye, and there'd ha' been dancing.' She swung her great bulk into a surprisingly light-footed jig, porter mug slopping in one hand. 'Ye-hee!' she yelled, with the mindless cry of the dancer in full fling, and linked her arm through Jessie's. Jess wrenched away in disgust.

'You're drunk again, Ma. And my weddin's to be ladylike. Like the gentry. I'm nae having a horde o' drunken fisherfolk sweatin' and squealin' like a sty o' Sandy Campbells,' she finished, avoiding the forbidden word. But behind the scorn there was a hint of regret.

'I'd ha' liked fine to have a bit o' a party,' she confessed to Rachel; 'a farewell, like, to the Square.' Then, recollecting herself, she added, 'But it wouldna be right. Nae for someone in *my* position. When I'm married, Fenton and I might give a

165

party for our workers,' she added condescendingly. 'You can come if you like. And James.'

'Thank you,' said Rachel, with quiet sarcasm. 'I will remind James to make a special note in our engagement diary.'

'Engagement? Ye're nae engaged, are ye?' she said, aghast, and Rachel savoured a moment's secret pleasure before saying, 'An engagement diary is a record of one's appointments and invitations for the future. I would have thought someone in *your* position would have known that.'

'I dinna need writin' in a book to tell me what to do,' snapped Jess. 'I'm nae dottled yet!' and she slammed out of the house.

But Rachel was glad there was to be no wedding party in the Square. She could not have borne to see James dance with Jess, as he was sure to have done; she remembered Old Yule and the figures behind the peat stack; remembered the sailing of the *Middleton* and Jessie's boasting; and though Jess was to marry another, Rachel knew, with cold certainty, that she had not finished with James.

The Square held plenty of curious eyes on the morning Jessie Brand moved out of it to higher places, but James Christie's were not among them. He and his brothers were at the quay, refitting the *Steadfast* for her next trip south. It was a grey, raw morning of lingering mist, the turf damp underfoot, the ships in the harbour mere wraiths in the haar which hung low over the water, shrouding sea and land alike. The deck of the *Steadfast* was clammy with moisture, the main mast with its drooping pennant scarcely visible overhead.

'Did ye not want to see the Brand lass go?' demanded Wee Alex, rolling a barrel of salt fish skilfully across the deck to the open hold. 'And her always wi' her eye on ye, Jamie? I mind the day she telt our Rachy to sew "Jessica" into yer shirt, and Rachy wouldna.'

'Watch and dinna stave yon barrel,' warned James sharply. 'And stow it well away from yon bale o' linen. That's best quality and I dinna want it tainted wi' fish-reek.'

But when the sound of carriage wheels came muffled through the mist, he turned his head with the others to watch it pass.

'She's planning to leave us in style, anyway,' commented Maitland, noting the decorated carriage and liveried driver.

'Jessie Brand was aye a show-off,' said William. 'And yon

Fenton Abercrombie a better catch than our Jamie,' added George.

'Richer, maybe,' grinned Davy, 'but not for long if Jessie Brand has the spending of it. And when the money's gone, I wouldna be yon Abercrombie lad for a' the tea in China.'

'She'll nae have a spending of it,' said Alex. 'They're nae like us. Yon Forbes lass was telling Ma the menfolk keep the money and the women get only what they choose to give 'em.'

'Then Jess would ha' done better to tak' our Jamie,' said William. 'I'd nae ha' lost my bet,' added George. 'And Jamie would ha' liked it fine, eh Jamie?' finished William with a dig of the elbow. 'She's a rare armful for any man, temper or no.'

'Shut your mou' the pair o' ye,' roared James, 'and see to your work.'

When the carriage returned half an hour later, the wedding party stowed inside, the wedding trunk out, and the harness bells jingling in the brightening air, James did not turn his head.

But Rachel and Annie had watched from their doorway, in company with every woman in North and South Squares.

'You mark my words, Rachel,' said Annie, as the wedding party turned the corner out of sight, 'we've not seen the last o' Jessie Brand, for all her fine words. She'll be back soon enough – if only to show us she's too good for the likes o' the Square, for she'll find little enough respect where she's going.'

But Jessica Abercrombie found herself the centre of attention, at least on her wedding day. Even Atholl Farquharson, the supercilious father-in-law of Fenton's cow of a sister, went out of his way to compliment her.

'An honour to meet you, Mrs Abercrombie,' he murmured and kissed her hand, just like a real gent wi' a real lady; and when he asked her about Fenton's work and the Christies' ship, what cargo they carried and for whom, he listened to her answers as if she were a duchess instead of just Bosun Brand's daughter. In fact, Jess noted with satisfaction, he paid her a deal more attention than he did Fenton's sour-faced ma. As for her own ma and da, she made sure they were packed off home at the first opportunity, not being fit folk to mix with her new in-laws in the city.

On the quay, the *Steadfast* lay quiet at her moorings, her hold battened down, her water barrels filled, everything in readiness for the morning's sailing. On the deck the twins squatted on their haunches, facing each other across the lantern-lit planking, throwing dice with rattling monotony, turn and turn about. Behind them, in the shadowed stern, Alex lay curled up asleep, his back against a coil of rope. In the inner basin more ships lay sleeping, packed edge to edge like herrings in a box, their bare masts bones against the night sky. Clouds shrouded the moon and there were few stars. Except for the snatches of merriment from some distant tavern, the rattle of dice, and the water's murmur, the night was quiet, until something detached itself from that far jollity and rolled truculently nearer.

'Too good for us she is, too high and mighty to drink wi' her ain Da . . .'

A shape materialized in the inner harbour, meandered past the Weighhouse, paused at one of the timber beams supporting the wooden balcony to relieve itself, and shambled onwards, declaiming its maudlin grief to the sleeping harbour and the night sky.

'Too good for us she is, too high and mighty to drink wi' her ain Da . . . her ain Da who nursed her as a baby . . . rocked her wee cradle . . . her ain Da.'

'It's Bosun,' warned William in a half-whisper. 'Drunk,' agreed George. 'Dinna move or he'll see us.'

But Bosun did not need to see. He knew where his friends were – here in the harbour, not in the cold, inhospitable city at his back.

'She telt me to gang hame,' he wailed, 'me and her ain Ma.' He clutched the bollard to which the *Steadfast*'s hawser was attached and, leaning on it, called loud into the night, 'My daughter married a toff! Nae agreeance. Nae whisky and cheese. Nae scones and butter for her Ma.' He hauled himself clumsily along the rope till he gripped the gunwale of the ship, his feet still on the quayside, a perilous yard of water between hull and quay across which his body sagged like a rotting bridge.

'He'll fall i' the harbour,' warned William. 'We'd best do something,' agreed George. 'Haul on the rope.'

Hastily George shortened the hawser till hull touched quay

and Bosun was once more upright. 'Drink wi' me, lads,' he pleaded. 'Let me aboard and we'll drink ma lassie's health as it should be drunk. See!' He fumbled with his pocket. 'I've whisky.' Brandishing a flask in George's face, he hooked a leg unsteadily over the gunwale and fell. William grabbed his arm and somehow stopped him slipping into the once-more widening gap between ship and quay, till George hauled on the rope and narrowed it again.

'He's nae coming aboard,' warned William. 'Jamie's orders.'

'Suppose we canna stop him?' For Bosun had recovered his footing and was once more attempting to board the *Steadfast*.

'Her ain Da and Ma packed off home wi' nae whisky nor dancin',' he rambled. 'But we'll dance, won't we lads?' He executed a lurching jig dangerously close to the water's edge and William vaulted the gunwale to the quay.

'Come on, Bosun,' he said, taking his arm. 'We'll drink wi' ye, won't we George?'

'But what about . . . ?' George jerked his head silently to the ship. 'Jamie said . . .'

'Wake Alex. We willna drink,' he added *sotto voce*, 'and we'll nae be long. For God's sake!' he added as Bosun attempted a Highland Fling too close to the quayside. 'Take his other arm, George, afore we have to jump in after him.' Then in a cheerful voice, he said, 'Come away home, Bosun, and we'll have a rare party, the three o' us.'

'Wi' whisky? And cakes for her Ma?'

'Aye, *and* dancing. We'll have a *real* wedding party, you'll see.'

Alex, kicked unceremoniously awake by George's sea-boot, watched, bleary-eyed, as the ill-assorted trio followed its erratic course towards the pierhead and the Square. He saw two tall lads and a smaller, fatter man whose feet were lifted periodically off the ground as his escort pressganged him home, then he saw only the empty quay and, with a contented sigh, resumed his sleeping watch in the *Steadfast*'s stern.

No one saw a shadow detach itself from the darkness of the Weighhouse steps, or heard the soft pad of bare feet on plank . . .

Rachel saw the plume of smoke above the headland of Girdleness against the turquoise paleness of the brightening sky and stopped in her tracks. It was too dark for cloud, too dense for chimney smoke. Besides, there was no house on the headland, she was certain. It must be at sea.

After they had watched the *Steadfast* sail on the morning after Jess's wedding, Rachel had taken Annie home to her own fireside and had left her with her knitting and the kale pot while she set out to the office to put the paperwork of the latest voyage to rights. The cargo of salmon was simple enough, but there were three separate shippers of Findon haddock, stockings from the Schoolhill manufactory, and a bale of fine woven cloth, stamped by the Linen Stamp Office as best quality, all to be costed and entered in the ledger. She would just have time to do it before her trip to the city to collect the next batch of wool for stockings. James disapproved of her knitting, and said so, but she could not sit idle and the money, little though it was, helped. Now, remembering James, she searched the sea for any sign of the *Steadfast*. She would have sailed north-eastwards first, into the bay, then swung southwards, beyond the Girdleness . . . and there was smoke where no smoke ought to be.

With gathering dread, she looped up her skirts and ran for the shipyard where Maitland, she knew, was at work on plans for the next brig.

The anchor was jettisoned in a scream of flying chain, sails rattled to the deck, roped buckets were thrown over the side, snatched up again and passed in a frenzied chain of slopping, swilling foam to the open hatch. Below deck the choking fumes of burning cloth held the first, faint hint of fish.

'God Almighty! The cargo!' James snatched up a belaying hook, pushed the twins aside with a shout of 'Keep the buckets coming – fast!' and dropped through the hatch to join Davy in the smoke-filled hold where he was positioned to catch the water bucket and direct it at the smouldering bale of cloth.

'Out of my way!' James thrust past him, between salmon barrels and packed stockings, latched the belaying hook into the burning bale and dragged it closer. As the air from the open hatch caught it, flame crackled suddenly from one corner and Davy collapsed in a convulsion of coughing as the smoke thickened with flakes of charred sack.

'*Fire?*' Maitland shot to his feet, scattering papers to the floor. 'Are you sure?' He did not wait for the answer, but ran out of the office and on to Pocra pier, from where the billowing smoke was clearly visible. Smoke . . . mercifully no flames yet . . . at least, was that not a tongue of orange in the grey?

'Ring the alarm bells,' he cried. 'Summon the lifeboat!' Oh God, the cargo lost . . . the ship lost . . . but of the two, the cargo was the more valuable and, moreover, not their own. 'Is Bosun Brand at sea?' But in spite of the previous night's excesses, the fishing boats had sailed before dawn, and would be far away. There was a chance one of them might see and go to the *Steadfast*'s aid, but . . .

'We'll launch our wee fishing boat, Rachy,' he shouted over his shoulder, as he ran for the cove and the sheltered stretch of beach where their fishing boat lay, upended in disuse. By now there was activity at the lifeboat house, where the team was manhandling the boat down the slipway, but Maitland collected his own volunteers by a single shout into the Square. Three men joined him on the instant, pulling on sea-boots and jerseys as they ran; and the little boat was righted by a concerted 'Heave!' and propelled across the sand. It took the water before the lifeboat and then both were away, oars pulling hard for the open sea.

'A rope!' gasped James. 'We'll heave the thing overboard – and keep the buckets coming.' Davy threw the next over James as a flame caught his jacket sleeve, then one over himself, before the fireball was jerked aloft in a trail of searing flame and was jettisoned, hissing, into the sea while bare feet stamped out sparks in rope and deck. Water buckets were hauled in with redoubled frenzy to douse deck and canvas. In the hold James hunted out every last scrap of smoking cloth and crushed it under his hands or stamped it out. Davy, choking and gasping in the poisonous air, kept watch for renewed attack.

But at last James pronounced the danger past, the fire out. Weak with coughing, Davy heaved himself wearily up the companionway on to the deck. Wincing with pain as his hands gripped the supporting ropes, James followed, just as Maitland's boat rounded the point of Girdleness and came leaping towards them, the lifeboat close on her tail.

'We need no help,' shouted James, his hands a funnel to his mouth. 'All's well!' With a raised hand of acknowledgement the lifeboat veered and made back to harbour. Maitland came on. Alex threw a rope and drew the little boat alongside.

'Come aboard,' said James. 'No, not all of you. Just Maitland.' His face was white with anger, his eyes cold.

'It's only the Baxter lads,' began Maitland, 'good friends and . . .' but James silenced him with a swift motion of the hand, and winced again as air lanced his burns.

'Come to the deckhouse,' he said. 'All of you.' And out of earshot of the men in the little boat alongside, James showed them a length of charred rope, shreds of scorched red and blue material still clinging to where they had been bound by oil-soaked twine.

'It was a fuse deliberately hidden behind the bale o' linen,' he said. 'Kindled, I would hazard, in the early hours of morning, so that the flame would not take hold till we were at sea.'

'You mean someone lit it?' said Alex, astonished.

'I am sure of it.'

'But how . . . ?' began the twins. 'We were on watch the whole . . .' then as one man their voices died away and they looked at Alex whose face had turned a deep, incriminating red. 'Did you sleep, Alex?'

But before the boy could answer, Davy was convulsed with a fit of coughing more violent than any they had seen and which ended in a torrent of blood. James laid him tenderly on the deck, folded jacket under his head, and mopped his brow with seawater, ice-cold and refreshing. 'Alex, bring water from the galley and the brandy bottle. Lie still, Davy lad, and dinna speak. We'll tak' ye home directly.'

'But the . . . bonus?' he began, his lips frothing blood.

'Hush, man, do ye hear?' James wiped away the fresh blood and moistened Davy's lips with a little brandy and water. 'Do as your captain tells ye. Maitland, ye'd best send yon fellows home again. You stay with us. We'll need ye to sail the ship.'

'Shall I not take Davy in the wee boat? It might be faster, and one of the men there can take his place?'

But James had stood too close to treachery. 'Send them away. I'll have none but Christies on the *Steadfast*.'

'Are you sure she's seaworthy? What about the fire damage?'

'I judge it to be only in the deck beams and a patch of floor timber, with the main hull untouched; but see for yourself, Maitland, before we weigh anchor. And by God,' he added, as he saw Davy's dead white face, 'I'll find the bastard who did this and *kill him*!'

They moored the *Steadfast* at Pocra, and while Maitland and Alex kept guard, the twins bore Davy between them on linked hands, James white-faced at their side. The Baxter lads had brought the news before them and when they reached the house in the Square Rachel had the kettle boiling, clean blankets on the box bed and had already sent a neighbour's child to find Mr Thomson, the minister.

Annie stood speechless and quivering as they laid Davy in the bed, and remained so while Rachel gently removed his blood-stained shirt and put a fresh one on him, sponged his face and beard, then his hands which were blistered and black with ash.

'You'll make a fine ma one day, lass,' he whispered, with an attempted grin, 'won't she, James?'

But James only urged him to save his breath lest the bleeding resume, and moved to Annie's side.

'It's the coughing, Ma,' he explained gently. 'The smoke brought it on, that's all. He'll be fine now, with fresh, clean air to breath.'

But even as he spoke the words, he knew they were lies. He read death in his brother's face as clearly as if the word had been burnt into his forehead by the flames. Annie Christie read it too and from deep in her chest came a low, monotonous moaning which chilled her hearers as nothing else had done.

'Hush, Auntie,' soothed Rachel, her arm around the older woman's shoulder. 'You'll upset Davy, and there's no need to mourn. The minister will be here soon. He has medical knowledge, and will tell us what to do.'

Andrew Noble, newly arrived in Aberdeen to take up a post in the hospital, hastened to call on his friend Fenton Abercrombie and Fenton's wife, Jessica, in their elegant apartment in Union Terrace.

'I am sorry I was not here for the wedding,' he apologized, 'but the diligence was held up at Perth. However, I hope I am not too late to offer you my congratulations, Fenton, and to pay my respects to your charming wife.'

Jessica simpered in what she considered a suitably ladylike fashion. Seated in the new brocade chair, her new sprigged muslin skirts carefully arranged, new china tea-service on new mahogany sofa-table, and the firelight dancing over newly polished floorboards and new India rug, she looked, thought Andrew, like a sleek and well-fed cat basking in undeserved comfort.

'Thank you,' she said, with condescension and extended a plump and well-ringed hand, apparently for him to kiss. Suppressing a smile, Andrew, with a bow, obliged.

'Tea?' she drawled, eyes half-closed, but he knew she was watching him with every sense alert, expecting compliments and envy. This time, he decided not to oblige.

'No thank you, Jessie.' He saw her wince at the old name and some mischievous memory prompted him to add, 'I've just come from the hospital where I was most handsomely fed.'

'*Hospital?*' Jess's new found composure vanished. She started from her chair and backed away to the far side of the room. 'Nae the fever hospital? I'll have nae fever doctor here. I'm nae wanting infection, nor Fenton neither.'

'Hush, my sweet,' soothed Fenton. He slipped a proprietory arm around her waist and led her tenderly back towards the fire. 'Do not upset yourself.' He dropped a soft kiss on the nape of her neck which her *décolletage* left plumply bare. 'Andrew carries no infection.'

Remembering her status as adored wife, Jess bit back the coarse retort and said only, 'I dinna like it all the same. Fever . . .' she shuddered with ancestral memory. 'It's nae right, coming among healthy folk.'

'I am sorry if I offend,' said Andrew. 'Perhaps it might be best if we withdrew to another room, Fenton? I have much to tell you of the College of Surgeons and . . .'

'Ye'll stay here,' ordered Jess, 'where I can hear what you're speaking about. Surgeons! That's cutting folk up. There was three students caught only last week i' Keith, Mairi telt me, wi' a body stolen fresh from the grave. Put in jail, the lot o' them, and good riddance. I know about your Medico-Society folk and I know ye're one o' them, Bookie Noble, but ye'll plot nae body-snatching i' *my* house.' Fenton opened his mouth to protest and she laid a hand on his arm. 'I'm nae having my Fenton involved,' she said, more softly and with an intimate look designed deliberately to recall the athletics of the night and Fenton's drained, adoring gratitude.

'I promise, my love,' he said, 'that we plan no such gruesome activity, but if it would make you happier, Jessica, we will talk of other things. Sit down, my dear. You too, Andrew.' He indicated a chair. 'Now tell us about London. Which coffee houses did you frequent? And did you visit the theatre?'

Before Andrew could answer, there was the sound of a commotion at the door, Mairi's protesting voice and a man's shouting. Mairi had been lent to them, against her will, until the new hiring fair. For Mrs Abercrombie had been long awaiting an excuse to replace her, as being both clumsily incompetent and a deal too fond of the master, and would listen to no pleas. 'Besides,' she told the girl firmly, 'Union Terrace is coming up in the world.'

The street may be, thought Mairi, but if Master Fenton's wife thinks she is too, she's another think coming. She'd take orders from Master Fenton, but nae from that Jessie Brand. At least, not without a fight.

It sounded like a fight in progress now, with Mairi defending the door against an onslaught of abuse; but it was George Abercrombie himself who roared into the drawing-room on a bow-wave of 'Villain! Murderous, scheming bastard!' with Mairi bobbing like an agitated jolly-boat in his wake.

Fenton leapt to his feet. 'What is it, Papa?' He stepped swiftly to Jess's side, prepared to defend her against whatever disaster threatened, but Jess had never looked less in need of a champion. For when Abercrombie roared into the room, his face scarlet with fury, his fists clenched, his great girth quivering with suppressed violence and the light of battle in his eyes, Jess felt the first excitement of her marriage. Quickly she set down cup and saucer on the little side table and leant forward in anticipation, though not before adjusting the folds of her gown to best advantage. Abercrombie had an eye for a pretty woman and she enjoyed his attention, especially now. She cast a swift sideways glance at her husband, and bit her lip to stop its involuntary curl. Fenton was gentle, considerate, tender, everything she was not and had no patience with: already she lusted for rough handling, for the excitement of battle, even for the violence which, it seemed, her father-in-law promised.

'Curse him for a devious, dastardly crook!' finished Abercrombie as he collapsed panting into the nearest chair. 'Mornin' to ye,' he added, seeing Andrew. 'Forgive me, but I've had a shock.' Andrew murmured something into Fenton's ear.

'Brandy, Papa?' Fenton said quickly, and, without waiting for an answer, moved to the decanter on the sideboard and poured a hefty measure. 'Drink that. You will feel better.'

Gratefully his father drank, but only to gather strength for renewed attack.

'Set fire to the boat, the sneaking rat! Might have killed them all.'

'Who, Papa?' inquired Jess sweetly, dark eyes alight with anticipation, full lips parted.

'Why that villain Farquharson, of course. But I'll get him, I swear it. He'll not ruin me and get away with it.'

'How has he ruined you?' persisted Fenton. 'I do not see . . .'

'Of course ye don't, ye daft loon! You see nought but that new wife o' yours – and quite right too,' he added, momentarily mellowed by Jess's warm eyes and splendid figure. My, but Fenton had got himself a beauty there – he only hoped the lad knew how to handle her. He wouldn't have minded a bit of handling himself, come to that. Hastily Abercrombie turned his mind back to sterner matters.

'How he knew beats me,' he resumed, 'unless . . . Jessica! You were talking to that rat Atholl Farquharson yesterday, weren't ye? What was he saying to ye, my dear?'

'Oh . . . he talked about this and that. Paid me compliments.' And treated me like a real lady, kissing my hand, opening doors for me, and listening to me as if what I said was special. *He* didn't sneer or patronize . . .' But her father-in-law was urging her.

'What else did he say? Think, lass.'

'Oh, I remember now. He asked how we were doing. How fast the *Steadfast* was. Who shipped goods wi' us, and what. So I told him.' At the look which came over Abercrombie's face she added defiantly, 'Why not? It wouldna ha' been polite not to answer when he was being so conversational and nice. I wasna having him thinking I was an ignorant quine wi' no knowledge of my husband's affairs. Besides, where's the harm?'

'None, my dear,' sighed Abercrombie, and closed his eyes. 'Except that someone put a slow fuse under the only bale o' linen in the hold and almost sent the *Steadfast* to Davy Jones's locker.'

'Good God!' said Andrew and Fenton together. 'The scoundrel! But what of the ship?'

'And James Christie?' asked Jess, her face suddenly pale.

'The Christies are safe enough – bar young Davy whose lungs are so tainted wi' the smoke I doubt he'll recover. The linen's lost o' course – threw it into the sea, and quite right. A smart lad, James. A barrel or two o' salmon ruined, but for the rest, charred planking and sailing time lost. No worse.'

'I'll go and see them,' said Andrew, making for the door. 'It sounds as though Davy could do with my help.'

'I'll come wi' ye,' offered Jess quickly. 'Fenton willna mind, will ye, and I'd like fine to see they're all right.'

'You stay here, lass,' said George Abercrombie, 'wi' your husband. He hasna had ye awful long yet and I'll warrant he needs your company.' He gave her a knowing wink. 'I only called for a moment, to give ye the news. Now I'll go again. Ye can come to the office later, lad, and we'll go over the damage together.' He heaved himself out of the chair and bellowed, 'Mairi! My hat and cane! I'll walk wi' ye a step, Andrew lad, and ye can tell me how ye fared in London.'

The Reverend Thomson had been and gone again, leaving little comfort, when Andrew arrived at the house in the Square. Davy lay propped on a pile of pillows, his face still ashen, his clean shirt already blood-spattered, a basin and rags at his side.

Rachel was busy preparing the poultice the minister had suggested to soothe Davy's chest, though no one placed any faith in its efficacy. The twins had joined Alex and Maitland on the *Steadfast* where they had already set about repairing the fire damage, but James remained, tormented by grief for his brother and anger against whoever had attempted to fire their ship.

'I'll kill whoever did this to you,' he vowed over and over, but Davy merely smiled weakly and managed, ''Tis no matter, Jamie. Tis the *Steadfast* ye must mend now, for I'm past mending. I reckon I was finished anyway, smoke or no.' He collapsed, coughing painfully, and Rachel sped to his side to support his shoulders and hold the basin for the bubbling blood. Afterwards, she washed him with tenderness and set his pillow to rights, while Annie sat motionless on a stool at Davy's bedside, her face as pale as his, her eyes dry, her gaunt frame gripped in rigid silence. She had not spoken since the minister left, so when James opened the door to Andrew Noble's knocking, her shriek terrified them all.

'*Get out!*' She scrambled to her feet and, her back to the bed, spread her arms in a gesture both of protection and defiance. 'Ye'll nae have my Davy for your Society. Get out! *Get out!*'

'It is only Andrew, Ma,' soothed James. 'Your sister Jeannie's lad from Cove. He's a doctor. He'll help us, Ma.'

But Annie had snatched up a knife and was advancing towards the door. 'I ken fine he's a doctor, and he's come for my Davy. He's come to cut him up. But I'll cut yon doctor-surgeon first if he steps one foot over my threshold. Butcher!' She lunged forward, knife raised. Andrew stepped nimbly back as James seized Annie from behind and simultaneously Rachel cried out, 'Leave her!' Too late. Annie, struggling to break free, slashed James's hand before he could prevent her, then as his blood gushed over her apron and spattered the trodden earth of the floor, the knife dropped from her hand and she began to cry. They were the easy, desolate tears of childhood, and as Rachel led her gently to her chair at the fireside she knew the last tenuous thread of Annie's equilibrium had snapped. 'It's all right, Auntie,' she soothed, 'it's all right. Be good now and sit quiet, till I come back.'

Then she snatched up a rag from beside Davy's bed and ran

178

to James who stood dazed in the centre of the room, clutching his left wrist with his right hand while the blood dripped with steady monotony onto the ground.

'Come through here,' she urged, steering him past the partition to the other half of the room, with the boys' bunks, the clothes kist, and Annie's dresser. 'Where she can't see. Sit down on the bunk and I'll fetch Andrew.'

But Andrew, waiting only to make sure Annie's violence had passed, had already slipped round the sailcloth partition to join them.

'Let me do it, Rachy,' he said. 'I'd best stop the bleeding before I look at Davy and Aunt Annie.'

'Go to her, Rachy,' said James, his face pale with loss of blood. 'See she's all right. I know she didna mean to hurt me. It was an accident.' He closed his eyes as Andrew lifted the pad of cloth Rachel still held to the cut.

'And another that burnt the flesh off your hands?' asked Andrew sternly. 'Why did you not have these attended to sooner?'

But James did not answer: pain, loss of blood, and the shock of the morning combined to defeat consciousness and he slumped back, senseless, on the bed.

'The best thing,' said Andrew briskly. 'Fetch boiled water, clean cloths and the needle case from my bag at the door. I can stitch this gash before he comes round, if I am quick, and dress the burns too. With your help. But you'd best have whisky ready for when he wakes. You'll not faint too, Rachy, will ye?'

Rachel shook her head. But when she saw Andrew draw the edges of slashed flesh together and push the needle through, she felt her head swim and closed her eyes till the thread was knotted, the ends snipped and the wound doused with ether to prevent infection. Then Andrew began on the burns which blistered palms and inside fingers of both hands, cleansing them gently with warm water and anointing them with balm from a china jar in his medicine case. Rachel, looking down at the helpless face and spread, wounded hands of the man she had never seen anywhere but completely in command, felt her heart swell with a new tenderness. Since Fiddly's death he had been called upon to bear too many burdens, alone and for them all.

179

Gently she laid a hand on his forehead and smoothed back his tumbled hair.

Beyond the sailcloth partition Davy was quiet, though she could hear the painful rasp of his breathing behind the whimpering into which Annie's sobs had changed. 'Will she be all right?' she asked Andrew when he fastened the last bandage and leant back on his heels to take breath.

Andrew looked up at her for a long moment before saying quietly, 'If you mean will she be violent again, I think not. But I doubt she will regain the full compass of her wits. You should have told me, Rachel, what she was like.'

'How could I?' she said simply. 'You were not here.'

'No.' He sighed. 'It seems to be my fate never to be at hand when I am needed.' He was remembering their shared childhood and the beatings she had suffered at his mother's hands, though always behind his back.

'You have your work,' she said loyally and added, with an attempt at levity, 'How else are you to win your house with many mansions?'

'I doubt I will ever do that, Rachy, and it was always Ma's wish, never mine. I have found my many mansions in the hospital. But what about you?' He had momentarily forgotten James, still insensible on the bunk beside them, but Rachel had not. Her hand still lay lightly on his forehead, gently stroking the soft hair, feeling the skin cool under her fingers, tracing the arch of brows, the fine lines of care. Love flowed through her fingertips, its tenderness lighting her eyes as she said quietly, 'My dreams are here, Andrew, with . . .' She stopped, blushed, and said simply, 'I want nothing more.'

'You're a good lass.' Andrew stood up, leant forward, and kissed her cheek. 'Stay with him till he comes round,' and he slipped past the partition to see to Davy.

But James was already stirring. When Rachel took up a water-soaked cloth and bathed his forehead, his eyes jerked open and he made to sit up.

'Take care,' she warned. 'Your hands are bandaged.' But he refused her offered help and attempted to swing his legs to the floor and sit upright.

He swayed, momentarily weak, and she put an arm round his

shoulders to steady him, then held whisky to his lips. 'Drink this. It will help you.'

'What would we do without you, lass?' It might have been imagination, but she thought he laid his head for the briefest moment against her breast before heaving himself unsteadily to his feet. He winced as hand touched wooden bunk, swayed again, but only for an instant, before pushing past the hanging sailcloth into the body of the room, Rachel anxiously following.

They found Annie still sitting where Rachel had set her, in her chair by the fire. She was no longer crying, but when Rachel approached, she looked up with a whimper of such witless yearning that the girl's heart ached for her and tears stung her eyes. 'Hush, Auntie,' she soothed, 'sit quiet. I'll be with you very soon.' Carefully she stood between Annie and the bed lest the sight of Andrew examining Davy's bared chest bring a return of violence. It seemed, however, that Andrew had been right. There was no strength left in Annie Christie, for violence or for struggle. After a lifetime of dogged endurance and unbending strength, she had snapped and was helpless as a child. With a long, shuddering breath Rachel shook off the last shred of her own childhood and in that moment assumed Annie's mantle.

With a nod she summoned James to keep his mother company.

'How is Davy?' she asked quietly as she followed Andrew to the doorway. 'Is there hope?'

Andrew shook his head. 'I fear the lungs are too far gone. The smoke has merely accelerated what was inevitable. Advanced consumption has no cure. I am sorry, Rachel,' he said gently as her eyes brimmed with tears. 'We can only pray it will not be long. He is in great pain. I will send morphine from the dispensary to help him sleep.'

'And . . . his body?' She remembered Davy long ago saying, *'Bodies dinna worry me. Ye can have mine, and welcome.'*

'He'll not be touched, Rachel, I promise you.'

'Thank you. And Aunt Annie?' She looked at him with helpless, pleading eyes, but this time he could offer no comfort.

'Look after her as you would a child. Be vigilant; guard

181

against accidents. And love her. There is no more anyone can do.'

There was no more anyone could do for Davy, either. By evening it was plain that, morphine or no, he would not survive the night. James sent the Baxter boys to guard the *Steadfast* so that the brothers could keep vigil together, but it was to Rachel that Davy made his special request.

'Tell her,' he whispered and choked on the blood which welled constantly now from between his colourless lips, '. . . she's the best lass . . . in . . . Scotland.'

'I'll tell her, Davy,' promised Rachel, tears blurring her eyes. She had no need to ask of whom he spoke.

'. . . and say I'd have liked fine . . .' he broke off to cough and a torrent of blood greater than any yet gushed into the basin Rachel held to his mouth. When it was over they all knew the end was near. Rachel had to bend close to catch the words and then all she could make out was '. . . my wife.'

'Hush, Davy,' she said. 'I'll tell her, I promise.'

He lay back on the pillow and closed his eyes. Then he said clearly, 'Tell Ma not to fret,' and with a long, shuddering sigh, Davy died.

The house was full for the funeral. Rachel baked scones and oatcakes, sent Alex for a cheese and butter from the market, while Abercrombie donated a flagon of whisky as well as attending himself. 'The least I could do,' he said gruffly when James thanked him. 'Fine lad, Davy.' The Baxters and Brands came (excepting Jess), with the whole of the Square, for Davy, like his father, had been well loved.

But, the funeral over, the Christie men resumed work on repairs to the *Steadfast*, even James with his bandaged hands. When Rachel protested, he brushed her aside with angry determination.

'There's work to do lass. The ship must sail within two days or we'll lose everything.' The cargo of salmon, boiled and preserved in vinegar, was still packed in barrels in the hold, except where space had had to be made for repair work to be carried out. They worked from before dawn till well into the night, cutting out burnt or suspect timber and replacing it with new. Abercrombie came to wish them luck, and left again. Rachel brought them food and, when the light failed, lanterns, and lent a hand to patch the scorch-marks in a sail. By the end of the day they were all exhausted, but they welcomed the necessity for work: it took their minds off Davy's death.

'I'll make the bastard pay,' vowed James as he helped Maitland hold a length of crossbeam in place while William and George rammed home the wooden nails. 'Abercrombie swears Atholl Farquharson was at the back of it, and it wouldna surprise me. Farquharson never could stand competition. If it was him, he'll pay for it, I swear it.'

'We've no evidence, James,' reminded Maitland. 'Save for that scrap o' burnt rope – and who's to say it wasna bound round the bale o' cloth in the first place?'

'He's right,' said William. 'Wi'out evidence, we're nowhere.'

'They'll say it was carelessness,' added George. 'A new ship, easy kindling.'

'I'm sorry,' said Alex for the hundredth time. 'I didna think I slept. It's all my fault.'

'No matter, lad,' said James wearily. 'They'd have found a way wi' ten of us aboard, if they'd a mind to. It's no more your fault than mine or anyone's. But I vow I'll get the bastard one day, somehow.'

'Aye,' agreed the twins. 'We'll ram him head down i' the harbour, killing our Davy.' But they all knew in their hearts that Davy would have died without the help of Atholl Farquharson.

'And be hanged for it like any sheep-thief?' said Rachel with deliberate scorn. 'A fine revenge that would be, and ye both too dead to enjoy it. Please,' she went on more gently, 'Take care. All of you. Do nothing rash. Aunt Annie has lost one son already; she could not bear it if she lost another.'

'Rachel's right,' said Maitland, the voice of reason. 'It would be best to watch and wait. Assume the fire was an accident, a careless spark, unnoticed till too late. That way we will lull suspicion – and when he tries again, as he surely will, we'll be ready for him.'

'Aye,' said James slowly, 'maybe you're right. And then – we'll *get* him.'

183

The following morning the *Steadfast* sailed on the early tide, and this time Rachel stood alone on the pierhead to watch them go.

From the deck of the *Steadfast* James saw the slim, forlorn figure, saw the dignity of her bearing, remembered the touch of her hand on his forehead while Davy was dying . . . Roughly he shook off the memory and turned his thoughts to the voyage ahead. For the moment, Maitland had taken Davy's place – it was too soon, said James, to trust a stranger aboard – and Maitland had not Davy's inborn skill. It would require all James's concentration to captain the ship safely to London within the promised time.

'I've guaranteed delivery by Saturday,' Abercrombie had told him. 'See you get there lad, and there's a healthy bonus for the pair of us – and one more nail in that bastard Farquharson's coffin.'

After Davy's funeral, in a rage of drunken grief and fury, Abercrombie had sought out Farquharson in the Lemon Tree Tavern and attempted to throttle him – and would have succeeded, had not the bystanders intervened. But with sobriety had come common sense. Without evidence nothing could be proved against Farquharson, and Abercrombie must bide his time and be watchful, as must they all.

But James needed no reminder. At the name of Farquharson his face had set in sombre determination. No one would fire his ship a second time.

On the day the *Steadfast* sailed, Rachel had a visitor.

'I came to see where he lived,' said the girl, a slim, fair-haired lass with sadness in her face, and the blue eyes and fair skin of her Viking ancestors, marauders on the Scottish Coast generations ago. She wore a beautiful lace collar over the rough cotton of her dress, and Rachel had no need to ask who she was.

'Come in,' said Rachel, standing back to allow the girl to enter. 'The men are at sea but Davy's mother is here.' She indicated the figure at the fireside. 'She is . . . not herself,' she explained in a low voice. 'Davy's going was a sore blow.'

'As it was to me,' said the girl, with such desolation in her voice that Rachel felt her own eyes blur. 'Will you take a cup o' broth?' she offered. 'It's a fair step to Stonehaven.'

184

But the girl shook her head. 'No I will not stay. I just wanted to see . . .'

Her eyes turned again to Annie, but Annie held a cloth bundle cradled in her lap and was crooning softly, lost in a world of her own. 'Here is a friend of Davy's, Aunt Annie,' called Rachel, 'come all the way from Stonehaven to see us.' Annie did not even turn her head and Rachel made a helpless gesture of apology. 'You see how it is. I am sorry.'

'No matter. I'll not disturb you longer.' She turned for the door.

'Wait.' Rachel laid a hand on her arm. 'Before he died, Davy gave me a message. He said to tell you . . .' She related, as best she could, poor Davy's message and added, for the girl's need, 'He loved you very much.'

'Thank you. You have given me all I hoped for.' With dignity, she turned and left. Only when her slim, brave figure had passed out of sight beyond the far side of the Square did Rachel realize she did not even know her name.

It was desolate in the Square with James and the others gone and Rachel's only companion poor, witless Aunt Annie. The days were friendless and drear, the cottage peopled only with memories. Beyond the sailcloth partition the boys' bunks stood empty, blankets unnaturally smooth, clothes folded and stowed away in the wooden kist. In the rafters, fishing nets and line lay neatly bundled or folded into creels, 'put away against the lean times' – for just as Annie had refused to let them sell the little fishing boat, she had also kept the tools of the fishing trade lest the new venture fail and they find themselves that dread thing, 'propertyless men'.

The sight of the nets brought wistful memories, and the faint smell which lingered in the air (though it was months since anyone had fished) of fish and seaweed and the tang of mussel flesh conjured up a past time, sweet and carefree in comparison with this. For Annie needed constant watching. She rose at midnight 'to put on the dinner', took down the fishing line and baited it with bread, set the table lovingly 'for Fiddly's supper'. Once Rachel found her on the Fittiegait, a creel on her back. 'I'm away to the market,' she told Rachel crossly. 'Dinna hinder me or the fish'll stink afore I get there.' But the creel was full of stones.

Sometimes Rachel woke to find Annie's bed empty, for since Davy's death she had refused to sleep in the box bed and slept instead in the truckle that had once been Wee Alex's. Then Rachel would scramble into her clothes and run until she found her wandering on the shore, with a mussel pail of seaweed and pretty shells, or ankle-deep in the shallows, singing. She was a constant anxiety to Rachel lest one day she come to harm, and Rachel watched her as she would have watched an irresponsible child.

'A breakdown of the nervous system,' said Andrew, 'brought on by shock after too many years of strain.' But whatever the reason and however much the irritation, Rachel never forgot that Bonnie Annie had taken her in when she was friendless and rejected, had cared for her as a daughter, and had loved her. She remembered those first days when she had marvelled at the happiness between Annie and her husband, remembered the grief of Fiddly's death and her heart ached with pity for the lost and lonely woman Annie Christie had become.

'A poor thing,' said the kinder women of the Square. 'Daft as a brush,' said others, while Jessie Brand Abercrombie, on one of her visits to the Square, ostensibly to call on her mother and her friend Rachel but really to show off her gig and her ever-changing array of clothes, condescended to offer to put in a word for her with the authorities at the Clerkseat Asylum. Andrew Noble, however, called at the cottage with a more practical suggestion.

'There is no need to put Annie away,' he told Rachel, 'as long as you can care for her – and I know you will. But that is not what I came to say. As you know, Louise Forbes and I have corresponded for some time now. She is a most able pupil and well qualified, though unofficially, in medical matters. She wanted me to tell you that she will be happy to visit you and give what help she can: should you wish to go out, for example, into the town, and leave your aunt in good hands. She thought it best that I ask you first, having known your aunt before . . .'

'She is very kind.' Rachel remembered Louise Forbes's visits, her aunt's animation, and the odd friendship that had sprung for a while between them. Miss Forbes had not visited the Square for many months.

'Louise has been much occupied,' explained Andrew, reading her thoughts. 'Who knows, the sight of her might restore something of Aunt Annie's interest; and if not, at least Miss Forbes will be company for you.'

Rachel was not sure she wanted Louise Forbes's company. Louise was confident and educated, and though she was no beauty, she was a lady. She was also Andrew's correspondent and, apparently, his friend. But remembering Miss Forbes's kindness Rachel bit back her unexpected jealousy and said only, 'I would be happy to see her, if you think it can do no harm.'

Louise Forbes proved a blessing. Without condescension or pity she talked briskly to Annie, encouraged her wanderings when they touched on Fiddly or Davy, asked her questions, and though Annie rarely focused enough of her mind to answer them directly, she seemed happy in Louise's company. When she drew herself up to her old height and announced sternly, 'I am late for the market,' Louise would tuck a shawl around Annie's shoulders and walk with her till her mind took a different direction. If Annie took up a knife to shell mussels 'for Fiddly's line', Louise would offer her a pail and say, 'We'll need to gather more. Let me help you,' and, like as not, before they reached the shore Annie had forgotten and could be led home again, content. Once Louise took her driving in her gig and the trip gave Annie such evident pleasure that it was repeated the following week, and the next. Rachel was not entirely free of anxiety on Annie's behalf – she wondered how long it would be before Louise Forbes tired of her charitable work – but the weekly visits eased her burden and gave her more time for the office on Pocra pier.

For after the first two or three trips with Maitland taking Davy's place, James had agreed to hire an extra hand and set Maitland free again to work in the shipyard.

'Ye're not the sailor Davy was,' he agreed, 'and ye'll be company for Rachel, wi' Ma how she is.'

Their mother's 'illness' was a subject too sensitive to mention between them. When the Christie boys were home between voyages, they behaved as if nothing had changed, ignored their mother's erratic behaviour, and turned a collective blind eye to her obvious infirmities. Only James said once, to Rachel, 'Care for her, Rachy. We rely on you.' And on another occasion, after a particularly trying scene when Annie had attempted to wake Maitland and the twins a mere ten minutes after they had gone to bed, urging them to put on their sea-boots and hurry lest their father go to sea without them, he had watched the patience with which Rachel steered Annie to her own bed, saying 'It's all right, Auntie, dinna worry, they'll go directly and Fiddly will wait for them,' and afterwards said, 'Thank you. You are good to her.'

Now, remembering his promise to see his mother end her days in comfort, he said roughly, 'There's better work for ye to do at home, Maitland. We've profits coming in steady now. We'll find the extra for a deckhand, and a carpenter to help you when you're ready to start.'

Work on plans for the new ship had slowed with Davy's death and the damage to the *Steadfast*. Maitland was still designing a bow which would combine speed and capacity in the best proportions, and until he was satisfied no start could be made, though they had timber enough left over from the *Steadfast* to begin as soon as the plans were complete. After much family discussion it had been agreed that the next ship would have cabins for passengers, a little galley, and a hold with enough space to make the trip worth while. Though with the harbour limitations they could not build too large: big ships could not berth at the quay and must unload at Pocra, or into lighters in the bay, though there was talk of deepening the channel one day.

Abercrombie was enthusiastic. 'I'll back ye with money, lads. I'll buy my share now, if it'll help and if I'll have a say in the ship's design. Something to beat Farquharson's *Flora*. Say, 300 tons?'

James was reminded again of Farquharson's treachery, of his mother's trouble and his brother's death, still unavenged. 'Aye,' he said grimly, '300 tons, and fast – and when the time's right, I'll hand over the *Steadfast* to the twins and join you, Maitland, in the yard.' The ship they built was to be named the *Bonnie Annie* and somehow, he knew, would be both his mother's comfort and his brother's revenge.

By October the plans were finished, the model made, and a carpenter hired to work with Maitland. The shipyard once more echoed with the sound of sawing and hammering, as the keel was laid and work on the hull commenced. As she had done before, Rachel carried food to them night and morning, staying only long enough to put down cooking-pot and flagon before hurrying back lest Annie wander too far from the Square and come to harm. The carpenter, on Maitland's urging, took on an apprentice, and steadily the new ship grew – cant timbers, transoms, futtocks, top timbers. Their only problem was space. The land was not big enough.

'If we could buy the tattie patch next door,' said Maitland, 'and have direct access to the quay . . .' But the lease of Dixon's patch still had a year to run.

'We'll get it one day,' said Abercrombie, 'dinna worry. You'll have first refusal as its for your yard, and you buildin' as fine a ship as any i' the harbour. But guard her well,' he warned as he took his leave. 'There's aye rats about, and I dinna mean only the four-legged kind.'

The turn of the year brought storms and shipwreck and such cold that there was even skating in the harbour. The body of a seaman was washed up between the piers and buried at Footdee. Other mariners, rescued, died later in the hospital of cold and fatigue, and in a wreck off Belhelvie seven out of ten crew were drowned. Even in the harbour there was danger: a carpenter fitting the cross-trees on the topmast of a new brig fell from the mainmast and fractured his skull. Annie, in her new simplicity, remained untroubled, while Rachel quaked with fear for those she loved. But the *Steadfast* kept harbour till the storms blew over, then, the seas safe again, resumed the London run.

Plans were put under way to improve the harbour, and with the prospect of a deeper channel shipbuilding flourished, till as many as twenty-two vessels were building up and down the quay, and in the Christie yard off Pocra pier the new ship steadily grew.

1818

At the end of January, Jessie Abercrombie gave birth to a large, black-haired, and red-faced daughter whom Fenton named Augusta and who screamed the house down. So, with a lusty lack of all inhibiting modesty and no attempt at fortitude, had her mother done, to her doctor's extreme annoyance.

Fenton had proved unexpectedly obstructive when Jess had demanded Andrew Noble. He had insisted she see only the family doctor who had attended himself and Clementina through the usual childhood ailments, an elderly, white-haired and painstaking fellow called MacLellan. Jess hated him.

'I'm nae having yon lecherous old devil wi' his hands up me,' she announced. 'I'd rather have my own Ma.'

But the Abercrombie clan united to block that idea. 'Dr MacLellan will attend you,' said Fenton firmly. 'No one else.'

It was Jess's particular revenge to remind him of this when, six weeks after the birth, she refused him. 'If ye'd let me have Dr Noble,' she pointed out, 'I'd nae be half so sore. I swear yon MacLellan ripped me on purpose, the randy old goat.' Jess had a vindictive streak which operated now in a refusal to let Fenton into her bed. 'For at least three months,' she told him firmly and added to herself, 'or forever.'

She did not particularly like Augusta, and from the noise the infant made whenever Jess touched her, she thought the feeling mutual. Fortunately Mairi and Augusta got on fine together. For Mairi, in spite of being 'lent', unwilling and rebellious, to the Fenton household, had stayed. Her rough incompetence suited Jess, who would have been made to feel inferior by a more accomplished maid, and when Mairi answered her back, Jess met her on her own ground with lusty insults in a succession of tussles which both enjoyed. So when Augusta proved a nuisance, Jess was happy enough to leave the upbringing of her daughter to the maid, particularly as Mairi knew all the right tricks to bring the child good luck and ward off evil.

'I wrapped the wee mite i' one o' the master's shirts,' she told Jess, 'so she'll marry happy, and I didna wash her palms so she's nae lost her luck.'

'Good,' said Jess. 'See ye dinna forget the candles,' but she was barely interested. Let Fenton and Mairi drool over the babe if they must: she would have preferred a son.

Two months after her lying-in, she confessed as much to Ma Brand.

'Never mind,' grinned her mother. 'Plenty more where yon came from, and plenty o' fun in the making of them, eh lass?' and she dug Jess vigorously in the ribs. Not for the world would Jess have admitted to her Ma that Fenton's love-making bored her, but as she looked on the huge, black-haired, black-whiskered woman who was her mother and remembered the grunts and squealing laughter emanating from the closed box bed, she felt the bile of jealousy sour her spirits and snapped, 'I'm nae having more and I've telt Fenton so. At least, not if I can help it.'

'Get on wi' ye,' jeered Ma Brand. 'Naebody can help it. Not wi' a man in her bed.'

But Jess had had enough. 'We dinna talk in yon coarse fashion in Union Terrace,' she said loftily, and swept out of the house.

Obeying his father's instructions to 'keep in with the Abercrombies', Robert Farquharson had invited Fenton and Jessica to dinner at his house in the West End, a separate wing of the Farquharson mansion. Atholl and his wife were also of the company though not, on the former's advice, the elder Abercrombies. Atholl had private reasons for avoiding George Abercrombie's company, not least the memory of that embarrassing scene in the Lemon Tree Tavern when Abercrombie had accused him of fire-raising and murder, and had had to be physically restrained from throttling Farquharson on the spot. A year later Atholl could still feel the strength of those work-knotted fingers at his throat, the whisky-laden breath in his face. An uncouth fellow, Abercrombie, grown more so with wealth. That shop of his continued to prosper, damn it, and now that he'd got a toe in the shipping door it was the same story. He'd elbow Farquharson out of the London trade, with his fast ship and his low rates, if they didn't watch out.

But Farquharson meant to do more than watch out. That first attempt had been intended only as a warning: that it had ended in the death of Davy Christie had been unintentional – he had no quarrel with the Christies except as Abercrombie's agents. Next time he must be more subtle. Best of all would be something actually *legal*. That brush with Abercrombie had unsettled him more than he cared to admit. He would get lawyer Forbes to work on it. Something legal *and* lethal . . . His eyes narrowed with calculation as he looked around his son's drawing-room.

A large, airy room, high-ceilinged in the newest fashion. That architect fellow had done well: the portico and drive were particularly imposing. But the venture had cost more than he could afford and, since the city's bankruptcy, money was tight. It would be tighter still if unwelcome competition were not dealt with, fast. His eyes fell speculatively on Fenton Abercrombie's wife. He remembered her wedding a year ago and a particularly illuminating conversation. Carefully, he set aside his coffee cup and advanced towards her.

'Have you seen the view from the window, Mrs Abercrombie?' he said, steering her skilfully away from the group at the fireside and into the window recess. 'One can see quite past the Dee to Cairn o' Mount. You are looking very lovely tonight, my dear,' he added. 'Quite the loveliest lady in the room. But I should not say such things to a married woman – pray forgive me.' He gave a courteous little bow of submission and Jess glowed with pleasure.

'I forgive you,' she said airily and looked coquettishly at him from behind her newest fan. 'Though others wouldn't.'

'Others, madam, have not your grace and charm,' replied Farquharson smoothly. 'Not every young man has the good fortune to marry beauty, grace *and* wit.' He glanced meaningfully towards the fireplace where his son Robert stood with Clementina. 'I remember thinking so the first time I met you, on the day of your wedding, when you talked so intelligently about shipping. Not every wife, I assure you, takes such an informed interest in her husband's occupation, more's the pity.'

'And more fools them,' retorted Jess. 'Where I come from a wife knows what her man's worth to the last farthing – and keeps her hands on the purse-strings.'

'And very pretty hands too, my dear.' Checking that the sofa stood between himself and his wife, he took one of her hands in his and stroked it gently. 'So soft and elegant,' he lied. 'So *ladylike*.'

'Oh la, sir!' said Jess coyly, repeating a phrase she had heard in somebody's drawing-room. 'How you do flatter me.'

Jess was enjoying herself. After months of snubbing by Mrs Abercrombie senior and Fenton's odious sister, it was balm to her ambitious heart to hear herself treated as an equal by a man of Farquharson's standing. He had pulled out her chair at table before she sat down, picked up her glove when she dropped it accidentally on purpose. And now he was talking to her just like in a play at the theatre.

'I assure you it is no flattery, madam,' said Farquharson seriously. 'You know as much about your husband's ships as he does. Is that not so? You could discuss freight charges and cargoes as easily as any gentleman in the room, and with far more charm and intelligence than *others*.' Again he looked pointedly towards Clementina.

'Well,' simpered Jess, 'I do know quite a bit, though I say it myself.'

'Such knowledge is worth rubies, madam,' he said solemnly, 'but then your neck is made for rubies and,' he added in low, caressing tones, 'I know a very good jeweller.'

'Atholl,' called his wife imperiously, 'of what are you talking? Bring your companion over here so we can all take part in the conversation.'

'Certainly, my dear.' He offered his arm to Jess with elaborate courtesy. 'Allow me, Mrs Abercrombie.'

Smirking with pride, Jess sailed across the drawing-room on Mr Farquharson's arm.

That was the first of many such conversations, sometimes at the Farquharsons' house, sometimes at Fenton Abercrombie's, and once at the Farquharson office off the Shiprow. For with Mairi in charge of baby Augusta, Jess took to her gig and the aimless driving which both satisfied vanity and passed the time. She drove to Broad Street to the shops, bought dresses she did not need, with bonnets and lengths of ribbon; paraded up and down the Union Street to show off her newest outfit; and visited the Christie shipyard, at first with Fenton, then alone, to inspect the company's new ship and 'check on progress'.

Atholl Farquharson treated her like a lady in the forefront of society, and with his protection she found herself grudgingly admitted to an increasing number of Aberdeen drawing-rooms. But there was one place where she found none of the new respect she craved and considered her due – and one man who continued to treat her as if she were still plain Jessie Brand. James Christie's unconcern both exasperated and excited her, till it became her over-riding aim to make James accord her the same esteem she received from Farquharson.

In consequence she pursued him with relentless mischief. She knew when he would be at sea, when ashore, and would arrive at the Fittiegait in the smart new gig her doting husband had bought her, alight, and swagger into the Christie yard, condescending and truculent, acting the manager and financial boss. 'Though 'tis the old Abercrombie, not the young who owns the shares,' grumbled Wee Alex, 'and then only a four-tenths part.' He was fiercely loyal to Rachel and knew, with no word said, that she dreaded Jess's visits. He remembered that incident, years ago, when he had overheard Jess threaten Rachel, urging her to stitch 'Jessica' into a shirt which belonged to James. James he idolized as only a younger brother can an older, and James, too, disliked Jess Abercrombie's visits.

'I see the work's coming on – slowly,' Jess would say, eyeing the frame on its wooden props. 'You're certainly taking your time.' Then, with a change of mood and a deliberately provocative look, 'I see I'll have to keep ye up to the mark, Mr Christie. We canna have ye slacking.' On another occasion she would change tactics and be the helpless, trusting innocent.

'Tell me, Mr Christie,' she would simper, her hand on his arm, 'what are those big pieces of wood called? The ones going up and out a bit?' and James would shake off her hand with irritable impatience, name hawse-piece or stanchion, and direct her to Maitland or one of the others, 'so I can get back to my work in peace'. But it was James whom Jess sought to torment, not the others, and thwarted of her prey she would drive off, dissatisfied and already planning the next foray. Her private pretext was to gather information with which to impress Atholl Farquharson, but, remembering how she had effected that conquest, she thought similar methods might win over James.

'Mr Farquharson is sending his *Flora* to the Baltic next, for a load o' cheap flax,' she would announce, or 'His *Dora* made London in one hundred and twenty hours last week, wi' a following wind.' James would listen gravely, thank her for her information, and turn his back. Or direct her to Rachel, saying, 'Rachel deals with that side of the business. You'd best talk to her.' Invariably Jess left frustrated and cross.

On one such occasion, in early May, when James rebuffed her, she retorted, 'Suit yourself. I thought ye might be interested in the competition. Since ye're not, there's others are.' She decided to call on her mother to work off irritation before returning home, but on the way she met Rachel and Annie Christie walking home from the shore.

'How is the baby?' inquired Rachel.

'Augusta? Fat and healthy o' course. We've good air in Union Terrace – none o' your whale-oil stink and mussel shells.' She sniffed scornfully, and eyed Rachel's dress where the sea-water had stained the hem. 'Been paddlin' wi' yer own baby?'

'Davy's late home again,' said Annie Christie reprovingly. 'I was looking for him. He should not stay out so late, not wi' his cough.'

'But he's *dead*, you dottled old cow!' shouted Jess, venting her frustration on the mother of its cause. 'He's been dead a year past.' Annie stared at her in bewilderment.

'Come, Auntie,' said Rachel. 'It is time to go home. The boys will be back soon for their supper.' To Jess she said, in a fierce undertone, 'You should be ashamed.'

'Ashamed?' Jess shouted with laughter. 'O' telling an old wifey she's dottled? She doesna ken what I'm saying anyway. Do ye, Daft Annie?' she bellowed, as if the poor creature were deaf.

'But *I* do,' warned Rachel, 'and I'll not forget it.' She hurried her aunt away home.

'What did she say about Davy, Rachel?' asked Annie, puzzled. 'Is he coming?'

'Soon,' soothed Rachel, still seething with anger at Jess's thoughtless cruelty. Or was it entirely thoughtless? Rachel remembered those words of long ago – *'I'll choose one for pride, the other for pleasure'*. She knew that 'other' was James, but how much of the boast had been jest, to tease and needle her, she could not tell. Surely now, with a husband and child, Jess would settle down and behave as any decent woman should?

Rachel set about diverting her aunt's attention with preparations for the evening meal, for with the *Steadfast* in port they were a full house, while her own mind went over and over the question of Jess's spiteful behaviour. She remembered the hare's foot years ago, hidden in Rachel's mussel pail, and knew, with sickening certainty, that behind the friendship Jess's jealousy still smouldered: it was not Annie she had sought to hurt, but, through her, Rachel.

The idea of Davy had lodged in Annie's mind, and that night, when the family slept, she crept silently out of bed and went to look for him. One of the South Square fishermen found her wandering in the dawn shallows clad only in her shift, her grey hair draggled about her shoulders and her limbs like ice. He brought her, protesting, home.

'I was speaking to my husband,' she told Rachel with dignity. 'I did not wish to come home.' Rachel looked questioningly at the fisherman who shrugged and said, 'Naebody in sight but the plingies,' and left.

Rachel remembered her own childhood loneliness when she had believed seagulls to be the souls of drowned sailors and had looked for her own parents among them, but all she said was, 'Fiddly would not want to see you with your hair wet and your clothes dripping. Come away in and let me dry them for you.'

James and the others stood helpless at the sight of their mother's ice-white limbs, the soaked linen clinging to the gaunt lines of her body, her bare feet green as death.

'Alex,' ordered Rachel sharply, 'warm a blanket for your Ma at the fire. You, Maitland, look in the kist yonder for a clean shift to her. James, mix whisky toddy, hot as ye can make it and see the kettle's on the boil.' At the back of her mind, voices of childhood echoed, wistful with memory, but she had no time to examine what they were. Others, however, remembered.

'Shall we take down the bath-tub,' asked William and George. 'We'll easy fill it for ye.'

But to bath Annie Christie before the fire like a half-drowned child would be too much indignity.

'No, William, thank you. But ye can see the fire's made up and the porridge hot. Folk'll need feeding just the same.' Even if a woman was dying, old before her time. Rachel feared death stood already in Annie Christie's face.

She packed the menfolk beyond the partition while she stripped her aunt, rubbed her vigorously with a hot towel and dressed her in a dry flannel shift, then called James to help her lift his mother into the box bed where Annie obstinately refused to go.

'But Fiddly was calling me,' she moaned when she was lying at last in the blankets Alex had warmed for her, a hot brick at her feet and another at her back. Her limbs were still ice-cold and Rachel feared she was chilled to the heart. 'Fiddly called to me,' she repeated, 'and Davy. Dear little Davy. He was aye a happy, loving child – as you could be, James.' She seized his hand and gripped it tight. 'If ye let yourself.' Then, as the heat of the blankets spread, she was gripped in a spasm of shivering so violent they feared it would shake the life from her. When it was over, she spoke again, with a sad despair. 'They were both there, and there was music. Such rare tunes as they played together . . . The house was aye full o' music when my Fiddly was here, and Davy had such a way wi' the mouthie.' Then she closed her eyes in exhaustion and slept. Gently Rachel tucked her aunt's hand back under the blanket and fetched another brick to warm the obstinate flesh.

'Shall I fetch the minister?' offered Wee Alex in a frightened whisper.

'No.' To James the minister's summons could mean only death. 'Rachel knows what to do.' And when I don't, thought Rachel, I will send for Andrew.

She packed Maitland and the twins back to the *Steadfast* with Alex. 'There's cargo to be stowed,' she said, 'and stores to check, and there's nothing you can do here. I'll send if you're needed.' James, she knew, would stay whether she told him to go or not.

Annie slept all day, rousing only long enough to drink a little warm milk at noon. The family ate their evening meal in anxious silence so as not to disturb the motionless figure in the

197

box bed. But before the meal was over, the noise of breathing grew suddenly stertorous and rasping. Rachel slipped quickly from table to the bed.

Her aunt's feet were no warmer, but the skin of her forehead burned dry and so hot that Rachel snatched back her hand in alarm. 'Alex! Run to the hospital for Dr Noble.' To James she said helplessly, 'I don't know what else to try.'

'There is little I can do,' said Andrew when he stood, an hour later, at Annie Christie's bedside. 'She is weak and has the fever in her lungs. I could bleed her, but . . .' He looked questioningly at Rachel who, in turn, looked at James's white, set face. He had not left his mother's side, except, protestingly, to eat, since the fisherman had brought her home.

'No, she has suffered enough. Let her at least die in peace.'

'Very well,' said Andrew quietly. 'She has little enough blood, I fear, to spare. I will leave you a powder, Rachel, to give her. It might reduce the fever and will at least help her to sleep. I am sorry I cannot do more.'

Rachel went to the door with him. 'Don't take it too hard,' he said softly. 'She is in no pain and I think, perhaps, she wants to go. I'll come again in the morning.'

Rachel lay down on the truckle bed but could not sleep. She remembered Jess's taunts which had caused her aunt's wanderings, remembered her aunt's loving kindness and later, her grief, and was torn between anger and an aching compassion. The sound of the older woman's breath as she tossed and moaned kept them all awake long into the night, for even Alex recognized that it might be their mother's last night on earth.

By morning she was no better, no worse. Andrew Noble came and went again, promising to return in the evening. All but James were sent, as before, to work. 'There is nothing for you to do here,' she repeated, 'except upset yourselves. I will send for you when the time comes.'

It was late in the afternoon, Rachel at the fireside knitting to keep back anxiety while at the same time tending the broth pot, James seated at his mother's side, face haggard, sleepless eyes on her waxen face, when Annie's eyes opened and she looked at him with all her old lucidity and strength.

'Rachel!' he cried, starting to his feet.

She set down the half-finished stocking, sped to the door and dispatched a neighbour's child, running, to the quay to summon the others. A moment later she was at James's side.

Annie's steady look shifted from James's face to Rachel's and she said clearly, 'Come closer, Rachel. Give me your hand.'

Rachel dropped to her knees at the bedside and took Annie's hand in both hers. 'I am here, Auntie. Tell me what it is you want.'

'I want nothing, child,' she retorted, with the old asperity, 'except to see you two as you ought to be.' Rachel dropped her eyes, acutely aware of James standing so close beside her that she could feel the warmth of him through the cotton of her gown. 'You have been better than any daughter to me, lass,' she went on, her voice fainter now, but unwavering. 'But you're nae my daughter, you're *nae blood kin*, and I know ye love him. I had hoped to be at Davy's wedding,' she went on wistfully, 'and to see my grandchildren, but it was not to be . . . Where are you, James? Give me your hand.' He reached out his hand, still scarred where the knife had slashed it, and took his mother's free one so that with one she held Rachel, with the other her son. 'Ah . . .' They heard her sigh with satisfaction before she said sternly, 'James, you must marry the lass.'

There was a moment's stunned silence before James said, faltering, 'Davy's lass, Ma?'

'Nae Davy's lass, ye daft loon! Rachel.'

Rachel held her breath and dared not move while behind her she felt James stiffen. He did not speak.

'Promise me,' went on his mother, relentless, 'promise me you will marry Rachel.'

'I promise, Ma.' His voice was hoarse and scarce above a whisper and Rachel's cheeks were burning now, with shame.

'Swear it,' persisted Annie and Rachel felt her fingers tighten over her own. 'By the fisherman's sacred oath.'

'I swear I will marry Rachel – or may my boat be a bonnet to me.'

The words hung in the air as if they had been blazoned there with fire, then Rachel felt her aunt's fingers relax and she fell back on the pillow, her face calm, her breathing suddenly quiet.

'Are we in time?' gasped Maitland, ashen-faced and breathless, the others crowding at his heels. Rachel nodded, moved back to let them take her place, but while Annie took her leave of her stricken sons, Rachel could think only of that solemn, empty vow.

Annie Christie died peacefully that night, in her sleep.

It was a strange funeral, muted and silent after the first torrent of tears. The twins had been inconsolable, Maitland openly weeping while Alex smothered his grief, face down, in the blankets of his bed. Only James remained dry-eyed, his face gaunt, his eyes distraught. He spoke only once to Rachel and that was to say, 'I failed her. I couldna even get her her house before she died.'

'She wanted no other house but this,' comforted Rachel. 'It was here that her memories were. She would have been lost without them.' But he did not seem to hear.

George Abercrombie came to the funeral, and Andrew Noble, with Miss Forbes. Seeing them together, Rachel wondered how long it would be before they married. Andrew had a good job at the hospital, a house of his own, and £100 a year. He could afford to marry whenever he chose. Looking at them as they stood side by side at the graveside, Rachel felt excluded and lonely, once more an unwanted orphan. The work of the fishing had been her reason for first coming to the Christie house; when that ended, Annie herself had been reason enough to stay. Now she had no useful purpose that some other woman could not serve equally well: even her work at the Pocra office could be done by any clerk. She had no right to stay – and nowhere else to go.

The funeral over, James and Rachel avoided each other's company. The vow his mother had extracted from him lingered always at the forefront of Rachel's mind, with the shame it had occasioned. She was sure its memory haunted James as it haunted her, but no words were spoken. Rachel wondered if the others had heard anything on that last day of their mother's life, and could not be sure. Maitland treated her with his usual affection and perhaps more solicitude than usual, the twins were touchingly anxious to help her and apparently grateful for any task she could give them, while Wee Alex turned to her as he had to his mother, in trust and unquestioning love. Alex would always be "Wee" though at fourteen he was already tall

200

as Rachel and would one day be tallest of them all. Only James stayed aloof and unapproachable.

But soon even that awkwardness was absorbed into the routine of work which they attacked with redoubled energy. The regular run to London was resumed, though now James hired the Baxter boys as crewmen so that Alex could help Maitland at the shipyard. When the major part of the hull was completed, James himself handed over the captaincy of the *Steadfast* to William and worked beside Maitland on the new ship.

All through the summer of that year and well into autumn they worked, cutting, hammering, measuring, fitting. Ordering ironwork for the deck, sailcloth, rope, all the paraphernalia of a sailing ship, with the added embellishments required for the cabins Maitland had designed. One of the carpenters made a fine box bunk with panelled, folding doors, and in the evenings Alex worked on designs for a figurehead. It was, by general agreement, to be another mermaid, though this time gilded with paper-thin sheets of gold leaf, carefully pressed into place over a coat of glue and smoothed with a soft cloth pad.

The masts were ordered, their height carefully calculated by reference to the ship's length and breadth; the crane which would lift them into place was booked for when the time came. Gradually the *Bonnie Annie* took shape, solidified, and changed from a frail skeleton of uprights to an imposing hull which gleamed in the autumn sunlight, glistened on a frosty morning under a crust of hoar frost, or shone sleek and solid through driving rain.

'Isn't she beautiful?' said Wee Alex. 'One day I'll be master o' this one: James has promised. I'll sail to Rotterdam and Campvere, Pictou, St John's, even the Mediterranean. And when the East India Company loses their China monopoly too, as James says they surely will, then I'll sail her to Foochow and come back loaded to the gunwales with the best tea, Rachy, for you.'

'Is she big enough to sail the China seas?'

'Aye, and if she's not, we'll build a bigger,' boasted Alex. 'We'll find a new shipyard when our lease runs out next year and build a ship as grand as any Hall's or the Duthie brothers can produce.'

The Christie men had all attended the launching of the *Castle Forbes* in March, had watched the grand ship slip into the harbour waters smooth and swift, joined in the cheering, been deafened by the exuberant band – and dreamed of beating the 440-ton East Indiaman in their own yard one day. Already they had orders for another *Steadfast* which they planned to build as soon as the current ship was finished, 'purely for sale and profit', and when the new vessel was launched and proved her excellence, Maitland had no doubt orders for her replica would flood in. He was well pleased with the workmen he had hired and was building up a reliable work force.

When the vessel was finished, James planned to leave the running of the shipyard largely to Maitland, and to concentrate his energies on the sea-going part of the enterprise; for at heart he was a seaman, happiest with the deck under his feet and the wheel under his hand. Rachel, with his guidance, had already mastered the necessary intricacies of quarantine laws, harbour dues, and pilot's fees, of lifeboat tax and Customs, and had in turn initiated Maitland and the twins, so that James was free to move from ship to shipyard to planning shed and know that work would continue to run smoothly wherever he chose to be. For the moment, however, he worked beside Maitland in the yard. Occasionally, when the itch became too strong, he would take over the *Steadfast* and race for London, delighting in the sea wind in his face, the little brig prancing and frisking under his hands, while the ice-green billows smacked in cascading glory from figurehead and arching prow, and the Christie pennant streamed, cracking, aloft.

In London, while the twins supervised the business of the cargo, James would stroll along the dockside eyeing bigger, further-travelled ships and, back in Aberdeen, would talk with Maitland of the vessels they would build for the international run.

Meanwhile Rachel carried food to the workmen in the little shipyard, lingering to collect offcuts of planking or wood-shavings for the fire or to help with paperwork on the days when the *Steadfast* was in harbour and there was loading and unloading to supervise and the galley to be restocked with oatmeal, cheese and salt fish as well as the fresh bread and fruit on which Rachel insisted. Then she would visit the Weighhouse and the quay, ostensibly to check the *Steadfast*'s cargo, but also to note what merchandise was arriving from where and for whom, which merchants favoured which ships with their custom and with what loyalty, noting those she thought might respond to favourable offers or a long-term contract. Later she would talk it over with Maitland, direct him to make the first approach, or would write out a handbill setting out their terms, and despatch Wee Alex to deliver it. On occasion, she would even deliver it herself.

By this means she had already won the Christies valuable custom with several merchants in the city. 'It's your face,' said Maitland, teasing. 'So deceptively innocent and honest! They're not to know ye're a hard-hearted lass when it comes to a bargain. I reckon they all leave the office thinking they've taken advantage of a sweet wee lassie wi' no idea o' business, and are so bemused by your looks they dinna realize they've walked straight into a trap.'

'It's *not* a trap,' she began indignantly, then laughed as she saw his expression. 'I would not cheat anyone, Maitland. I only want the best for us, that is all.'

'I know, Rachel, and you've given us of your best, un-stintingly, especially since Ma died.' He paused, remember-ing, before continuing quietly, 'Do not work too hard, Rachel. I don't know what we'd do if you . . .' he faltered helplessly, to a stop, and Rachel said briskly, 'I work no harder than you do, Maitland, or any of you. There is no cause to worry on my behalf.' *Besides*, she admitted silently, *if I do not work, I think – and that way lie unhappiness and turmoil*.

Work was a panacea for all of them in the months after Annie Christie's death, but in spite of the blanketing exhaustion which ended each day, there was still a tension in the house, a strange uneasiness of eyes that avoided hers, of low voices and muted conversation, as if a barrier had been thrown up between herself and the Christies. Annie's death, however, had removed a barrier for Jessie Brand.

Rachel was setting out to the shipyard on a crisp October morning with the boys' bread and cheese and a pan of broth, when she found her doorway blocked by Jessie, resplendent in peacock silks and ribbons, a scarlet cashmere shawl with tassels of gold thread, and a bonnet creaking under a fistful of purple cherries.

'I have come to pay a morning call,' she announced with exaggerated refinement.

'I am so sorry,' said Rachel, equally correct. 'I am not at home.' She had not forgiven Jess for the cruel words to Annie, which she was sure had led directly to her death.

'Course ye are, ye daft quine. I can *see* ye,' said Jess, surprised. 'Well, aren't ye going to ask me in?'

'I was just leaving for the shipyard,' said Rachel, indicating the broth pan, 'so if you will excuse me . . .' She waited pointedly for Jess to leave, but instead Jess adjusted her shawl, touched a complacent hand to the curls at her temples and announced, 'Then I'll come with ye. It's time I inspected yon ship of ours again. I havena seen her lately.'

The 'ours' filled Rachel with a jealous and simmering anger. 'There is no need to trouble yourself,' she said coldly, 'with things you do not understand.'

'Oh, it's nae trouble,' said Jess and added mischievously, 'It will be a *pleasure*.'

Rachel bit back her anger, and stepped into the Square. Jess followed, gorgeous as a Spanish figurehead in her brilliant silks and ribbons. Rachel, in contrast, felt thin and pale, the soft grey of her dress overshadowed to insignificance. Jess had said 'pleasure' and again Rachel remembered that conversation which had so shocked her: '*I'll choose one for pride – the other for pleasure.*' As it had done in childhood, what she thought of as the grey stone rolled over her heart and pressed down with choking pain. But she held her head high, on her face an expression of proud unconcern.

At the yard they found James in the office with Maitland, both bending over the floor plan and checking measurements against the figures in Maitland's book.

'I've come to see over our boatie,' announced Jess, fixing James with challenging eyes. 'I thought I'd best check you're doing things right, wi' the Abercrombie money involved, and all.'

'Very kind of you,' said James solemnly. 'We were just saying, weren't we Maitland, that we needed expert advice. You can save us a deal of trouble, Mrs Abercrombie, by telling us how many three-inch planks we need to deck an area pointed to 101 feet 5 inches, and 24 feet at greatest width.'

But if he expected to baffle Jess with incomprehensible measurements, he failed.

'You'll soon see when ye run out,' she said airily. 'And I didna come to study your measurements,' she went on, giving James a deliberately flirtatious look, 'not *this* time. I came to see our ship. Take me over her, Mr Christie,' and she held out her arm.

For a moment Rachel thought he would refuse, then with a mocking bow he took her arm in his and led her out into the yard. Watching them go, the tall, dark-haired, bearded young man and the over-dressed, flamboyant girl, Rachel knew that she was powerless to stop whatever current ran between them – and that there *was* some secret current she was sure. It had been there for as long as she could remember: when James had given Rachel a shell and Jess, too, had demanded an Old Yule gift; when she had seen them together behind the peat stack and Annie had separated them; when they had kissed on the quayside and Jess had announced they would marry; even now, with Jess married to Fenton Abercrombie, the same current was there, however James might fight against it. But perhaps, with his mother dead and the burden of that unwilling vow upon him, he would no longer fight?

Rachel bit her lip and turned her back on the yard. 'I brought your dinner,' she said to Maitland in a colourless voice and set the pot down on the table.

'It'll keep hot enough, dinna worry,' said Maitland, but he looked at her with new concern. 'You're tired, Rachel, aren't you? You work too hard for us all.'

Rachel could not answer, lest the gentleness of his voice release the anger or the tears. 'Dinna grieve,' he said softly, a comforting arm around her shoulders. 'It will be all right one day, you'll see.'

She leant her head against his chest to draw brief comfort before straightening her back with determined courage. 'I am not tired, Maitland. I do little enough, and it was not easy for Aunt Annie after Fiddly died. She is at peace now, so why should I grieve?'

'That was not what I meant, Rachel, and you know it.' He

spoke gravely, and as she looked down at the plans on the table, the lines of keel and sternpost, transoms and top timbers, blurred into a cobweb, dew-sparkling and indistinct.

'How is Andrew?' Maitland said, changing tack. 'He has done well for himself. He will be wanting a wife soon.'

In spite of her misery, Rachel laughed. 'Matchmaking does not suit you, Maitland. If Andrew wants a wife, he will find his own, and I doubt he will look for her in the Square. Now tell me about these plans you were studying,' she added with determined cheerfulness. 'I'd like to know how you make your calculations.'

Eagerly Maitland explained the cabin design and where it should fit into the decking, and soon they were both absorbed in the intricacies of the new ship's structure, emotional turmoil for the moment forgotten.

But when Rachel looked through the open door some ten minutes later and saw James and Jess returning, their arms still linked and Jess leaning unnecessarily close, jealousy returned with redoubled pain. Jess's face was flushed, her eyes were darting mischief, and though she released James's arm on reaching the office, the tension still vibrated strong between them.

'It's a fine ship,' she announced, like a judge pronouncing a looked-for verdict. 'You've done well. I hadna realized she was sae big,' she went on conversationally. 'Ye'll have a rare job to get her into the water. How do ye plan to do it? It's a fair step to the quay.'

There was a moment's silence in which Rachel detected a sudden shocked wariness, before James said slowly, 'There's ways and means – and wagons. We'll do it when the time comes. And now, Mrs Abercrombie, unlike the fine gentlefolk in the city, we working lads have to eat. So, if you will excuse us?' With a mocking bow he stepped back and indicated the door.

'Thank you, my man,' she said, sweeping past him, and she added over her shoulder and with a deliberate look at Rachel, 'It has been a pleasure.'

'Silly cow,' said Alex, arriving with the twins in time to see her leave. 'What did she want this time?'

'Two tippens she's after our Jamie again!' George and William pushed each other playfully in the ribs. 'And her a married woman.' 'Poor fool him.' 'Where's the dinner? We're starving?'

But when they had crowded companionably round the trestle table in the office and Rachel had helped them to broth and bread, James said worriedly to Maitland, 'She's right, Maitland. We should have thought of the launching. We canna pull her on rollers this time.'

'We'll build a rolling platform,' said Maitland. 'No bother. With men and ropes, we'll pull her easy.'

'But which way?' said Rachel, increasingly anxious. 'We can't take her down the wee lane like the *Steadfast*.'

'Rachel's right,' put in Alex. 'She'd wedge tight wi' her breadth and the rolling platform, and we'd need to cross Dixon's yard to reach the quay direct.'

'Dixon'll nae mind,' said James. 'I'll speak to him tonight.'

But when he returned, late, to the house in the Square, it was with an air of mingled disappointment and excitement. 'Dixon'll give us permission, nae bother, but his lease runs out at Martinmas. He's taken a wee croft past the Denburn and he doesna plan to renew.'

'Then we must take it over,' declared Rachel. 'We've long wanted more land, and it'll make a fine big yard with what we have already.'

'Aye,' said Maitland, 'we'd best see Dixon tomorrow.'

'But he canna just hand the lease over to us,' explained James. 'The owners willna let him. It's to be put to roup.'

'Then we must bid for it ourselves,' said Rachel.

'Or better still,' put in Maitland, 'ask Abercrombie to do it for us. He knows the Lemon Tree. He'll know the best way to go about it.'

'Aye.' Wee Alex had caught the general excitement. 'And when we have it, we'll build an East-Indiaman better than any i' London!'

'You'd best get to your bed,' reminded Rachel, 'or you'll not be up betimes in the morning. Have we the money?' she asked quietly when Alex, protesting, had retired beyond the partition.

'If we haven't, we'll borrow it.' James sounded more cheerful than he had for many weeks. 'Pray God we get the land,' breathed Rachel, surreptitiously touching iron as Annie had done in moments of anxiety. 'Not only for the launching, but for the future of the Christie yard.'

James echoed her thoughts. 'Just think, lads, with that land, the Christie shipyard will be well away. We'll have space to build ships to order, not just for ourselves. We'll expand, take on more staff, and one day Alex lad,' he called over his shoulder, 'you'll get your East-Indiaman, I promise you.'

'Aye lads,' said Abercrombie, 'I'll bid for ye, and gladly. It's time ye had more space. Jess told me of your problem wi' the launching. Smart lass, sometimes, and I curse myself for not thinking of it sooner. But we'll put in for yon land and we'll get it, nae bother. You leave it wi' me lads, and dinna worry.'

But it was four weeks to Martinmas, and worry was inevitable. Suppose they were unsuccessful?

'If we dinna get the lease o' Dixon's land,' James reassured them over and over, 'there'll be other land on the market, and there's nae hurry. No doubt whoever does get it will let us through just the same.'

'Sure to,' said Jessie airily. She had taken to visiting the office regularly since she had paid her social call on Rachel and accompanied her to the yard. She was following the progress of the ship, she said, for her father-in-law; but after the first routine question and non-committal answer, she would settle down in the office should James be working there; if he were not, she would follow him about the yard, leaning on his arm, 'lest I slip wi' all these wood shavings,' and goading him with suggestive questions. One day, tormented beyond endurance, he turned on her. 'What is it ye want of me, woman?'

They were standing in the open yard, the huge timber hull at their backs, the smell of sawdust and fresh-cut wood sweet on the crisp November air, and from the depth of the burgeoning ship men's voices and the sound of hammering.

'You're daft as your Ma, James Christie, if you canna see what I want.' She looked him up and down with slow invitation and added, 'You.' Then she laughed with the full-blooded, derisive laugh of her mother and sauntered away, feathers bouncing, wide hips swaying in their sumptuous skirts, ridiculous parasol twirling impudently over one shoulder, out of the yard to where her gig waited, tethered on the Fittiegait.

A slow blush of shame and anger spread upwards from neck to brow as James watched her go. She had insulted his mother in death as she had in life. She was a wicked, cruel woman, and a whore. A blatant, adulterous whore. She had always set her cap at him, pursued him, bullied him, and now she was married she was no better. But most shameful of all, whore that she was, he wanted her and she knew it. Angrily, James slammed into the office and, when Maitland asked what was the matter, swore.

He swore again a week later when Abercrombie himself arrived at the yard.

'I didna get it,' shouted Abercrombie and crashed a fist onto the table. 'Dixon paid £5 a year for yon lease and today it went for £25! I wasna paying that, not for a wee bit tattie patch without even a decent fence.'

'Who bought it?' asked James quietly.

'That lawyer Forbes, "acting for a client". But it's my belief he'd been authorized to pay *anything* to get it. £25! You could get a fine stance in Union Street for that. It's lunacy. Or treachery.'

And on the day after Martinmas, when workmen moved in to strengthen and enlarge the fence between the Dixon land and theirs, the Christies knew it was the latter. James dictated a letter which Rachel wrote to the new owner, care of Mr Forbes, lawyer in Correction Wynd, requesting permission to move the hull of their ship across his land for the purposes of launching from the quay, but they already knew in their hearts what the answer would be.

'*My client regrets extensive fencing newly erected and work already in progress makes such access out of the question. Had you informed my client earlier, of course he would have been happy to oblige. As it is, he is sure you will understand he cannot allow disruption to the work in progress. He hopes, however, that you will have no trouble making other arrangements, and remains etc. etc.*'

There was a moment's silence before James exploded, 'Work in progress? It's nae but a bloody tattie field!'

'And yon fencing could come down and up again, nae bother,' said Wee Alex.

'We'd best get Abercrombie to see what he can do,' said Maitland. 'There might even be a public right of way.'

'Perhaps I could ask Miss Forbes to speak to her father on our behalf?' suggested Rachel.

'A waste of time,' said James. 'You can be sure there'll be no right of way. No, whoever is behind this has done it deliberately, and I don't need Abercrombie to tell me who that is. I owe the bastard still for Davy's death, and by God I'll kill him if he blocks the launch.'

'Be careful, James,' warned Rachel, alarmed. 'You'll not assault him.'

'Rachel's right,' said Maitland, a hand on James's arm. 'To end up in the Tolbooth or on the end of a rope would solve nothing. No, we must think this over carefully, and somehow we must find a way.'

For the moment, Abercrombie was as angry and as helpless as they were, and, baffled, the Christies retreated to their ship to continue work on the almost-completed hull and worry out some sort of plan by which to circumvent the obstacle.

'It's nae fair!' declared Wee Alex when the *Steadfast* docked the following morning early, and William and George joined the others in family conclave.

'We could uproot yon fence,' said William. 'And replace it after,' added George, 'and no harm done.'

'Except that to move a 300-ton ship on a wheeled platform will take an hour or two to manage,' said Maitland sarcastically, 'and yon lawyer mannie would have the law on us before we were half-way across Dixon's patch.'

'I'll get him somehow,' growled James. 'I'll drag the bastard here and *make* him sign permission,' but they were empty threats. As Maitland said, 'What would be the use? He'd have the law on us the moment we set him free. If we do anything, it must be something which leaves us free and blameless – or undetected – and our ship over the quay and safe afloat.'

'But *what?*' demanded James for the hundredth time and crashed down his fist in impotent fury.

Short of criminal violence, neither Maitland nor James nor Wee Alex could think of a solution. It was left to the twins, with one brain shared between them, to find the answer.

On that dark November afternoon, with the storm clouds low on the horizon and the sea growling deep with threat, Jess Abercrombie's gig drew up on the Fittiegait, and, lifting silken skirts to expose a length of hand-made kid walking-boot and shapely, stockinged calf, Jess herself descended, fur-collared and fur-muffed, with a feathered hat big as a ship's wheel on her thick-piled hair. As she had hoped, she found James alone. The twins were on the quayside, checking the loading of goods for the next trip, Wee Alex with them, and Jess had already ascertained that Maitland was at the sailmakers confirming measurements for topsails and main. The workmen were deep in the hold of the new ship, preparing the sockets to receive the masts, so that when she stood at the office door and looked round the jumble of the little shipyard there was no one in sight – only a cat prowling furtively in the woodstack, and, from the hold of the ship, muffled hammering. Inside the office a lantern had already been lit, and in its warm glow she saw James's dark head bent over an open ledger, a quill pen in his hand.

Softly, Jess opened the door of the office and stepped inside, closing it behind her.

'Busy?' she inquired, looking over his shoulder. She stood so close at his back that her full breasts pressed against his shoulders: he smelt sweat and orris-root and the warmth of her hair. She put her arms round his neck, plump wrists crossed over his chest, and leant forward so that her cheek rested against his head. 'What is it ye're doing?'

Roughly he slammed the ledger shut, broke away from her clasp, and stood up to face her. 'Trying to work,' he said slowly, his eyes bright and hard, his mouth dry. He moistened his lips with a nervous tongue and she laughed, a low, provocative laugh that set his blood racing.

'It's all ye ever do, James Christie, and a poor way to spend your time when ye could be *working* . . . wi' me.'

'Get back to your husband where ye belong.'

'But he sent me himself. He's worried about ye.' She took a step closer and reached a hand up to touch his cheek. 'Ye're looking awful pale. But I'm to tell ye my father-in-law'll do all he can for ye.' Her hand was caressing him now, mesmerising him so that he could not move, and had no wish to. 'Of course,' she went on, easing closer, her fingers at the neck of his shirt, 'when Atholl played yon trick on him, at the roup, Mr Abercrombie was furious . . . we all were . . .' Her fingers were caressing the nape of his neck now, sending fire through his blood, 'but I told Atholl it wasna fair, right from the start. "It's nae fair," I telt him, "if yon lads canna launch their boatie and . . ."'

'*What*?' James gripped her shoulders and shook her with a force which drained the colour from her cheeks. '*You* told him? You treacherous bitch!'

'I didna mean it,' cried Jess, terrified by James's homicidal fury. 'Honest I didn't. It was only con . . . conversation.' Tears of pain started to her eyes as his fingers dug into the flesh of her shoulders. 'I didna mean ye any harm, Jamie. *Please*,' she finished on a sob of terror, convinced now that he would kill her.

But as suddenly as it had arisen, James's rage was spent. His hands dropped from her shoulders and he turned away. 'What's the use? The harm's done. I'm sorry,' he added gruffly as she stood flushed and trembling, rubbing her bruised shoulders, 'I don't know what came over me.'

'It was my fault,' said Jess warily. 'I was stupid, that's all. I opened my big mouth once too often. But Mr Farquharson likes to talk about his ships and things, and I saw no harm, honest I didn't. I wouldn't have harmed you for the world, Jamie.' She looked at him from dark eyes still brimming tears of pain, her full lips parted a little and trembling. 'Say you forgive me?' She laid a soft hand on his chest and moved closer. 'Please?'

James had never seen Jessie cry and the sudden tears were more appealing than all her bold advances. He felt her warm breath on his cheek, then her full breasts were pressing gently against his chest, and suddenly honour, self-respect, even antagonism were meaningless. His mother was dead, himself plighted against his will, his ship's launch was blocked, all his hopes and plans were shattered. What use was there in fighting any more? When she looked up at him, half trusting, half fearful, and repeated softly, '*Please?*' he knew he was lost.

With a silent cry of triumph, Jess knew it too. When she ran a caressing hand over his chest and whispered, 'I am truly sorry, Jamie, really I am. Say you forgive me?' there was nothing he could do but kiss her. And when her fingers moved to loosen the first button of his shirt, he merely reached out a hand to douse the lantern and wedge fast the door.

On the deck of the *Steadfast* where she lay moored against the quay below the Weighhouse, William and George kept watch. In the gloom of early evening the lighted window of Atholl Farquharson's office dabbed the dark block of buildings in the Shiprow with welcome warmth. Below, the lantern-light above his entrance cast a similar glow over cobbled street and arching alleyway, and they had had no difficulty watching the comings and goings of his visitors, including the arrival, half an hour earlier, of Jessie Brand Abercrombie.

Now they watched her leave Farquharson's office, mount the step of her gig, drive out of the Shiprow and past the shadowed balcony of the Weighhouse towards Pocra pier.

'See that, William? She's away to see our Jamie again.'

'Aye, George. 'Tis time.' They turned briefly to summon Wee Alex from below deck. 'Keep watch, Alex, and wait for us.' Then, with studied nonchalance, they vaulted the gunwale to the quayside and strolled, shoulder to shoulder, towards the Shiprow.

Atholl Farquharson was well pleased: £25 was more than he had intended to pay for a scrubby square of tattie patch, but he would have paid double that, if necessary, to get what he wanted – and he wanted Abercrombie and the Christies stopped. His pale eyes narrowed as he remembered Abercrombie's threats in the Lemon Tree after that last débâcle: he'd pay Abercrombie back for that. *And* for poaching his best customers, for undercutting his rates, and for boasting he operated a swifter, more efficient service with his one boat than Farquharson provided with three. Aye, he'd pay him back . . . a mere £25 was nothing for the pleasure of that.

Smiling with satisfaction at another bargain struck to his advantage, Farquharson put away his papers, locked his desk, took up walking cane and tall hat, and finally turned out the lamp. Then, locking the door behind him, he made his way down the forestair to the close and the archway into the Shiprow.

'Good evening, Mr Farquharson.' Two voices spoke in unison, two tall shadows merged to block his way. Farquharson stopped in alarm, looked swiftly right and left, seeking night-watchmen or town guard, but no one lingered in the evening darkness, preferring light and warmth to the dank gloom of a gathering haar.

'Excuse me,' he said, making to pass, but the two men stepped back only to step forward again, one on either side of him, pressing uncomfortably close.

'I think we're going your way.' 'We'll walk wi' ye a whilie.' 'No, no, Mr Farquharson, nae up the Shiprow.' '*This* way.' 'And ye dinna need yon cane.' There was the sound of splinter-ing wood and a distant splash. Then, taking an arm each and half lifting him from the ground, the two men swung him southward towards the quay.

'But I want the Castlegate! I've a hansom waiting! Unhand me this instant or I'll call the watch,' he protested, terror raising his voice an octave. 'The town guard! Unhand me, I say! Let me go!'

'What does he say, George?' 'I canna quite hear, William.' 'Perhaps he wants to hurry?' They lengthened their stride, the small, once-dapper man with his brocade waistcoat and nan-keen breeks squealing now with terror, his legs scrabbling two inches from the ground. The twins were tall men both, Farquharson a head and shoulders smaller.

'Where are you taking me, you blackguards? You'll pay for this, I promise you.'

'Ye're aye asking questions about the Christie ships.' 'So we thought we'd show you, like, for yoursel'.' They were on the quay now, the ships in the basin to their right resting gunwale to gunwale, sails furled, riding lights winking through the mist on the rise and dip of the swell. Ahead of them, past the Weigh-house and secured to a bollard fore and aft, lay the dark hull of the *Steadfast*, a single lantern gleaming from the after-deck. William put fingers to his lips and whistled. A head appeared above the gunwale.

'We're coming aboard, Alex.' 'Is everything ready?' 'Aye.'

'Come away in, Mr Farquharson,' and they heaved him suddenly upwards to soar in ignominious and involuntary flight on to the *Steadfast*'s deck.

'Welcome aboard.' 'Ye've aye wanted to visit us, haven't ye, sir?'

'What are you going to do to me?' gibbered Farquharson, pale and purple by turns. 'I'll have the law on you, you . . . *help*!' But his high scream was smothered by an instant hand.

'Naughty,' warned William, 'and us being so kind to ye.' 'Showing ye over our own ship that ye've always been so interested in. Is the hatch open, Alex?'

'Aye. Everything's ready.'

'We thought ye'd like to see the hold first, Mr Farquharson.' 'There's nae ladder the night, so we'll just help ye down.' Swift as thought the twins dipped, seized an ankle each, and stood up again, whisking Farquharson upside down in a single, concerted movement and holding him by the shins, hat flying and head clearing the deck by a mere two inches.

'We've lit a lantern for ye.' 'So's ye can see.' So saying, they lowered Farquharson head first into the hatch, striking his hands away when he tried to grab hold of the coping, until he was suspended midway between deck and bilge.

'Can ye see yon charred patch at the stern?' called William. Farquharson gurgled, face purple and eyes bulging with the pressure of blood. 'Yon's where your wee fire burned.'

'See the planking?' added George. 'Where the new bits fit sae neat into the old? Yon's where ye smoked our Davy to his death.'

'I didn't . . .' spluttered Farquharson. 'It was not . . .'

'Someone put a rope fuse in our hold and lit it,' said William. 'If it wasna you, I wonder who it was? My, but this leg's getting heavy to hold . . . how's yours, George?'

'Awfu' heavy, too, William. I'll wager a silver button I let go afore you do.' 'And I'll wager two buttons from his bonny waistcoat that I let go first. I'm getting cramp i' my fingers.' 'Me too.' 'Two silver buttons and a tie pin . . .'

'For God's sake,' gasped Farquharson, 'pull me up!'

'Did ye say ye'd remembered who lit yon fuse?' 'Was it you?'

'No, no. It was a man of mine.'

'Ye paid him, did ye?'

'Yes, yes, I paid him. Now pull me up before I choke.'

'He paid a man, George.' 'Well, well. Did ye hear that, Alex? He paid a man.' 'Paid him to light the fuse, did ye, Mr Farquharson?'

'*Yes*, curse you. For God's sake . . .' Farquharson jerked and struggled in contorted agony as his head seemed to swell to pumpkin size.

'Did ye hear all that, Alex? Wee Alex has a rare memory. He can remember anything, word for word. Isn't that right, Wee Alex?'

'Aye, I can. Especially when it concerns our Davy.'

'I didn't mean to kill anyone,' squealed Farquharson, convinced he was close to death himself. 'As God is my witness . . . the fuse burnt too slow.' His voice echoed strangely hollow in the depths of the half-empty hold and his shadow swung weirdly distorted in the lantern light.

'What did ye mean then, Mr Farquharson?' 'Did ye think to warm our feet when the wind blew cold?' 'Or was it to sink us, maybe?' 'Or ruin our cargo?'

'Yes, yes,' gasped Farquharson. '*Please* . . .' he ended in despair, and at last, satisfied, the twins lifted him slowly, inch by inch, up on to the deck again, where they laid him, terrified and cringing, till his blood resumed its proper course.

'I'm right glad ye told us,' said William, 'but ye really shouldna' have killed our Davy.' 'Jamie will be glad to hear it too,' added George. 'You've been awfu' unkind to our Jamie.' 'And the shock of our Davy's death took our Ma's wits away and killed her.' 'Aye. Ye shouldna have killed our Ma.' 'And ye made our Rachy cry.'

Towering huge as retribution against the grey night sky, they stood on either side of Farquharson's prostrate figure. Mist had gathered thick now over the water, shrouding masthead and tenement, muffling sound. Farquharson knew he had no hope of rescue. A man could disappear without trace on a night like this, skull smashed in or throat cut; could fall into the harbour and drown. Looking up at the Christie twins, he put all his terrified venom into five words. 'I'll get you for this!'

'Nae without evidence,' reminded William, 'as we couldna get you for yon fire.' 'But we have the evidence now,' added George.

'Shall I go yet?' asked Alex, eager for the next part of the plan.

'In a minute. Tell me, George, don't ye think Mr Farquharson's looking awfu' hot?' 'Aye, William, he's gie red i' the face.' 'He'll be sweltering, like as not, poor man, and him wi' all those clothes on.' 'We canna have him too hot, now, can we, William?'

With the single purpose which had united them all their lives, William and George bent over Farquharson, unfastened his waist buttons and, taking a leg each, drew off shoes and breeches in a single movement, leaving Farquharson in his shirt tails on the deck.

'There! Are ye feeling cooler now, Mr Farquharson?' 'He doesna look it, George, he's gone purple.' 'We'd maybe best take off his coatie, too.'

'Don't touch me!' Farquharson locked his arms tight across his chest, rolled on his side and drew up his knees to shield his nether parts.

'There, he's sleeping like a baby, William. We'll maybe leave his coatie.' 'Aye, it looks kind o' smart wi' yon shirt tails flappin'.' 'I knew he'd feel better, wi'out his trousers.' 'Awful hot, trousers can be.' 'Especially when ye've nae long had them on.' 'Let's help ye to yer feet, Mr Farquharson.'

Atholl Farquharson was mortified, furious, humiliated, ashamed, and above all so gripped with terror that he thought he would vomit any minute. 'Give them back,' he gasped. 'This instant!'

But Alex held the offending garment by finger and thumb over the side of the ship. 'Shall I drop 'em in, William?' he asked eagerly.

'Nay, Alex, they might be *evidence*. I've a better place to put them. Ye mind yon gig that went past?'

'Jessie Abercrombie's?'

'Aye. It's parked on the Fittiegait next to Dixon's yard. I reckon ye'd best slip his breeches into yon gig to warm the seat. I reckon he's warmed the owner's seat already, eh, George?'

Farquharson blanched at this new horror and spluttered ineffectual threats, but the twins' part of the plan was over and Alex was growing impatient. 'Hurry,' he urged. 'Somebody might come, or Jamie might have gone.'

'Right, Alex, away ye go! Fetch Rachel wi' a clean sheet o' paper and her best pen. We'll meet ye at the office in the yard. And dinna forget yon breeks.'

Farquharson's nankeen breeches in one hand, Alex vaulted lightly on to the quay and disappeared into the darkness in the direction of Pocra pier.

'Come along, Mr Farquharson, on wi' your shoes.' 'We'd best be going too.' 'I reckon the *Steadfast*'ll be safe enough wi'out us, considering.'

Taking an arm each, as before, the twins swung their captive between them over the gunwale and on to the quay, jumping nimbly after him. They made a strange trio, two tall seamen in seamen's jerseys and thigh boots, and between them a once-dapper city gentleman, neat frock coat and brocaded waistcoat over flapping shirt-tails and scuttling stockinged legs.

Rachel was setting the table for their evening meal when Alex arrived, panting and excited, at the door.

'You're to come at once, Rachy, to the shipyard and bring paper, pen and ink. Hurry!'

'What is it, Alex?' she cried, gripped with sudden fear. 'What has happened?'

'You'll see. Just hurry. I want you to be there afore they arrive so ye can see Jamie's face.'

Dropping bowl and platter on to the table she snatched up her shawl and ran. But when they reached the Christies' shipyard the office window was in darkness, the workmen gone. Mist hung over the timber stacks and trailed through the posts which supported the dark hull of the resting ship. The ground under their feet was already crusted with ice where moisture from the mist had settled over earth and mingled sawdust. There was a dank smell in the air, and at the boundary of the Christie land the posts of the new fence rose black and menacing as pikeshafts between yard and shore. Rachel shivered and drew her shawl closer about her shoulders. 'We'd best go home, Alex. There's no one here.'

But as they hesitated, someone turned up the lamp in the shipyard office and Wee Alex let out a breath of relief.

'They've got here before us,' he cried, breaking into a run.

He burst through the door, Rachel at his heels, only to stop dead in shocked confusion. James, his face flushed and hair unkempt, was tucking checked shirt back into navy breeches, the buttons still undone. Behind him Jess, exultant, in a blur of purple taffeta and dishevelled hair, was fastening the bodice of her dress.

Rachel went white with shock, followed by a rush of cold anger so violent it robbed her of breath. Alex flushed scarlet with shame and fury. James looked startled, momentarily abashed, then defiant, while Jess after a glance of triumph directed straight at Rachel, began to hum quietly to herself while she continued to set her dress to rights.

For a moment no one spoke, then James said, without looking at her, 'You'd best go now, Jessica.' She was twisting her hair up into an unruly chignon, hair pins held between her teeth, and did not answer, though the humming continued, taunting and unabashed.

James whirled on her in sudden fury. '*Get out*, will you?' He seized her hat, rammed it on her head and pushed her towards the door.

'Tut, tut,' she said archly, one eye on Rachel, 'a while back ye werena so anxious for me to leave ye.' She set her hat at a better angle, took up her cloak and with deliberate slowness adjusted its folds and bits of fur to her satisfaction.

'What are you waiting for?' asked Rachel, and the icy quietness of her voice brought every eye to her ashen face. Then, as Jess stroked the pelt of her muff with a taunting half-smile, and still made no move to go, Rachel said in a voice of frightening control, 'Has he not settled with you? That is because I have the key.' Before anyone realized the implication of her words, she had jerked open the drawer where she kept the cash for small everyday purchases and scooped up a handful of coins. Deliberately she counted them out from one hand to the other, then slammed them on to the table. 'That, I believe, is the usual rate. Take it and go.'

For a moment, Rachel thought Jess would choke, then as James made no move in her defence the paroxysm passed and she laughed her old, coarse laugh.

'Keep it,' she said with a shrug, and ran her eyes languidly over James from head to toe before looking directly at Rachel

219

again. 'It was my *pleasure*.' Then with a toss of her splendid head she pushed past them and out into the night.

With her exit, tension snapped. 'You bastard, James!' spluttered Alex, almost incoherent with fury, and for the first time in his life he swung a fist at his brother. James parried with a raised forearm and as Alex sprang forward in renewed attack, Rachel cried '*No!*' and swayed with sudden faintness. Both stopped and looked at her, but it was Alex who put his arm swiftly round her waist and led her tenderly to a chair. 'It's all right, Rachy, I'm here,' he soothed, and over her head directed a look of such hatred at James that he had the grace to blush.

But before anyone could speak, there was the sound of a commotion in the yard and the twins arrived, their ill-dressed companion still struggling between them, and Jess, William's free hand firmly gripping her arm, at their side.

'We found her i' the yard,' said George cheerfully. 'Going home wi'out her boy-friend,' added William, 'and him wi' his legs all cold.' Then they stopped, looked from face to face in puzzlement and said together, 'What's ado?'

Alex took charge. 'Nothing,' he snapped. 'We're tired o' waiting, that's all, and Rachy was not feeling too well. Are you better now, Rachy?'

'Fine,' she said, regaining composure, though where her heart had been was an aching void, grey, cold, and friendless. Straight-backed she took up her pen and dipped it carefully into the ink-well.

'Just write what I tell ye in your best script, Rachel,' said Alex, 'and Mr Farquharson will sign it.'

James, all initiative drained, stood in the shadow at the back of the office and watched as his brothers took over.

'*I, Atholl Farquharson, confess that on the night of 28 April 1817, I did feloniously cause a lighted fuse of rope and twisted cotton to be concealed in the hold of the brig* Steadfast *of Aberdeen, joint owners Christie Brothers and George Abercrombie, in recompense for which I hereby grant permission to the said Christie Brothers and George Abercrombie to cross that piece of land known as Dixon's yard at any time of day or night for the purposes of launching any ship, of any size, which they might build or cause to be built, from this day forward and for all time. Signed this 20th day of November, 1818.* Leave a space there, Rachy, "*and duly witnessed . . .*"

Now Mr Farquharson is going to sign it for us, Rachel, if you will just hand him the pen.'

'Dinna sign,' drawled Jess from the doorway, where she leant against the doorpost, her exit firmly blocked by George. 'Not without they give ye back yer breeks. Yon legs o' yours would disgrace a barnyard hen, let alone the fine city gentleman ye set yersel' up to be,' and she laughed.

Atholl's weasel face flushed bilious with mortification and fury. 'I'll get you for this, all of you,' he vowed. 'One day I'll get you, as God is my witness.'

'Harken to the brave wee laddie,' said William. 'He claims he and God are bosom friends.' 'Then he'd best ask God to give him back his breeks.' 'Or bless him wi' a better pair o' legs.'

But Alex had no more stomach for the twins' tormenting. 'Sign!' he ordered and, as William forced Farquharson into a chair, put the quill into his hand. 'Neatly now,' he warned as Farquharson hesitated. There was silence but for the faint scratch of nib on paper, then Farquharson threw the pen down with an oath and pushed back his chair.

'Curse the whole stinking pack of you for the thieving bastards you are,' he spat, 'and if you think you have me beaten, you'd best think again.'

'The witness,' said Rachel, 'should be outside the family.'

Alex understood. 'Witness,' he ordered, thrusting the pen at Jess.

For the first time in her life, they saw Jessie Brand at a loss. 'I canna . . .' she protested, burying her hands in her muff.

'You can and will. Bring her, George.' Jess did not even struggle. But when the pen was in her unprotesting fingers she still hung back. 'Sign,' ordered Alex and at last, shame-faced and deflated, Jess's hand moved to guide the pen in an ill-made, wavering cross.

'No matter,' said Rachel calmly. 'I'll write "*Jessie Brand Abercrombie, her mark*" beside it.' Carefully she formed the letters in her best script.

'Why did ye not say ye couldna even write your name?' said Alex after a shocked moment. But Rachel knew why: this time when she caught Jess's eye the other looked away in confusion before saying, blustering, 'Because ye didna ask!'

It was small enough triumph, and was powerless against the

desolation which filled Rachel now to the marrow of her being, like the slow, chilling death of an Arctic sea. She hardly heard Jess's parting words of, 'God rot the lot o' ye!' spat out with sudden venom, hardly registered her passage as she flounced to the door and freedom, for this time no one blocked her path. Rachel sat, immobile, her face expressionless, her eyes glazed with shock, as William said, 'Ye'd best run after her Mr Farquharson if ye hope to get your breeks afore she drives away,' and with a parting oath, Farquharson took the twins' advice.

It was in the moment's silence which followed his undignified departure that Maitland at last arrived, anxious and apologetic.

'It took longer than I thought to settle the business,' he explained, looking from one silent face to another, 'and then the fellow offered me a bumper in the Bay Tree to seal the bargain, and what with one thing and another . . .' his voice trailed into momentary silence before he said, 'Is anything the matter?'

Without a word, James pushed past him and strode out into the night.

'He'll come back, Rachy,' comforted Maitland when, after a silent supper, James had still not returned. Rachel did not answer. What was there possibly to say? She scoured the cooking pots, banked the fire, checked the porridge pot against the morning and finally slipped, desolate, into bed while '*one for pride – the other for pleasure*' echoed over and over inside her head, like the slow tolling of the funeral bell.

James Christie manhandled the last of the water barrels into place in the hold, then stood back to check his handiwork. Months of loading the little *Steadfast* had taught him the importance of a secure and well-stowed cargo – all the more important in this ship, bound for Newfoundland. Five weeks or more at the mercy of the Atlantic, with a hold full of emigrants, sea-sick and miserable, as well as deck cargo, stores, and an assortment of bales and crates sent by the burghers of Aberdeen to find a market in the new world, demanded careful planning and meticulous execution. Though James Christie was no more than an ordinary seaman here, he cast a captain's eye over the arrangements below deck.

After two days of loading, every space on board was filled, if not by crate or barrel, then by human freight – crofters and their families, with no hope of improving their lot at home, seeking farmland and independence across the sea; younger sons seeking similar betterment; artisans and tradesmen, lured by tales of greater opportunity; women and children, sent for to join their menfolk abroad. James looked at the tight-packed mass of hopeful humanity, with their bundles and their babies, and sought an answering hope in his own breast.

Home held nothing for him now. Nothing. He had been right to sign on with the first ship that would have him. When he had slammed out of the Christie office and strode blindly towards the inner basin and the quay, he had had no plan, no aim. All he had known was that he could not stay another moment in the same room as those reproachful, accusing eyes.

But fate had been kind. The *Osprey* was to sail the next day for Canada, and one of their seamen had fallen into the harbour that very night and drowned. Without a moment's thought, James had signed on in his place.

Canada was the answer. Like these emigrants, he would find a new life there. He would start afresh without family, without obligation, above all without that strangling death-bed vow. The others did not need him – look how well they had managed already without him: that signed confession of Farquharson's would open every door. He hoped Rachel had made a copy of it, and hidden the original away safe somewhere. That bastard Farquharson was sure to try to get it back. But it was none of his business now. Besides, they had probably arranged all that already, as they had arranged everything else.

No, they had no need of James. As for that vow he had made to his mother . . . how could there ever be anything between himself and Rachel now? Not after Jess. Not ever.

James was coiling rope, checking the knots which held the barrels in place. He remembered the hold of the *Steadfast* and the fire which had led to Davy's death, and cast a swift eye over passengers and floor. No tobacco fumes. No dangerous debris. He swung up the companionway to the open deck.

It was afternoon, the winter sun low in the west. After yesterday's mist the air had cleared to leave a crisp, fresh sky, cloudless and brittle. There would be stars tonight, and frost.

James looked aloft to where seamen already swarmed over the masts, legs crooked over yard or clamped akimbo to the upright, ready to loose topsail or main at the first signal. On shore, a small crowd had gathered to see them sail – relatives and friends come to wave the emigrants on their way. Ropes had been loosened from bollards and held only by a single twist. The pilot boat was already in position to see them safely out of harbour and into the open sea. Soon that harbour would be no more than a bump on the horizon behind them.

And good riddance, thought James, his jaw set. Good riddance to the lot of them. He swung into position on the yards of the mainmast from where he could see over the heads of the crowd and along the quay to Pocra and the Christie shipyard. The *Steadfast* lay quiet at her moorings, no sign of anyone aboard. He frowned briefly – they should not leave her unattended – before remembering it was no longer any concern of his. Nevertheless, when he detected movement on the *Steadfast*'s deck he felt relief. Impatiently he turned away from memory, to see a flash of scarlet in the crowd. Unbidden, other memories came rushing back: Jess kissing him farewell when the *Middleton* sailed, and his mother, with Rachel and the others, waving.

Jess. Already the exhilaration of their lovemaking had faded and in its place had come a needling suspicion that she had used him. The memory of her defiant '*It was my pleasure*' obliterated the touching tears of her apology – tears which he had accepted, wonderingly, as evidence of a tender, softer Jess beneath the brash exterior. Now he was not so sure. The more he thought about it, the more tears and apology seemed out of character. In the effrontery of her parting words lay the true Jessie Brand.

She used me, he realized with growing shame. She set out to get me years ago. She told me so, in my own shipyard. And she won.

With a shudder of self-disgust, James reached upwards to the yards of the topsail and swung higher, his bare feet nimble in the ropes, his bare hands firm on the looped canvas of the sail. Good riddance to Jess, too.

'Cast off!' came the cry from the deck far below, and he saw ropes snake over the widening gap between quay and ship.

'Raise the foresail!' Canvas flapped as the sail unfolded, and

James felt the wind fresh in his face. The *Osprey* was gathering speed, slipping steadily downstream on the evening tide.

But the noise under the bowsprit was wrong. It should have been lighter, sharper, as bow wave parted over mermaid curves. The singing of wind in sail was wrong – too deep a sound, too rough. And instead of the helm under his hand, James felt only alien ropes. Resolutely he thrust memory aside. That part of his life was *over*.

The *Osprey* was in the channel now, sweeping on the ebb tide, swift and true, towards the neck of the harbour and the open sea. Quay, customs house, boatyards, all were receding fast as the brig gathered speed. Now they were passing the *Steadfast*. James saw the open hold, saw William – or was it George? – manhandling a bale of cloth towards the gap. He hoped to God they'd checked that bale for contraband. Then that, too, was slipping behind them, with the Christie boathouse and the last stretch of Pocra pier. Another minute and he would be free of them all – free to start afresh. Deliberately James turned his face to the sea.

But as the channel narrowed between the southern breakwater and the wave-washed wooden pillars of the north pier, something made him turn his head for one last look at the homeland he would never see again. The headland, where his mother used to stand and wave, was empty. Only the low thatched roofs of the Square and the bent grass, rustling in the wind.

Empty . . . Unexpectedly, James felt an unbearable anguish, and a desolation which he knew, with terrifying certainty, would be his, now, for ever . . .

Then a movement caught his eye, a flash of blue from the pier near the *Steadfast* . . . a woman's dress?

'Raise the mainsail!'

The cry went unheeded. James dropped to the deck, leapt for the gunwales, stood poised for a brief moment over the widening gap – and jumped.

It was late in the afternoon before Rachel made her way home at last, alone, leaving Maitland and the twins in the shipyard, still at work. Alex had been put in charge of the little *Steadfast*, at anchor further up the quay and already loaded for her next voyage. He and the twins were to sleep aboard and keep watch, turn and turn about. James need not have worried that their vigilance would slip: Farquharson's signed confession might have opened the way for the launching, but the new ship was not completed yet, and the *Steadfast* was still vulnerable.

Only Maitland would be at home that night, and as Rachel approached the cottage which had once held so many of her adopted family, she felt the weight of an ancient sadness over her heart. The last of the daylight had already faded, seagulls cried into the evening melancholy, and the sound of the sea came soft as secret weeping from beyond the cottage walls.

So it was with shock and alarm that she stepped over the threshold and saw a figure in the gloom of banked firelight and shadow.

'Rachel? I thought you would never come.'

At the sound of the familiar voice she stood silent, trembling with a turmoil of overwhelming emotion.

'Can you not even say "welcome"?' His voice was edged with a sorrow which touched her heart, armoured though it was against him, with pride. She could find no words.

'I was to sail for Canada, Rachel. But I jumped ship and swam ashore.'

'Then you will be wet,' she managed and, with speech, regained self-possession. Without looking at him, she slipped the shawl from her shoulders and began to fold it carefully. 'You had better change your clothes.'

'I have already done so.'

There was a moment's silence, then James said, 'Are you not going to ask me why I came back?'

She crossed the neat-swept, earthen floor, laid the shawl on her bed and took up an apron in its place.

'Last night . . .' He swallowed, then said in a rush, 'I could not help it, Rachel, I swear it. It was a torment . . . a fire . . . a devil if you like . . . that drove me. None of my own volition. Afterwards I wanted to escape. Not just from you with your wounded, accusing eyes, but from everything. I was ashamed.'

He looked at her steadily now, his face grave, as confession gave new dignity to his bearing. He is asking my forgiveness, she thought dully, and my understanding. But the memory of that scene in the shipping office was too vivid still, too sharp with pain. How can he expect it, after . . . ? She turned away from him, took up a taper and held it to the embers. It was time to light the lamp.

'I was ashamed, Rachel,' he repeated. 'Not just of that, but of everything. I had vowed revenge and done nothing. I had left it to the twins and Wee Alex to do what I should have done myself. I had failed you – all of you. So when I found a ship bound for Newfoundland and in need of a deckhand, I signed up. I thought to emigrate, to start afresh with no ties, no memories, no obligations. I thought to be *free*. But when I saw our shipyard and the *Steadfast*, everything I love, slipping away from me, I found I could not do it. So I came home.

'Thirty-three days to Pictou, they said,' he went on, as she made no answer. 'I was talking with the crew. But when our new ship is fully rigged, I reckon we'll be able to make it in less. The *Osprey*'s owners have a contractor there, for best yellow pine. We could do the same, we could start our own timber yard here, next the shipyard, on . . .' He hesitated before saying deliberately, 'on Dixon's patch. We must expand, build more and better ships. We'll sail the seven seas one day. The Christie pennant will . . .' He broke off as she touched taper to crusie lamp and for the first time he saw the implacable mask of her face.

'Rachel!' He stepped forward and gripped her shoulders, hard. '*Listen to me*. No, do not look away. I know I hurt you. I know I do not deserve anything of you, least of all forgiveness, but at least *listen*.'

At last she allowed herself to look him full in the face, and resentment fell away. He was tall as she remembered him, but thinner and haggard-faced, and she noticed for the first time that his dark hair was touched with grey at the temples, flecks of premature white in the red of his beard. But the eyes, one brown, one blue, were as enigmatic and disturbing as they had always been.

'Before Ma died,' he said slowly, and Rachel knew that the moment she had dreaded could no longer be avoided, 'I made her a vow. You were with me. You know what it was.'

'You promised to marry me,' she said, surprised by the calmness of her voice, the steadiness of her heartbeat and her

227

own lack of emotion. 'But I release you from all obligation.' She looked at him unwaveringly, and when he did not speak, repeated, 'You are not obliged to ask me.'

'As you are not obliged to accept.'

'No.' His hands dropped from her shoulders and he turned away. She took down a measure from the pot-shelf and began to ladle oatmeal from the tub into a pan for the morning porridge.

'You should marry Maitland.' His voice was bitter, though not, she knew, against his brother. 'He is kind and honest. And he loves you.'

'If Maitland asked me to marry him,' she said calmly, adding salt to the pan, 'I would refuse.'

'But I thought . . . I thought you and he . . .'

'He has his work to occupy him. Besides,' she paused and for the first time since their meeting, smiled, 'he does not really love me that way. He only thinks he does. He and I are friends, that is all. And I think he does not need a woman.'

'And what of me? Do I need a woman, Rachel?' Her face clouded again and he added quickly, 'Not that way. I said a *woman*, not a whore. You do not answer.'

'What is there to say?' She continued to stir the porridge pot with slow, mesmeric strokes until his control snapped.

'*Leave it!*' He snatched the spurtle from her hand and flung it aside. 'I will tell you what there is to say. Say you forgive me. Say you understand. Say you . . .' His voice faltered momentarily before continuing in gentler tones. 'Say you love me, Rachel? A little? Say you can find room in that valiant, faithful heart of yours for a man who may have wounded you, humiliated you, but who did so unintentionally and begs your forgiveness – a man who loves you more than his own pride?'

She stared at him in wonder, searching his face for truth.

'Do not look at me like that, Rachel! Do you doubt my word so much?'

'I . . .' She shook her head slowly in mingled disbelief and joy. *He had said he loved her.*

'Listen to me.' He reached out a hand and took hers, unwilling, in his. 'And hear the truth. When the *Osprey* was slipping through the channel I thought of a thousand things – of responsibilities no longer mine, of burdens shed, of troubles left behind me. I told myself I was free at last, to do as I chose,

228

where I chose. But I saw the *Steadfast* at anchor and remembered who had been the driving force behind the little ship. I saw the Pocra shipyard and remembered who had worked so selflessly and tirelessly there in the office, as well as here at my own hearth. I saw the headland where you and Ma used to stand, waving, and it was empty. Then I saw your dress. It *was* yours, for it was blue as this one,' and he drew her closer till she felt his breath on her upturned cheek. 'And I knew that wherever I went would be empty as that headland unless you were with me.'

Still Rachel said nothing, while her searching eyes looked deep into his.

'Do you still doubt me? Oh Rachel, I have hurt you even more than I thought.' He clasped her suddenly tight against his chest. 'Forgive me.' Gently his hand caressed her hair. 'And believe that I ask you not because I made a vow to Ma, but of my own free choice. Will you be my wife?'

It was not as she had imagined it would be. She had dreamt only of a husband who would love her as Fiddly loved his Annie, of a house with no empty corners and no loneliness. Those childhood dreams had held no place for treachery. But memory would fade and what was her life without James but a loneliness worse than any of her childhood? Love drowned the last vestiges of pride as she said quietly, 'Yes, James. I will.'

He breathed a long sigh, cradled her head against his chest, and said, 'It is as it should be. I know that you are my destiny, Rachel. I think I have always known it, from the moment I saw you, naked as a mermaid, skinny, bruised, with your hair flowing down your back and your great fearful eyes. The day you came to us, half-drowned and terrified, I knew it was me you had come to.'

'And I . . .' She lifted her face to his and kissed him.

'One day,' he murmured dreamily when the lamp had burned low and the only light came from the slumbering fire, 'when the *Bonnie Annie* is launched, I will take you with me, Rachel. We will sail, you and I, together, to Mandalay and Rio. I will buy you silks and oriental perfumes and fill the hold with unimagined glories – to sell to the worthy burghers of Aberdeen at a wicked profit, while Maitland stays at home to build us better, faster ships. Then we will race to Foochow and back again, swifter than any other ship, with a cargo of the finest tea. Or to the West Indies for sugar and tobacco for Abercrombie's high-class shop. Oh Rachel, what a future there will be for us and for our children . . . But come, we must go and tell the others.'

He pulled her to her feet and, tucking her shawl about her shoulders, drew her tenderly under his encircling arm. Outside, the first bright evening star was shining, and as he opened the door the sea wind blew fresh and clean with promise.

'Perhaps now,' he added, laughing, as they stepped out into the Square, 'my brothers will forgive me – and Wee Alex might even speak to me again!'

Author's Note

The background material relating to Footdee and the development of Aberdeen harbour is as authentic as my sources allow, but all characters in the story are fictitious and, though there will inevitably be similarities, are in no way intended to represent actual shipbuilding families of Aberdeen. Folklore does record that in the early nineteenth century an eight-year-old child, 'Cove Eppie', was sent up the coast to Aberdeen to help out a widowed aunt with nine sons, though what became of her or the sons I have not been able to discover.

For details of life in Footdee I am particularly indebted to Dr James Duthie's lectures on Aberdeen's maritime history, to *Aberdonia, Footdee in the Last Century*, by a Lady, (Mrs Allardyce) 1872, and *Fishing Boats and Fisherfolk of the East Coast of Scotland* by Peter F. Anson. For shipbuilding, to *The Shipbuilder's Repository: or a treatise on marine architecture etc.*, 1788. For medical history, to *The Book of Aberdeen* ed. David Rorie, 1939, and *Studies in the History of the University*, P. J. Anderson. Finally, for a storehouse of contemporary detail, to the files of the *Aberdeen Journal*.

I would like to record my thanks to Mrs Vivienne Forrest, for steering me towards valuable source material; to Miss Hilda Duthie of Stonehaven, for her illuminating conversation, for most valuable information about the Duthie shipbuilding company and for allowing me access to family papers and memorabilia; to Dr James Duthie, Curator, Aberdeen Maritime Museum, for dealing uncomplainingly with my innumerable inquiries; to the staff of Aberdeen Public Library, Linksfield Branch and Local Collection, and finally to the staff of King's College Library, Special Collections, in the University of Aberdeen, for their unfailing courtesy, encouragement and help.